TFS NAVAJO

The Terran Fleet Command Saga – Book 3

*****

Tori L. Harris

ISBN: 978-0-9961796-6-9
TFS NAVAJO
THE TERRAN FLEET COMMAND SAGA – BOOK 3
VERSION 1.1

Written and Published by Tori L. Harris
AuthorToriHarris.com

Edited by Monique Happy
www.moniquehappy.com

Cover Design by Ivo Brankovikj
https://www.artstation.com/artist/ivobrankovikj

War is the continuation of politics by other means.

Major-General Carl von Clausewitz

Chapter 1

"Don't even think about it, Admiral," Doctor Chen scolded as Rugali Naftur attempted to rise from his grav chair to return the salutes being rendered on the bridge view screen. "You've been out of emergency heart surgery for … what? Just a few hours at this point?" Both her tone and the firm pressure of her hands on his shoulders left little room for argument.

Naftur scowled, then softened his expression and glanced at Captain Prescott, clearly seeking both an ally against Doctor Chen as well as permission to respond directly to Commander Takkar aboard the *Hadeon*. Even with Takkar and the ten other Wek visible on the view screen still kneeling after having addressed Naftur as "Your Highness," this was still Tom Prescott's ship — and the *Hadeon*, for the moment at least, was still an enemy combatant with which they were engaged in an official parley.

Prescott, still taken aback by the *Hadeon's* response to Admiral Naftur's appearance on his bridge, started to reply, then checked himself as the implications of the rapidly evolving situation unfolded in his mind.

"Sir, the *Baldev* has been designated as Bravo 1," Lieutenant Lau announced from Tactical 1. "She's still headed in this direction with shields and weapon systems powered up."

"Will they honor the parley already in progress?" Prescott asked, still staring at Admiral Naftur.

"If it is indeed the *Baldev* and she is still under the command of Ditanu Yagani, I am confident that she will not open fire without warning. Bear in mind, however, that Captain Yagani is not obligated to participate in our negotiations, and since he is now the senior Resistance commander on the scene, it is within his prerogative to order the other vessels to end their participation as well. If that is his intention, it would be appropriate for him to inform us accordingly and allow us to withdraw from the immediate area before taking any hostile action."

Prescott shifted his gaze back to the spectacle playing out on the bridge view screen before looking back at Naftur. *This is what we came here to do, so let's see how this plays out,* he thought ... *and quickly, I hope.* With an upturned palm, he gestured from Naftur towards the view screen. "Please," he said, inviting the Wek admiral to proceed.

"Thank you, Captain Prescott," Naftur began again, his voice surprisingly strong given what he had been through over the past twelve hours. "Commander Takkar and crew, please rise. You honor and humble me with your gesture. I apologize for not rendering a proper response, but I must remain seated under the explicit orders of the two surgeons who saved my life earlier this day." On referring to the two doctors, Naftur had nodded towards Nenir Turlaka while at the same time reaching back to place his huge hand over that of Jiao Chen, still resting on his shoulder. Caught somewhat off guard by the admiral's gesture and the odd sensation of his touch, she jumped involuntarily at first, then squeezed his shoulder gently in reply.

"Your servant, Gracafürst," Takkar replied, still obviously a little overwhelmed by Naftur's presence, "but you should be aware that the news of your death at the hands of the Humans has been widely reported throughout the Collective for several months. In fact, I believe most Wek who have joined the Resistance, myself included, would cite your death as one of their primary motivations for doing so."

Naftur's leonine face had taken on an uncharacteristically troubled expression, his eyes dark with a mix of concern and barely controlled fury. "Thank you, Commander Takkar," he growled. "We must content ourselves for now with addressing the results of this treachery. We can also take heart in the knowledge that deceit on such a scale invariably leads to the deceivers' undoing.

"Here is what I want you and all other Wek to know regarding the Terrans. While I have studied them for years, it is only over the past month that I have finally had the opportunity to spend time with them. During that time, I have spoken at length with many of their leaders, sharing frank conversations concerning the strengths and weaknesses of both their people and ours. I have fought by their side, and found them to be formidable warriors who fight with bravery and a cunning audacity I have rarely seen equaled on the field of battle. Finally, I had the honor of saving the life of one of their most senior military leaders earlier today, and in turn had mine saved through the tireless efforts of a great many Humans. They came to my aid — not because of who or what I was, but because I needed help. This they did without hesitation, simply because they recognized a need and it was in their nature to do so.

"The Terrans have done nothing to indicate that they pose a threat to the Collective, Yuli, and treating them as enemies out of some misplaced sense of fear would forever veil our alliance within the pale gloom of cowardice."

"I understand," Takkar replied, inclining his head briefly with his eyes closed as if offering his own heartfelt apology for his actions. "Sir, Captain Yagani is hailing us. With your permission, I will explain the situation to him. I am sure he will want to speak with you once he realizes that you are … *here*."

"Be cautious, young Commander, and do not assume that the motivations of other members of the Resistance movement are the same as your own."

"Of course, sire."

"Admiral is fine, Commander Takkar. As you know, since our world's accession into the Sajeth Collective, the dynastic houses of Graca no longer hold any real authority. Our titles are largely historical relics used for ceremonial purposes at this point."

"I will, of course, address you in any way you wish, Admiral Naftur. But as for me and my house, you will always be Gracafürst, the one who should be king. Takkar out."

With that, Commander Takkar's image disappeared from the view screen, followed by stunned silence on *Theseus'* bridge. Every officer in the room who could do so without completely turning around in their seats stared in astonishment at Admiral Naftur.

"Well, this is indeed a bit awkward, is it not?" he said after a few moments, smiling in spite of himself. "I will be more than happy to beguile you with tales of the ancestral Wek monarchy another time … any of you with the patience to listen to such arcane topics, that is. For now, just know that I have intentionally avoided references to this topic because it is really nothing more than an unnecessary distraction at this point."

Nenir Turlaka cleared her throat, staring at Naftur with a disapproving expression on her face.

"Now, now, Ambassador, the only relevant context with which I undertook my mission to the Sol system was in my capacity as a Sajeth Collective admiral. I would encourage all of you to take the conversation you just heard as nothing more than a historical point of reference. I am no more and no less than the officer you have come to know over the past month. Regarding the urgent business at hand, the *Baldev* is the lead ship from our most powerful warship class. I urge you to ignore all other distractions and prepare yourselves accordingly."

"Is there anything you can tell us about the ship itself in case we find ourselves in combat?" Prescott asked.

Naftur sighed audibly, once again finding himself in a morally ambiguous situation. Revealing bits of classified information to the Humans, under the circumstances, seemed like a reasonable and necessary sacrifice in the fight against an enemy of his people. In his role as a fleet admiral, however, he had no authority to make such decisions on his own. He also knew that doing so had the potential to produce unpredictable, damaging results in the future. Until just a few weeks ago, such circumstances would have seemed completely outside the realm of possibility — an interesting scenario in a leadership ethics course perhaps, but not one that would ever occur in the real world.

"I was not directly involved with the *Baldev*-class development program," he began cautiously, "but I did hear rumors that, like the *Gresav*, the first ship in the class was used as a testbed for a special weapons project."

Prescott stared expectantly into the old admiral's eyes, but said nothing. He was aware of the internal struggle that must be taking place in Naftur's mind, and knew instinctively that pressing the issue was unlikely to yield the result he was hoping for.

"I am afraid I can provide little detail, but my understanding is that she has an array of modified gravitic field emitters capable of projecting some sort of beam at enemy warships. I have no idea what the effects of such a weapon might be, but she is obviously a huge ship with tremendous power generation capabilities." With that, Naftur's shoulders sagged and he seemed to visibly slouch in his chair as both physical and emotional fatigue finally started to get the better of him.

"Thank you, sir," Prescott replied respectfully, hoping to express his gratitude while at the same time acknowledging the difficult decisions the Wek admiral was being forced to make on their behalf.

SCS Hadeon, Location Dagger
(3.3 light years from Earth)

Yuli Takkar took a moment to ensure that he would not be overheard, then glanced at his second-in-command in the chair to his right. "I want you to know that, regardless of what transpires from this moment on, I will not further dishonor myself and my family by betraying Rugali Naftur. If that requires you to relieve me of command at some point, so be it," he said, receiving a solemn nod in return.

"Captain Takkar, I have Captain Yagani aboard the *Baldev* standing by," a Wek lieutenant announced from the Communications workstation. "He would like to speak with you privately, sir."

Takkar breathed deeply and tried to gather his thoughts. Much had transpired since the inept Damaran Commander Woorin Miah had been placed in command of the four-ship detachment tasked with guarding the Resistance task force's original rally point. Takkar knew, however, that the question foremost in Captain Yagani's mind would be precisely how four Sajeth Collective cruisers ended up on the losing end of a skirmish with a single Terran ship — most likely classed as a mere destroyer, given her size — along with a smattering of fighters. Takkar also found himself in the uncomfortable position of needing to explain why he had removed Commander Miah from command — particularly since he had been hand-picked for the role by the Resistance task force commander, Commodore Naveen Sarafi, after having served as his executive officer.

"I will take it in the ready room," Takkar said, nodding to his second-in-command to let him know that he had the bridge. Takkar then squared his shoulders and headed aft with a renewed sense of confidence he had not felt for some time. In spite of the potentially career-ending situation he found himself in at the moment, a single thought filled him with new hope: *Rugali Naftur lives.*

As Takkar entered the ship's ready room, the *Hadeon's* AI recognized his presence, secured the room, and emitted a warning chime to indicate that his vidcon was standing by. "On-screen, please," he commanded, while seating himself at the room's ornately carved conference table. Seconds later, the scowling face of Captain Ditanu Yagani filled the display screen.

"Good evening, Captain Yagani, I am Commander Yuli Takkar, acting captain of the *Hadeon*," he began, thinking this was as good of a way to begin a difficult conversation as any other.

"And to you, Captain Takkar," Yagani answered, offering the younger officer the courtesy of referring to him as a fellow captain. "That is, I *hope* it turns out to be a good evening for the both of us. From what I can decipher of the situation outside, however, it is not at all clear to me exactly *what* has been happening here today. Would you care to provide me a brief update? Please begin with the status of the cruiser *Babayev*. She is obviously heavily damaged, and I can see that rescue operations are currently underway."

"Of course, sir. Yes, the *Babayev* was heavily damaged in a brief battle with the Terran ships, but she has been stabilized … for the moment, at least. Her life support systems and structural integrity fields are operating on emergency reserve power. Unfortunately, she is unlikely to be capable of moving under her own power again without significant repairs."

"So I assume you are in the process of evacuating her crew, then."

"Yes, sir. We are utilizing every available shuttle and should have everyone safely aboard the other three cruisers within the hour. Captain Prescott aboard the Human warship *Theseus* has given his word that they will not interfere with our efforts along those lines."

"Let us hope, then, that he is a man of his word. Now, please briefly tell me of the events that led up to this point."

Takkar took in a deep breath as his mind raced to piece together a summary of the past twenty-four hours — hopefully in a manner that would not result in his joining Commander Miah in the brig.

"Shortly after the task force began assembling at this location," he began again, "we were discovered by a formation of two Terran scout ships. The new perimeter defense drone system performed well, allowing the *Hadeon* to destroy the two vessels at something approaching the maximum range of our energy weapons. Shortly thereafter, Commodore Sarafi communicated that the bulk of the task force would be moving to the secondary rally point, which I assume your AI has at this point ..."

On the display screen, Yagani looked to his right for confirmation that the command and control systems aboard the *Baldev* had successfully synchronized with those of the *Hadeon*. In addition to the location of the secondary rally point, Captain Yagani and the crew of the *Baldev* now had access to virtually every event that had taken place aboard all of the task force's ships over the past several days. Though, in theory, this rendered their current conversation somewhat redundant, there was still no substitute for a face to face briefing from a competent, on-scene commander. Returning his attention to Takkar, Yagani simply nodded in reply.

"Very good, sir. Commodore Sarafi also ordered that our detachment of two *Shopak*-class cruisers and two *Keturah*-class BD cruisers would be assigned to guard the original rally point and direct additional ships to the secondary location as they arrived."

"*Guard* it? I am not sure I understand your meaning. In situations such as this, data transfer is typically handled by deploying a simple comm buoy. As I am sure you are aware, their data streams are encrypted, and they do not transmit at all until they receive an interrogation signal from a friendly ship. That, coupled with their small size, yields a highly secure means of transferring critical data — particularly something as simple as a routine change of orders. In fact, information such as the coordinates of an alternate rally point is precisely what the system was designed to handle. Sarafi must have had something else in mind when he elected to leave four of his ships alone at this location. He provided no additional information?"

"No sir, he did not. He also sent his executive officer, Commander Woorin Miah, to take command of the detachment."

"I know of Commander Miah. He is a Damaran, correct?"

"Yes, sir."

Captain Yagani furrowed his brow and gazed deeply into the younger officer's eyes. "Well, Captain Takkar, this story grows more puzzling and disconcerting by the moment. Where, pray tell, is Commander Miah now?"

"Regretfully, I was forced to relieve him of command and confine him to quarters."

"Hah! I doubt very much you regret it, although you may yet live long enough to do so, young Captain," Yagani laughed. "He is a fool, as you have obviously discovered for yourself. Let me see if I can guess the remainder of your story. The Human warship arrived and requested a meeting under a flag of truce. Miah ostensibly agreed, then manufactured some sort of excuse for opening fire after attempting to lure the enemy vessel into optimum weapons range."

"All correct, sir. His excuse for doing so, however, is one you probably would not expect. The Humans claimed to have Admiral Rugali Naftur aboard. Commander Miah accused the Humans of lying, then opened fire shortly thereafter — an unprovoked and cowardly violation of the rules of war."

"I see," Yagani said evenly. "Based on the state of the *Babayev*, I surmise that the ensuing battle did not go well."

"No, sir. The Human ship has highly effective shielding of a type that we have not encountered previously. In addition, their ships appear to be capable of rapid, consecutive hyperspace transitions ... as do their missiles."

"Their *missiles*? Are you certain of this, Captain?"

"I am. We detected a salvo of twenty-four missiles launched from their fighters at an initial range and velocity that should have rendered them easy targets for the *Hadeon* and *Keturah's* battlespace defense systems. Just before the fire control AIs plotted solutions and opened fire, all twenty-four missiles transitioned to hyperspace. As best we can tell, they reemerged into normal space *inside* the *Babayev's* aft shields, completely destroying her propulsion section. Even before the missile strikes, the Human destroyer had already caused a great deal of damage with kinetic energy weapons fire."

"So I am to understand that the Terrans appear to be much farther along in their integration of Pelaran technology than our intelligence apparatus has led us to believe," Yagani said, stating the question as a fact.

"Yes, sir, to say the least. I have read everything I can get my hands on regarding the Pelaran cultivation program, but I have never seen any references to the capabilities I have witnessed firsthand today."

"Humph," Yagani grunted. "Yet another triumph of Damaran intelligence gathering. I wish I could say that I am surprised. How many more Resistance vessels are we expecting?"

"Two more *Baldev*-class battleships, the *Zhelov* and the *Serapion*. As far as I know, the two of them are still traveling together. Based on the most recent data I have seen regarding their estimated position, I believe we can look for them to arrive shortly."

"Excellent. Once they do, Captain Takkar, I hope you agree that we will enjoy an overwhelming advantage … in spite of the surprising capabilities the Humans seem to have acquired. We will capture or destroy their warship as well as their fighters and then proceed to the new rally point for the attack on Terra."

"What I have not yet told you, Captain Yagani, is that during the aftermath of the battle, I was able to confirm that Rugali Naftur actually *is* onboard the *Theseus* … as is Ambassador Nenir Turlaka. Sir, if I may be so bold, I recommend that you speak with him yourself. You can do so privately, if you wish. He spoke highly of you after the *Baldev* arrived, and surely you know him to be an honorable man with the best interests of Graca foremost in his heart."

Yagani simply stared at Takkar for what seemed like a long time before glancing down at his desk — a look of fatigue mixed with sadness clouding his normally proud features. "Their presence aboard the Human vessel is unfortunate, Yuli, but I am afraid that having a conversation with Admiral Naftur at this point would change nothing. I do believe that Naftur is an honorable man, but he and his kind are nothing more than remnants of a bygone era that will never return. Graca cannot stand alone against the Humans and their Pelaran masters. Our very survival depends upon all of the Collective's worlds uniting against their systematic form of aggression. Bringing about that alignment is the reason for the Resistance movement, as you know very well, and the reason we find ourselves here today."

"Please reconsider, sir," Takkar urged. "Admiral Naftur has spent time with the Humans and does not believe them to be our enemy. Like us, they recognize the threat posed by the Pelarans. Perhaps this could provide us with an unprecedented opportunity to ally ourselves with a world already in possession of a significant amount of their technology."

"Unfortunately, the pattern is always the same, Captain Takkar," Yagani said with a weary sigh. "While the Humans may not see us as their enemy today, they are clearly in the process of being offered membership in the Pelaran Alliance. The Guardian spacecraft always boast that there has never been a world that has declined such an invitation. Why do you think that is? The Pelaran's technology … their influence … their *power* … act upon a world like the most addictive of drugs. Make no mistake, the Humans are not simply in *possession* of Pelaran technology. The entire fabric of their civilization is interwoven with it at this point. Indeed, their world has become all but inseparable from it. And even if they were willing and able to cast all of the trappings of that technology aside, do you believe the Pelarans would simply leave them in peace?"

"I suppose not. But could we not provide the Humans with an alternative via membership in the Sajeth Collective?"

"While that does sound like a reasonable approach, the Pelarans would never allow such an alliance. No, Yuli, our only hope in instances such as this is to find a means of intervening in the cultivation process — destroying their Guardian spacecraft once we are able to do so or, as a last resort, eliminating their proxy civilizations. The Pelarans do not appear to be fond of undertaking large-scale military operations on their own, so perhaps over time we will succeed in convincing them that this section of the galaxy is unsuitable for their cultivation program."

Takkar appeared to be preparing to mount another argument in favor of Admiral Naftur and the Humans, but Yagani held up his hand to signal that their conversation had come to an end. "For better or worse, Captain Takkar, you and I have cast our lot with the Resistance. It is a profoundly unsatisfactory situation in which we find ourselves, to be sure. After being forced into making such a decision, I believe it is perfectly natural for us to question our own motives — to wonder if we have done the right thing — but at this stage, I believe we have little choice in the matter. We must follow the path set before us and hope for the best."

Chapter 2

TFS Navajo, Earth-Sun Lagrange Point 2
(Combat Information Center - 1.5×10^6 km from Earth)

"He intends to attack," Captain Ogima Davis said flatly. After shepherding the *Navajo* along with the carrier *Jutland* and three *Ingenuity*-class frigates to an assembly point at Lagrange point 2, Davis had joined Admiral Kevin Patterson in the flagship's CIC. There was little else to be accomplished on the bridge at the moment, and over the past several days, it had become increasingly evident that the long-anticipated confrontation with the Resistance task force would most likely not occur within the Sol system at all. "Captain Yagani is just waiting for their rescue and/or salvage operations aboard Charlie 1 to conclude. Then he'll get all of his shuttlecraft back under cover and let fly. The only question in my mind is whether Naftur is right about his providing some sort of warning before doing so."

"Well, aren't you a ray of sunshine this morning?" Patterson replied without shifting his gaze from the holographic table in the center of the room. "I can't say I disagree with you, but he doesn't seem to be in too big of a hurry for a commander preparing to execute an attack. Other than keeping his shields and weapons online, it doesn't appear that he has done anything to prepare the remaining three cruisers for further action. Charlie 2 and 3 haven't moved a muscle since the *Baldev* arrived, and Charlie 4 is still moving steadily downrange."

"Like she wants us to think that she's out of the fight?"

Patterson furrowed his brow as he looked up at his flag captain. "Maybe," he replied. "Here's what bothers me, Captain. If Yagani thinks he has an overwhelming tactical advantage — and he almost certainly does, given the size of his ship and the fact that he still has three undamaged cruisers at his disposal — why wouldn't he just officially end the parley and demand Prescott's surrender?"

"That may still happen, sir, but I think we can take the presence of Naftur aboard the *Theseus* off the table as a decisive factor at this point. Commander Takkar was clearly impressed, perhaps even to the point of switching sides, but quite a bit of time has passed since we last heard anything from him. I'm afraid that may be an indication that Captain Yagani aboard the *Baldev* was less enthusiastic. Otherwise, I feel certain we would have heard from one or the other of them by now."

"So you think he's just waiting to finish up the evacuation of Charlie 1 then?"

"At best, yes. Otherwise, I'd say he's purposely dragging his feet … almost as if he's waiting for something."

Patterson stared back at the holo table. Even with all of the technology he had at his disposal, the prospect of managing two simultaneous combat operations was a daunting one. The destroyer strike package he had dispatched to the secondary Resistance rally point at Location Crossbow would be prepared to execute their attack momentarily, yet he was unwilling issue their "go order" until he had established real-time comm at their location. Once that happened, a number of additional options would open up, including the opportunity to reinforce the *Theseus* and her fighter escorts back at Location Dagger, if necessary.

Patterson knew all too well, however, that such opportunities always came with an associated cost. Reinforcing Prescott at Location Dagger, for example, might quickly lead to TFC's first significant military victory. Unfortunately, that same action might well result in his ceding the opportunity to decisively engage the bulk of the Resistance forces at Location Crossbow prior to their attack on Earth. Such an opportunity might not present itself again, and he could not afford to waste it — even if it meant sacrificing Prescott's forces at Dagger.

Dammit, he thought sourly. "Ensign Fletcher!" he called in the general direction of the closest Communications console.

"Yes, Admiral," came the immediate but uncharacteristically grave reply.

"Signal the CAGs aboard the *Philippine Sea* and the *Ushant*. I want an additional forty-eight F-373s on the way out to reinforce Captain Prescott's *Theseus* at Location Dagger as quickly as possible … and I want them on-scene in no more than thirty minutes. Let them know that it doesn't matter if one carrier needs to send more than the other. You can also answer for me that, yes, I am well aware that this will probably leave both carriers with very few operational *Reapers* aboard once we take maintenance issues into account. The *Jutland* has already sent twenty-four of hers, so they shouldn't be in any worse shape than she is. This is urgent, Katy, so transmit it as an Emergency OPORD."

"Four eight *Reapers* to Location Dagger within one five minutes, aye, sir," Fletcher replied.

"Any guesses as to how much time we have?" Patterson asked, turning his attention back to Captain Davis.

"If I'm reading the situation correctly, I'd say not much."

TFS Karna, Location Crossbow
(In hyperspace - 5.93×10^{11} km from Location Dagger)

As they awaited their orders to attack, the bridge view screens aboard all seventeen *Theseus*-class destroyers comprising the alpha strike group displayed the abyssal black void associated with remaining stationary in hyperspace. Otherwise, there was no visual indication that they had successfully traversed the roughly thirty-one trillion kilometers between Earth and Location Crossbow within a period of time so small as to be imperceptible to their crews. This was, in fact, the location to which a single F-373 *Reaper* designated as "Gamble 22" had followed the particle trails left by a total of twenty-six Resistance task force ships. And, since no departing hyperspace transitions had been detected, confidence was high that the enemy vessels would still be in the immediate vicinity.

Unfortunately, Gamble 22 had expended its payload of communications beacons at Locations Dagger and Willow, so Admiral Patterson's first order of business for the strike group was establishing real-time communications with the rest of the fleet. Accordingly, less than two minutes after her arrival, the outer doors of the *Karna's* inboard starboard plasma torpedo tube retracted. What followed was an extremely low-energy rendition of the same sequence executed during the launch of a plasma torpedo. The comm beacon itself was encased on one side in a device that was similar in many ways to the sabots once used to position kinetic energy rounds in the barrels of railguns and traditional artillery pieces. As voltage was applied to the rails lining the inner walls of the torpedo tube, a Lorentz force slowly accelerated the sabot down the rails towards the vacuum of space. Upon reaching the end of the rails, rather than being discarded like a traditional sabot, the enclosure simply stopped, thus allowing the comm beacon to gently exit the torpedo tube.

Within thirty seconds of release, the device had stabilized itself and begun the process of exchanging data with the *Karna* as well as the other TFC ships in the immediate vicinity. Synchronization with the NRD network would subsequently occur just five minutes later, once again expanding the range of Fleet's situational awareness. In an unprecedented feat of combat communications, Admiral Kevin Patterson would now have the capability of both assessing and responding to multiple threats in multiple locations separated by vast, interstellar distances. With a total of only eighteen destroyers and a smattering of fighters capable of crossing such distances quickly enough to go on the offensive, the stage was set for the ultimate test of Humanity's understanding of the principles of war.

TFS Theseus, Location Dagger
(3.3 light years from Earth)

Under the most strenuous protest the exhausted Admiral Naftur could muster, Doctor Turlaka insisted that he return to the medical bay, where she undoubtedly intended to sedate him in order to prevent his attempting to return to the bridge without her permission. Both Captain Prescott and Commander Reynolds had repeatedly assured him that his brief appearance had already produced the desired effect among the Wek military personnel manning the Resistance ships in the area. In the end, however, it was Jiao Chen who abruptly concluded the discussion with the pointed observation that his dying "due to sheer stubbornness and stupidity" on *Theseus'* bridge would serve no purpose whatsoever.

"Captain," Lieutenant Dubashi reported from the Communications console, "I have Flash Traffic from the Flag, sir."

Even before Napoleon Bonaparte's network of over five hundred semaphore telegraph stations ushered in a new era of "real-time," long-haul communications in 18th century France, flag officers had long recognized that information, not artillery, was the true king of the battlefield. The problem had always been one of balance. While senior officers located kilometers (or, in this case, light years) away might well be in possession of key pieces of information capable of turning the tide of battle, there was always an opportunity cost associated with putting that information in the hands of an on-scene commander. At best, officers in the field became keenly aware that every one of their decisions were being watched … evaluated … and, quite often, second-guessed.

Unfortunately, history was also replete with cases where senior military and/or political officials had attempted to subvert the chain of command — micromanaging, or even taking direct control of a battle from the comfort of a posh conference room hidden deep within the corridors of power. Admiral Kevin Patterson, by contrast, had spent his professional lifetime studying both the art and science often referred to as C4ISR — Command, Control, Communications, Computers, Intelligence, Surveillance, and Reconnaissance. Understanding the fine balance required to support his battlefield commanders, the admiral usually chose to simply convey information rather than issuing specific operational orders — thus leaving both the authority and the initiative required for decision making precisely where it belonged.

"Captain's eyes only?" Prescott asked, looking up from his screen.

"No, sir … TFS *Theseus* general."

"We probably all need to hear it then. Please send a copy to everyone's console and forward it to our fighters as well. Then go ahead and read it aloud if you would."

"Aye, sir," she replied, rapidly entering the required commands. "The message reads as follows:

Z2123
TOP SECRET - MAGI PRIME
FM: CNO — ABOARD TFC FLAGSHIP, TFS
NAVAJO
TO: TFS THESEUS

INFO: SUSPECT IMMINENT ATTACK —
ADDITIONAL FIGHTERS EN ROUTE

1. DELAY IN FURTHER COMMUNICATIONS WITH
RESISTANCE WARSHIPS MAY INDICATE INTENT
TO ATTACK.
2. ENEMY BEHAVIOR SUGGESTS THEY EXPECT
REINFORCEMENTS.
3. TWO SQUADRONS OF F-373 FIGHTERS EN
ROUTE YOUR POSITION — ETA 30 MINUTES.
4. REDEPLOY FORCES AT YOUR DISCRETION TO
IMPROVE TACTICAL SITUATION.
5. IF HOSTILITIES RESUME, DESTROY OR
CAPTURE SCS BALDEV, IF POSSIBLE.
6. ALPHA STRIKE PREPARING TO ENGAGE
RESISTANCE FORCES AT SECONDARY RALLY
POINT (CROSSBOW).
7. NO ADDITIONAL CAPITAL SHIPS AVAILABLE
AT THIS TIME. GODSPEED THESEUS. ADM
PATTERSON SENDS.

"Thank you, Lieutenant. And our status, please?"

"All systems in the green, Captain. The ship remains
at General Quarters for combat ops and is ready to C-
Jump. C-Jump range 100.7 light years and stable.
Sublight engines online, we are free to maneuver."

"Very well. Please acknowledge Admiral Patterson's
message, then get me a comlink with Captain Zhukov
and Commander Waffer."

"Aye, sir."

"Ensign Fisher?"

"Yes, sir!" the young helmsman responded enthusiastically.

"From now on, if we're at General Quarters for combat ops, make it a standing order to have an emergency C-Jump plotted and standing by to execute. Let's go with three zero light seconds for now. At the moment, that seems like it's far enough to ensure that we are out of immediate danger without wasting power unnecessarily. You also have permission to position the ship as required to ensure we have a clear path for our C-Jump."

"Aye, sir. Thank you. That was actually going to be my next question, since the *Baldev* is currently blocking our escape trajectory."

"And I assume that's intentional. You can't blame them for trying, of course, but let's not make things quite that easy for them. Just give us slow rotations about our vertical or lateral axes to keep our path clear. Any questions?"

"No, sir. Repositioning now."

"Slow and easy, Ensign. They almost certainly know what we're up to, so we need not make it look like we're about to do something unexpected. Oh, and one more thing, we tend to make emergency C-Jumps in emergency situations, so, in spite of Fleet's insistence on proper terminology, I might just say 'jump.' Make sense?"

"We'll be out of here before you can even get to the 'uh,' Captain," he chuckled.

"Alright, XO, here's what I'm thinking," Prescott said, shifting his attention to Commander Reynolds in the command chair to his right. "I'd really like to give those additional fighters time to arrive on station before the shooting starts again. Do you agree?"

"If we have a choice, absolutely, sir," she replied.

"Well, if we start to reposition *Theseus* without some sort of nonthreatening pretext for doing so, it will probably be seen as either provocative, or in the very least an indication that we are expecting more trouble. Our fighters, on the other hand, have remained fairly active since the shooting stopped. I'm thinking we might just get away with allowing each flight of twelve to get themselves into position for a quick strike, if necessary, without drawing too much attention to what they're doing. I'd also like to slave six of our *Hunters* to each flight of *Reapers*. That will give each flight a total of eighteen spacecraft — and an additional forty-eight missiles to fire."

"Hmm … I doubt the Resistance ships will appreciate seeing our fighters setting up for another attack run either. That still seems pretty provocative to me. Don't you think they will respond?" she asked.

"They might … and they could well see it as an aggressive move, but I'm sure everyone on both sides realizes that at some point, this conflict has to come to some kind of a conclusion. We either agree to break contact while remaining under a flag of truce, or we reengage. Admiral Patterson obviously believes that Captain Yagani intends the latter. And if he really is expecting more Resistance ships to arrive, delay works in *their* favor, not ours."

"And what about Commander Takkar and the *Hadeon*? You saw his reaction to Admiral Naftur. Do you really believe he will fire on us at the risk of killing a man he clearly idolizes?" Reynolds asked, directing this question to both Prescott and Ambassador Turlaka.

"There is no question that he would feel conflicted in doing so," Turlaka answered, "but if he truly believes that his duty to protect both Graca and the Sajeth Collective lies with the Resistance …"

"Sir, I have Captain Zhukov and Commander Waffer — audio only," Dubashi interrupted. With the two pilots wearing heavily instrumented helmets and lying in utter darkness within the armored fuselages of their *Reaper* aerospace superiority fighters, there was little point in a vidcon feed.

Prescott simply nodded at Dubashi, followed shortly thereafter by the familiar chime indicating that an active comm channel had been established.

"Good evening, gentlemen. Thank you very much for your help so far. That was some nice shooting. I assume you saw the Flash message from Admiral Patterson?"

"Thank you, Captain Prescott, and a good evening to you as well," Zhukov replied. "Yes, we did. We were discussing very nearly the same thing right before we received the admiral's message. We took a look at Commander Reynolds analysis of the Resistance ships' aft shield vulnerability. From what we have seen thus far, Bravo 1 seems to have a significantly smaller gap between her shields and engine nozzles than the cruisers do. I am afraid she is going to be a tough nut to crack. Commander Waffer's flight is repositioning now to get a better view of her drive section."

"Well, that's not good news, but also not unexpected. We noted that Admiral Naftur's ship, the *Gresav,* has a smaller gap as well. So it seems like this is a vulnerability they have been working hard to overcome in their newer ship designs. In any event, the admiral's orders are straightforward. If hostilities resume, we are to capture or destroy the *Baldev*. Given what we know at the moment, I believe our strategy should be to finish off the cruisers first, starting with Charlie 2. It remains to be seen whether the two newer cruisers, Charlie 3 and 4, will reenter the fight, so do not fire on either of them until I designate them as hostiles. If that happens, we will target Charlie 4 first, then Charlie 3 before finally going after the *Baldev* herself. Based on Commander Takkar's interaction with Admiral Naftur, I think there may still be a chance that the *Hadeon* will leave the area entirely. Either way, I want all three of those cruisers out of the fight as quickly as possible. So if you see me designate one as a hostile, don't hesitate to hit them hard and fast."

"And what about the 'grav beam' that Admiral Naftur mentioned?" Reynolds asked.

"I'm not sure there is much we can do to address it since we have no idea what the weapon even does," Prescott replied. "We could speculate that it induces some kind of sheer forces when it comes into contact with a ship's hull, but that's just a guess. We also have no idea of the weapon's range or its effectiveness against our shields. So, for now at least, I'm going to say that we should keep it in mind, but we can't plan for something we know nothing about."

"Captain," Lieutenant Commander Schmidt announced from the Tactical 1 console, "all three cruisers just changed course, sir. Charlie 2 and 3 appear to be taking up flanking positions, and Charlie 4 has turned back in this direction and is accelerating."

"Have they concluded their rescue operation?"

"Looks like it, sir. They had several shuttles ferrying survivors and equipment back and forth. All of them have now returned to either Charlie 2 or Charlie 3."

"Understood. Go ahead and slave the AIs from six of our *Hunters* to Captain Zhukov and Commander Waffer's fighters. Let me know immediately if anything else changes."

"Aye, sir."

Outside, two groups of six RPSVs disappeared in small flashes of grayish-white light, immediately reappearing in extended formation with each flight of twelve F-373 fighters. On the right side of *Theseus'* view screen, the tactical plot momentarily displayed all twelve *Hunters* as if they were operating in autonomous attack mode. Seconds later, the text block accompanying their icons merged with that of the *Reapers* as the two lead pilots' neural interfaces seamlessly took command of the additional spacecraft.

"Alright, Badger 1 and Badger 2 Flights," Prescott continued, "you two have the *Hunters*. Once you are in position, I'm going to hail the *Baldev* and let Captain Yagani know that I am willing to accept either his cooperation or his surrender."

"That wasn't at all what I was expecting you to say," Reynolds said with a nervous smile.

"Good. Hopefully Captain Yagani will have the same reaction. If he's hoping for reinforcements, there's no question that he will be less confident prior to their arrival — particularly after we just bested four of their cruisers. If they do open fire first, expect *Theseus* to C-Jump away and reposition for an attack on Charlie 2. If you find yourselves under heavy fire, I suggest you do the same. We may well be outgunned here, but if we use a combination of tactical C-Jumps and our shields to their full advantage, we should be able to wear them down and gain the upper hand. Does anyone have any questions?"

"I do not think so, Captain," Zhukov responded. "Please give us a couple of minutes to reposition. If you like, our AIs can relay the most critical of our tactical comm calls during the battle. This will allow you to hear when we arrive at designated locations, fire weapons, etcetera."

"Perfect, please set that up for us. Good hunting, Badger flights. Prescott out."

Suddenly feeling a little claustrophobic at being strapped in his command chair, Prescott released his restraints and stood. "Ambassador Turlaka, this young man will see you back to the medical bay," he said, turning to gesture towards the Marine sentry near the aft bridge entrance. "There are adjacent sleeping quarters available for medical staff that utilize the same environmental systems as the operating room, so you can rest without the need for restraints. I'm sure you will also want to keep close tabs on Admiral Naftur."

Nenir opened her mouth as if she were about to protest being dismissed in this manner, but the look on Prescott's face made it clear that his words, while phrased as a courteous invitation, were intended to ensure that she would not be present on the bridge to witness another battle with warships from her own world. "Thank you, Captain Prescott," she replied graciously as she rose from her chair. "I really could use some rest at this point." Without further comment, she headed in the direction of the Marine sentry and quickly left the bridge.

Reynolds glanced at her captain under raised eyebrows and simply nodded.

"I'm afraid this time we may not have the option of showing the restraint we displayed during the first engagement," he said by way of reply.

"Badger 1 ready … Badger 2 ready," came the terse, tactical comm calls from the two flights of fighters over the bridge speakers.

"Captain," Lieutenant Dubashi reported, turning to look at Prescott with an impish grin, "Badger 1 and Badger 2 Flights report that they are in position."

"I heard. Thank you, Lieutenant," he smiled. "As long as the AI is relaying their tactical comm, you need not repeat their calls unless you think we missed something important. Please go ahead and hail the *Baldev*."

"Aye, sir, hailing."

After a short delay, Captain Ditanu Yagani appeared in the center of the bridge view screen.

"Hello, Captain Prescott," he said, wearing a confident smile. "Commander Takkar of the *Hadeon* speaks highly of you, so I am pleased to have the opportunity to meet you myself."

"Thank you, Captain Yagani. I'm sure his enthusiasm has more to do with his conversation with Admiral Naftur. I regret that our two surgeons have since insisted that he return to the medical bay to rest, but I am confident he will want to speak with you as soon as he is able to do so."

"I had the honor of meeting the esteemed admiral once before, but I doubt he would remember me. In any event, I am sure you have contacted me at this time so that we can arrange a peaceful and mutually beneficial end to this confrontation. Let me say from the outset that I appreciate the fact that you showed remarkable restraint in dealing with Commander Takkar and in allowing our rescue teams to evacuate the damaged cruiser *Babayev*. At this point, however, I hope you will agree that the *Baldev's* arrival has shifted the balance of power in our favor. Accordingly, I would like to propose a simple end to hostilities at this point. You have my word of honor that you and your crew will be treated with the utmost respect and provided with the same accommodations as our own personnel. Come, Captain Prescott, we have both been busily positioning our forces in preparation for further combat, but there is no need for any additional bloodshed on either side."

Prescott breathed in deeply and commanded himself to respond with as calm a demeanor as possible. "Look," he began in an almost sympathetic tone, "I have only recently had the opportunity to get acquainted with your species, and I don't mind telling you that I already consider the first two Wek that I met to be good friends. I'm confident Admiral Naftur will tell you the same — as evidenced by the fact that he very nearly sacrificed his own life to save one of our officers. I believe the reason our people seem to have a natural affinity for each other is very simple — we have a lot in common and share many of the same values. And since I know that to be true, I don't believe for one second that you would ever see surrender as a viable option if our roles were reversed. We are here defending our homeworld, Ditanu, so you know that I must decline your offer. Having said that, Admiral Naftur will also tell you, as he told Commander Takkar earlier, that we are *not* your enemy. I agree wholeheartedly that additional bloodshed is unnecessary. Let us both stand down here and now, prevent the Resistance attack on Earth, and then address the Pelaran threat together."

Yagani stared at Prescott for a long moment, appearing to be giving serious consideration to his proposal. Ultimately, his face seemed to cloud as if he had encountered some unassailable obstacle that prevented further progress along this line of thought.

"Under different circumstances, I might well be inclined to agree with your proposal, Captain, but today my duty obliges me to take a different path. Know that I take no pleasure in this course of action, but I must insist that you surrender your vessel or be destroyed. Since we were operating under a flag of truce, I will allow you a period of two minutes to reposition your vessel or to withdraw completely if that is your choice."

"I am saddened to hear it, Captain. We are acting in self-defense, so a withdrawal is not an option for us. If, at any point during our engagement, you reconsider and decide that you would like to either surrender or cooperate, my offer will remain open."

"As will mine, sir. Yagani out."

"Tactical, range to the *Baldev*, please," Prescott said. With the decision made, his voice had taken on a much harder edge than during his conversation with Captain Yagani.

"Just over three hundred thousand kilometers, sir," Lieutenant Lau responded.

"Helm, you have two minutes to double that distance and put us in a position to either C-Jump clear or attack Charlie 2. Sublight engines only, please."

"Aye, sir."

In a display intended to give the much less maneuverable Resistance warships pause, Ensign Fisher increased *Theseus'* engines to maximum power — heading initially in the direction of the *Baldev* before gracefully rolling the ship inverted relative to her former flight path and executing a tight Split S turn to head in the opposite direction. Throughout the maneuver, her remaining twelve *Hunter* RPSVs maintained perfect formation in two groups posted slightly below and to either side of her flight path. The ship accelerated steadily away from the enemy vessels until reaching nearly five percent the speed of light, then reversed thrust — her massive sublight engines providing a smooth deceleration to arrive at her chosen destination well before Captain Yagani's two-minute warning had expired. The impressive demonstration of the destroyer's power sent the clearest possible message to the enemy vessels — the Terrans came prepared to fight.

Chapter 3

TFS Philippine Sea, Earth Orbit
(Primary Flight Control)

"Attention on the hangar deck, this is the Air Boss. Stand by for a twenty-four-spacecraft launch event. This will be a rapid-turn, simultaneous launch utilizing all eight elevators — one F-373 per elevator, eight ships per cycle, and three launch cycles. Spacecraft-handling officers report readiness and expect a green deck in zero three minutes."

As remarkable as it seemed for a single carrier to be performing at a reasonable level of efficiency during only her second day in space, flight operations were progressing without a hitch on *both* of TFC's most recently launched *Jutland*-class carriers. So far at least, there had been no serious equipment failures, and it also appeared that neither the *Philippine Sea* nor the *Ushant* suffered from the same installation problem that had rendered the lead carrier's two largest spacecraft elevators inoperative.

With the first cycle of the launch event now imminent, automated warning announcements from *Philippine Sea's* AI echoed throughout the hangar deck: *"Attention ... launch event commencing. Clear elevators one through four and elevators five through eight for immediate departure. Lift operation in six zero seconds."* On the floor of the hangar deck, eight "bear" spacecraft directors stood poised next to their respective elevator platforms with one arm in the air to indicate that their area was clear and safe for lift operation. On each elevator, the pilots of the first eight *Reapers* (closely monitored by their onboard AIs, of course) quickly ran through their final pre-launch checklists — ensuring that their reactors, engines, weapons, and flight systems were fully online and prepared for combat. All twenty-four of the fighters departing from the *Philippine Sea* had been configured for a heavy anti-ship strike. Accordingly, every weapons station on the spacecraft capable of mounting a missile had been utilized. In addition to their dorsal and ventral railgun turrets, each fighter carried a payload of six HB-7c missiles within their internal weapons bays and another eight on pylons beneath their wings.

"*Attention, launch event initiated. Lift operation in five ... four ... three ... two ... one ... mark,*" the ship's AI announced. "*Stand by for launch cycle two, commencing in three zero seconds.*"

All eight of the carrier's flight elevators rose simultaneously until each platform's surface was flush with the flight deck. Less than two seconds later, after a final confirmation check of each fighter's primary systems, the carrier's AI granted autonomous control to each individual spacecraft. Each *Reaper's* onboard AI then took an additional few seconds to run their own final set of pre-launch systems checks before signaling their pilots that they were cleared for launch. Scanning the area around their fighters with synthetically enhanced vision, each pilot then released the clamps holding them in place. On a final signal from their flight lead, all eight spacecraft rose simultaneously from the flight deck before rotating in place and heading off to a nearby assembly area to await the remaining members of their squadron.

Ninety-four thousand kilometers away, on the opposite side of the planet, an identical scene played out above the flight deck of the carrier *Ushant*. Less than ten minutes after the launch event began, a total of forty-eight F-373 *Reaper* aerospace superiority fighters synchronized their departure vectors and made final preparations for their C-Jump to Location Dagger.

TFS Navajo, Earth-Sun Lagrange Point 2
(Combat Information Center - 1.5×10^6 km from Earth)

"All forty-eight fighters are formed up and ready for C-Jump on your mark, Admiral," Captain Davis reported. "Once they arrive, the squadron from the *Philippine Sea* will merge with Badger 1 Flight under Captain Zhukov. The ones from the *Ushant* will become part of Badger 2 Flight under Commander Waffer."

"That's a squadron and a half — thirty-six fighters each. Should we reasonably expect our two squadron commanders to manage that many spacecraft at one time?" Patterson asked.

"It shouldn't be a problem. They occasionally run massed attack training exercises where they coordinate even larger numbers of ships. The neural interface they're using is similar to the one our special ops troops use in their EVA combat armor, so it's designed to handle complex operational scenarios with lots of moving parts ... once you get the hang of it, that is. Other than the twelve *Hunters* from the *Theseus*, these are all crewed fighters anyway — with their AIs there to back them up in case they do anything … uh … *unexpected*. Worst case, Zhukov or Waffer can always make the decision to designate additional flight commanders, if necessary."

"Well then, I'm sure Prescott will be happy to have the extra help … I'll be surprised at this point if he doesn't end up going toe to toe with three cruisers and a Wek battleship. Please issue final clearance to depart."

A photo-realistic representation of the Earth nearly two meters in height, complete with current weather patterns (as well as real-time surface activity when zoomed in far enough to display it), currently dominated the center of the CIC holographic table. On either side of the planet, icons representing the two carriers were paired with those of their respective fighter squadrons awaiting orders from the flagship. Immediately upon receipt of the admiral's "go order," the icons representing the fighters disappeared in forty-eight simultaneous flashes of grayish-white light.

"Alright, I'm afraid that's about all we can do for Prescott and company for now," Patterson said, quickly reconfiguring the holographic table to display the location of the secondary Resistance rally point. "We should begin receiving data from Crossbow anytime."

As if on cue, the space above the table shimmered slightly, then refocused to show two large, spherical outlines. Although hyperspace and "normal" space technically occupied the same physical location, the holographic table was often configured to display each as its own distinct region. Currently, the larger of the two spheres — representing "normal" space — displayed a blinking red icon near its center to indicate that, for the moment, there was no available data. The second, smaller sphere displayed a cluster of blue icons representing the seventeen *Theseus*-class destroyers awaiting the admiral's orders in hyperspace at Location Crossbow.

"Are you planning to wait and see what happens at Dagger before ordering them to attack?" Captain Davis asked, nodding to the assembled ships.

"Originally, yes, I was. My hope was that Admiral Naftur's presence combined with a show of force from *Theseus* and her fighter escorts might have persuaded the remaining Resistance forces to stand down," he replied, uncharacteristically leaning with both hands spread wide against the side of the holo table. "Hell, all of this is seat of the pants, Ogima. You understand that, right?"

"I know what General Eisenhower said, sir: 'No plan survives contact with the enemy.'"

"He probably did say something like that," Patterson chuckled, standing up straight once again and rubbing his eyes without bothering to remove his glasses, "but that's not his quote. That particular maxim paraphrases German Field Marshal Helmuth von Molkte the Elder. What he actually said was more like 'No plan of operations extends with certainty beyond the first encounter with the enemy's main hostile force.' Eisenhower, on the other hand, said 'In preparing for battle, I have always found that plans are useless, but planning is indispensable.'"

"Alright, alright," Davis laughed, raising both hands in mock surrender. "You'd think I would have figured out by now that I shouldn't make historical references in the presence of the ultimate military history buff! What I meant to say is that we're doing the best we can with the time and resources we have at our disposal."

"True enough, I suppose. I definitely don't think we would have ever planned for anything like this particular scenario, though, regardless of how much time we had available. I've gone over this whole situation in my mind a thousand times, but there's still something that doesn't quite add up for me. It's almost as if the Resistance ships never really had any intention of attacking Earth outright."

"Sir?" Davis asked.

"I don't know … it's probably nothing. It just seems like they're going about it as if they have other, competing objectives in mind, that's all. Never mind me, Captain. If a man runs on Navy coffee long enough without getting much sleep, his inner monologue tends to turn into a running commentary that no one really wants to hear. Back to your original question … since Naftur does not seem to have had the impact we were hoping for at Location Dagger, I don't believe waiting for a resolution there is worth the risk of losing our opportunity at Location Crossbow. Go ahead and authorize the alpha strike with no changes from the original plan. Oh … and send Gamble 22 back to Location Crossbow as well. Tell him to remain in hyperspace while the destroyers conduct their attack. If those Resistance ships decide to make a run for it, I'd at least like to know what direction they went."

"Aye, sir. Transmitting now."

SCS Gunov, Location Crossbow
(5.93×10^{11} km from Location Dagger)

Commodore Naveen Sarafi stared with satisfaction and no small degree of wonder at the display screen in his ready room. Although long-range communications had been a reality for Sajeth Collective vessels for centuries, the underlying technology had advanced surprisingly little during that time. Although, by and large, the systems had proven themselves to be effective and reliable over the years, they were also unwieldy and somewhat impractical from an operational standpoint. At one time, in fact, the original deep space communications network had relied solely on fixed, planet-side installations coupled with geostationary satellites to connect far-flung governmental and military organizations across the Sajeth Collective. Unfortunately, even after countless attempts to miniaturize components of the system, the equipment still took up copious amounts of space. While entire buildings filled with comm gear were perfectly acceptable at sprawling governmental facilities, such had never been the case aboard ships of war, where every cubic centimeter of space was sorely coveted. Perhaps worst of all, the equipment had often forced captains to choose between either remaining out of communications or sitting stationary for extended periods (sometimes days at a time) while the system synchronized and established connectivity with the nearest node on the network.

At long last, the equipment providing the video feed and tactical information currently displayed on Sarafi's screen represented a much needed and long promised quantum leap in communications technology. From the moment he had first been briefed on the system's revolutionary capabilities, he had realized that, once widely deployed, it would usher in a new era of ubiquitous, real-time comm for the Collective and provide a tremendous advantage for its military forces. This fact had not been lost on the military oversight committee of the Sajeth Collective's Governing Council, which had classified the most sensitive details at such a high level that very few officers who worked with the equipment every day were aware of its true capabilities.

Among the Resistance task force's officers, only the commodore had been granted full access. And not for the first time, Sarafi found himself wondering if, under the circumstances, this might be a case where violating information security made more sense than potentially putting their entire mission at risk. After all, there were already hundreds of officers aboard his task force who were familiar with the Pelaran-derived surveillance drones being deployed by the newly commissioned Battlespace Defense cruisers. They knew the drones were capable of setting up a real-time defensive perimeter around their forces extending out to well over a billion kilometers. They knew that the system relayed detailed surveillance data — allowing the fleet to maintain nearly complete situational awareness, including live video, from any location inside the perimeter. In fact, he rationalized, the only thing they really did *not* know was the system's range. And, in truth, neither did he. The Collective's scientists did believe that there was a theoretical limit to the distance between nodes, but it was something on the order of one hundred light years — perhaps even more. In any event, when compared with the limitations imposed by the old

Sajeth Collective network, the new system had virtually unlimited range.

From a practical standpoint, the decision to share certain details of the system's capabilities was his alone to make. The mission to the Sol system had been put together so quickly that the new surveillance drones did not yet allow for continuous oversight of his activities by his masters on the Governing Council. Yet as isolating and problematic as it was for him to be the only member of his task force with access to the drones' data, Sarafi admitted to himself that it was a bit intoxicating to be the only officer possessed of what felt like a nearly omnipotent view of his battlespace. At the relatively short distance of 22.9 light days, the *Gunov* had reestablished contact with the surveillance drones at the original rally point in less than an hour. Since then, he had simply watched and waited. In the interim, two additional *Rusalov*-class battleships had arrived and been forwarded on to the secondary rally point without incident. The longer he had waited, however, the more he had begun to wonder whether the loathsome Commander Miah had been correct. Perhaps the Humans were either unwilling — or even unable — to send additional ships to investigate the loss of their scout vessels. If that were indeed the case, his move to the secondary rally point had been an unnecessary precaution.

Contingencies wrapped within contingencies, he mused. In Sarafi's opinion, there were far too many allowances for such things in the mission plan he had been given. The whole thing read like nothing more than a long series of conditional "if-then" statements, some of which were based on scenarios that he thought so unlikely as to border on the absurd. Then again, the first seemingly unlikely event had already taken place — the Humans had located the original rally point — forcing him to alter the original, simple plan (which he favored) in a manner he never would have predicted. Rather than simply allowing all of his forces to arrive at the original rally point, then proceeding to Terra for a quick, devastating strike (any interference from the Guardian notwithstanding), the plan now required him to use a portion of his forces as "bait" in hopes of enticing the Humans to attack. Otherwise, there was little if any military justification for leaving several ships to "guard" the original rally point. While sacrifices were sometimes required in battle, Sarafi was still somewhat uncomfortable with the idea that so many lives were being placed at risk in pursuit of what amounted to nothing more than a grand political agenda.

The Resistance leaders with seats on the Governing Council realized early on that the biggest single risk inherent in the expedition to attack Terra was that their forces would be completely wiped out by the Guardian spacecraft, the Humans, or a combination of both. Their concern, however, was not for the loss of their naval forces so much as the potential for wasting the opportunity represented by such a monumental crisis. A "victory," from their perspective, required at least some of the task force to return home carrying a precious cargo of data — *propaganda*, Sarafi corrected himself. Depending on what events had transpired in the Sol system, that data would be leveraged to either justify the destruction of a nearly defenseless civilization, or to prove just how dangerous the Terrans had already become. The former would solidify their place in history as defenders of the Collective, the latter would most likely tip the balance in favor of all-out war in defense of their member worlds.

After what seemed an interminable period of waiting, the Humans had finally arrived at the original rally point. Watching events unfold from 593 billion kilometers away, Sarafi initially feared that the Resistance leaders' strategy had backfired. Surely, with only a single Human ship arriving on the scene, there was little chance of anything more dramatic than an immediate surrender. Just as anticipated, however, Commander Miah — that fool of a Damaran — had somehow managed to provoke a confrontation. Unfortunately, the result, while exactly what the mission planners had hoped for in one sense, had hardly provided the raw material needed to portray the Humans as bloodthirsty savages bent on the destruction of the Collective.

The relatively small, Pelaran-enhanced Human vessel, along with a small group of fighter spacecraft, had easily defeated four resistance vessels, any one of which should have been more than their equal in battle. Precisely how this had been accomplished was still a bit of a mystery. The Human fighters had fired twenty-four missiles at the *Babayev* at a range that should have allowed them to be easily intercepted — even for one of the older, *Shopak*-class cruisers. Yet, for whatever reason, it appeared that none of the missiles had been intercepted by energy weapons fire or blocked by the ship's shields. Once again, Sarafi silently cursed the rigid security measures governing the use of the new surveillance drone system. Since none of the officers aboard the Resistance ships at the original rally point had been granted access, their AIs were likewise not authorized to share their invaluable, on-scene tactical analyses or even their comm feeds with the *Gunov*. Instead, Sarafi was limited to the data-gathering capabilities of the surveillance drones themselves which, while considerable, paled in comparison to the warships that had launched them.

The longer he watched, the more unacceptable the situation became, and, in response, Sarafi began composing the official justification he would use to render the normally inflexible security protocols a bit more pliable. At least, he hoped, sufficiently pliable to avoid being prosecuted for improper handling of classified data. The notion that he still had to be concerned about such things seemed patently ridiculous at this point anyway — considering that he was currently in the process of leading a technically extralegal, officially unsanctioned military expedition against the homeworld of another civilization. Laws governing such things, he knew, were often ignored, or in some cases reshaped to indemnify those in positions of power.

In any event, it was not necessary for Sarafi to clear *all* of his personnel for access to the classified information. Even if he could justify something as simple as allowing the *Gunov's* tactical officers to analyze the raw surveillance drone data feeds, he felt certain that they would be able to quickly determine why the Human attack had been so successful. If he did *not* do so at some point, would he not be held equally accountable if the Humans then managed to execute the same sort of attacks against the bulk of his forces?

Perhaps worst of all for the political component of his mission was what he had observed after the *Babayev* had been rendered defenseless in the aftermath of the skirmish with the Human warship. *Hadeon*, obviously surprised to find herself at a tactical disadvantage, had ceased fire and shortly thereafter begun launching her shuttles in the direction of the stricken cruiser *Babayev*. The only scenario Sarafi could imagine to fit what he had observed was that Commander Miah had fired first, then promptly surrendered to the Human vessel as soon as he had suffered his first loss. Once the shooting had stopped, the Human warship had shown remarkable restraint, allowing the Resistance vessels to conduct their rescue operations when it would have been entirely within their rights to destroy every enemy vessel in the area.

Sarafi had been considering the idea of sending in additional Resistance warships to provoke the Humans into continuing the battle when the *Baldev* arrived. Surely, this was the best possible scenario for accomplishing the political portion of his mission objectives. If the Human warship managed to destroy four cruisers as well as the lead vessel in the newest class of Sajeth Collective battleships, he would certainly capture all of the data necessary to convey the nature of the threat back to the Governing Council. If, on the other hand, the Human vessel was destroyed, Sarafi felt confident that he could proceed with the original mission to attack Terra with a reasonable assurance of success.

At that moment, the distressing sound of what he now recognized as a defense perimeter violation alarm interrupted his deliberations.

"Commodore Sarafi to the bridge," his communications officer announced urgently over the ship's intercom system.

Chapter 4

TFS Theseus, Location Dagger
(3.3 light years from Earth)

"Multiple new contacts!" Lieutenant Lau announced from Tactical 1.

"Did we detect hyperspace transitions?" Prescott asked, glancing quickly at the tactical plot for confirmation.

"No, sir ... stand by ... confirmed, the *Baldev* is launching fighters."

"Understood. Let's try to stay clear of them if we can. Let me know when you have a total count."

"Aye, sir. Ten so far and still launching. It looks like they are just forming up to one side of Bravo 1 for now."

"Commander Schmidt, it occurs to me that the Wek aren't big believers in point defenses, so if those fighters happen to get within range of ours at some point ..."

"The sea-whiz will make believers out of them, sir."

"Very good. Be watching for the opportunity. You might have to tweak the AI's settings a bit. Otherwise, if we switch the railguns to point defense mode, it will primarily be looking to stop inbound missiles rather than taking down fighters."

"Aye, sir," Schmidt replied, sensing that his captain's unusually specific instructions were a sign that he was perhaps a bit more apprehensive than during previous engagements.

"Both Badger flights are standing by, sir," Dubashi said from the Communications console.

"Excellent. Signal them to —"

"Multiple contacts, multiple hyperspace transitions. These are *behind* us, sir!" Lieutenant Lau interrupted, this time in an even more excited, urgent tone.

"Easy, Lieutenant Lau," Prescott soothed. "They're ours, right?" Still staring at the tactical plot, he could see that the latest contacts were represented by two yellow icons, each with an "UNK" indicator to show that the precise number of contacts had yet to be determined. Seconds later, both icons changed to blue with accompanying text blocks designating twenty-four additional F-373 fighters each for Badger 1 and Badger 2 Flights, respectively. –

"Yes, sir, they're ours," Lau said sheepishly. "And they just C-Jumped again — right into an extended trail formation with the original two flights."

"Dubashi, signal the fighters to commence their attack," Prescott ordered. "Helm, steer in the general direction of Charlie 2, and follow our fighters in case we need to finish her off. Don't crowd them, though. Hang back and let's allow the situation to develop a bit before we go charging in."

"Aye, sir," Fisher and Dubashi replied in unison.

Although Ensign Fisher had immediately adjusted course to follow Badger 1 Flight, he need not have done so. Within seconds of receiving their order to attack, both groups of fighters transitioned to hyperspace.

"Badger 1 and Badger 2 Flights have transitioned, sir," Lau reported.

Before Lieutenant Lau could finish his sentence, thirty-six *Reaper* fighters reappeared in normal space, roughly seventy-five thousand kilometers aft of Charlie 2. The flight had executed their C-Jump so that they arrived in a stacked, line-abreast formation, providing every spacecraft a clear line of fire in the direction of the cruiser's vulnerable stern.

"Badger 1 Flight - Fox Charlie!" came the tactical comm call from Captain Zhukov, indicating that his formation was firing C-Drive-equipped missiles — in this case, two HB-7cs from each of the flight's thirty-six fighters. As soon as the missiles were clear of the formation, every spacecraft pitched down slightly to clear their flight paths, followed shortly thereafter by Zhukov's call of *"Badger 1 Flight is Juliet."* With that, the entire flight transitioned to hyperspace once again. Although each individual ship was still under the direct control of a single pilot, each of those pilots was trained to interact on an almost subconscious level via their neural interface. This interaction took place not only with their own fighter and its AI, but also with every other ship in their flight, particularly with their flight commander, Captain Zhukov. The result was much more than a mere merger of "Human and machine." Instead, it was truly more of a coupling of Human and artificial intelligence at such a fundamental level that their performance far eclipsed what either was capable of achieving without the other.

At precisely the same instant that Captain Zhukov's fighters had appeared behind Charlie 2, Commander Waffer's flight had split into two separate elements. The largest of the two groups, with twenty-four spacecraft, appeared aft of Bravo 1, quickly confirmed that Charlie 3 and 4 were still designated as noncombatants, and then immediately executed a "probing attack" against the *Baldev. "Badger 21 Flight - Fox Charlie!"* Commander

Waffer called as a total of forty-eight anti-ship missiles streaked away toward the distant battleship.

The smaller group, composed of twelve fighters, flashed aggressively into normal space so close to the *Baldev's* fighter escorts that their targets were already well within optimal railgun range. The *Reaper* formation slashed directly through the middle of the still-assembling Resistance fighters behind a deadly wall of fragmented kinetic energy rounds that raced away from the F-373s at nearly ten percent the speed of light.

"Badger 22 Flight - Guns Guns Guns!" came the call from the lead pilot in the second element of Badger 2 Flight. Each pilots' announcement of weapons releases, while somewhat helpful in keeping *Theseus'* crew updated on the progress of the attacks, came at such a rapid pace that it was difficult to follow the battle, even while staring at a real-time tactical plot.

"Badger 2 Flight is Juliet," Commander Waffer called, as both elements of his flight C-Jumped away to regroup and assess the damage from their first attack run.

All of the Resistance fighters unfortunate enough to have been caught in the path of Badger 22 Flight's railgun attack — which turned out to be a total of nine — were ground into rapidly expanding clouds of dust by the barrage of fragments laid down by the Human fighters. Like an afterthought tinged with bitter regret, the *Baldev* herself had finally opened up with her energy weapons, but her response was far too late to even test any of the *Reapers'* shields.

"My God. Are you able to keep up with what's happening?" Reynolds asked quietly. "I feel like I'm five minutes behind this battle and it just started thirty seconds ago."

"The violence and speed of the attacks is a key element of their strategy," Prescott said. "Don't get too hung up on the comm calls. In fact, we can discontinue them if they are too distracting. Just continue using your tactical plot like you always have and focus on the AI's battle damage assessment."

"One two zero friendly missiles in flight, Captain," Lieutenant Lau reported from Tactical 2, "they are transitioning ... stand by ... impacts! Multiple impacts on both Charlie 2 and Bravo 1."

"Enhanced views of each, please," Prescott ordered, after which two windows opened on the view screen displaying zoomed-in, light-amplified views of both ships. The image of Charlie 2 had barely stabilized on the screen before the entire aft end of the ship was cleaved into two sections. At the same time, the massive cruiser's outer hull appeared to be in the process of being peeled back from the stern as a result of incredibly violent explosions deep within her drive section. For a moment, it looked as if she, like her sister ship the *Babayev*, might be taken out of action while remaining largely intact, but it was not to be. As *Theseus'* bridge crew watched in awe, the entire image bloomed forth in brilliant white light, temporarily obscuring their view as the entire ship exploded in a colossal ball of antimatter-induced fire.

"Charlie 2 destroyed," Lieutenant Commander Schmidt reported calmly.

"Badger 22 Flight - Vampire Vampire Vampire!" the lead pilot in the second element of Badger 2 Flight called

over the tactical comm channel, indicating that they had detected the launch of hostile anti-ship missiles.

"Confirmed, Captain," Schmidt said, "I have a missile launch from Charlie 4. Zero eight enemy missiles in flight. They're targeting us, sir. Estimated time to impact, three three seconds. No friendly missiles in flight at this time. Damage to Bravo 1 unknown."

"Just eight? Anything from Charlie 3?"

"No, sir, not yet, although she still looks to be putting herself in a position to fire. None of them are even bothering with their energy weapons at the moment — just the salvo of missiles from Charlie 4. Wait one … disregard what I said about Charlie 3, she just transitioned to hyperspace."

"Understood," Prescott replied. "Advise immediately if she returns to the area. Designate Charlie 4 as an enemy combatant. Helm, we're going to let the fighters worry about that last cruiser for now. Plot a C-Jump to a position in the neighborhood of where Badger 21 Flight launched their missiles at the *Baldev's* stern. We should be getting updated battle damage assessment data forwarded from the fighters shortly. Hopefully, that will give us some idea of what we're up against."

"Estimated time to impact, one three seconds," Lieutenant Commander Schmidt reported from Tactical 1.

"Helm, execute your C-Jump when ready."

"Aye, sir. Tactical C-Jumping."

On the bridge view screen, *Theseus'* AI displayed a "flyby" of the debris that had until recently been Charlie 2 before passing rapidly over the top of the *Baldev*. After transitioning back into normal space, Ensign Fisher once again pushed the destroyer's sublight engines to full power, beginning a vertical climb as if to perform a loop. As the ship passed over the point where the maneuver began, he performed a half-roll to complete an Immelmann turn and headed the ship back in the direction of its target.

"Enemy missiles are no factor, sir," Lieutenant Commander Schmidt said. "They are still in powered flight, but have switched to search mode."

"Thank you, Schmidt. Just keep an eye on them. I doubt they will reacquire us, but their ships may have the capability to issue commands that will send them in the direction of new targets in a situation like this."

"We've got Badger 21's data," Reynolds said, issuing commands via her touchscreen to display the new information via a tactical assessment window on the port side of the bridge view screen. Multiple views of both Bravo 1 and Charlie 4 were displayed with all known vulnerabilities highlighted. "As noted earlier, Charlie 4 has the same old vulnerability near her engine nozzles — which is not surprising since her hull configuration is similar to the older cruisers. Don't get me wrong, she's still a significant threat, but I'm satisfied the fighters should be able to make short work of her. The *Baldev*, on the other hand ... take a look at this."

The tactical assessment now displayed two rotating three-dimensional depictions of the *Baldev's* drive section. After an exhaustive analysis of the battleship's engine configuration and shield energy output, the AI had highlighted a small, but still significant gap between the ship's sublight engine nozzles and her aft shields.

"The first view is based on sensor readings the fighters took *before* launching their attack on Bravo 1's stern. Note that, as we discussed earlier, the gap is smaller than it is on their cruisers — more like what we saw on the *Gresav*-class ships — but it's still there and we can still jump a bunch of C-Drive-equipped missile inside that gap. The second view," she said, nodding towards the view screen, "is based on readings taken *after* the fighters launched their attack."

"Looks like they've solved their aft shield problem," Prescott said quietly. "Maintain this range for now, Fisher — evasive maneuvers only."

"Aye, sir."

"To a degree, yes they have," Reynolds continued, "and it's a pretty simple solution at that. It looks like they just added a ring of additional shield emitters around the entire drive section."

As Reynolds spoke, the AI zoomed in on the battleship's stern — the additional shield emitters now highlighted in red and flashing to further emphasize their locations. The AI then removed the fields generated by all of the other aft shield emitters, clearly revealing the designers' intentions.

"As you can see, these new emitters create a field that is very nearly tangent to the outermost edge of the ship's sublight engine nozzles."

"Simple enough, I suppose. Given the severity of the vulnerability, you have to wonder why it took them so long to implement such a straightforward solution."

"That's just it, sir … that's actually the one bit of good news I have to offer. They fixed one problem, but in the process they created another. We theorized all along that this shield gap issue had something to do with the output of their sublight engines. Today's data confirms that theory in a big way. Running these new shield emitters closes the gap, but at the cost of seriously degrading their engine output. The AI's best guess is that they lose something like ninety-four percent of their effective thrust when they engage this supplemental field. Since their engine nozzles are gimbaled, it's also a safe bet that they will lose quite a bit of their maneuverability as well."

"So the question now becomes one of how we take advantage of this new vulnerability without getting ourselves ripped apart in the process," Prescott said, glancing over at the tactical plot to confirm the locations of the fighters. "Badger flights, *Theseus*-Actual."

"Badger 1 … Badger 2," came the immediate replies from Zhukov and Waffer.

"As I'm sure you have seen by now, the *Baldev* has the capability to reconfigure her aft shields. The good news is that once she does so, she should lose much of her ability to change course and speed. I need some of your fighters to put themselves in a position to maintain a constant threat against her drive section so that she's forced to keep those supplemental aft shields engaged. With any luck, this will allow us to work on wearing down her shields while limiting her ability to maneuver in response to our attacks. If the shield gap opens up again at her stern, I want them to hit her with everything they have."

"Understood, Captain," Commander Waffer replied. "That won't be a problem. We will also take care of

Charlie 4 momentarily. But, sir … I'm concerned we're being set up here."

"We're all ears, Commander," Prescott replied after a brief pause.

"After our first round of attacks, we C-Jumped to a safe distance, but we took no significant fire from either vessel during the time we were in range."

"I'm not sure I follow you," Prescott said. "The *Baldev* did open fire on your element that hit their fighters. Don't you think you were just in and out before they had a chance to adequately respond?"

"Maybe, Captain, but based on the data we have on those defense platform cruisers like Charlie 4, we're all well within range of their energy weapons right now, but they still aren't firing. I'm sure you also noted that Charlie 4 fired only eight missiles before you C-Jumped. I'm not sure what they're trying to accomplish, but they're up to something, sir."

"You may be on to something there, Commander, but don't you think that allowing their cruisers to get picked off without even putting up much of a fight seems like an ill-advised strategy?"

"Without a doubt, but they probably realize there isn't much they can do to prevent that from happening anyway. The fact that Charlie 2 and 4 didn't jump away leads me to believe they have been ordered to lure the *Theseus* in closer, regardless of the cost."

"Alright, Commander Waffer, thank you for pointing this out. What you're saying makes sense to me as well, but it's really just speculation at this point. The truth is that we *are* about to get closer, primarily because we don't have much of a choice. Please keep a close eye on us when we start slugging it out with Bravo 1. I suspect we'll be in need of your assistance at some point."

"We'll be there for you, *Theseus*. Badger 21 Flight will be C-Jumping momentarily to a position well beyond your current location to cover Bravo 1's stern. Expect our attack on Charlie 4 to commence in three zero seconds."

"Thank you, Badgers. *Theseus*-Actual out."

"One last thing," Reynolds said, "as far as we can tell, the *Baldev* is still vulnerable to kinetic energy weapons, and, as usual, there are no indications that she is equipped with any sort of point defense system."

"Humph. I suppose they consider that to be of little consequence if enemy ships can't penetrate their shields. Helm, plot a C-Jump for an optimum range railgun and plasma torpedo attack run on Bravo 1's stern. I have to believe that's still where we need to be focusing our attention. Tactical, set up the railguns for preferential targeting on this new ring of shield emitters. If we can get lucky and open up that shield gap again, Badger 21 Flight will know exactly what to do next."

"Aye, sir," all three officers at the center bridge console replied.

"Badger 1 and Badger 21 Flights have transitioned, sir," Lau reported, paused momentarily, then added, "Badger 21 Flight is now on station to cover Bravo 1's stern. Badger 1 Flight is beginning its attack on the remaining cruiser."

The fighters' attack on Charlie 4 began in a nearly identical fashion to the previous attacks that had destroyed both Charlie 1 and Charlie 2. Once again, all thirty-six fighters transitioned back into normal space roughly seventy-five thousand kilometers aft of their target. This time, however, immediately after each fighter had once again loosed two HB-7c missiles, the space astern of the warship was lit by an intense barrage of energy weapons fire as Charlie 4 — the *Keturah* — finally opened up with every available weapon that had a clear line of fire at the pursuing fighters and their lethal cloud of anti-ship missiles. At a range of only one quarter of a light second, the cruiser's fire control AI had little difficulty plotting a firing solution for every missile targeting their vulnerable drive section. With surgical precision, the ship's beam emitters were assigned a precise amount of energy to deliver to each inbound missile before moving on to the next threat in their queue. The cruiser itself, now clearly aware of the tactics being employed by the Human fighters, dipped sharply by the stern as her eight massive sublight engine nozzles blazed forth with a brilliant blue glow. In just seconds, the ship was in a steep climbing turn to starboard relative to her original course.

Realizing that he had temporarily lost the initiative and unwilling to push a bad position, Captain Zhukov ordered his fighters to once again transition to hyperspace. *"Badger 1 Flight is Juliet,"* he announced over the tactical comm channel. Fortunately, only a small fraction of the BD cruiser's weapons banks had been in a position to fire when his flight had been detected by the *Keturah*. Although a few had taken shield hits, none of the valuable fighters had been lost to enemy fire before C-Jumping safely away. Their attack, on the other hand, had been a dismal failure. Of the seventy-two missiles launched at the *Keturah's* drive section, sixty-five had been destroyed by her fierce hail of defensive energy weapons fire. The remaining seven had survived long enough to execute their C-Jumps, but the extraordinarily precise positioning required to transition inside the cruiser's aft shields before impact had been thwarted by her aggressive maneuvers. Only one missile managed to actually reach its target, proximity detonating upon its closest approach to the outer dorsal edge of one of the ship's sublight engine nozzles and yielding only superficial damage.

"Wouldn't it make more sense to fire the missiles from a much greater range?" Reynolds asked, scowling at the still-maneuvering *Keturah* on the tactical plot.

"If you could be assured that your target would either remain stationary or maintain a constant course and speed, absolutely. Unfortunately, the greater the range, the greater the chances that the enemy vessel will do something unexpected and invalidate your firing solution. The biggest downside to the HB-7c missile when it's fired in this manner is that it essentially becomes an unguided weapon for a period of time before it transitions to hyperspace — and that period gets longer as the range to the target increases. So if the target accelerates or makes even a gentle turn, you could well end up with a clean miss. It also takes time for the missiles to stabilize on their course before making their C-Jump. As Charlie 4 just demonstrated, they are vulnerable to being intercepted at any time prior to making their jump, so shorter range attacks have their drawbacks as well. In any event, now that they know what we're about, I expect it's going to get a lot more difficult to score an easy kill."

Chapter 5

TFS Theseus, Location Dagger
(3.3 light years from Earth)

"Should we press on with our attack on the *Baldev*?" Reynolds asked.

"For now, yes," Prescott replied. "Assuming Waffer's Badger 21 Flight remains on station to cover her stern, Zhukov still has a total of forty-eight fighters and six RPSVs at his disposal. I suspect he'll find a way to take down Charlie 4 directly. If he can't, we may not fare much better ourselves. Tactical, slave our remaining twelve *Hunters* to Badger 21 Flight. There's no need to expose them to enemy fire at this point. Once we start this run, we need you to take down as many of those new aft shield emitters as you can. I don't expect this is going to be pleasant, so let's try to minimize the number of runs needed, if possible. Helm, straight at Bravo 1's stern, please."

Before the three officers even had time to acknowledge the order, *Theseus* surged forward as Fisher rapidly advanced her sublight engines to full power. For the first time since transitioning out of *Ingenuity*, the bridge crew felt themselves being pushed back in their seats as the ship's inertial dampening systems lagged slightly behind her acceleration curve.

"Lieutenant Lee, how do we avoid more of those low angle of incidence shots that tend get past our shields … assuming the *Baldev* starts firing at some point, that is?" Prescott asked.

"We will need to develop a profile of each ship's firing pattern so that we can avoid putting ourselves in a position where incoming fire hits our shields at angles approaching the perpendicular, sir," Lieutenant Lee answered from the Science and Engineering console. "We probably won't be able to avoid that situation completely, but our data will improve every time they fire. Captain Zhukov's last attack run did a pretty good job of fleshing out Charlie 4's aft firing pattern, for example. When we start taking fire, the AI will provide the helm console with a graphical indication of where we should avoid flying, if possible. In general, we should avoid passing directly over or under the target and try to keep our course line from pointing directly at their main weapons banks."

"Thank you, Lieutenant. That's good info, although it sounds a little like dodging raindrops during a thunderstorm," he chuckled. "You heard him, Fisher, we need you to modify the definition of 'straight at 'em' just a bit. Alter your course line to avoid perpendicular fire, as often as you possibly can."

"Aye, sir, I'll do my best," the young helmsman replied noncommittally.

"I'm sure we'll be fine. As soon as our weapons no longer bear on the target's stern, C-Jump clear and set us up for another run."

"Optimal weapons range in two five seconds, Captain," Lieutenant Commander Schmidt reported from Tactical 1.

"Very good. Lau, I need you to pound the hell out of those emitters with penetration rounds from the railguns. Hopefully, they will still be able to get through the added shielding. Schmidt, try a point location attack with a full spread of torpedoes and energy weapons."

"We could sure use the *Navajo's* big guns right about now," Reynolds muttered to herself.

"For the moment, we've got the biggest guns Fleet has to offer our here, Commander. But if we can blunt their attack and force them to withdraw from the system —"

"Then if and when they do come back, things will be different," she concluded.

"I hope so, yes. With any luck, our carriers and cruisers will be able to join us if we have to face the Resistance again … or whoever else decides to show up, God forbid. For now, though, it's up to us to find a way to stop them, or at least convince them that an attack on Earth is more trouble than it's worth."

Prescott glanced over at the tactical plot, noting that the AI was automatically emphasizing *Theseus'* optimal weapons range by surrounding the ship with a green circle. As the edge of their range bubble rapidly approached Bravo 1, he saw that the AI was also displaying a corresponding estimate of the battleship's weapons range. Just as Commander Waffer had noted, his ship had been within the *Baldev's* range since their attack run began. *Why the hell aren't they firing?* he thought, suddenly feeling the hair stand on the back of his neck.

"Optimal weapons range reached," Lau reported. "Firing."

At that moment, nine of the destroyer's fifteen railgun turrets were in a position to target the battleship's drive section, and all nine now spewed forth steady streams composed of tens of thousands of penetrator rounds flying at nearly ten percent the speed of light. Based on the firing pattern selected by Lieutenant Lau, *Theseus'* AI attempted to converge the outbound railgun fire into two separate streams, slowly tracing each around the perimeter of the drive section in an effort to destroy as many shield emitters as possible. Although not entirely effective at stopping the incoming railgun rounds, the heavy shielding in place over the *Baldev's* stern still interacted with each one as it approached the hull, reducing its velocity and causing a significant percentage of the rounds to miss their target entirely. Without the shields, the fusillade would have easily transformed most of the warship's stern into a glowing mass of molten metal as each individual round delivered its destructive cargo of kinetic energy to the target.

Simultaneously, Lieutenant Schmidt had initiated his attack against a two-meter by two-meter target near the edge of several overlapping emitter streams that, according to *Theseus'* AI, corresponded to the lowest mean field strength of any location on the battleship's stern. Using a technique reminiscent of an artillery tactic developed in the mid twentieth century known as Multiple Rounds, Simultaneous Impact (MRSI), the destructive power of multiple weapon systems were coordinated by the ship's AI to converge at a single location at a precise moment in time. Accordingly, as Schmidt gave the command to fire, the AI intentionally delayed the discharge of its energy weapons until its salvo of five plasma torpedoes had reached just over two-thirds of the distance to the target. With just two one-thousandths of a second remaining until impact, fully half of the destroyer's readily available power was shunted to its energy weapons, delivering a maximum power discharge from the twenty-five beam emitter locations currently bearing on the targeted location. Just as it had done with its railgun turrets, *Theseus'* AI took into account the locations of the emitters in play, allowing the individual beams to converge at the designated point of impact.

With Badger 21 Flight remaining aft of their target, *Theseus* received continuous streams of data from several different locations, presenting its crew with a detailed assessment of the damage they had inflicted — even after the target's drive section was no longer visible from their location. Real-time light and thermally enhanced imagery of the *Baldev's* stern was immediately presented on the bridge view screen, with the effect on the target's shields highlighted on the tactical assessment display. The results, while hardly catastrophic for the colossal battleship, were better than expected.

"Captain, we took out several of the new shield emitters down the starboard side of Bravo 1's drive section," Lau reported. "The additional shielding is still in place, but it looks like we forced their AI to modify its configuration to compensate for the damage."

"C-Jumping," Ensign Fisher reported as *Theseus* concluded her first attack run and altered course to avoid passing directly beneath the huge battleship. As his practiced hands quickly executed the required commands, a series of unfamiliar, but urgent-sounding warning tones issued from the Helm console. "Uh, sir ..."

Outside, with *Theseus* now at her closest approach, energy weapons fire burst forth from what looked like hundreds of locations across the entire starboard and ventral surfaces of the *Baldev*.

"Fisher, emergency C-Jump!" Prescott yelled, the normally controlled tone of his voice deserting him entirely. In the background, the sound of the ship's reactors and sublight engines also rose sharply as she attempted to fend off the massive torrent of incoming fire.

"I'm trying, but I'm getting some kind of field integrity fault that I've never seen before … the C-Drive is offline, sir!" he replied in near panic.

With little else any of them could do at the moment, the entire bridge crew held its collective breath, each person sending nervous glances in Fisher's direction as they silently willed their ship to complete its C-Jump. For the next several seconds, his hands moved frantically across the surface of the Helm console as he continued his vain attempts to transition the ship while simultaneously executing a series of high-speed evasive maneuvers.

"Bridge, Engineering," Commander Logan's voice boomed from the overhead speakers.

"Prescott. Go, Commander!"

"We are being bombarded by a focused gravitic beam with a waveform that looks a lot like what our inertial dampeners produce. It's not enough to cause hull damage, but it's more than sufficient to prevent our hyperdrive from creating a field that's stable enough for a transition."

"I need options, Logan."

"For now, we just need to run!" his chief engineer replied in an uncharacteristically urgent tone. "We're way too close to be able to count on our shields to protect us."

As if to underscore Logan's point, *Theseus* shook violently with multiple impacts as several of the *Baldev's* bolts of focused, orange-tinted energy managed to avoid being intercepted by the destroyer's shields, instantly vaporizing sections of her outer hull armor.

Without further prompting, Ensign Fisher selected a course indicated by the AI to minimize the potential for shield penetrations, then pushed the ship's Cannae sublight engines to emergency power, temporarily allowing them to deliver twenty percent more thrust than their design maximum. *Theseus* responded without hesitation, accelerating away from the battleship in a tight arc as if it were a stationary target.

"Warning, initiate Anti-G Straining Maneuver to prevent G-induced loss of consciousness," the ship's AI announced.

"AI, Prescott. Discontinue G-force warnings," he ordered impatiently. Out of habit, he had begun tensing the muscles in his legs and abdomen as soon as his helmsman had started the series of aggressive turns. "Watch the Gs, everyone," he grunted, trying to sound more in control of the situation. "We can't afford to have anyone passing out right now."

"I guess we just found Admiral Naftur's gravitic beam weapon," Logan continued over the intercom, resuming normal breathing as the ship stabilized on its new course.

"Maybe so," Prescott said. "Let's hope that's the only trick they have up their sleeve. Any idea what kind of range we're talking about?"

"Not really, no. The *Baldev* has a number of heavy gravitic emitters mounted at various locations on her hull, so I can't even tell you at the moment which ones are responsible for the beam," he replied, sending a high resolution image of several examples to the bridge view screen. "But I *will* take a wild guess that they have a pretty substantial range ... probably a few hundred thousand kilometers at least. If they didn't, I can't imagine there would be much point in mounting them on a warship in the first place. I can also tell you that she has arrays like the ones I just sent you on both her ventral and dorsal surfaces, so we're unlikely to find much of a 'dead zone' where they can't hit us."

"Thank you, Commander. Keep the shields up and the engines running, please."

"As if my life depended on it, Captain. Logan out."

"Sir, Charlie 4 is firing on us now as well," Schmidt reported from Tactical 1, "but so far, she doesn't appear to be giving chase."

"Insult to injury at this point," he replied, glancing up at the hull impacts counter below the tactical plot, which now stood at thirteen. The ship had taken six additional hits to its hull thus far since beginning its attack run against the *Baldev*. Fortunately, with the distance between the *Theseus* and the two remaining enemy ships rapidly increasing, her shields had once again become highly effective at deflecting the incoming fire. "Helm, I think it goes without saying, but get us as far away from that battleship as you can, as fast as you can, and as soon as you get a stable hyperdrive field, execute your C-Jump."

"Aye, Captain," Fisher replied, still rapidly entering commands at the Helm console.

Even with the *Keturah* now sending a sizable fraction of her considerable firepower in their direction, the intensity of the incoming energy weapons fire had lessened somewhat from what it had been just moments ago. With *Theseus'* stern now facing the enemy ships, shield intercept events continued to occur at a rapid pace behind the destroyer as she streaked out of the area. Each interaction with an incoming bolt of energy produced a brief flash of light in the visible spectrum, resulting in a ghostly, white glow that seemed to ebb and flow like flashes of lightning revealing a whitecapped, following sea.

"Okay," Reynolds said, looking up from her touchscreen, "the AI had originally misidentified the *Baldev's* gravitic weapon as a problem with our own field generators. The good news is that the effects of the weapon are relatively easy for us to detect since we have an extensive network of sensors in place to monitor the various gravitic systems we use onboard. From now on, the tactical plot should display a warning indicator when we detect the beam. The Helm console's C-Drive interface should also display the same warning and trip the flags indicating that hyperspace transitions are unavailable. You can see them now, right Ensign Fisher?"

"Yes, ma'am. Got it. Thank you."

"Good work, Commander. Tactical, range to the *Baldev*, please?" Prescott asked.

"One niner zero thousand kilometers, Captain," Schmidt replied. "Just passing .05 c and still accelerating."

"I'm going to be optimistic and venture a guess that we'll be able to transition to hyperspace once our range exceeds three hundred thousand kilometers."

"I'm not so sure about that, sir," Reynolds replied. "It apparently doesn't take much interference to prevent the hyperdrive from doing its thing. I'm thinking more like double that. It's a good thing Bravo 1 can't come after us. They're pretty much hamstrung as long as our fighters are covering their stern."

"Dammit!" Prescott swore under his breath, realizing that he had neglected to update the fighter squadrons regarding *Theseus'* status. "Badger flights, *Theseus*-Actual."

"Badger 1 ... Badger 2," Zhukov and Waffer replied in their typical, businesslike tone.

"I'm not sure how much of our situation you were able to piece together over the past couple of minutes, but the purpose of the gravitic beam Admiral Naftur warned us about is to prevent a ship from transitioning to hyperspace. They've been hitting us with it ever since we finished our attack run. We are unable to C-Jump at the moment, but believe we should be able to do so once again after we put sufficient distance between ourselves and the *Baldev*. The presence of Badger 21 Flight off their stern does appear to be forcing them to keep their supplemental shields engaged — and that, in turn, prevents their giving chase. Since I'm pretty sure coming after us is something they would very much like to do, I believe you should expect that they will focus their attention on you once we transition out of the area."

"Badger flights copy. Be advised that we are still showing an operational status on all of our C-Drives, so they may only have the capability to target one ship at a time. What are your intentions, Captain?" Zhukov asked.

"Glad to hear it. Assuming we can clear their grav beam, we intend to C-Jump thirty light seconds downrange, take a quick look at the battle damage assessment, then set up for another attack run on Bravo 1's stern."

"Range to Bravo 1 now three zero zero thousand kilometers," Schmidt updated in the background.

"Sir, if I may," Waffer interjected, "our AI has been chewing on the data from your attack run and it looks like it was significantly more effective than our models predicted. I believe if you execute the same type of attack against Charlie 4, you will at the very least succeed in bringing down her shields so that we can finish her off. You may even destroy her outright. That gets us back to our original plan of being able to focus everything we have left on Bravo 1."

Prescott glanced at his XO, who nodded her emphatic agreement under raised eyebrows. "Alright, Badger flights, we'll go with your suggestion. We won't be gone long once we C-Jump, so be ready to back us up once we return to start our next attack run. By the same token, don't hesitate to C-Jump away yourselves if you come under fire."

"Will do, *Theseus*, Badgers out."

"Captain, Commander Waffer is definitely right about our attack," Lau said from Tactical 2. "I was so focused on taking down shield emitters that I didn't really notice the results of Lieutenant Commander Schmidt's ordinance until now. Bravo 1's aft shields remained intact overall — other than the supplemental field reconfiguration I mentioned earlier — but our point location attack seems to have placed so much energy in one spot that some of it managed to impact her hull."

"That's very good news, Lieutenant. Did we do any damage?"

"C-Jumping," Fisher interrupted from the Helm console.

"And that's even better news," Prescott chuckled.

The sound of the destroyer's reactors decreased in volume as the rate of shield intercept events instantly decreased from hundreds per minute to zero. With the Resistance warships now just over nine million kilometers astern, Ensign Fisher finally decreased power to the sublight engines and began the process of decelerating in a wide arc that would ultimately head them back in the direction of the battle.

"What was our range to Bravo 1 when we finally cleared their gravitic beam?" Prescott asked, supplanting his earlier question.

"Between five and six hundred thousand kilometers, sir," Schmidt answered.

"Well, there you go, Commander," he said, smiling broadly.

"I would have been fine with being wrong on that one, sir," she replied. "It just surprised me how little energy it takes to keep us from making a hyperspace transition. I have to believe there is some way we can counter it, though."

"Let's hope that's the case since it essentially nullifies one of our biggest tactical advantages. Lieutenant Lee, damage report, please."

"We've got some hull damage, sir," he replied without looking up from the Science and Engineering console, "but so far it seems to be limited to our outermost layers of armor plating. It also doesn't look like we have lost any close-in weapon system turrets or shield emitters. Engineering is still conducting their survey to confirm. Otherwise, all systems are still in the green. Once we complete our turn, we are ready to C-Jump. Range 99.3 light years and stable."

"Don't ever let anyone tell you that luck isn't a real thing," Prescott muttered. "Ensign Fisher, how long until you have us in a position to C-Jump back?"

"Three seven seconds, sir."

"Excellent. Lieutenant Lau, please continue with your battle damage assessment … but be quick about it, please."

"Aye, sir. You were asking if Lieutenant Commander Schmidt's point location attack caused any damage. I'd have to say yes, but in an area that probably didn't have too much of an effect on their sublight engine nozzles or shield emitters. The significant lesson learned is that putting enough energy in one spot at one time appears to overload their shielding to some degree. So when we go after Charlie 4, I think we should allow the AI to choose the weakest shield location again, but this time have it correspond with one of her engine nozzles."

"So we allow the AI to open a hole with the energy weapons and then thread the needle with the railguns …"

"Yes, sir. I also think we should try mixing in some fragmentation rounds with the penetrators. I don't have a computer model for anything like this situation, but I'm hoping we might get some kind of a rebound effect between the shields and the hull."

"We might at that. Nice job, you two. Set it up quickly and let's get this done. Keep in mind that Admiral Patterson warned us that they might be expecting reinforcements. If that's the case, time is most definitely *not* on our side. Lieutenant Dubashi, what's the comm delay back to our fighters from here?"

At the Communications console, Dubashi quickly executed an NRD network latency query, which, in addition to a great deal of additional information regarding the status of the network in general, provided a readout of the comm delay from *Theseus'* current position to the nearest ten Fleet assets.

"Only about seven seconds, Captain. Our current location, as well as that of the Badger flights, are each only about one million kilometers from the nearest comm beacon."

"Thank you, Lieutenant. Alright, Ensign Fisher, Charlie 4's position as currently displayed on the tactical plot is being relayed from our fighters, so it's delayed by about seven seconds. Keep in mind that she is not equipped with supplemental aft shields like the *Baldev*. As you can see, she is still maneuvering and I think we can safely assume that she will continue to do so in order to prevent another C-Drive-equipped missile attack on her stern. That means it's up to us to either put a stop to her maneuvering or take her out completely, so I need you to C-Jump us as close as you can without putting us in danger of transitioning inside her hull. Once we arrive, close with her as quickly as possible, match her maneuvers turn for turn, and give Tactical a chance to execute their attack. Make sense?"

"Yes, sir. I think I just heard you say that you want me to dogfight that cruiser."

"Well ..." Prescott chuckled, realizing that there was quite a bit of truth in the young ensign's statement, "yeah, I guess that's exactly what I want you to do. Just keep in mind that she will be hammering away at us with her aft weapons banks, and most likely Bravo 1 will open up on us again as well. Do your best to avoid hits that might get past our shields — although I'm sure that's going to be pretty tough once we're behind the target. I'm also pretty confident that Bravo 1 will prevent us from C-Jumping again, so be prepared to make a run for it, just like last time."

"Aye, sir. Got it."

"Anyone else have any questions on what we're doing?" Prescott asked. Hearing nothing, he continued, "Dubashi, send our fighters a time-indexed warning that we will be C-Jumping in two zero seconds on your mark, then give the Helm console a countdown timer."

"Aye, sir," she replied, entering the required commands before transmitting the message. "Mark ... message transmitted. C-Jump in one eight seconds and counting."

"Everyone take a deep breath ... stay relaxed and focused. We've done just fine so far, but it's up to us to finish this fight," Prescott said as calmly as he could manage.

"First and best, sir," Dubashi replied nervously.

"Here we go again, folks," Fisher said. "C-Jumping in 3 … 2 … 1 …"

Chapter 6

SCS Gunov, Location Crossbow
(5.93×10^{11} km from Location Dagger)

"Report!" Commodore Sarafi barked as he emerged from his ready room.

"A single ship has transitioned from hyperspace, Commodore," his tactical officer responded. "Range to the target is just over six hundred thousand kilometers. She is slightly larger than the *Gunov* at six hundred twenty-five meters in length and appears to be heavily armed — beam emitters, kinetics, and vertical missile launch cells are all in evidence. Thus far, however, we have detected no shields in use. The fire control AI cannot identify the specific vessel type, but has classified her as 'probable Terran' in origin based on a number of similarities to their small scout vessels. Per the most recent rules of engagement for the secondary rally point, the battlespace defense system has not opened fire since it was unable to make a definitive hostile identification. Shall we authorize the system to engage, sir?"

Sarafi's eyes had remained fixed on the light-amplified and thermally enhanced image of the Terran warship as he made his way to his command chair. The vessel was clearly of the same class as the one he had been observing for some time back at the original rally point, and he briefly entertained the thought that it might be the exact same ship. But no, that could not possibly be the case, could it? The data stream provided by the remote surveillance drones was delayed by less than thirty seconds before reaching the display screen in his ready room. This was clearly a different ship, but the idea of the Terrans possessing a significant number of such vessels was a troubling prospect indeed. These were powerful, advanced warships — easily more than a match for older Sajeth Collective cruisers or perhaps even a *Rusalov*-class battleship. How many of these did the Terrans have at their disposal? Two? Ten? Were there other, even more powerful ships that his forces had not yet encountered?

"Make no mistake, they are almost certainly equipped with shielding of some sort. Have they hailed us?" he asked his communications officer without taking his eyes off the view screen.

"No, sir."

"Are they closing on our position?"

"No, sir," his tactical officer responded once again. "They are maneuvering to some degree, but their range has remained steady since they arrived."

"Hmm. Well, at this point, we have given them more than enough time to perform a thorough reconnaissance of our forces, if that was their intent," Sarafi remarked, half to himself. "Comm, go ahead and try hailing them. Perhaps having witnessed the extent to which their forces are outnumbered, their captain will be ready to discuss terms."

"Aye, sir. Hailing."

After a brief pause during which the two vessels' AIs synchronized for real-time translation services, the face of a surprisingly confident-looking Terran male appeared on the *Gunov's* view screen.

"I am Commodore Naveen Sarafi of the Sajeth Collective flagship *Gunov*. With whom do I have the honor of speaking?"

"This is Captain Bruce Abrams of the starship TFS *Karna,* here on behalf of Terran Fleet Command." Like Prescott, Abrams had been uncomfortable having his crews address him as "commodore" during his independent command and privately thought the title both unnecessary and pretentious. "*Commodore*, I am afraid I have the unpleasant duty of informing you that the presence of your warships in such close proximity to the Sol System is seen as an act of aggression by our people. We have recently established diplomatic relations with the Sajeth Collective and have every reason to believe that our worlds will enjoy a long and prosperous friendship. I am sure you understand, however, that the space in the immediate vicinity of our homeworld is sovereign Terran territory. In the interest of our security and yours, we ask that you withdraw your forces immediately."

"My sympathies, Captain. It is an unpleasant errand indeed on which your vessel was dispatched. Unfortunately, my orders are even less agreeable. I suspect you already know why we are here, do you not? It is our wish to avoid unnecessary violence, however, and I am optimistic that we can do so if you and whatever other forces you represent will agree to stand down."

"I do have a pretty good idea why you are here, Commodore Sarafi, so I am not sure I am ready to accept your assertion that you would like to avoid unnecessary violence just yet. I implore you to take advantage of this opportunity to affirm and strengthen our new relationship. It is within your power to make Humanity a permanent ally today, sir, rather than run the risk of creating a dangerous enemy."

"Under normal circumstances, I would like that of all things, Captain Abrams. Regrettably, that decision has already been made and it is beyond my power to countermand it at this point. Now — please — you are hopelessly outnumbered. Allow your vessel to be taken peaceably and no harm shall come to your crew."

Abrams sighed audibly, looking down for a moment as if considering Commodore Sarafi's offer. Seeming to come to a decision that, like his adversary's, was largely made by others well in advance of today's meeting, he looked up and regarded the Wek officer through narrowed eyes. "It is true, sir, that we are outnumbered, but I think you will find that we are far from hopeless." With that, Abrams looked off to the side and nodded to an unseen member of his crew.

"Multiple contacts!" Sarafi's tactical officer growled as eight separate two-ship formations of *Theseus*-class destroyers transitioned from hyperspace at locations around the perimeter of the Resistance task force. "A total of seventeen warships, Commodore … all with a configuration similar to the original contact."

Sarafi paused, allowing his forces precious seconds to prepare for a confrontation with the Terran vessels. *"Well*, Captain," he began again with a calculating smile on his face, "I suppose now I am obligated to ask you to state your intentions. Surely, we are both reasonable and clever enough to come up with a resolution that does not require the senseless deaths of thousands of our people."

"That depends entirely on you at this point, Commodore. I am authorized to allow you to withdraw your forces. Your ships will be tracked until they have reached a distance of at least twenty-five light years from the Sol system. Beyond that, we will attempt to pursue a diplomatic solution to the current situation via the Sajeth Collective Governing Council."

"And if I refuse?"

"Then I am authorized to cause the senseless deaths of thousands of your people," Abrams replied, mirroring Sarafi's smile. "But I sincerely hope that you will choose the former. I am sure you understand that we cannot allow —"

With a quick gesture to his communications officer, Sarafi terminated the tedious and clearly pointless conversation with the petulant Terran captain. Here was a situation that was truly as unfortunate as it was unexpected. There was plenty of evidence at this point that the Humans had fielded far more formidable forces than originally expected — in numbers, speed, and firepower. That being the case, perhaps it was reasonable to assume that they had sent every available vessel out to meet the Resistance threat once the location of their task force had been discovered. Keeping ships in reserve to defend the planet from attack certainly made sense if there were sufficient ships available to do so. What might a Terran admiral do, however, if he were presented with an opportunity to decisively engage the enemy, but had only twenty or so ships at his disposal? Sarafi felt sure that he knew what *he* would do in that situation, but thus far, the Humans had proven both resourceful and unpredictable, had they not?

And what did this development portend for the attack on Terra itself? The location of his task force's rally point had been largely dictated by the capabilities (or lack thereof) of the older ships under his command. At this distance, even the most modern Sajeth Collective ships like the *Gunov* were still a full day's travel from the planet. Even if he chose not to face the Human vessels here, and instead departed immediately for Terra, he had every reason to believe that these same enemy warships would be waiting for him when he arrived. No, under the circumstances, he had no choice but to destroy the Human ships here and now, then press on with the remainder of his mission with whatever forces he had remaining after the battle. Worst case, the *Gunov* herself was fully capable of completing the planetary attack alone — although doing so was an option Sarafi hoped to avoid, if possible.

"Sir, we are detecting multiple missile launches in progress from all of the Human vessels," Sarafi's tactical officer reported. "The fire control AIs from our two battlespace defense cruisers are now tracking nearly three hundred inbound missiles!"

"Understood. Comm, send from Flag to all vessels as follows: 'Engage and destroy all Terran vessels. Coordinate attacks per battlespace defense AI to avoid inadvertently targeting friendly forces.'"

"Aye, Commodore."

"The Human vessels have transitioned to hyperspace, sir," Tactical reported.

"Yes, that appears to be a favored tactic of theirs," he scoffed. "They will not have gone far. We need to take advantage of this time to intercept those missiles."

"Aye, sir, the BD system has already developed firing solutions for all two hundred seventy-two enemy missiles utilizing beam and kinetic weapons from twenty of our vessels. They are relatively slow missiles, sir. The probability of intercept is ninety-four percent or greater for all inbound ordinance," the tactical officer reported with a triumphant tone in his voice. "In fact, they are so slow that the system is pausing to all allow the missiles to reach optimal kill range."

In a terrifying flash of situational awareness, Naveen Sarafi realized what he had missed while watching the Human ships at the original rally point so easily disable the *Babayev*, a massive and heavily shielded *Shopak*-class cruiser. "Tactical, override the BD system and order all ships to open fire now!" he roared. "Flag to all vessels, emergency, break to starboard, break to starboard, break to starboard!"

At an average distance of just over four hundred thousand kilometers from their intended targets, seventeen individual groups composed of sixteen HB-7c missiles each reached their predetermined velocity setpoints, engaged their miniaturized C-Drives, and transitioned to hyperspace.

It took mere seconds for all twenty-six Resistance ships to respond to the commodore's order to take emergency evasive action. In an impressive display of Sajeth Collective command and control capabilities, each vessel rapidly increased power while immediately beginning a turn to the right of their previous course. Simultaneously, each vessel tasked with engaging one or more of the inbound missiles opened fire with all weapons that currently had a clear line of sight to their targets. Unfortunately, by the time the first, orange-tinted bolts of energy arrived at their projected points of impact, they passed harmlessly through the empty space that should have contained Terran missiles.

As fate and timing would have it, there were precisely the same number of cruisers present in the Resistance task force at the moment as there were Human destroyers available to target them. Fifteen of these were of the original *Shopak*-class design, while the remaining two were the critical *Keturah*-class BD cruisers — currently tasked with coordinating the task force's efforts to defend against the Terran intruders.

The last thought that ran through Commodore Sarafi's mind before the Human missiles found their targets was that he had managed to well and truly succeed in accomplishing at least part of the mission envisioned by the damnable politicians.

TFS Theseus, Location Dagger
(3.3 light years from Earth)

"Transition complete, Captain. Range to Charlie 4, two hundred kilometers … adjusting course and speed to park us on her six," Ensign Fisher reported from the Helm console as the still-maneuvering enemy cruiser appeared as a small dot that rapidly expanded to fill much of the bridge view screen.

"Alright, Tactical, as soon as Fisher has you in position, execute your attack. I don't have to tell you that the quicker we can take her out of action, the better," Prescott said.

As if either officer manning the Tactical console needed further convincing on this point, the noise level on *Theseus'* bridge rose sharply as a number of events occurred simultaneously. The first sound they heard was a series of urgent-sounding chirps from the Helm console indicating that the ship had once again been targeted by the *Baldev's* gravitic beam.

"Bravo 1 has acquired us with her grav beam, sir," Fisher reported immediately. "Hyperspace transitions unavailable."

"Thank you, Ensign. That's unfortunate, but not unexpected. Stay with your target," Prescott replied evenly.

Next came the now all-to-familiar cacophony of sounds associated with incoming energy weapons fire — first from the aft weapons banks of their chase, then followed shortly thereafter by Bravo 1. Once more, *Theseus'* reactors responded immediately, providing the vast amounts of power required to handle the steadily increasing number of shield intercept events occurring all around her hull.

"Only sporadic fire from the battleship so far, Captain. They're probably worried about hitting their cruiser," Schmidt observed from Tactical 1.

"As well they should be. I'm counting on their realizing at some point that when they *miss* us, there is some danger of hitting Charlie 4, but when they *hit* us, there's an even better chance that our shields will deflect their rounds right into the cruiser's drive section."

"Bravo 1 has launched more fighters — a total of twenty-five now — and they appear to be heading in the general direction of Badger 21 Flight," Lieutenant Lau reported.

"Is Badger 21 Flight still in a position to cover the *Baldev's* stern for us?" Prescott asked.

"Yes, sir, but they may get distracted shortly."

"Tactical, I need both of you stay focused on your attack run. Lieutenant Lee, please coordinate with all three Badger flights to make sure they keep Bravo 1 pinned down. They may not need our help handling the enemy fighters, but we'll see what we can do after we deal with Charlie 4."

"Aye, sir," Lieutenant Lee responded from the Science and Engineering console.

For such a large warship, the BD cruiser *Keturah* was still surprisingly nimble. As Ensign Fisher maneuvered to stay on her tail, *Theseus'* AI dutifully gathered a wide array of performance data in the hopes of revealing a vulnerability that might later be exploited to bring about her demise. Everything from the cruiser's acceleration and turn rate/radius to minute changes in the apparent power output of her engines and shields while firing her energy weapons was measured, analyzed, and cataloged. With such a wealth of new data to work with, it didn't take *Theseus'* AI long to begin passing along various pieces of valuable information via the tactical assessment displayed on the bridge view screen. The first of these was an indication that the enemy vessel's Wek designers had achieved significant improvements in maneuverability and power generation capacity over the original cruiser designs encountered previously.

"Fisher, the AI reports that your target is nearly thirty percent more maneuverable and has twenty-five percent more power output than the older cruisers we've run into before. I just thought you'd want to know," Commander Reynolds chuckled. Time and again, she had seen Captain Prescott exhibit his sometimes quirky sense of humor at what seemed like the strangest of times. What she had come to realize, however, was that allowing crewmembers to fixate and become too intense in the heat of combat was a major performance killer. Glancing at her captain for a reaction, she received a knowing grin and a wink in reply.

"Uh … many thanks to the AI for that, ma'am," Fisher replied. "That helps a lot … I guess. Seriously, though, I'm almost there, I just need a few more seconds."

Although *Theseus* was clearly the more maneuverable of the two warships, matching the enemy cruiser's aggressive and seemingly random changes in speed and direction was turning out to be a bigger challenge than the young helmsman had expected.

"Missile launch!" Lieutenant Lau reported from Tactical 2. "Bravo 1 just ripple-fired three two missiles from her ventral launch tubes. Time to impact, three eight seconds."

"Lieutenant Lee, launch countermeasures. All weapons to point defense mode," Prescott responded without hesitation.

"Countermeasures, aye. Beam and kinetic weapons switching to point defense mode. Sea-whiz online and tracking inbound missiles," Lee replied.

"Now would be a good time, Tactical," Prescott said, the first hints of urgency creeping into his voice.

"They must think they've got us in a pretty tight spot to risk hitting their own cruiser with a stray missile," Reynolds said, leaning to her left so that only Prescott could hear.

"They probably do, and they're probably right. They know we can't transition, and they also know we'll be reluctant to break off this attack in an effort to avoid their missiles."

Reynolds glanced at the tactical plot, noting the positions of the decoys designed to duplicate the emissions characteristics of the destroyer and fool the incoming missiles into chasing them instead. Thus far, all thirty-two inbound missiles appeared to be ignoring the decoys and heading directly for the *Theseus*. As she watched, the display updated to display the rapidly closing missiles in an ominous pulsating red that sent a chill of déjà vu coursing down the length of her spine.

"Time to impact, two niner seconds," Lee updated.

***

At a point roughly halfway between the *Theseus* and Bravo 1, all thirty-six fighters assigned to Badger 1 Flight transitioned into normal space. Just as before, every spacecraft was positioned so that it was afforded a clear line of fire — this time at the anti-ship missiles fired by the *Baldev*. Realizing the destroyer's tenuous position, Captain Zhukov allocated a total of four HB-7c missiles for each enemy missile targeting the *Theseus*. Just three hundred milliseconds after the *Reapers* transitioned, one hundred and twenty-eight of the multimission-capable missiles leapt from their underwing pylons and accelerated rapidly away from the fighters."

"Badger 1 Flight - Fox Alpha!" Captain Zhukov announced over the tactical comm channel. By convention, the "Alpha" designation was an indication that the versatile missiles were being launched in what would have once been considered "air-to-air" mode. At such close range, the missiles' onboard C-Drives were unnecessary. Instead, each weapon received initial targeting instructions from its fighter before launch, then relied on a sophisticated suite of internal sensors to ensure a successful intercept of its target.

A reactionless Cannae drive, without the blazing engine nozzle still used in similar Wek-designed weapons, propelled each Terran weapon along a short, predetermined course towards the location where its flight path would intercept one of Bravo 1's missiles. Accordingly — in the visible spectrum at least — the Human missiles were all but invisible as their onboard processors made final, minute course corrections in an effort to achieve clean, "skin-to-skin" hits on their targets.

Perhaps even more difficult to detect, however, were two cylindrical pods deployed by two of the *Baldev's* original nine fighters shortly before they had been destroyed by Badger 22 Flight. Designed originally to operate autonomously, each Carrada Area Denial Weapons pod was capable of positioning itself within a designated anti-access zone in the hopes of complicating the efforts of enemy forces attempting to achieve tactical superiority — particularly with small, fighter-class spacecraft. In this case, the *Baldev's* fighters had simply released the pods at a location roughly half the distance to the *Keturah* in anticipation of precisely this sort of opportunity.

Using data provided by the battlespace defense system to calculate the closest approach of Badger 1 Flight, each pod now pivoted in the direction of the oncoming fighters and fired three kinetic energy interceptors. Rather than relying on their own source of propulsion — which would have dramatically increased the size and complexity of the system — each interceptor was fired from a rail launcher not unlike those used by railgun and plasma torpedo mounts aboard TFC vessels. While somewhat limited in power due to their size, each pod was equipped with a gravitic generator capable of counteracting the inertia of its projectiles during launch. This allowed each interceptor to cover the relatively small distance to their targets at a speed of over seven thousand kilometers per second.

At a distance projected to disperse a precise quantity of fragments across the volume of space occupied by the oncoming fighters, each interceptor detonated a small set of charges along its length. Milliseconds later, six rapidly expanding cones of submunitions merged with Badger 1's flight path at a combined speed of nearly five percent the speed of light.

Like the *Theseus,* each F-373 fighter was equipped with a gravitic shield capable of simultaneously deflecting a significant (albeit unknown) number of incoming munitions. The engineers had warned, and combat experience had now proven, that kinetic energy rounds were the most difficult ordinance to deflect, particularly when they approached from angles nearly perpendicular to the hull. Now, as the stacked formation of fighters encountered the cloud of deadly fragments very nearly head-on, their shields were forced to handle a situation that was suboptimal in almost every respect. Worse still, as the lead spacecraft successfully deflected the first series of fragments it encountered, a great many of the rounds were sent careening directly into other fighters in the formation — also at angles approaching ninety degrees. A mere fraction of a second later, the shields of the fighters nearest the front of the formation were overwhelmed — leading instantaneously to their complete destruction. As their rapidly expanding debris clouds stretched out towards the other ships in the formation at relativistic speeds, the additional fragments only served to enhance the Carrada's destructive power.

Of the original thirty-six *Reapers* assigned to Badger 1 Flight, only six survived unscathed, including Captain Zhukov's ship. Twenty-three F-373 fighters were completely destroyed, as were the accompanying (and unshielded) six *Hunter* RPSVs detached from the *Theseus* at the onset of the battle. No emergency locator beacon signals emanated from the debris field — the fighters having been destroyed with such violence that even the heavily armored "bathtubs" designed to protect their pilots were ground into fragments. The remaining seven spacecraft, while all more or less in one piece, were incapable of continuing the battle — and only three still possessed operable C-Drives.

Even before the pilots of the remaining operational *Reapers* had become fully aware of the grievous damage inflicted against their flight, their AIs had coordinated and settled on a response designed to prevent the loss of additional spacecraft. Under such extreme circumstances — when both lives and valuable equipment were likely to be lost unless action was taken at a pace far exceeding their Human pilots' capabilities — the AIs were authorized to act autonomously. Having already located the source of the weapons that had attacked them, the two closest fighters instantly opened fire with both their dorsal and ventral railgun turrets — their own kinetic energy penetration rounds streaking away towards the two Carrada weapons pods at just under ten percent the speed of light. Only seconds after Badger 1 Flight had been decimated in the unexpected attack, both area denial weapons pods simply disappeared in two expanding clouds of metallic dust. With the immediate threat neutralized, the *Reapers'* AIs executed a quick search of the immediate area for additional weapons pods. Finding none, they continued the routine business of operating the sophisticated fighters while awaiting additional orders from their still stunned Human pilots.

Seconds later, recovering somewhat from the initial shock of the attack, Captain Zhukov ordered another quick sweep of the area for additional survivors. Then, with his remaining fighters' active sensor suites still scanning for additional area denial weapons, he and the other five fully operational fighters began the slow process of escorting the damaged members of their decimated flight out of the immediate area.

Chapter 7

TFS Theseus, Location Dagger
(3.3 light years from Earth)

"Missile launch!" Lau reported once again from Tactical 2. "Tracking one two eight friendly inbound missiles fired from Badger 1 in antimissile mode."

"Is there still time for Badger 1's missiles to make the intercept?" Prescott asked.

"I believe so, sir, and apparently so does Charlie 4. They are shifting their fire to try and take out the friendlies. The original group of three-two anti-ship missiles from Bravo 1 is still two three seconds out."

Without any sort of intervention required of its crew, the BD cruiser *Keturah* had made the determination that the most effective method of either destroying the Human vessel outright, or at least temporarily removing the threat to its own vulnerable stern, was ensuring that the *Baldev's* salvo of anti-ship missiles successfully reached its target. Accordingly, all of the warship's aft beam emitters shifted their fire in a last ditch attempt to destroy the Human missiles during their final seconds of flight before they in turn intercepted the *Baldev's* missiles. Performing precisely the task for which she had been designed, the cruiser's fire control AI advanced rapidly through the enormously complicated calculations required to identify, target, and destroy one hundred and twenty-eight unimaginably fast targets — continually refining its firing solution even as the first bolts fired from its aft energy weapons banks were already streaming downrange at the speed of light. At such short range, the *Keturah's* beam emitters had little difficulty slicing through the Human HB-7c missiles — the destruction of each making it ever more likely that at least some of the *Baldev's* missiles would reach the *Theseus*. In the very short amount of time she had been provided, the BD cruiser managed to significantly improve her own situation by significantly complicating that of her enemy. Out of the one hundred and twenty-eight missiles fired by Badger 1 Flight, only forty-two survived the *Keturah's* energy weapons barrage. Unfortunately for the *Theseus*, a significant percentage of the remaining friendly missiles scored double and triple hits against inbound anti-ship missiles — ultimately allowing twelve of them to continue on course.

"Multiple successful intercepts, sir, stand by … one two anti-ship missiles still inbound. One eight seconds to —"

"Point location target acquired and locked," Schmidt interrupted hurriedly. "Firing!"

Just as it had during the previous attack on the *Baldev's* drive section, *Theseus'* AI selected a single location on Charlie 4's stern where a lack of uniformity in field strength at the junction between emitter streams offered a slight advantage. Once again, the AI timed the impact of a full spread of five plasma torpedoes to precisely correspond with a maximum power discharge from all beam weapons currently bearing on the target. This time, however, the AI also sent a combination of kinetic energy penetrator and fragmentation rounds streaming from nine of the destroyer's railgun turrets to precisely the same location on the enemy ship's stern —

directly over the *Keturah's* huge number four engine nozzle.

Cascading waves of energy coursed outward from the BD cruiser's drive section, traveling along the entire length of the hull as her shield systems struggled to cope with the massive quantities of energy being concentrated against one small area of her stern. The *Keturah's* entire shield flickered momentarily — just long enough to allow the relentless streams of railgun and energy weapons fire to inflict significant damage to the targeted area — then appeared to recover to some extent. At the site of the number four engine nozzle, however, even this brief interruption in shield continuity resulted in the immediate destruction of four shield emitters, causing what amounted to a catastrophic, albeit localized, shield failure.

This was precisely the opportunity for which *Theseus'* ever-watchful AI had been waiting.

Shifting her fire slightly to exploit the new vulnerability, *Theseus'* energy weapons and railguns slammed directly into the unshielded sublight engine nozzle, instantly tearing the relatively delicate structure to pieces. Just as Lieutenant Lau had hoped, the addition of fragmentation rounds from the railgun turrets had the added effect of dispersing the damage across an even larger area of the cruiser's stern. Ultimately, however, it was Lieutenant Commander Schmidt who delivered the coup de grâce. In preparing for their attack run, he had instructed *Theseus'* AI to fire a second volley of plasma torpedoes as quickly as the weapons could be recharged. With Ensign Fisher aggressively maintaining the destroyer's position astern of the *Keturah*, five compressed bolts of plasma once again slammed into the now unshielded portion of her drive section, fusing most of the area into a brightly glowing mass of molten metals. Just a few short seconds after *Theseus* had opened fire, six of the cruiser's eight sublight engines had been completely destroyed. Shortly thereafter, the brilliant blue glow issuing from her remaining two engines decreased sharply, then disappeared altogether.

Seconds later and hidden from *Theseus'* view, massive, forward-facing doors mounted amidships on both sides of *Keturah's* hull slid quickly into recessed cavities to reveal a single sublight engine nozzle even larger than her eight main engines mounted astern. Without further delay, both engines blazed into life at their maximum rated thrust.

"Inbound missiles have cleared our point defense barrier," Lieutenant Lee announced. "Three more destroyed! Time to impact on the remaining nine, one three seconds. Sea-whiz is firing."

At fifteen locations along *Theseus'* stern, a combination of mini railgun and energy turrets began filling the relatively small space between the destroyer and the rapidly approaching missiles with a lethal curtain of kinetic energy rounds and bolts of focused energy.

With so much activity taking place at one time on his bridge, Prescott's ability to divide his attention between every urgent demand was strained to the point of distraction. Faced with such an unreasonable burden, the Human mind tends to fixate on a single subject, and in this case, the incoming anti-ship missiles topped Prescott's mental priority list. Many years earlier, a young Ensign Prescott had been warned repeatedly of this understandable, but potentially deadly tendency — traditionally referred to as "boresighting" by combat pilots. Now, perhaps only a second or two off his normal mental pace, Captain Prescott's mind became fully aware of a new and potentially disastrous threat.

"Fisher, you're too close!" he yelled. "Down, down, down! Mark three one five *NOW!*"

During his efforts to match the BD cruiser's movements, Ensign Fisher had been "hand flying" the ship. In this configuration, *Theseus'* AI, while never completely relinquishing control to its helmsman, took slightly longer to augment Human control inputs or, when necessary, to override potentially dangerous commands. With the destroyer operating in such close proximity to its target, the loss of the *Keturah's* main engines, followed immediately by her application of full reverse thrust, created a situation that was not anticipated — either by *Theseus'* young helmsman or her AI.

"Holy *shit*!" Fisher swore as he instantly reacted to force his ship's bow below the *Keturah's* heavily damaged drive section.

"Seven more missiles destroyed!" Lieutenant Lee shouted. "Two remaining —"

"All hands brace for contact!" Prescott interrupted — immediately repeated by the AI throughout the ship.

Nimble though she was for a warship of nearly five hundred thousand metric tons, *Theseus'* Cannae thrusters pushed her massive bulk downward at an agonizingly slow pace as the ship closed the remaining distance to the rapidly decelerating *Keturah*. Once the gap between the two warships had narrowed to only fourteen hundred meters, the destroyer's gravitic shields began interacting with the hull of the cruiser in exactly the same manner that it normally handled incoming kinetic energy rounds or missiles. While incapable of preventing a collision between the two vessels, the field strength at the point of closest approach quickly increased until reaching the maximum power handling capabilities of the system's gravitic emitters. As *Theseus'* AI violently shifted the grav fields to induce destructive shear forces all along the *Keturah's* hull, the most significant result was the utter destruction of nearly all devices protruding above the surface — most notably shield and beam emitter emplacements — immediately collapsing what remained of the cruiser's aft shields. When physical contact finally did occur between the two ships, the impact itself was brief but still quite violent. The top of *Theseus'* hull just forward of amidships struck a glancing blow against the outermost ventral surface of the *Keturah's* drive section, crushing the cruiser's two remaining sublight engine nozzles. Surprisingly, other than carving an impressively long but somewhat superficial gouge out of her dorsal surface's armor plating, the destroyer managed to escape the encounter with no additional damage.

Just as the two ships began to ease slowly apart, the two remaining anti-ship missiles fired by the *Baldev* reached the point where they began interacting with *Theseus'* aft gravitic shields. The body of the first missile was instantly distorted beyond recognition, resulting in a violent explosion of the weapon's propellant and oxidizer mixture so energetic that its warhead never received an instruction to detonate from the onboard processor. The second and final missile approached *Theseus'* stern with a slightly upward trajectory relative to the ship's longitudinal axis. As was the AI's preference, gravitic distortions were placed along the missile's flight path such that its trajectory was altered ever so slightly upward. Unable to react quickly enough to the unintended change of direction, the missile's warhead was ordered to detonate in a last ditch attempt to inflict as much damage as possible to its target. Faithfully executing its final instruction, the warhead exploded in a massive nuclear fireball … twenty-three milliseconds after penetrating the *Keturah's* drive section.

"Nuclear detonation close aboard, Captain!" Lieutenant Lau reported. "They hit Charlie 4! No additional inbound ordinance at this time."

"Helm, get us away from that ship!" Prescott ordered. "Her reactors could go at any moment."

"Aye, Captain," Fisher replied, still generally amazed that they were still alive.

Designed to focus its powerful shaped charge of nuclear fire in a relatively small area, the anti-ship missile's explosive power was insufficient to destroy a ship as large as the BD cruiser outright. Instead, the detonation occurred just as the warhead entered the ship's engineering section, gutting the most critical of the warship's internal spaces while exposing much of the rest to lethal radiation levels. The *Keturah's* massive, forward-facing sublight engines immediately ceased operation, as did all of her key systems with the exception of emergency life support in the areas not already exposed to the hard vacuum of space.

SCS Gunov, Location Crossbow

(5.93x10^{11} km from Location Dagger)

Although Commodore Sarafi's Resistance forces had been under standing orders to execute regular changes in speed and direction in an effort to avoid a "Before Light Arrival" attack from the Guardian spacecraft, the tactic proved completely ineffective against the Terrans and their hyperdrive-equipped missiles. Ironically, it had been Commodore Sarafi who provided the time needed for the Human warship, TFS *Karna*, to survey his entire assembly area with her passive sensor suite — supplying her powerful AI with all the data it needed to predict the locations of every Resistance vessel to within a few centimeters at the time of the attack. Sarafi's order for evasive action, while faithfully executed, was far too late to save the bulk of his task force.

In a spectacle that eclipsed even the most ambitious science fiction movies ever produced by Hollywood, two hundred and fifty-nine HB-7c missiles transitioned from hyperspace inside the shields protecting their targets' vulnerable drive sections — each one traveling at precisely the same speed as before its initial transition. An infinitesimal period of time later, all two hundred and fifty-nine — over ninety-five percent of the anti-ship missiles launched by the Human destroyers — found their marks. Most of the weapons simply exploded on impact, completely destroying all eight of the huge thrust chambers making up the externally visible portion of the cruisers' sublight engines and wreaking catastrophic damage to their power generation and engineering spaces. It was the remaining one-third of the missiles, however, that caused by far the greatest damage. The warheads themselves were designed to act much like the kinetic energy penetrator rounds fired by Human railgun turrets. Their shape, composition, and tremendous speed now worked in concert to punch directly through to their targets' "soft" internal spaces before detonating their compact antimatter warheads. In all but three cases, the series of internal explosions within what were essentially enormous pressure vessels resulted in complete structural failure — often accompanied by the spectacular visual effect of blast fronts passing through the warship's hull to exit on the opposing side. The most dramatic effects, however, occurred in those ships whose emergency containment systems failed to prevent the large quantities of antimatter housed within their reactors from coming into contact with regular matter. Within the hearts of each of these warships, large-scale atomic-level annihilation events created spectacular flashes of light in the visible spectrum as the once-powerful vessels were blown apart from the inside at relativistic speeds.

Of the fifteen *Shopak*-class cruisers targeted, all but two were destroyed outright. Both of these were left helplessly adrift — without power and in need of immediate assistance to prevent the loss of all hands. The two *Keturah*-class battlespace defense cruisers fared slightly better, due in large part to improvements in their outer armor. Like the other two surviving cruisers, one of these was heavily damaged and adrift with only emergency power available. This left only one of the seventeen vessels attacked by the Human destroyers still in the fight. Purely by coincidence, she had been in the process of coming about — with her captain having ordered an increase in power and a turn to starboard —

just as the attack began. Although she had still taken three hits, they had been glancing, off-axis blows that, while still doing minor damage to her drive section, had not penetrated the ship's hull.

The devastation was on a scale never before experienced by Sajeth Collective forces … even during the protracted period of interstellar warfare that ultimately led to the formation of their alliance.

"Silence on the bridge!" Sarafi bellowed, the savage tone of his voice leaving little doubt of what would happen to the next member of the crew who dared to speak out of turn. "Clearly, the Terrans' first attack was highly effective — much more so than any of us had expected. But now I need each of you focused and executing your duties flawlessly. Do so, and we may yet prevail. Fail, and we will be lucky to survive, even with the advantages afforded us by the *Gunov*. Am I making myself clear?" There were muted grunts and growls of approval around the bridge in response.

Now, at last they have a real enemy and a reason to fight, he though grimly. "XO, hold your status report for a moment. Tactical, have the Terran vessels returned?"

"No, Commodore, not yet."

"At least one of them will do so in order to assess the results of their initial attack. Comm, notify all ships that they are to hold their fire until they hear otherwise from the Flag. Tell the *Rusalov*-class battleships to stand by to launch all available fighters and prepare for a focused kinetics cannonade. For the remainder of this battle, the *Gunov's* fire control AI will be designating targets and controlling their main guns. Also let them know that the Humans have hyperdrive-capable missiles accurate enough to transition inside our shields. The *Rusalovs* should activate their aft shield augmenters. All other ships should execute random evasive maneuvers per Annex-Three of the TACPLAN."

"Aye, sir."

"Now ... I need a quick summary of our task force status, please," he said, drawing in a deep breath and closing his eyes to clear his mind.

After a brief pause, Sarafi's new XO, a steady, formidable Wek female called Ragini Freyda, spoke up. "Sir, based on the information we have thus far, thirteen of our *Shopak*-class cruisers have been completely destroyed. The two remaining standard cruisers are heavily damaged and requesting our immediate assistance."

"That will, regretfully, have to wait for the time being. And what of our *Keturah*-class BD cruisers?"

"One of them is also requesting our aid. The other is reporting minor damage to her propulsion section, but she is still underway, able to maneuver, and her BD system is still operational."

"Inform the captain of the remaining operational cruiser that he is to feign heavy damage. Make it look as if his ship is adrift without steerage way. I also want him to lower his shields and reduce his power output to the minimum required to operate the BD system. Tell him that I expect the Terran ships will launch a large number of the scout vessels we encountered at the original rally point as soon as they transition back into the area. From what we have seen, the scouts are not equipped with shields and are incapable of rapid hyperspace transitions. If that happens, he is to take control of all remaining energy weapons as well as the Carrada Area Denial System to execute his attack. He may only get one chance, so tell him I fully expect his ship to eliminate the enemy scout vessels completely, if possible. The *Rusalovs* are to delay launching their own fighters until after the BD cruiser has completed its attack, then scramble them as quickly as possible. Once on station, the fighters are to clean up any remaining enemy scout vessels and then assist in our larger attack on the Terran destroyers. Understood?"

"Yes, sir," his XO responded, entering the necessary information at her Command workstation to relay Sarafi's orders while wondering at the commodore's newly found prescience. While not a bad officer per se compared to some she had had the misfortune of serving under, Sarafi had never struck her as particularly imaginative in his thinking. "Transmitting now."

"Instruct the other two *Gresav*-class ships to form up with us. We will operate in support of each other and concentrate our firepower while directing that of the battleships."

"Aye, sir."

Sarafi sat back in his command chair momentarily while considering what else he might do to improve his odds against the Terran ships. *How many more of my decisions this day will result in such an appalling loss of life?* he asked himself. *And how many of my own people am I willing to sacrifice for the sake of this mission?*

In spite of the urgency of the current situation, another part of his mind strayed to the notion of how much better off his homeworld might be at the moment if they were allied with these Terrans rather than with the

Damarans and their ilk. Their strategy thus far had been brazen — almost elegant in its simplicity — and yet there was certainly no arguing with the results they had achieved. Even after having suffered such grievous losses, however, Sarafi had confidence that he would regain the upper hand and exact a heavy toll against the Human ships. Nevertheless, he was forced to concede that Naftur might have been right about them all along. When required, they fought like a cornered Zakula, while at the same time being capable of offering compassion and mercy to a vanquished enemy. There were contradictions here — a great many of them in fact — and Sarafi once again promised himself that he would spend more time thinking through them for himself when time, circumstance, and *duty* allowed.

"Contact," the tactical officer announced. "Same range as before, sir … just over six hundred thousand kilometers. The AI indicates that it is the same vessel that hailed us before, the *Karna*."

"And she is hailing us again," the comm officer announced.

"These Humans talk nearly as much as the damned Damarans," Sarafi snarled, temporarily overcoming the rather bleak mood on the *Gunov's* bridge and drawing a few muffled sounds of amusement in response. "We will indulge them once more to give our comrades a few additional moments to prepare, then we shall allow our weapons to speak on our behalf." This time, there were more raucous sounds of approval from the bridge crew in response to their commodore's defiant tone. He smiled with more enthusiasm than he felt at the moment, then allowed the room to settle before continuing. "Put the Terran captain back on the screen, please."

Once again, Captain Abrams appeared on the forward display screen, this time wearing a decidedly somber expression considering the success of the Humans' first attack.

"Hello again, Captain. I presume you are calling to offer us the opportunity to surrender?"

"Yes, I am, sir. I also want to assure you unequivocally that the destruction of your vessels that has occurred thus far need not lead to a wider conflict. We will make no apologies for defending our homeworld, but we also have no interest in seeing additional bloodshed on either side. I urge you to stand down and allow us to assist you with rescue operations. Once they have been concluded, we will provide whatever additional aid you require before escorting your remaining forces out of the area."

Sarafi stared broodingly at the Human captain for a moment, unsure what to make of his seemingly sincere offer. "I am afraid my response is unchanged, Captain Abrams. I, too, am here to defend my homeworld, as well as the six others that are part of our alliance. I must also caution you of the dangers associated with becoming overconfident in ships and their weapon systems to such an extent that you underestimate your opponent's leadership. Now that I have seen your 'trick,'" Sarafi paused, staring at Abrams through narrowed eyes, "I can assure you that it will no longer avail you. So, once again, I am obligated to extend you the same offer … which you will, of course, decline. Let us put a stop to all of this unnecessary chatter and settle this like warriors, rather than bootlicking diplomats."

"As you wish," the scowling Human captain responded curtly. "Abrams out."

"Sir," the tactical officer reported, "our other two destroyers have formed up to port and starboard and slightly aft of our current position. Also, the Terran vessel has transitioned to hyperspace again."

"Understood. Comm, warn the other two destroyers that we are getting underway and that they should expect repeated Annex-Three type maneuvers. Helm, in thirty seconds, begin a smooth acceleration to our best maneuvering speed. Make your first relative bearing three five zero, up forty-five on the bow. Once you see that our sister ships are maintaining their positions, begin your evasive maneuver series. Inform me immediately if they are unable to stay in formation."

"Aye, sir."

"Commodore, during the first Terran attack, all seventeen of their ships were coplanar," Freyda observed.

"They were indeed. As were ours, for the most part," Sarafi responded, pleased that his young protégé had noticed not only the manner in which their enemies had executed their attack, but also his response to it. "I am uncertain that we can depend on their doing the same thing again, but they *are* new at this game, are they not?"

"That is certainly our assumption, yes, sir," she replied, smiling conspiratorially.

"With any luck, however, the success of their first attack may encourage them to make somewhat more of a bold stroke when they return. Everything I have seen so far leads me to believe that their hyperdrive missiles require stationary, or at least predictable, targets. I just explicitly told them, as if they did not already know, that we will not fall prey to another of their hyperdrive missile attacks. I am sure Captain Abrams and his ship's AI also noted several of the changes we have already put into motion to prevent them from using that particular type of attack again."

"So you believe they might reenter the battle using a similar formation, but attack in a different manner?" she asked.

"I think they will have little choice but to close with our vessels and fight it out. Executing what amounts to a sneak attack using their missiles is one thing, but attacking a group of warships that are completely out of their class is quite another. So, I intend to put the three vessels we have remaining that are most nearly their match at the center of the battlespace … and above the plane of their previous attack. That will also place us almost directly over our surviving BD cruiser and very nearly equidistant from all six of our *Rusalov* battleships around the perimeter."

"There are no warships in our inventory whose shields can withstand an attack from three *Gresav*-class destroyers simultaneously," Freyda observed, proudly "not even the new *Baldevs*."

"If our computer models are to be believed, that is certainly true," Sarafi smiled.

"We have detected no shields being used by the Terran vessels. Are you certain that they are so equipped?" she asked with a sidelong, suspicious glance.

"I am. But I can say no more on the subject for the moment."

"Contacts!" the tactical officer interrupted. "All seventeen Terran vessels have returned, sir. They have broken into six groups. Each group appears to be headed for one of our *Rusalovs*. No sign of fighters thus far."

"Well, well," Sarafi drawled with a savage smile, "their formations look strikingly similar to their first attack, do they not? I will say this for the Humans, what they lack in experience, they seem to more than make up for with reckless courage. Comm, signal the battleships with a reminder that the fire control systems for their main guns will be under the control of the *Gunov's* AI for the remainder of the battle. Whenever possible, they should also concentrate their secondary weapon systems on the targets designated by the Flag."

"Commander, you will direct the cannonade from the *Rusalovs* while I manage our three *Gresavs*. Your first priority is to remove Terran vessels from the fight. It matters not if they remain largely intact. Shift your fire as quickly as possible after you disable one of their number."

"Aye, sir."

"And we shall begin," he said, staring intently at the tactical situation display, "with *this* one."

Chapter 8

TFS Theseus, Location Dagger
(3.3 light years from Earth)

As soon as there was sufficient distance between the hulls of the *Theseus* and the *Keturah*, Ensign Fisher executed a maximum performance turn to place the stricken Resistance BD cruiser dead astern, then once again pushed the destroyer's Cannae sublight engines to emergency power. With his situational awareness increasing once again in the aftermath of the near disastrous collision, he adjusted the ship's departure vector to place the damaged enemy cruiser between their position and the now distant *Baldev*. For the moment, his tactic seemed to be working — the battleship had yet to resume its energy weapons fire.

"Helm, keep increasing the distance to Charlie 4 just in case, then maintain course until we're out of Bravo 1's grav beam and can make another tactical C-jump. Thirty light seconds again is fine. Execute as soon as possible."

"Aye, sir. Projecting six one seconds to C-Jump on this heading."

"Captain, we detected some type of projectile launch from the dorsal side of Charlie 4 at about the same time the *Baldev's* missile hit her drive section," Lieutenant Lee reported from the Science and Engineering console. "Based on its emissions, I'm betting it was one of her reactor's containment units. In fact, I'd have to say that it was probably all of them at once since we've seen only minimal power levels from her since then."

"Good catch, Lieutenant. It almost had to be. Otherwise, I don't think there is any possible way she could have avoided a breach. I'd say that's another major improvement over the earlier cruisers based on what we saw happen to Charlie 2. Really extraordinary engineering when you think about it …" Prescott said, shaking his head. "Status report, please."

"Moderate damage to our dorsal armor plating, sir. The damage looks pretty ugly on the monitors, but it's largely superficial from what we can tell so far. We lost two close-in weapon system turrets and one emitter from our primary dorsal energy weapons array. Otherwise, all systems are still in the green. No hull breaches reported and no injuries reported."

"Tactical?"

"Badger 21 Flight has their hands full with the *Baldev's* fighters, Captain," Schmidt replied. "There are now four six enemy fighters in their general vicinity, so, for the moment, they're outnumbered almost two to one."

"What about Badger 1 Flight? Aren't they assisting?"

"Badger 22's twelve fighters are headed that way now, but I'm having some trouble locating all of Badger 1 Flight. I think some of them must have transitioned … stand by." There was an uncomfortable silence as Lieutenant Commander Schmidt confirmed and reconfirmed the distressing information being displayed on his console.

"Is there a problem, Schmidt?"

"Yes, sir, there is. Badger 1 Flight is reporting a combat ineffective status."

"What? How is that possible?"

"I'm showing only one three of their original three six fighters. It looks like they are also trying to distance themselves from Bravo 1. If we adjust our course slightly, we can intercept."

Prescott swore silently to himself at the realization that a significant portion of the forces under his command had simply ceased to exist without his immediate knowledge. Glancing at the tactical plot, he noted that the same information Schmidt had just reported was also reflected in the order of battle summary, but it really wasn't much of a surprise that no one on *Theseus'* bridge had noticed during the heat of combat. The primary purpose of the tactical plot was to highlight the threats deemed most urgent by the ship's AI — not to provide a strategic-level view of the battlespace. He also knew that the CIC duty staff aboard Admiral Patterson's flagship (if not Admiral Patterson himself) were monitoring every aspect of the battle and would not hesitate to redirect his actions if they deemed it necessary. *Think — focus — respond!* he raged inwardly, furious that his mind was already busily convincing itself that their deaths had nothing to do with any actions he had taken ... or had failed to take.

"Lieutenant Dubashi, are we detecting any emergency locator beacon transmissions?"

"No, sir."

"Go ahead and try contacting Badger 1 — text only. See if they require immediate assistance and ask them to open a comm channel if able."

It took only a few seconds for Captain Zhukov to reply.

"Theseus, Zhukov."

The fact that Captain Zhukov was no longer using his flight's "Badger 1" call sign made the hair on the back of Prescott's neck stand on end.

"Zhukov, *Theseus*-Actual. What can we do to help, Captain?"

"I have four ships in need of an exfil as soon as possible, Captain. Shortly after we transitioned in to take out the missiles targeting the *Theseus*, we triggered some sort of anti-access weapon system. It used a type of fragmentation warhead that overwhelmed our shields. We lost most of our fighters before we even realized that we were under attack. I had also brought along the six RPSVs you assigned to our flight with the intention of positioning them for use in much the same manner as the weapon that attacked us. Unfortunately, all six of them were destroyed as well. I was left with a total of six fully operational and seven critically damaged 373s. I sent the three damaged ships that still had operable C-Drives back to their carriers, but the remaining four are marginal at best. We have been escorting them out of the immediate area as quickly as possible, but I fear at least one of them will end up needing to eject at some point. Can *Theseus* accommodate four *Reapers* in her hangar bay?"

With everything else running through his mind at the moment, Prescott simply looked at Commander Reynolds for an answer to Zhukov's question.

"I think so, yes," she nodded, "but we'll have to recover them one at a time and get their wings stowed so that we can move each one out of the way for the next. I doubt we'll be able to also embark all twenty-four … well … eighteen of our *Hunters*, but they can C-Jump back to Earth on their own, if needed. Captain Zhukov, how long can your pilots survive if they have to eject?"

"Indefinitely … in theory at least. Our survival pods are equipped with a dedicated power supply and we have sufficient water and rations available to last several days at least."

"And the status of the pods on the four damaged fighters?" Prescott asked, understanding from personal experience how unpleasant it would be for the pilots if they were forced to remain inside them for an extended period of time.

"All are in the green so far," Zhukov replied.

"Alright, Dmitri, we're going to alter course and attempt to rendezvous with your flight. Since our encounter with Charlie 4, however, I think the only reason we haven't been taking fire from the *Baldev* is that she doesn't have a clear line of fire at us without potentially finishing off the cruiser. So when we change course to meet you, we may draw their fire again. If that happens, we won't be able to recover your fighters until after we finish off Bravo 1 … it's just too risky for your pilots. Have your damaged ships stay together and continue on course at their best possible speed. If someone has to punch out, remind them to activate their locator beacon. I really can't see Captain Yagani firing on survival pods or defenseless ships, but it will be up to the remaining pilots to decide whether they stay with the downed pilot or continue on course. One way or another, someone will pick them up soon, and with any luck, it will be us. In the meantime, we need you and your remaining operational fighters back in the fight. It looks as though Waffer might have a fight on his hands."

"Understood, Captain. I will relay your instructions and we will be on our way momentarily. One last thing … after we were attacked, we destroyed the two anti-access weapons pods that hit us. We then completed a thorough scan of the immediate area out to a radius of about five light minutes with our active sensors. At the moment, I do not believe the Resistance ships have any more of these weapons pods deployed, but please be aware that they are small and difficult to detect. Based on their location, I assume the ones we encountered were most likely released by the first group of fighters we destroyed earlier."

"Thank you, Captain Zhukov. Will do. Prescott out."

"Commander, the longer this fight goes on, the more the situation favors the Resistance. We've got to do something decisive and get ourselves in a better situation to be able to handle their reinforcements *before* they arrive."

"Yes, sir," Reynolds replied. "Our point location attacks have been the only truly effective tactic so far. Another high speed run at Bravo 1's drive section might at least force them to drop their supplemental shields. Frankly, I think that's still our only option at the moment."

"Agreed. Fisher, time to expected C-Jump, please," Prescott asked.

"Zero eight seconds, sir."

"Belay that C-Jump for the moment, please. I assume you also have a course plotted to pick up our damaged fighters?"

"Yes, sir. Ready on your mark."

"Very well, let's try it. If we start taking fire, correct back to the original course and put Charlie 4 between us and Bravo 1 again. Any questions?"

"No, sir, but the farther we get from Charlie 4, the harder it's going to be to stay out of their line of sight. I think the only reason it has worked so far is because Bravo 1's supplemental aft shields are preventing them from maneuvering."

"That may be true, but it was exceptional thinking on your part and may well have saved our collective arses. Besides, we'll take whatever advantage we can get at this point. Execute your course correction, please."

"Thank you, sir. Aye, sir."

As Fisher entered the required commands to alter *Theseus'* course, the ship's bow slowly rose above her former flight path in response while simultaneously easing into a slight turn to port. It took only moments for the *Baldev* to respond with a renewed hail of energy weapons fire streaming downrange to slam into the destroyer's aft shields.

"Correcting back, Captain," Fisher reported immediately. "We are also free of Bravo 1's grav beam. C-Jump range 100.4 light years and stable."

"Understood. Execute your C-Jump when ready. Dubashi, inform Captain Zhukov that we are unable to attempt a recovery mission at this time and will be transitioning for another attack on Bravo 1."

"Aye, sir," both officers replied in unison.

The message from Captain Yagani was clear — he would allow the damaged remnants of Badger 1 Flight to slowly make their way out of the combat zone unmolested, but ships that were still in the fight were fair game and subject to immediate attack for as long as the battle continued. For the moment at least, all damaged ships, both friendly and hostile, were simply on their own.

SCS Gunov, Location Crossbow
(5.93×10^{11} km from Location Dagger)

"Tactical and Helm workstations …" Commodore Sarafi announced.

"Yes, sir," both Wek officers announced as one.

"I have designated the first formation of three Terran ships that we shall attack. Helm, you are to coordinate with our two sister ships and ensure that they are able to maintain their positions in formation. The AIs should assist you to some extent, but as the lead helmsman, formation integrity is largely your responsibility. Understood?"

"Yes, Commodore."

"Very good. Tactical, each time we attack one of the ships in their formation, make your target the starboard ship. As I instructed Commander Freyda, your primary goal is to remove Terran ships from the battle, not destroy them completely … not yet, at least," he smiled. "I will assist you in determining when to move on to the next target. Whenever possible, I want you to attack from either above or below their flight path until I tell you otherwise. After we hit them a time or two, we should be able to assess the effectiveness of their shields and adjust our tactics, as required. Any questions from either of you?"

"No, Commodore."

"Then let us get about the business of avenging our comrades, shall we? Execute your attack."

"Aye, sir," both officers answered intently.

With the *Gunov* and her two consorts currently in a climbing turn to port relative to the other Resistance warships, the helm officer noted the position of their first target, then began the process of reversing their turn while smoothly increasing their angle of attack through the vertical. The three *Gresav*-class destroyers continued their maneuver until completing what their Human counterparts might refer to as a modified Cuban Eight. All three ships then rapidly accelerated, heading towards a location in space projected to be almost directly above their targets once they reached the optimum range for their energy weapons.

For her part, Commander Freyda was working at a near frenzied pace at her Command workstation. While her role of directing the fire of the task force's six *Rusalov*-class battleships seemed simple enough, issuing the series of commands required to properly coordinate their attack required more time than she actually had available — particularly with the Terran warships rapidly closing on their remaining forces. After what seemed to her like an interminable period of time had passed, and during which she noticed Commodore Sarafi glancing impatiently in her direction at least twice, she finally completed the long series of required tasks and issued the order to open fire.

Having remained in active service for over one hundred Terran years past their expected lifetimes, the *Rusalovs* were, in many ways, relics from a bygone age. Designed by Wek engineers before energy weapons had reached a level of power output and reliability deemed worthy of their most powerful warships, the *Rusalovs'* main armaments had originally included traditional, two-stage gas-powered main guns only marginally more advanced than those relying solely on gunpowder to launch their projectiles. While effective enough for short range space combat and planetary bombardment, the weapons could not propel their shells at sufficient speeds to eliminate the need for explosive warheads. In fact, these weapons had more in common with Terran ocean-going battleship guns dating back to the early twentieth century and beyond than they did modern, kinetic energy weapons. As the Sajeth Collective expanded, however, their designers gained access to increasingly advanced technology, and steadily upgraded existing ship designs to take advantage of the corresponding improvements in weapon systems. For the *Rusalov*-class battleships, this decades-long progression ultimately led to an interesting hodgepodge of systems — anachronisms extended and enhanced to ultimately become some of the most powerful ever produced by the shipyards of Graca.

Perhaps the most significant upgrade, and the one most responsible for keeping the *Rusalovs* active in the Sajeth Collective fleet, was the replacement of the ships' original main guns with electromagnetic projectile launchers that the Wek now referred to as simply "kinetics." In spite of their "modernization," the weapons still hurled massive shells at distant enemy targets — and at over eight hundred kilograms each, the projectiles rivaled the largest ever fired by seagoing battleships. Once fired, the *Rusalovs'* self-guided rounds proceeded downrange at a comparatively glacial pace of only five thousand kilometers per second — technically placing them squarely in the archaic "hypervelocity" category. What they lacked in speed, however, the weapons did their best to make up for in terms of mass, accuracy, and the addition of a nuclear warhead approximately five times as powerful as those carried by most Sajeth Collective anti-ship missiles. While the Wek engineers knew all too well that speed trumped mass when it came to kinetics weapon design, the huge guns were still deemed viable. Ironically, this was partially due to the ongoing development of a *defensive* system still in the early stages of development when the battleships were first commissioned — shields.

In the years that followed, Wek shield systems had proven so effective that point defenses had been all but eliminated from most warship classes. The same was true of "small caliber" kinetics — such as the railguns favored by their Human rivals. This was in large part due to the practical difficulties associated with allowing steady streams of projectiles to pass through the shields on the way to their targets. This problem had been relatively easy to overcome for energy weapons by coordinating the phase and frequency of the beam emitters used. For kinetic energy weapons, however, the solution turned out to be much less exotic: fire fewer rounds and drop the shields for each. The *Rusalovs'* main guns were, after all, only capable of firing at the leisurely rate of one round every thirty seconds. Accordingly, the designers had taken the eminently practical approach of switching off specific field emitters during the forty microseconds it took for a shell to pass through the space normally occupied by the vessels' shields. In an effort to prevent an enemy from predicting the precise instant when this would occur, the ships' AIs inserted random intervals of time between successive salvos. Otherwise, the mighty battleships relied on an impressive three meters of armor to render their enemies' attacks a bitter exercise in futility — or so they hoped.

With the six *Rusalov* battleships now largely slaved to the *Gunov,* many of their hopelessly outdated command and control systems were rendered largely irrelevant as they became mere extensions of the flagship's vastly more sophisticated AI. Now, as the Terran ships reached optimal range, the two massive "gunhouse" turrets mounted dorsally amidships rotated in the general direction of the lead ship in each enemy formation, paused momentarily, and opened fire.

"Will the Humans not simply execute a rapid series of transitions to avoid the incoming rounds?" Freyda asked, growing uncharacteristically nervous under Sarafi's intense scrutiny.

Sarafi raised his eyebrows thoughtfully, as if he, himself, were considering the question for the first time. "Perhaps they will, but they most likely have gathered some data at this point regarding the effectiveness of our shields. If that is indeed the case, they will realize that executing rapid transitions will not be a particularly effective tactic. They cannot hope to destroy any of our remaining ships without first bringing down its shields … and they cannot hope to bring down our shields without a sustained, heavy bombardment. No, Commander, I suspect that they will attempt to utilize the combined firepower from each of their formations for that very purpose … relying on their own shields to protect them from the battleships' main guns. Let us hope that doing so will prove a fateful mistake for the Humans."

Freyda looked up from her Command workstation and stared openly at her commanding officer under a furrowed brow. She was becoming increasingly convinced that Sarafi had access to a great deal more information regarding the capabilities of the Terran forces than she did, which seemed equal parts confusing, troubling, and downright irritating from her perspective.

Noticing the look on her face, he leaned closer and spoke in a low tone that only she could hear. "We will discuss this topic at length when we are at leisure, Commander Freyda. For now, I would ask that you listen carefully to what I am able to tell you and take what I say at face value."

"Understood, sir," she replied after a moment's consideration.

Seconds later, as the first thirty-six projectiles fired from the *Rusalov* battleships reached the attacking Terran warships all around the battlespace, all but eight (nearly eighty percent) of the massive shells breached their enemies' shields and struck within just a few meters of their intended points of impact. Four of the six targeted Human warships suffered a minimum of four hits each, and the results were beyond Commodore Sarafi's most optimistic expectations. All four were completely destroyed, with gigantic sections of their broken hulls spinning off into space in multiple directions. A huge section of one of the vessels even managed to collide with the neighboring ship in its formation — almost certainly removing it as an immediate threat in the current battle. The hulls of the final two ships targeted by the initial salvo remained intact, but both appeared to be heavily damaged and likely to be permanently dispatched with only minimal additional effort.

Glancing at the tactical situation display at his workstation, Sarafi called up the AI's real-time analysis of one of the Terran vessels in the moments before it had been destroyed. As he had suspected, its shields, while obviously employing an entirely different type of technology than that used by Sajeth Collective vessels, were equally vulnerable to attacks from such large projectiles. A distant part of his mind mused momentarily that effective shield design perhaps wasn't as simple as merely dissipating kinetic energy. Indeed, the huge shells fired from the *Rusalov* battleships carried less energy than the dramatically smaller projectiles fired by the Terran ships — which, by contrast, were traveling at relativistic speeds. Was there something about the sheer physical size of the shells that posed a greater challenge … and for both types of shield systems? Not for the first time, Sarafi silently cursed the shortsightedness of the bureaucrats who had steered the Governing Council's military planning committee into largely abandoning kinetic energy weapons aboard all of their newer warship classes.

"I can now confirm *Rusalov* main battery hits on six of the Terran warships, sir." Freyda reported. "Four have been completely destroyed. Three others appear to be heavily damaged … one of these was from collateral damage caused by a collision with debris."

"Well done," Sarafi replied. "The rest will likely get much more difficult to hit now that they realize how effective our guns are against their shields. Once they have time to accelerate, the Terran ships are much faster than the *Rusalovs'* shells, after all. Get as many hits as you can as quickly as you can."

"It will be my pleasure, sir," she replied. "The second volley is already in flight. Time to impact, one six seconds."

Sarafi barely heard his XO's response, having already shifted his attention to the three-ship destroyer attack on, as luck would have it, one of the two Terran "formations" that was now composed of only a single warship. Understandably, the enemy ship had broken off to port after the other two vessels in its small group had been destroyed — seconds after beginning their own attack run on the nearest *Rusalov* battleship. In response, the *Gunov's* AI had adjusted their course and speed to arrive at a point directly above their target — diving to close the remaining distance while offering the maximum number of beam emitter emplacements a clear line of fire.

"They have obviously detected our approach," Freyda observed. "Why have they chosen not to open fire?"

As if in response to her question, all of the remaining Terran ships still capable of doing so transitioned into hyperspace in ten simultaneous flashes of grayish-white light.

"They have transitioned again, sir," Sarafi's tactical officer reported.

"All of them?"

"There were ten hyperspace departure signatures. They appear to have left their three damaged warships to fend for themselves. Two of these appear to have lost power. The third is moving away from our forces using their sublight engines."

"Time to intercept the third vessel from our current position?"

"She is very nearly on the opposite side of our perimeter, Commodore and accelerating rapidly at the moment. We can still catch her without transitioning to hyperspace, but it will take a while — approximately six minutes at her current rate of acceleration."

"Very good, do it."

"Begging your pardon, sir," Freyda interjected, "but can we not simply transition to a point just beyond the target to perform our intercept?"

"Ordinarily, I would say that is precisely what we should do, but, based on the fact that the Humans located our second rally point so quickly, we must assume that they have developed the capability to track our vessels in hyperspace. If we transition, we could very well be telegraphing our intentions. Have you not also noticed that they appear to be making lengthy transitions without significantly changing their locations?"

"Between their first and second attacks? Yes, sir, I did."

"As you know, we have used such tactics ourselves at times, but doing so requires us to relocate our forces to an intermediate location, then transition back to the combat zone."

"And you believe that they are simply entering hyperspace, remaining stationary — perhaps even repositioning their vessels — before returning to normal space? I realize that such a thing is possible, but do you believe them capable of that kind of technological prowess so recently after achieving interstellar travel? Our own ships cannot do so … even after centuries of hyperdrive development."

"We cannot do so at the moment, no, but our scientists and engineers fully grasp the underlying physics regarding why that is so. We understand many such things from a theoretical perspective. We have simply not yet dedicated sufficient time and resources into translating that knowledge into practical application," Sarafi replied, his voice taking on a more harsh, menacing tone. "You used the word 'achieve,' Commander. Bear in mind that the Humans have 'achieved' very little of their current technological capabilities on their own. So, yes, I believe them capable of many things that would, under normal circumstances, remain well beyond their grasp for centuries to come. That dangerous paradox of capability without the discipline and knowledge required for achievement is fundamentally why we are here, is it not?"

"Well said, Commodore. It is indeed," Freyda replied solemnly.

"Have the closest *Rusalovs* target the two disabled Terran warships and destroy them immediately."

Freyda hesitated, looking up from her Command workstation to stare into her commanding officer's eyes, hoping she had somehow misheard what he had said. She knew better than to question Sarafi's orders in front of the bridge crew, particularly when he began speaking in that distant, angry — almost patronizing — voice that he tended to slip into at times. *The truly dangerous thing about zealots,* she thought, *is not so much that they are completely wrong but rather that they passionately believe themselves to be completely right.*

"Ragini," he began again in a much more conciliatory tone. "I understand and share your reluctance to destroy the damaged Terran vessels. If, however, we still believe that our reasons for ever contemplating this mission in the first place were and remain just, then we have little choice in the matter. It is my belief that the Humans currently possess only a few vessels with the capabilities demonstrated by the ships attacking us now. In fact, what we are facing here today may well constitute their entire fleet. If that is the case, we must do everything within our power to eliminate them now if we are to have any chance of success once we launch our attack on Terra."

Freyda continued to stare back at him, a look of uncertainty mixed with a hint of disappointment clouding her normally confident face. "I am sorry, sir, I …"

"No, Commander, you need not apologize. You show both courage and wisdom in questioning such orders. In fact, dealing with the potential repercussions of such a morally ambiguous action is a burden that I should bear alone."

With that, Sarafi quickly entered the necessary instructions at his own Command workstation to direct fire at the two disabled warships. Just three seconds later, the two closest *Rusalov* battleships completed the loading cycle for their main guns and immediately fired six rounds at each target.

"Twelve shells in flight," the *Gunov's* tactical officer reported after placing windows displaying both of the damaged Terran warships on the port side of the bridge display screen. "Time to impact, one four and one six seconds, respectively."

"Thank you, Lieutenant."

As the remaining seconds before impact ticked slowly past, not a word was spoken on the *Gunov's* bridge. Each officer present did their level best to affect an air of the routine — busying themselves with their individual tasks as if doing so might somehow insulate them from the atrocity to which they had now become a party.

On the bridge display screen, six simultaneous explosions erupted along the entire length of the first Terran ship, followed shortly thereafter by an almost identical scene as the second ship also took six direct hits. The light and thermally enhanced images on the screen did little justice to the nuclear-induced hell that had just been unleashed aboard the enemy vessels, but it was clear enough that the fire spewing like geysers from each point of impact represented only a tiny fraction of what was taking place inside their hulls. Although both vessels remained intact, it was obvious that both were now little more than gutted hulks — adrift without power and, in all likelihood, with no survivors.

"Both enemy warships destroyed, Commodore," the tactical officer finally reported after allowing what he hoped was an appropriate amount of time to pass. "The last Terran ship is maintaining course and has stopped accelerating. Time to intercept: four minutes."

Chapter 9

TFS Theseus, Location Dagger
(3.3 light years from Earth)

"Transition complete, Captain," Lieutenant Dubashi reported. "All systems in the green. C-Jump range 100.3 light years and stable. Sublight engines online, we are free to maneuver."

"Tactical, what's the status of Badger 2 Flight?" Prescott asked.

"Commander Waffer still has them broken out into two separate elements, Captain," Lieutenant Commander Schmidt reported. "Badger 21 is still in the same general area as before — and still in a position to cover the *Baldev's* stern — but they have taken a few casualties. I'm showing two zero of the original two four fighters remaining. Badger 22 has lost one as well, but they have now been reinforced by Captain Zhukov's six spacecraft for a total of one seven. Both elements are still engaged with Bravo 1's fighters, but they do appear to have the upper hand at this point."

"Are they taking fire from Bravo 1?"

"Sporadic fire only, sir. Our ships have remained in pretty close proximity with theirs, so Bravo 1 isn't getting much of an opportunity to take a shot."

"Are you still showing eighteen *Hunters* remaining?"

"Yes, sir. They're still attached to Waffer's Badger 21 element. Once Bravo 1 started launching fighters again, he sent all of the *Hunters* in the opposite direction. It looks like he intends to hold them in reserve for the time being."

Prescott paused, weighing the potential benefits of assisting the remaining fighters versus another attack on the *Baldev* herself.

"What are you thinking?" Reynolds asked after a few moments.

"That we could probably transition pretty close to Badger 21 Flight and take out the remaining enemy fighters, possibly avoiding any further losses in the process."

"But ..."

"But in so doing, we would most likely make ourselves and our remaining fighters vulnerable to attack from the *Baldev* herself. As much as I hate to continue ignoring them, our only path to victory requires the *Theseus* to take out the battleship ... or at least her supplemental shields. Do you concur?"

"I do, sir. And I don't think you've been ignoring our fighters. Looking out for each other is one thing, but as soon as destroying the enemy is no longer the number one priority, defeat becomes a near certainty."

"That's pretty good, Commander. Did you just make that up?"

"Thank you, I did," she smiled. "Now let's get this over with before any more Resistance ships show up. The way things are going, I'm sure it will be more battleships."

"Agreed. Ensign Fisher, how long until you have us in a position to C-Jump back?"

"To put us in a good position for another attack on the *Baldev's* stern, six three seconds, sir."

In spite of his usual efforts to maintain as relaxed an air as possible on his bridge, Prescott was beginning to feel the effects of prolonged, battle-induced stress. At the edges of his consciousness, there was a blurring of his normally keen perception coupled with an emotion that he rarely experienced in any significant measure — fear. It was not a fear born of physical cowardice so much as the crushing weight of responsibility now resting on his shoulders — the dread of failure magnified in the tired mind of a man who had rarely done so. Above all, it was the fear of making a mistake — even the simplest oversight or omission — leading immediately to the deaths of thousands and shortly thereafter to the deaths of billions.

Although, intellectually, Prescott knew the comparison to a little on the silly side, what kept coming to mind was the hopeless, sick feeling he had always experienced when stepping into the batter's box as an eight-year-old child playing Little League baseball. He had hated baseball — had played mostly because he thought (incorrectly) that his father expected him to — and his utter lack of prowess on the field had borne witness to his corresponding lack of interest. Now, however, his childish anxiety of appearing foolish in front of his family and friends had been replaced by the stark reality that a mistake here could well mean the loss of … everything.

This will be the third time Yagani has seen us execute an almost identical attack, he thought. *Is this what it feels like right before you get yourself and all the people who depend on you killed?*

Swallowing hard to counteract the taste of bile rising in the back of his throat and a growing uneasiness in the pit of his stomach, he closed his eyes and breathed deeply before continuing.

"Alright Helm ... Tactical," he said in as close to his normal tone as he could manage, "with any luck, this will be the last time we have to do this. I want this attack run to play out like a combination of our first two. The first time we hit Bravo 1's stern, we did more damage than expected, taking out a number of their supplemental shield emitters. But then we blew past them before we could capitalize on the effects of Schmidt's point location attack. We corrected that problem during the attack on Charlie 4, but doing so forced us to remain under fire for an extended period of time. Probably the only thing that saved us from significant energy weapons damage was Charlie 4 shifting her fire to take out our fighters' missiles and Bravo 1 holding her fire for fear of hitting their cruiser. I think we can all agree that it's a very bad idea for us to spend that much time astern of Bravo 1. So this time, I want us to coordinate our attacks with a large-scale missile attack from our remaining RPSVs. Lieutenant Lee, I'd like you to handle the *Hunters*, please."

"Aye, sir," he replied confidently.

"Lieutenant Dubashi, before I go into more detail, please warn our fighters that we will be retaking control of our RPSVs and executing another attack on Bravo 1's stern — ETA: zero two minutes. Tell them to launch their own missile strike on the battleship immediately if they see the supplemental shields drop."

"Aye, sir," Dubashi replied.

"We already know that a bunch of missile impacts aren't enough to bring down Bravo 1's shields on their own, but I do think we've established a pretty consistent pattern that there are limits to what they can withstand — particularly when we deliver an overwhelming amount of energy to a small area. So *this,*" he said, nodding towards the port view screen, "is what I want you to hit …"

Once again, the tactical assessment displayed a three-dimensional depiction of the *Baldev's* drive section. After a brief pause, the AI zoomed in and placed a flashing red oval over an area where the supplemental shield emitter ring intersected with a cluster of additional emitters that appeared to be of a slightly different configuration.

"As you can see, in this section the supplemental emitter ring crosses through what the AI believes is one of the arrays for their primary aft shields. It's also very close to their number three sublight engine thrust chamber. If we can concentrate our fire and punch through like we did on the first two attacks, I think we'll have a pretty good shot at taking out everything in the area. As we saw with Charlie 4, even a momentary breach of their aft shields will allow a significant amount of our ordinance to reach their hull … hopefully resulting in another cascading series of failures and a dead battleship. Even if all we can do is destroy the supplemental emitters between here and here …" out of habit, Prescott pointed to the view screen, but the AI was already highlighting the referenced emitters in red as he spoke, "it should be enough to take down their additional shielding and open the gap for another C-Drive missile strike."

"During our first two attacks, the AI chose points near the edge of overlapping emitter streams with reduced field strength," Schmidt observed. "Is that the case here as well?"

"Unfortunately, no," Prescott replied, shaking his head. "And if there's a downside to targeting this area, I'd say that's it. The *Baldev's* designers seem to have done a pretty good job ensuring that those slightly weaker points do not occur over the most vital sections of the stern. This time, however, we're going to add seventy-two missiles to our side of the equation, so, hopefully, that will more than make up for the slightly improved shielding at the target location."

"Ready to C-Jump, sir," Ensign Fisher interjected after having his attention drawn back to the Helm console by a series of electronic chirps.

"Is everyone clear on what we're doing?" Prescott asked, looking each of them in the eyes and hoping that his own face wasn't reflecting what he was feeling in his gut at the moment. "Ready, XO?"

"All departments still reporting combat ops readiness, Captain."

"Alright, Fisher, let's do this one last time."

"Aye, sir. C-Jumping in 3 … 2 … 1 …"

On the bridge view screen, the relative positions of the *Baldev* and her fighters as well as both elements of Badger 2 Flight were indicated by several sets of red and green brackets along with accompanying blocks of informational text. Inside the red brackets labeled "Bravo 1," the battleship grew quickly in size as *Theseus'* AI provided a visual representation of their nine-million-kilometer approach as if the entire journey had occurred in normal space.

"Transition complete, Captain," Fisher reported as he rapidly advanced the destroyer's sublight engines to full power and made a quick series of adjustments of their flight path towards the huge warship.

"Point location target acquired and locked," Schmidt reported from Tactical 1. Optimum weapons range in three niner seconds."

"They're hitting us again with their grav beam, sir," Fisher said as the now-familiar warning tones sounded from the Helm console. "The hyperdrive is offline."

During *Theseus'* previous attack on the *Baldev's* drive section, Captain Yagani had waited until the destroyer had reached its point of closest approach and was about to attempt a transition to hyperspace before opening fire. His primary goal in doing so had been to lure the *Theseus* in as close as possible in order to assess the effectiveness of his ship's gravitic beam system against the Terran hyperdrive. He also believed at the time that the Human warship posed little if any threat to the *Baldev* with the possible exception of their hyperdrive-equipped missiles — and these he had easily nullified by engaging the supplemental shields now protecting his stern. This time, however, Yagani was under no such illusion. Having now observed two examples where the Human destroyer had managed to concentrate nearly all of its considerable firepower at a single location, he had no intention of allowing a third. Accordingly, the *Baldev*, lead vessel of her class and arguably the most powerful warship ever fielded by the

Sajeth Collective, unleashed her full fury against the approaching Terran ship.

"Fox Charlie!" Lieutenant Lee announced excitedly as all eighteen of the remaining *Hunter* RPSVs fired half their payload of HB-7c missiles. "Seven two missiles inbound. The AI has control of their C-Jump timing from here."

As if Lee's announcement had somehow invoked the ire of a vengeful deity, *Theseus* shook violently from a series of impacts as the *Baldev* lit the space between the two vessels with orange-tinted energy weapons fire and the white flashes of light induced by shield intercept events.

Prescott's attention was once again drawn to the tactical plot and its accompanying hull impacts counter. At first glance, the counter displayed twenty-three impacts, but rapidly increased to twenty-seven as the intensity of the incoming fire seemed to increase with every passing second.

"Helm, can you alter course to improve shield performance?"

"Negative, sir, not without breaking off our attack," Fisher replied, raising his voice over the increasing din. "The AI is telling me 'don't fly here' in every direction at the moment."

"Optimum weapons range in one one seconds," Schmidt reported.

***

From locations flanking *Theseus'* approach course, two Carrada Area Denial Weapons pods rotated slightly on their vertical axes, leading their target just enough to ensure maximum submunitions coverage at the predicted point of intercept. Although not generally designed for use against such large warships, the system's earlier success against the Terran fighters had been noted by one of Captain Yagani's tactical officers. Since the larger Human ship appeared to be equipped with similar shields, he had suggested that the Carrada might also prove effective as an additional layer of protection for the *Baldev's* stern.

A relatively recent addition to the Sajeth Collective's arsenal, four of the Carrada pods had recently been deployed aboard each of their newest warships. Captain Yagani, agreeing that the Terrans would likely attempt another attack against his drive section, had ordered his final two area denial pods be released by the last wave of departing fighters just minutes before the Human warship had transitioned back into the area.

With the *Baldev's* engines operating at reduced power due to the activation of her supplemental aft shields, the two Carrada pods had little difficulty maintaining their positions well astern — essentially acting as tiny escorts for the gigantic battleship. Now, as the Terran vessel reached optimal range, each pod fired its entire payload of twelve kinetic energy interceptors.

***

"Sir!" Lau yelled, "I've got two of Zhukov's anti-access pods dead ahead …"

Lieutenant Lau's warning had come far too late for Fisher to take evasive action. At such close range, the

Carrada's interceptors had taken less than five seconds to complete their brief flights across the destroyer's path. And with *Theseus* following a relatively predictable course towards its target, all twenty-four interceptors disbursed their cargo of submunitions with deadly accuracy — instantly enveloping the entire ship in a thick cloud of fragments. Tens of thousands of small but nearly simultaneous impacts merged with the continuous hail of heavy energy weapons fire from the *Baldev,* completely overwhelming the destroyer's shields.

"Shields offline!" Lau yelled. He had been forced to wait what seemed like several seconds until the deafening sound of hull impacts had subsided somewhat before making his announcement. Even now, the sound of multiple alarms as well as energy weapons fire slamming directly into the ship's hull continued at such a frightful pace that it sounded as if she could literally fly apart at any moment.

Prescott struggled to push forward in his restraints so that he could lean quickly over to the side opposite Commander Reynolds and vomit, his stomach finally overcoming his best efforts at maintaining control. "Stay on target!" he bellowed, wiping his mouth with his sleeve before straightening in his Command chair once again. "Continue the attack run!"

"Firing, Captain," Schmidt reported, "but we missed the window for a coordinated attack. Our missiles are still in flight. The AI belayed their C-Jump."

With multiple weapons offline and the ship well past the point of optimum weapons range, *Theseus'* AI struggled to compensate for the damage while still salvaging the attack — hitting the designated point location target with three plasma torpedoes as well as roughly half the beam weapons and railguns that had been used during the previous attack on Charlie 4. Not surprisingly, the *Baldev's* shields maintained their integrity, dutifully channeling the incoming fire as glowing waves of energy traveled along the entire length of the enormous ship's hull.

"The weapons pods that hit us have been destroyed, but the attack on Bravo 1 was ineffective, sir," Schmidt reported. "Their supplemental aft shield field strength dropped by about twenty percent, but it's already back to normal levels. No significant change in their primary aft shields."

"Did we at least destroy some of their shield emitters with the railguns?"

"Yes, sir," Lau answered, "but several of our beam emitters and railgun turrets went offline when we got hit, so we didn't get as many of them as we did on the first run."

"Helm, take as much evasive action as you can while you put us back in position for another run," Prescott ordered.

Fisher turned around in his chair to confirm what he was hearing, an unmistakable look of fear mixed with confusion on his normally confident face.

"NOW, Ensign!"

"Sir, we can't —" Reynolds began.

Prescott turned to his XO with an expression leaving little doubt that further discussion was not an option. "Lieutenant Lee, damage report."

"Those weapons pods effectively shot-blasted most of the surface area of our hull, Captain. We have mostly superficial, ablative damage where the fragments impacted, but the hits from the *Baldev's* energy weapons are doing much more significant damage — every one of those is penetrating a meter or more into our armor."

"The *shields*, Lee, why are the *shields* offline?" Prescott asked impatiently.

"Best guess, sir, there were just too many fragments for the system to intercept them all. All those additional hull-mounted gravitic emitters that make the shields work are not very heavily armored. Quite a few of them are offline and most likely destroyed."

"So they're not just temporarily down, they're not coming back at all, right?"

"Yes, sir, that's right."

"Tactical," Prescott continued, still raising his voice over the tremendous sound of his ship's hull being pounded by the *Baldev's* energy weapons fire, "have any of our inbound missiles been intercepted?"

"No, sir," Schmidt answered. "They remain outside of Bravo 1's energy weapons range … she may not have even detected them yet."

"Can you keep them in a holding pattern of some sort until we get another opportunity?"

"Yes, sir. The AI did that automatically when we missed our first time on target. As long as they don't get destroyed, we can re-task them at any time."

"Helm, how soon will we be back in position for another run?"

"Uh …" Fisher hesitated, struggling to focus in spite of the incessant noise and violent shaking, "six niner seconds, sir."

"Right. Tactical, this is probably your last shot. Get your missile strike coordinated again and make this one count. Fisher, I'm sure I don't have to tell you to run like hell after this next pass and C-Jump as soon as possible … assuming we're still able."

"No, sir, you definitely do not, and as far as I can tell, the C-Drive is still working so far."

"Glad to hear it. Engineering, bridge," Prescott called.

"Commander Logan here. Go, Captain!"

"Any chance we can get the shields back online … or at least some of the weapons that didn't fire on that last run?"

"The shields are mostly a no-go, sir. We lost too many emitters. I might be able to replace enough of them to get some of their functionality back without a depot-level maintenance facility, but it's going to require quite a bit of EVA work. It does look like the system is still active from about the leading edge of our 'wing' section aft, though."

"That's better than nothing, I guess. And the weapons?"

"You should have most of them back now. The AI had all but decided that we were about to be destroyed, so there was a lot of automated rerouting of power going on. I've tweaked those settings, so it shouldn't happen again. Other than that, we've got quite a bit of hull damage, so I wouldn't count on everything working. I know for sure we've lost a couple of railgun mounts and two of our forward plasma torpedo tubes."

Prescott scowled and swore to himself. Having lived through the previous attack, he now felt oddly at peace with the prospect of ultimately not surviving the current battle with the *Baldev*. But with such a significant reduction in available firepower, could he even justify the risk of one more run?

"Anything else I need to know?" he asked, making a conscious decision to push the lingering doubts from his mind.

"No, sir. Just keep in mind that it's only a matter of time before they do enough damage to hit to something we can't do without ... or breach our inner hull, God forbid."

"Understood. Just one more run, Commander. Prescott out. Alright, everyone," he shouted, addressing everyone on the bridge, "we're only going to get one more shot at this —"

"Contact!" Lieutenant Lau interrupted.

On the tactical plot, the new contact, which the AI had immediately classified as a probable Sajeth Collective cruiser due to its size and emissions characteristics, was initially displayed with the yellow icon reserved for unknown contacts. A moment later, the icon's color changed to green, indicating that the AI now recognized it as a known neutral vessel — or one manually designated as a noncombatant.

"It's Charlie 3 again, sir, the *Hadeon!*" Lau announced as the accompanying block of identifying text appeared on the screen, then immediately began flashing to indicate that a live video stream was available.

"Commander Takkar is hailing us, Captain," Lieutenant Dubashi reported from the Comm/Nav console.

"On-screen, please," Prescott replied, hoping that he wasn't about to receive another recommendation that he surrender to Captain Yagani and the *Baldev*.

Seconds later, a vidcon window displaying an earnest-looking Commander Yuli Takkar opened in the center of the bridge view screen.

"Hello again, Captain Prescott," he began in his rather formal style. "My sincerest apologies for leaving your ship alone to face the *Baldev* and the *Keturah* earlier. On behalf of my entire crew, I would like to pledge the *Hadeon* in support of Admiral Naftur and his house. Until he returns to his duties, we will assist you and your crew to the best of our abilities."

Prescott paused momentarily, unsure of what to make of the Wek officer's proclamation of support. Was this type of "defection" from the Resistance movement what Admiral Naftur had hoped would happen on a larger scale? As he struggled to process the implications of what Takkar was saying, a particularly savage jolt — one that would easily have thrown him from his chair had he not been restrained — vividly reminded him of the urgency of the current situation.

"We have taken quite a bit of damage, Commander, and are in the process of preparing for another attack. Are you truly willing to fire on your own vessel in order to help us?"

"We pledge our lives and our ship to Gracafürst and his house," Takkar repeated. "Once this conflict has concluded, we will submit ourselves for whatever disciplinary action he deems appropriate. We have, all of us, behaved in a dishonorable fashion and see this as our only path to atone for our misconduct."

Prescott stared directly into Takkar's huge gray eyes, incredulous, but detected no hint whatsoever of deceit or false pretense. "We welcome your assistance," he replied, thinking darkly to himself that if the Wek commander were lying it would probably do little more than hasten their demise at this point anyway. "You will receive targeting information shortly. Can you be in a position to fire on the *Baldev's* stern in … Fisher?"

"Three eight seconds, sir," he replied instantly.

"We have a firing solution from our current position," Takkar answered, "but will close to improve it as best we can during the time remaining. Please do not alter your approach flight path in our direction to ensure that you avoid our incoming fire."

"Understood. Good luck, Commander."

"To us both, Captain. Takkar out."

"Missile launch!" Lieutenant Lau reported from Tactical 2 just as the vidcon window closed on the bridge view screen. "Two four … correction four eight missiles fired from Bravo 1 — both her ventral and dorsal launch cells this time. Time to impact, one niner seconds."

"Countermeasures again, Lieutenant Lee. All weapons to point defense mode," Prescott responded. "No matter what happens, I want every weapon we have available back in normal mode in time to execute our attack."

"Aye, sir," Lee, Lau, and Schmidt responded as one.

"Countermeasures away," Lee announced shortly thereafter.

"Beam and kinetic weapons firing in point defense mode," Lau added. "Sea-whiz is tracking ... *sir*, the *Hadeon* is firing!"

At this range, the BD cruiser's fire control AI had easily detected and locked on to all forty-eight missiles fired by the *Baldev* before they had even completely cleared their launch cells. Just as the two groups of missiles reached the point where they were beginning to alter course in the direction of their target, the *Hadeon* had opened fire. With her starboard side facing in the general direction of the *Baldev*, Commander Takkar had positioned the cruiser to present her entire broadside of energy weapons banks to the battleship, thus creating a very nearly ideal case for an anti-missile barrage.

"*Whoa*," Lieutenant Lee remarked in awe as what looked like two distinct, fan-shaped groupings of orange-tinted energy weapons fire streaked both above and below Bravo 1's hull to engage the two groups of departing missiles simultaneously.

With cold, methodical precision, the *Hadeon's* AI worked through its list of targets, initially designating each one to receive as many as three separate impacts from its heavy beam emitters. As the list of targets quickly dwindled, each was assigned progressively more weapons fire until the list was reduced to zero. Within eight seconds of the anti-ship missiles leaving their vertical launch cells — and well before any had reached the curtain of kinetic energy rounds being laid down by the *Theseus* — the *Hadeon* had destroyed all forty-eight of Bravo 1's anti-ship missiles.

"All inbound missiles destroyed!" Lau reported excitedly."

"Securing all weapons from point-defense mode," Schmidt added. "Optimum weapons range in one one seconds."

"Well, I guess that settles the question of whether or not Commander Takkar was serious about helping us," Reynolds said without looking up from her touchscreen.

"Maybe so," Prescott replied. "I guess I'll be more convinced when I see them open fire on their own ship."

Even with much of her once proud hull now scorched and marred by a combination of the damage inflicted by the Carrada weapons pods and the relentless pounding from the *Baldev's* energy weapons, TFS *Theseus* still managed a graceful, sweeping turn to begin her final attack run on the distant battleship.

"Point location target acquired and locked," Schmidt reported from Tactical 1. "All seven two HB-7c missiles confirming re-task order. Firing all weapons."

Before Schmidt had even finished executing the required commands at his console, the *Hadeon* opened fire on the *Baldev's* drive section with all of her starboard energy weapons banks — now configured for an anti-ship strike and converged on the point location designated by her new ally. The center of the targeted area blazed forth with brilliant, white light surrounded by an angry, orange glow as massive amounts of energy were delivered to a roughly four square meter area of the battleship's aft shields. Milliseconds later, *Theseus* added her diminished but still powerful salvo of three plasma torpedoes along with focused fire from twenty-three beam emitters and seven railgun turrets.

The barrage continued for what seemed like an eternity to the crews aboard both attacking ships, each of which continued to take a ferocious pounding from the *Baldev's* powerful aft and starboard energy weapons. In reality, however, only a few seconds passed before the battleship's already weakened supplemental shields lost several additional emitters to kinetic energy weapons fire, leading to a localized failure in the targeted area. The opportunity was immediately detected by *Theseus'* AI, which commanded all seventy-two of the inbound HB-7c missiles to strike the now-vulnerable area — calculating that at least a few would manage to transition inside the battleship's primary shields.

Chapter 10

SCS Gunov, Location Crossbow
$(5.93 \times 10^{11}$ km from Location Dagger$)$

"We will reach optimal energy weapons range to the remaining Terran vessel in just under two minutes, Commodore," the *Gunov's* tactical officer reported.

With nearly six minutes now having elapsed since most of the enemy warships had transitioned to hyperspace, Sarafi was growing increasingly anxious that he was either running out of time, or, worse, being led into a trap by the fleeing Human ship.

"This is taking far too long," he said gravely. "We need to finish off this last target and return to the confines of our defensive perimeter as quickly as possible."

"If their damage is significant, perhaps a spread of anti-ship missiles might finish them off before we are forced to engage with energy weapons," Commander Freyda suggested. Although still not comfortable with the idea of destroying damaged enemy vessels that were clearly no longer a threat, this one was attempting to leave the area rather than surrender. In her mind, the simple act of failing to yield and face capture rendered them fair game for additional attacks.

"Do it. And make it a spread of eighteen — six from each ship," Sarafi growled, chiding himself for being so distracted that he had not considered this simple tactic several minutes before.

"Six missiles from each ship, aye, sir," his tactical officer repeated. "Both ships acknowledged — firing."

Atop each of the three *Gresav*-class destroyers, small sets of doors above six vertical launch cells swung open. Immediately thereafter, bright plumes of fiery exhaust gas escaped from the adjacent vents as anti-ship missiles climbed silently above each destroyer atop a pillar of flame.

"Missiles away," the tactical officer reported. "Time to impact, twenty-nine seconds."

"Should we risk a turn back towards our perimeter now?" Freyda asked.

Sarafi considered her question momentarily. It was certainly not a foregone conclusion that the missile attack would destroy the remaining Human vessel, especially given that they were equipped not only with shields, but also formidable point defense weaponry. Continuing this seemingly endless pursuit of a single, damaged enemy ship while potentially endangering the most critical remaining members of his own task force, however, was beginning to feel very much like the errand of a fool.

"A wise question, Commander," he replied, "and I am of your way of thinking entirely. Helm, set a course back to the point where we began the previous engagement — directly above our remaining cruiser, please."

"Contacts!" the tactical officer announced yet again. "I have two of the Terran vessels dead ahead, sir, to either side of the damaged ship. They appear to be laying down defensive fire."

"Helm, belay my previous order. Continue on course towards the damaged vessel. Tactical, if they succeed in shooting down our missiles, concentrate all of our formation's energy weapons fire on the damaged vessel first. Once we eliminate that one, we will move on to the other two. XO, I suspect the remaining Terran vessels will resume their attack on the *Rusalovs* momentarily. Be prepared to —"

Before Sarafi could complete his sentence, the *Gresav*-class destroyer immediately to port and slightly aft of his ship exploded in a brilliant white ball of fire as fifteen HB-7c missiles transitioned from hyperspace inside her aft shields, penetrated her hull, and detonated their compact antimatter warheads.

"Helm, break left!" he roared with a level of fury beyond anything the members of his bridge crew had ever experienced from their Commodore.

Thrusters all along the *Gunov's* starboard bow blazed into life and immediately began pushing the huge warship to port, even as her gimbaled sublight engine nozzles vectored the tremendous thrust required to bring her stern around while simultaneously increasing to maximum power. Even before the destroyer was fully established on her new course, the second volley of fifteen anti-ship missiles — originally intended for her vulnerable drive section — transitioned from hyperspace where their target had been located just moments before. The missiles continued ahead harmlessly for a few additional seconds before being automatically targeted by the *Gunov's* AI, which quickly dispatched the entire group with murderously accurate energy weapons fire.

Right up to the moment before the *Gunov* had made her dramatic turn to port, her remaining consort to starboard had been dutifully maintaining her assigned position in the three-ship formation. Caught completely off guard by Commodore Sarafi's frantic evasive action, she found herself alone, continuing along the same course she had been following for the last several minutes. As her helmsman hesitated, unsure of whether to attempt a left turning rejoin with the *Gunov*, she was an easy target for the third and final salvo of fifteen anti-ship missiles.

***

After the stunning success of his first attack against the Resistance cruisers, Captain Abrams had not expected to find himself in a situation where the same tactics might once again prove effective. Having suffered his own grievous losses to the Resistance battleships' heavy guns, however, he had been looking for any opportunity to once again gain the upper hand — preferably while avoiding the necessity of another frontal assault.

The fleeing *Theseus*-class destroyer, while temporarily unable to transition and in grave danger of being destroyed, had nevertheless provided an unexpected, and much needed, bounty of real-time battlespace intelligence data. Armed with this precious information, Abrams had been granted the luxury of assessing the situation to determine his next move within the relative safety of hyperspace.

As difficult as it had been to watch helplessly as the Resistance warships ruthlessly eliminated the two most seriously damaged members of his task force, it was Commodore Sarafi's next move that had finally provided the opportunity Abrams had been waiting for. In his haste to eliminate the third and final damaged Terran ship as a potential threat, Sarafi had allowed his three-ship formation to be drawn away from the bulk of his forces — drawn away at a predictable speed along a direct flight path towards his fleeing prey. Although Captain Abrams had dared not hope that this situation would remain in place long enough to be exploited, he had nevertheless gambled that placing two additional ships in Sarafi's path might entice him to continue on his present course — with any luck, long enough to be targeted for a C-Drive-equipped missile strike.

At a range of approximately five light seconds (1.5 million km), three *Theseus*-class destroyers had transitioned back into normal space and immediately fired five HB-7c missiles each at the first of Sarafi's three ships. As the missiles accelerated towards their distant target, control had been seamlessly transferred to one of the friendly warships directly in Sarafi's flight path, which immediately began transmitting the precise targeting data the missiles required to successfully execute their C-Jump.

Abrams was well aware that he would need every weapon at his disposal for the coming fight against the Resistance battleships, and had initially considered waiting for a damage assessment before firing additional missiles. Realizing that he would almost certainly not be afforded an opportunity like this one again, however, he quickly fired the second and third salvos of fifteen missiles. Less than thirty seconds after the initial volley of missiles had been fired, the dramatic effects of the attack were graphically displayed on the tactical plots aboard all eleven of the remaining *Theseus*-class destroyers. No crewmember aboard any of the Human vessels had been more surprised by the results than Captain Bruce Abrams.

***

"Commodore, the three Terran vessels have destroyed all eighteen of our anti-ship missiles," the *Gunov's* tactical officer reported sheepishly. Although it was his job to report such things in a timely fashion to whomever was in command of the ship, the youngish Wek lieutenant was completely unwilling to report the obvious destruction of the other two *Gresav*-class destroyers that had until recently been members of their three-ship formation.

"Helm, maintain maximum power to the sublight engines and head back towards the remainder of our forces," Sarafi ordered, ignoring his tactical officer and speaking in a surprisingly calm voice given his barely controlled rage of just moments before. "Continue random evasive maneuvers per Annex-Three of the TACPLAN and do what you can to prevent the Terran warships from closing on us."

The words were like ash in his mouth at this point. With the knowledge in his possession at the outset of this battle, he knew that there was no excuse for his allowing the Humans to take advantage of their damnable hyperdrive-equipped missiles — not once, but twice. And there was no question in his mind that the blame for the tremendous losses suffered thus far would fall squarely on his shoulders. In Sarafi's mind, only one path remained open that would salvage his career and indeed save his own life at this point. The attack on

Terra must end in either the destruction of Human civilization, or in the very least a last stand worthy of uniting the Collective against them as well as their Pelaran benefactors.

"Aye, sir. Executing now," he heard his Helm officer acknowledge from what seemed like a great distance.

With his task force now reduced to something approaching the minimum number of warships required to mount any sort of conventional attack on Terra, Sarafi realized that he could no longer afford to risk additional losses. While he fully expected that the very same ships he had engaged here would, in all likelihood, be waiting for him when he transitioned from hyperspace near the target, his task force's arrival would immediately force the Humans into a defensive role. This alone, he hoped, would go a long way towards mitigating some of the losses he had already suffered.

"XO, see that the navigation systems from all remaining vessels are coupled to the *Gunov's* and inform all vessels that we will transition to hyperspace momentarily. There will be no intermediate destination. We will proceed directly to Terra and execute our attack per the original plan. Once we are on our way, we will have roughly two Terran days in transit. During that time, I will communicate with our captains and address any last minute issues. Understood?"

"Of course, Commodore," Freyda replied, doing an admirable job of hiding whatever reservations she might have had regarding their prospects for successfully completing their mission at this point.

"Very well. I will give you a few moments to complete your task, then I would like you to be a witness when I knowingly and purposely violate a number of Sajeth Collective security regulations."

"I, uh ..." she began hesitantly, "as you wish, sir."

At his Command workstation, Sarafi worked quickly to bypass the security restrictions intended to prevent him from displaying classified information on a screen that was clearly not located in a secure location. He then removed the electronic safeguards intended to prevent data from being transferred between the Pelaran-derived surveillance drones at each of his rally points, then explicitly granted the *Gunov* full access to the AIs of every Resistance vessel at both locations. With that accomplished, he called up the same video surveillance feeds from the original rally point that he had been monitoring from the privacy of his ready room as well as a tactical situation display provided by a combination of ships' AIs near the original rally point.

What he saw sent a series of involuntary chills running down the length of his spine. The situation was confused at best, but at first glance it appeared that the *Baldev* had been heavily damaged and might even be adrift based on its apparent movement. The *Hadeon* appeared largely undamaged — *leave it to the Damaran to avoid any potential for damage,* Sarafi thought bitterly. Her sister ship, the *Keturah,* looked to be in much the same shape as the *Baldev*, perhaps worse by the looks of her mangled stern. As for the two *Shopak-* class cruisers that were previously assigned to the detachment, the floating hulk of the *Babayev* was still in the same general area as before. The other vessel, the name of which escaped Sarafi at the moment, was nowhere to be seen. The Human warship, for its part, was an appalling mess to behold, but nevertheless gave the impression of still maneuvering under its own power — no doubt delivering far more damage to his forces than it had received.

"Comm, please hail Commander Miah aboard the *Hadeon* if you please," Sarafi ordered.

"Uh, sir …" the comm officer began tentatively after a momentary pause, "begging your pardon, sir, but we have not yet established long-range communications with our vessels at the original rally point."

Sarafi looked up from his display screen with a savage, but somewhat amused look on his face. "Please indulge me by following my orders, Lieutenant," he replied. "Perhaps you will be surprised by the results."

"Of course, Commodore, right away," the young Wek officer said.

After a few moments of rapidly entering commands at his workstation, the communications officer turned in his chair to face Sarafi again. "I am sorry, sir, but the *Hadeon* is not responding." Unsure if his commanding officer was simply mistaken or if he actually believed that they should be capable of contacting the BD cruiser from over half a trillion miles away, he stared earnestly at Sarafi and simply waited for a response.

"Unfortunately, that does not surprise me, Lieutenant. Try the *Baldev* please, and do it quickly. We need to depart for Terra as soon as possible before our enemy has time to organize for yet another attack."

"Aye, sir," he replied immediately, willing to do just about anything at this point to avoid further irritating the commodore.

"Sir, we have successfully coupled our navigation system to those of our remaining vessels," Freyda reported. "All are prepared to depart on our signal."

"Thank you, Commander. I expect we will do exactly that momentarily. Is the remaining BD cruiser capable of transitioning to hyperspace?"

"Yes, sir. As are all six *Rusalov* battleships for a total of eight."

"It will be enough, Ragini. In any event, we have little choice in the matter at this point, eh?" he said with an ironic smile.

Freyda regarded him for a moment, thinking that such comments seemed oddly misplaced under the circumstances, then continued, "I also feel obligated to remind you of the three damaged cruisers requesting our assistance."

Sarafi seemed shaken by her statement, and the distant look in his eyes led Freyda to believe that he truly had forgotten about the thousands of lives hanging in the balance aboard the stricken vessels.

"This is an active war zone, Commander," he finally said. "It is indeed a regrettable situation, but rescue operations are simply not possible while the remainder of our ships are under attack. I fear we would end up losing more lives than we could possibly save. With any luck, the Human vessels will feel some obligation to assist them once we depart."

Right. Just as we "helped" their damaged vessels? Freyda wondered.

"Commodore, I have Captain Ditanu Yagani of the battleship *Baldev* at our original Rally point," the comm officer reported triumphantly.

"Nicely done, Lieutenant. I had every confidence that you would make it so," he smiled. "On-screen, please."

There was a momentary pause while a window opened on the bridge display screen to reveal Captain Yagani, a look of what might be described as surprised anguish on his face.

"Hello Captain. I am Commodore Naveen Sarafi aboard the Pelaran Resistance flagship *Gunov*. I regret not having the opportunity to speak with you before now and apologize in advance if I seem abrupt and direct. Our forces are under attack from the Terrans at the secondary rally point just as you appear to be at the first. I am unable to offer you any assistance at this time, but we will be departing for our attack on Terra momentarily. Is the *Baldev* still capable of hyperspace flight?"

"Commodore," Yagani said, inclining his head respectfully. "No, unfortunately, we are unable to transition to hyperspace. We have taken heavy damage to our propulsion section, and many of our engineering and power generation spaces are unpressurized at the moment. All but one of our reactors jettisoned their containment units once our aft shields collapsed, so we have only minimal power available. Most of our engineering staff is missing and presumed killed, but the ones we have remaining tell me that we may lose power altogether. Captain Prescott of the Human vessel *Theseus* is offering to assist us, and I fear that I may have little choice but to accept."

"I assume you have heard nothing from the other two *Baldev*-class battleships, *Zhelov* and *Serapion*?"

"I have not, although even their late arrival would be most welcome."

"Alright, Captain Yagani, I need you to listen carefully to what I require of you, then I must depart for Terra with the remainder of our task force. Unfortunately, I believe we must assume that your ship will be under the control of the Humans by the time the *Zhelov* and *Serapion* arrive. Accordingly, I want you to launch a communications buoy that will relay the instructions I am about to transmit to your ship's AI. Once the task force at the secondary Rally point transitions to hyperspace, the Terran ships here might well be sent to your location to assist the *Theseus*. Unfortunately, we cannot afford to risk the loss of any additional ships until we begin the attack on Terra itself."

"So are saying that you intend to order the *Zhelov* and *Serapion* to depart for Terra as soon as they arrive without engaging enemy forces here?" Yagani asked evenly.

"I am afraid we have little choice at this point, Captain. The *Baldev*-class ships are twice as fast as the older *Rusalovs* we will be traveling with, so as long as they arrive within the next twenty-four hours, they should have little difficulty rendezvousing with the remainder of our forces at Terra in time to participate in our attack."

"Understood," Yagani replied with a scowl that clearly portrayed how he felt about the current situation.

In the already chaotic background noise aboard the *Baldev*, a new and urgent-sounding alarm sounded and immediately drew Captain Yagani's attention to something not visible on Sarafi's screen.

"I wish I could be of more assistance, Captain," the commodore continued, "but perhaps the best thing I can do for you right now is let you get back to attending to your ship. Ah yes, one more thing before you go … what can you tell me of the BD cruiser *Hadeon*? She looks relatively undamaged, but I have been unable to contact Commander Miah."

"The *Hadeon* has be … Com … at …" After a few additional seconds of sporadic, choppy video with no sound, the vidcon window on *Gunov's* bridge display screen closed.

"The transmission was terminated at the source, sir," the comm officer reported. "Shall I try establishing contact again?"

Sarafi thought about what he had just seen and heard, attempting to formulate some sort of logical explanation for how the *Baldev* and three other warships had been very nearly destroyed while the *Hadeon* — which was still in the immediate area — had suffered little if any damage. No scenario that came to mind seemed to fit the facts as he knew them at the moment, which was as frustrating as it was disturbing.

"Your thoughts, Commander Freyda?" he asked.

"Anything I might offer would be wild speculation at best, sir," she replied, "and most likely wrong anyway. As you saw, however, Captain Yagani has his hands full trying to hold his ship together. Since we have nothing additional to offer him, I recommend we immediately depart for Terra before we come under renewed attack."

"Contacts!" the tactical officer announced. "Eight of the Terran ships just transitioned back into the area, sir. It looks like they intend to remain in a single group this time."

"Their range to the closest *Rusalov*?" Sarafi asked.

"Just over five hundred thousand kilometers."

"Humph," Sarafi grunted. "Perhaps they have learned to respect the *Rusalovs'* main batteries. No missile launches detected?"

"No, sir. Stand by ... all eight are launching fighters."

"As you said, Commander Freyda, it is time we made our exit. Comm, please provide all warships with a thirty second transition warning and specifically remind the *Rusalovs* that the AI will need to disengage their supplemental shields before aligning them with our departure vector."

"Aye, sir. Signaling now."

Seconds later, with their twelve massive sublight engines now unencumbered by additional shielding, all six *Rusalov* battleships rotated smartly on their vertical axes and accelerated under maximum power at a rate that seemed to defy their tremendous size. Unable to resist the opportunity, each of the eight Terran warships immediately fired four anti-ship missiles in the direction of the nearest battleship. Just as the missiles tipped their noses over in the direction of their target and prepared to execute their C-Jump, however, the starfield around each of the Resistance ships blurred momentarily before the entire remaining task force disappeared in eight simultaneous flashes of gray light.

F-373 "Gamble 22," Location Crossbow

(In hyperspace - 5.93x10^{11} km from Location Dagger)

"Outbound hyperspace transition signatures detected!" the fighter's AI reported excitedly, causing its pilot to jump involuntarily.

"Wow, seriously? What was wrong with just saying 'contacts' like everyone else aboard every other ship since — forever?"

"That's fine. But when I just say 'contacts,' I'm not providing you with any information about what I'm referring to. That forces you to say things like 'clarify,' or 'classify,' or else you get all nautical on me and say things like 'where away?'"

"Alright, alright — I get it, whatever," the pilot replied, quickly running through the series of tasks required for what he assumed would be an immediate departure. "It just seems a little weird to me that you would get so excited about it this time. We've been sitting here this whole time watching everything that's been happening with Captain Abrams' task force, so it's not like it was a surprise or anything. You saw the Resistance ships transition just like I did."

"True, but are you aware that this is the first time one of our ships has actually been able to actively gather data from hyperspace during a transition event? This could literally lead to our gaining a better understanding of —"

"Of how our own C-Drives work? Awesome. But as fascinating as that truly is, I'm pretty sure we're about to get very busy again very quickly. Show me your 'outbound hyperspace transition signatures,' please."

"Designated. You should see them now to port."

"Yeah, I got 'em," the lieutenant replied, looking off to his left and noting the now-familiar grouping of red ovals pulsing urgently within his field of view. "Why are there no course indicator lines this time?"

"I'm still working on that. I should have initial departure vectors for you shortly. When the ships first transition, it creates a fairly intense burst of the same particles we followed to find the secondary rally point. At first, it looks like nothing more than a bunch of noise, but that dies down pretty quickly. Once the smoke clears, so to speak, there's a fairly distinct indication of the direction of flight."

"Uh huh, well I don't see any smoke, but we both know that's going to be the first question we get asked, so —"

"Got it," the AI interrupted as a series of red lines extended from the points of transition displayed within the lieutenant's field of view. All eight lines pointed at a conspicuously bright yellowish-white star — the fourth brightest in the sky at this distance.

Although not surprised by this result, the pilot nevertheless experienced a sudden and unexpected feeling of anxiety at the thought of powerful enemy warships heading in the direction of everything and everyone he had ever known.

"Get me Admiral Patterson, please."

Chapter 11

TFS Theseus, Location Dagger
(3.3 light years from Earth)

"I'm not entirely sure I follow what you're telling me, Commander Takkar," Prescott said, astonished by what he thought his new Wek ally was attempting to explain. "Captain Yagani is responding to *your* hails — while still ignoring mine — all while denying our offer to render assistance? It's possible we're losing something in the translation here, so please allow me to explain to you in simple, direct terms exactly what I want you to pass along to the good captain of the *Baldev*. Our offer to assist is not optional. It was presented as such as a matter of tradition and courtesy, but in fact, it's really not an 'offer' so much as a demand. Furthermore, we extended this courtesy based on our previous understanding that Captain Yagani wished to surrender his vessel and avoid further loss of life. We respect, honor, and wholeheartedly agree with his decision to do so, but his surrender must be complete and unconditional."

"My apologies, Captain Prescott," Takkar replied, clearly uncomfortable with being placed in the role of mediator. "I will endeavor to make your position very clear to Captain Yagani when I speak with him again momentarily."

"Thank you, Commander. While it truly is my intention to be as helpful as possible, this *is* still an active combat zone, and we obviously have other, urgent matters demanding our immediate attention. Based on what you have told me regarding the imminent arrival of two additional Resistance battleships, I hope that it is not his intention to simply delay until they arrive and then withdraw his offer to surrender. If that happens —"

"Yes, sir, I understand. Although I had not met Captain Yagani before today, I do not believe that is his intention. Other than preferring to communicate through me, he has been generally cooperative thus far. In fact, as strange as this sounds, he has asked me to inform you that he has been ordered by Commodore Sarafi, our task force commander, to launch a communications buoy."

"Wait … ordered by your task force commander? You mean just now?"

It seemed to Takkar that every action he took and every word that came out of his mouth — regardless of the forethought involved or the intent in his heart — moved him inexorably closer to outright treason against his people. As he paused to consider how much detail he should offer, however, his mind continually returned to the same thought: *Gracafürst trusts these Humans. Who am I to doubt his judgment?* Intellectually, he knew that such rationalizations in no way relieved him of his own personal responsibilities. At the same time, however, he firmly believed himself to be doing the right thing — and with a moral clarity that he had not experienced for many months.

"Yes, Captain," Takkar continued. "Sarafi's flagship, the *Gunov*, apparently has access to a new type of long-range communications technology. I am sorry, but I have no additional details to offer, other than the fact that he was aware of what was taking place here and, in response, issued this order to Captain Yagani."

"And what is to be the purpose of this communications buoy? Is it part of this new long-range system?"

"No, sir, not to my knowledge. These buoys are not particularly sophisticated and have been in use within the Sajeth Collective fleet for a hundred years or more. They are often prepositioned to transmit orders to ships that have been traveling in hyperspace for extended periods. In this case, the intent is to transmit revised orders to the two battleships I mentioned, the *Zhelov* and the *Serapion*. The buoys are far too small to generate the power required to communicate via our deep space network. Typically, they are programmed to detect the electronic signature of specific vessels in the immediate area, then establish an encrypted communications channel to deliver their message."

"It's interesting that Commodore Sarafi didn't choose to utilize a buoy of this type when he moved the bulk of his task force to the second rally point," Prescott remarked. "Did Captain Yagani have any idea what message is to be delivered to the two battleships?"

"Yes, sir, and I made precisely the same observation at the time. I suspect, however, that the commodore's decision to leave four vessels behind at the original rally point was made *for* him well in advance," Takkar said with a disgusted tone. "There was clearly no military advantage to be gained by doing so. Frankly, I suspect we were left there as a means of enticing any Terran vessels that came looking for their missing scout ships to attack."

"He was using you as *bait?*" Reynolds asked, incredulous. "With no intention of sending reinforcements to assist you when we showed up? I'm thinking the Resistance movement might start having a little trouble with their recruiting efforts if word of that ever gets out."

"Indeed," he replied, the hint of a smile forming at the corners of his mouth for the first time. Takkar had to admit that he was beginning to understand some of what Admiral Naftur had seen in these Terrans. They were obviously determined, quick-thinking adversaries on the battlefield, but there was also an openness about them — a willingness to find humor even in the midst of a stressful situation — that he rather liked. "As to the actual encoded message," he continued, "Captain Yagani was not provided access, but he was told that the two battleships were being ordered to avoid contact with enemy forces here and depart immediately for Terra."

"Holy cow," Reynolds remarked, shaking her head in disbelief, "this just keeps getting better and better. No wonder Yagani was willing to come clean about the comm buoy. It sounds like Commodore Sarafi totally hung you guys out to dry."

For the next several seconds, Takkar furrowed his brow while struggling to make sense of his AI's attempt at translating Commander Reynolds' last remark. "I believe we have experienced a bit of a translation problem," he finally said, chuckling to himself at the imagery brought to mind by the AI's rather imaginative interpretation. "But yes, while not normally one to question his superiors' orders, Captain Yagani is beginning to have his doubts about the legitimacy of the entire Resistance movement. Intentionally placing our military forces in a position where they are likely to be destroyed — almost certainly to advance a cynical political agenda — is a degree of corruption unlikely to be tolerated by Wek officers. This should be true regardless of the underlying cause or the motivation of those issuing such orders."

"Commander Takkar, please excuse us for just a moment," Prescott said, nodding to Lieutenant Dubashi at the Comm/Nav console. Although Takkar's image remained in place on the view screen, symbols appeared indicating that the audio and video feeds from *Theseus'* side had been temporarily suspended.

"What do you think?" Prescott asked.

"Well, I guess the obvious question at this point is — given that we have no way of knowing precisely what information Sarafi placed aboard the comm buoy — should we even allow it to be launched?" Reynolds said. "For all we know, he issued orders for the *Zhelov* and the *Serapion* to attack and destroy our forces before they set off for Earth."

"That was my first thought as well," Prescott replied. "But my gut tells me we should allow Yagani to press on with the launch. Even if the battleships receive orders to attack us, we're really in no worse shape than we would have been otherwise. Besides, they may attack even if we *don't* allow them to get the message. In fact, if the situation were reversed, I'm pretty confident that's exactly what we would do — although figuring out precisely what had been taking place immediately before our arrival might have posed a challenge. The truth of the matter is that we would be heavily outgunned in a battle against two of the *Baldev's* sister ships. So if Sarafi really is sending them on their way without a confrontation, that might be the best possible scenario for us at this point."

"That assumes, of course, that Admiral Patterson doesn't order us to hold them here at all costs."

"I guess we'll have an answer to that question shortly, but I don't think he will ask us to hold the line here unless he can reinforce us. If he does end up with additional ships he can send our way, however, I'm sure he would prefer that we attempt to prevent those two *Baldevs* from ever reaching Earth. I took a quick look at what's been taking place at the other rally point and, although it looks like the combat is over for now, they took some pretty heavy losses. If we're going to get reinforcements at this point, that's where they will have to come from, and I really don't see that happening in the near term. Is there anything else you need to say in confidence before we bring Takkar back in?"

"No, sir, but if you think he's trustworthy, I like the idea of his babysitting Captain Yagani and the *Baldev* while we finish recovering our damaged fighters and find out what Admiral Patterson expects us to do next."

"Right, well — as to his being trustworthy — I have absolutely no idea. But I also don't see where he had anything to gain by siding with us against the *Baldev* other than a desire to follow Admiral Naftur. Tell me if you think I'm missing something, but at the moment I'm inclined to proceed under the assumption that we can take him at his word. I don't believe Commander Takkar and the *Hadeon* have the option of rejoining the Resistance at this point, even if they wanted to, so I think it's unlikely he will suddenly attempt to side with the *Zhelov* and the *Serapion* when they arrive. The *Baldev*, on the other hand ... although she isn't much of a threat at this point, I honestly have no idea what we should do with her."

"Tell me about it," Reynolds sighed. "We have no idea of her casualties yet, but the data we received from the *Hadeon* indicates that she has a complement of over twelve thousand personnel. Of that, about twenty-five hundred make up something similar to one of our Marine Expeditionary Units."

"Yeah, we are in no way equipped to handle anything on that scale. So that needs to be an Admiral Patterson question for sure."

"Yes, sir, that's why they pay him the big bucks," she smiled.

"Okay, Lieutenant," Prescott called, getting Dubashi's attention once again. With a single keystroke at her console, the vidcon on the screen became active once again.

"Sorry about that, Commander Takkar," Prescott said. "I know that you don't have a precise ETA for the *Zhelov* and the *Serapion,* but can you tell us about how long will it take for them to receive a transmission from the communications buoy once they arrive?"

"Yes, Captain. The ships' AIs will scan for a communications buoy immediately upon their arrival. The procedures our ships follow when arriving near an existing assembly area requires a large exclusion zone to provide separation from vessels already on station."

Takkar nodded to his communications officer off-screen. Shortly thereafter, Lieutenant Dubashi received an additional data stream from the *Hadeon* and displayed the resulting graphic in a window directly beside

Commander Takkar's image. The slowly rotating, three-dimensional plot depicted a view of the exclusion zone relative to the current locations of all the other ships in the area.

"Depending on where they arrive within the zone relative to the location of the buoy," Takkar continued, "there might be a brief comm delay, but they should still receive their instructions pretty quickly."

"And do you expect that they will comply with the order to depart for Terra immediately, even taking into account the situation here?"

"Sajeth Collective naval doctrine requires captains to respond to orders received in this fashion immediately. I don't know either of these captains, and there is always the possibility that they will do something unexpected, but if they are following standard procedures they will ignore what they see here and proceed to Terra without delay."

"I know I've been asking you questions that most likely involve classified information, and I'm not sure how I would respond if our roles were reversed. It would be very helpful, however, if we knew how long it will take the two battleships to arrive at Earth. Flag Captain Jelani aboard the *Gresav* told us the trip would take approximately twenty-six hours. That equates to a speed of about eleven hundred *c*. Our assumption is that, as one of the Collective's newest ships, the *Gresav* is probably also one of the fastest. Can we assume that the *Baldev*-class battleships can travel at roughly the same speed?"

Takkar face darkened as he breathed in sharply, then released his breath with the deep, mournful sound Prescott had heard a number of times from Admiral

Naftur. "I am unsure about the accuracy of the translation, but the word 'classified,' is by no means adequate to describe the sensitivity of the information we have been openly discussing. My actions here today, even if ultimately deemed proper and necessary, will almost certainly require a pardon of some sort in order to spare my life."

Prescott regarded the Wek officer sympathetically and could clearly see the multiple layers of conflict registered on his expressive face. Takkar was obviously a creature of conscience, which, ironically, was precisely what had led him down the winding path lined with competing allegiances and moral ambiguity to reach this point in time. Prescott wondered if, faced with the same set of difficult choices, he would have the courage of his convictions required to set aside a lifetime of expectations and preconceived notions — the courage to chart an entirely new course based solely on what he believed to be right. Takkar had now done so twice, and the heavy burden of his decisions was painful to behold.

"I won't insult you by pretending to understand the conflict you face, Commander. I will say, however, that where this single piece of information is concerned, you're not really giving us anything we don't already know. You're simply confirming information we already have in hand."

"And, in so doing, providing a key piece of information that will give aid to those who were, until just a few hours ago, my sworn enemies," he said in a distant, distracted tone. "At least that is how those in positions of power and influence within the Resistance movement will put it."

"If you will permit me, Yuli, we Humans were never your 'sworn enemies.' Surely, that distinction belongs only to those who actively seek to do your people harm. We didn't even know you existed until just over a month ago, and have absolutely nothing to gain by making enemies of the Wek, or any other members of the Sajeth Collective, for that matter. That is unless they ruthlessly attack us without provocation — in which case I think they will find that we are capable of our own unique brand of savagery when circumstance require us to defend ourselves. Indeed, we have everything to gain by cultivating an enduring partnership between our worlds … sorry, poor choice of words there, but you understand my meaning, I'm sure."

"Humph," Takkar grunted, his face seeming to brighten once again.

"We're a planet of traders, Takkar. I'm definitely no statesman myself, but I'm pretty sure our primary goal in dealing with the worlds of the Collective will be to negotiate mutually beneficial business arrangements. Well … mutually beneficial, but hopefully just a little more beneficial for us than for you," Prescott said with a cunning smile. "Actually, you may need to do business with us for a few years before you make up your mind on the question of whether we qualify as sworn enemies," he laughed.

"There are most definitely none like you within the Sajeth Collective," Takkar replied, shaking his head slowly. "In fact, other than the Pelarans themselves — about whom we still know very little — I do not believe we have ever encountered a civilization that seems to encompass such a wide range of … attributes, if you will. You might be surprised to learn that many species, at least in my opinion, have a tendency to fit within a fairly narrow archetype."

"Thank you … I think," Prescott smiled, "and, yes, that does surprise me. I would like nothing better than to discuss the topic with you at length when we are at leisure. For now, however, I think we had better move this along before we find ourselves in a fight that we have no hope of winning. Can you tell us when we can expect the Resistance ships to reach Terra?"

"Of course, Captain," Takkar said resignedly. "The information you mentioned is indeed accurate. There are, in fact, only two primary hyperdrive designs currently deployed aboard active duty Sajeth Collective naval vessels. As you inferred, the faster of the two is installed aboard *Gresav*-class vessels, as well as most other warships fielded within the past two decades or so. This includes the *Hadeon*, which is a member of the *Keturah*-class, as well as the *Baldev*-class battleships. They typically do travel at approximately one thousand one hundred times the speed of light, although higher speeds are possible over shorter distances or in an emergency. The older design is capable of only about half this speed and is installed aboard many of our older vessels including the standard *Shopak*-class cruisers like the *Babayev*. The bulk of Commodore Sarafi's task force is made up of vessels utilizing the older hyperdrive design. At last count, he had at least fifteen standard cruisers at his disposal as well as six *Rusalov*-class battleships."

"So you believe he will be traveling at around five hundred and fifty *c*, then?" Prescott asked.

"I cannot say for sure, Captain, but I cannot imagine a situation where he would be willing to leave so many of his ships behind. Unless …"

"Yes, Commander?"

"While I have not seen the specifics of Commodore Sarafi's attack plan, based on the ships at his disposal I believe we can safely assume that he will execute a relatively conventional, extraorbital bombardment. By 'conventional,' I do not mean to imply that no nuclear weapons will be used — indeed, a great many will be required if his intent is to render the planet uninhabitable — but I would expect most of these will be in the form of nuclear-tipped artillery rounds like those fired by the older *Rusalov*-class battleships. This kind of 'conventional' attack requires a number of ships to remain in the general area of the target for a period of time. If, before the attack on Terra commences, Sarafi's losses turn out to be heavier than expected, however, there is the possibility he might attempt to execute a 'special weapons' attack."

"What, you mean like a chemical or biological weapon?" Reynolds asked.

"Biological, yes — horrifying, deplorable weapons, genetically engineered to target a specific species. Such abominations have been banned on Graca and aboard all Wek vessels for centuries, so, by extension the same has always applied to all Sajeth Collective ships. Research into weapons of this type has long been conducted by the Lesheerans, however, and occasionally proposed as a means of 'compassionately' ending a conflict by simply exterminating the enemy. The Lesheerans have often boasted that they possess the capability to very specifically target their weapons. They supposedly have the technology required to kill only those within a certain race, with a specific ancestor in their lineage, or even to target something as arbitrary as a physical characteristic such as eye color. Perhaps the most insidious characteristic of these weapons is that they leave the enemy's territory — in this case the entire planet — fully intact and ready for colonization."

"Dear God," Reynolds muttered to herself.

"So you believe the leaders of the Resistance may have decided to ignore the long-standing ban and equip Sarafi's ship with these biological weapons?" Prescott asked.

"I have no specific information on the subject, but it would not be a surprise to me if that were the case. The Lesheerans typically remain in lockstep with their closest ally, the Damarans. Representatives from these two worlds on the Sajeth Collective Governing Council were the original instigators behind the Resistance movement."

"Thank you, Commander Takkar," Prescott said earnestly, "I think we've heard enough for now, but I'm sure we will have additional questions for you later. With any luck, the information you have provided will save countless lives — both in the Sol system and ultimately in the Sajeth Collective as well. Now, for the time being, I would like you to continue coordinating with Captain Yagani aboard the *Baldev*. After he launches his comm buoy — which needs to happen immediately — you are to make it absolutely clear that we demand his unconditional surrender. Direct him to immediately recover all of his remaining fighters and stand by for further instructions. Beyond that, I would like you to render *only* the aid required to prevent the immediate loss of additional life aboard his ship. I want to make myself very clear on this point, because I'm sure the *Baldev* will require quite a bit of help from us over the next few days. For now, however, offer them whatever urgent assistance you can provide quickly, then stand off from the exclusion zone to the same general area as the *Theseus*. We are still in the process of recovering our own damaged fighters, so I believe our current location is far enough away to avoid an immediate attack in case the *Zhelov* and the *Serapion* elect to ignore Commodore Sarafi's instructions. Do you have any questions for me?"

"Yes, sir. Have you received any communications from the other damaged cruiser, the *Keturah*?"

"We have not. We believe she jettisoned her reactor cores after being hit by the *Baldev's* missile. Since then, we have seen only minimal energy readings from her, and there are indications of multiple hull breaches. We will do everything we can to help them once the *Zhelov* and the *Serapion* have cleared the area."

Takkar paused momentarily, glancing downward as if gauging how best to respond. "Begging your pardon, sir, but since we are providing some minimal level of assistance to the *Baldev*, should we not extend the same courtesy to the *Keturah*? *Theseus* is the closer of our two vessels. Perhaps you can dispatch a shuttle of some sort to at least assess whether there are any survivors. If members of her crew are trapped in isolated areas, our providing emergency supplies may save many lives."

Prescott thought for a moment about how the damaged F-373s would likely be stowed in *Theseus'* hangar bay and whether it might still be possible to quickly launch two of their *Gurkha* Assault ASVs — or even the two *Sherpas* for that matter — without interfering with the ongoing recovery operation.

"Yes, of course, Commander. We'll do what we can, but I don't want either of us to risk additional lives in what may be a futile attempt at providing emergency aid. If the two battleships arrive while you are in close proximity to the *Baldev*, you are to transition to hyperspace, proceed to a safe distance, and contact me for further instructions."

"Thank you, Captain Prescott. I understand what you have asked of me and I will join you shortly. We will also provide you with information regarding the *Keturah's* external access points momentarily."

"Move quickly, Commander. If possible, I don't want you anywhere near the *Baldev* when those additional battleships arrive. Prescott out."

"I assume you'll want Lieutenant Jacks to handle the emergency relief op?" Reynolds asked, already issuing orders to prepare the required supplies for loading aboard one or more of their available ASVs.

"Yes, and I would prefer to send two of the *Gurkhas*, if possible, so they can at least have the option to C-Jump clear if they find themselves in a bad situation."

"Understood. I'll take a look at the current state of the hangar deck shortly," she replied, looking up from her touchscreen.

Prescott paused to take a deep breath, then stared at his XO while slowly shaking his head in wonder at everything they had experienced over the past several days.

"You okay?" Reynolds asked quietly.

"Yeah, I'm fine. I'm just not too keen on all of these 'fate of the world on your shoulders' kinds of situations. You?"

"Same," she smiled. "Knock on wood, but I think we're doing fine so far. Besides, would you trust anyone else but us to deal with this mess?"

"Oh, hell no," he replied, chuckling. "On that subject, did you see that it was Bruce Abrams leading the alpha strike at Location Crossbow? You remember him from the Live Fire Training Range, right? He had *Diligence* until about a week ago when Admiral Patterson transitioned his entire crew into the *Karna* the same way he did ours."

"Ah, that's right. I didn't make the connection though. I guess the admiral has quite a bit of confidence in him, then?"

"I'd say so, yes. He's a good man ... and a solid choice for that mission. I'm also guessing his crew has more experience on the range than any other at this point, which is probably the other reason they were transitioned over to a *Theseus*-class. Okay, Commander," he said, quickly refocusing on the urgent business still at hand, "what's our status?"

"The good news is that there have been no significant changes since the last update from Commander Logan. Other than the damage to the shield system as well as the loss of two of our forward plasma torpedo tubes and two railgun turrets, we're in surprisingly good shape. All other systems in the green. C-Jump range 101.1 light years and stable."

"Remarkable," Prescott replied, shaking his head again. "And where are we on recovering the damaged fighters?"

"When Flight Ops realized what kind of shape they were in, they went ahead and did an emergency egress and recovery for all four pilots. They all appear to have made it through their ordeal just fine, but they're being checked out in the medical bay just in case. Recovering their *Reapers*, however, has been a little more difficult than expected. We've got remote maneuvering units attached to all four, so getting them to the aft flight apron hasn't been a problem, but they all pretty much look like they've been dropped into a meat grinder. With so much damage, most of their systems aren't working at all. Just as an example, we finally got the first two aboard and stowed, but their wings wouldn't fold up properly, so they had to be removed."

"Removed … you mean as in disassembled?"

"No, removed as in detached from their fuselages using plasma torches."

"Hmm … well it's obviously preferable for us to recover the spacecraft, if possible, but if we find ourselves under attack again, discontinue the effort immediately and have the AI initiate a containment breach on any remaining fighters as soon as we're at a safe distance. We cannot risk having any of them captured, particularly one that's still largely intact."

"Understood. If you think I have time before our vidcon with Admiral Patterson, I'd like to head down to the flight deck and take a look for myself. There's only so much you can see on a video monitor."

"That's probably a good idea, but make it quick."

"Will do, sir," Reynolds replied, already heading for the door.

"Lieutenant Dubashi, please signal Zhukov and Waffer and ask them to check in for an update as soon as they have a moment."

"Aye, sir."

Prescott took another deep breath, his mind still struggling to come to grips with the problem of prioritizing dozens of equally urgent matters, each one demanding his immediate and undivided attention. The task that grabbed his attention next, however, made him laugh inwardly at his apparent inability to determine precisely what to do next.

"Lieutenant Lee, can you please reset the hull impacts counter? I think we may have broken it," he said, nodding to the starboard view screen. Since the nearly catastrophic encounter with the two Carrada Area Denial Weapons pods — which had largely taken the ship's shield systems offline — the AI had no longer possessed the capability to register an accurate count of weapons impacts on the outer hull. The counter, now flashing red beneath the tactical plot, still displayed the final count from the moment *Theseus* had plowed through the deadly cloud of fragments.

"Oh, yes, sir, no problem," Lee responded. "It's no longer getting data, so I can just disable it."

"Thanks, it's a little distracting for some reason. Is that count accurate, by the way?"

Lee took notice of the number for the first time, which stood at thirty-three thousand two hundred and forty-two. "Wow, that's pretty impressive, but, yes, it probably was accurate up to the point where most of the shield emitters and sensors got stripped off the hull. I'm sure once we're back at Yucca, they'll be able to provide an accurate count of total impacts. Clearly, Science and Engineering will need to head back to the drawing board on hardening those key components, particularly against fragmentary weapons like the ones we encountered."

"That would be great, but we're still alive, so you'll get no complaints from me."

"Captain," Lieutenant Dubashi interrupted, "message from the Flag, sir — text only. It reads: 'Continue salvage and rescue operations, as practicable, but do not, repeat *do not* engage in further combat operations unless TFC reinforcements arrive your location. If additional enemy forces arrive first, destroy all damaged TFC assets and C-Jump back to Earth immediately. Vidcon with Flag at 0815Z."

"Thank you, Lieutenant. Please acknowledge all," Prescott said, gratified once again by Patterson's unfailing ability to provide the information he knew his commanders needed without interfering with their ability to do their jobs.

"Will do, sir. I now have Captain Zhukov and Commander Waffer standing by."

"Thank you. Put them through please."

"Aye, sir," Dubashi replied, issuing the required commands at her console before nodding to indicate a live audio connection.

"Badger flights, *Theseus*-Actual."

"Badger 21 … Badger 22," came the immediate replies from Waffer and Zhukov, respectively.

"Captain Zhukov, all four of the pilots from your disabled fighters are now safely aboard *Theseus*. They are getting checked out in medical, but all four appear to be fine."

"That is indeed good news, Captain Prescott. Thank you."

"Commander Reynolds is down on the flight deck checking in on the recovery operation. Hopefully, we will have all four of their ships secured in our hangar bay shortly. Do you have any additional spacecraft in need of assistance?"

"Negative, sir," Commander Waffer answered. Even though he was junior to Captain Zhukov, he remained in command of Badger 2 Flight, which had now absorbed all of Badger 1's remaining six operational fighters.

"We do have six ships that are 'Winchester,' however," Waffer reported, indicating that the fighters had expended all of their primary ordinance. "Captain Zhukov's ship is one of those, sir. Recommend we go ahead and send them back to their carriers for a quick turn."

"Agreed. I will, of course, leave it up to you to decide whether to double-turn the pilots or swap them out for crew rest, but it's likely we'll need their fighters flying around the clock for the foreseeable future."

"Yes, sir. We'll take a look at who we have on deck before sending them back out."

"Very good. Any change in the *Baldev* since the shooting stopped?"

"Nothing significant, no. We've been monitoring their recovery operations since Captain Yagani signaled his surrender."

"We were surprised by the number of fighters she had onboard. What was the final count?"

"They launched a grand total of five three, of which we destroyed two niner. Based on the size of the ship, I'm guessing that has to be something close to their total complement. As far as we can tell, the fighters themselves are a lot like our *Hunters*, but a little larger and more heavily armed."

"Unmanned then?"

"As far as we can tell, yes, and with no shielding. They're tough, though — fast and highly maneuverable. All but seven of them are now back aboard the *Baldev*. We have no way of knowing whether they are intentionally dragging their feet on recovery ops, but one of their flight aprons appears to have been completely destroyed, so it's not surprising that it's taking them a while to embark the remaining fighters."

"They're short on power as well," Prescott observed. "Just keep an eye on them for us and let us know if anything changes."

"Will do."

"Oh, one other thing, the *Baldev* will be launching some sort of communications buoy shortly. In short, it's supposed to notify their two additional battleships due to arrive shortly that they are to immediately depart for Earth."

"I see," Waffer replied. "Is that a good thing?"

"Well, no, not really," Prescott chuckled, "but in our current state, we would stand very little chance against two more ships like the *Baldev*. Sending them on their way gives us a little time to tie up some loose ends here and then face them as a combined fleet near Earth."

"That sounds like a bad idea on a number of levels, but I don't suppose we have much of a choice at this point. Do we know how long it will take for them to arrive at Earth once they leave here?"

"If we assume their commander, Commodore Sarafi, intends to attack with all of the forces he has at his disposal, we should have just over four eight hours. If he presses on with only his fastest ships, it cuts that time in half."

"And do we have any reason to believe he would do that?" Waffer asked.

"The truth is that we have no idea what he plans to do. I suspect Admiral Patterson will be preparing for the worst case scenario, but given that the Guardian is still in the area, it seems logical to me that Sarafi will want to utilize every ship he has at his disposal during the attack."

"Agreed. Do you have any other instructions for us?" Waffer asked.

"No, that's all I have for you at the moment. I assume you will both be joining Admiral Patterson's vidcon at 0815Z?"

"That's affirmative, Captain."

"Very good. Thank you, gentlemen. Prescott out."

Chapter 12

(0815 UTC - Combat Information Center - 1.5×10^6 km from Earth)

"Okay everyone, Admiral Patterson is attending to some last minute business, so he asked me to get our briefing started. I think I've probably met most of you before, but I'm Flag Captain Ogima Davis of the admiral's flagship, TFS *Navajo*. As usual, this vidcon is classified Top Secret, code word MAGI PRIME. All recipients of this data stream are responsible for ensuring that a secure environment, appropriate for this classification level, exists at your location.

"I'm going to run through a quick overview of what has been taking place over the past twenty-four hours. In the interest of time, I'll be glossing over or simply leaving out most of the details, but please hold your questions until the end, if you would. In summary, combat operations have been taking place against elements of the Pelaran Resistance task force at two separate locations. The first, Location Dagger, is roughly three and a third light years from Earth and is the site of the enemy's original rally point. The second, Location Crossbow, is just under twenty-three light days from the original rally point at Location Dagger and was being used by the Resistance as a secondary staging area after their first was discovered by one of our *Hunter* recon flights."

As Davis spoke, the holographic table highlighted the locations to which he was referring with its customary pulsating green spheres. Although all of the briefing's remote participants could clearly see the *Navajo's* CIC holo table on their view screens, its three-dimensional characteristics were somewhat diminished when viewed on flat, two-dimensional monitors. To compensate for this loss of fidelity, the *Navajo's* AI crafted a separate presentation in real-time to accompany Davis' remarks, displaying it in a separate window at each participant's location.

"Initially, we sent a single F-373 to deploy a number of comm beacons in the vicinity of where we believed our two *Hunters* were lost. During the deployment, the fighter detected the hyperdrive signatures of twenty-four departing enemy ships, followed shortly thereafter by two more. The fighter's AI was able to determine the departing ships' direction of flight — which, thankfully, was not towards Earth at the time — leading Admiral Patterson to believe that the Resistance task force might be waiting for additional reinforcements to arrive before commencing their attack.

"In response, a reconnaissance in force mission was undertaken with two primary objectives. One: to determine what, if any, Resistance forces remained at Location Dagger, and two: to provide Wek Admiral Rugali Naftur the opportunity to make contact with those forces in the hope of convincing their leadership that an attack on Earth was unnecessary. Now I know that second objective sounds like a bit of a long shot, but we have recently learned some things about the admiral that make it seem significantly less far-fetched than we originally thought. I'm sure there will be more details on that subject going forward.

"For the reconnaissance portion of the mission, TFS *Theseus* was dispatched to Location Dagger with a contingent of twenty-four F-373 fighter spacecraft. The fighters were ordered to stand by five light hours away at Location Willow, here," Davis said, pointing to one of the five spheres hovering in space above the holographic table.

"As I'm sure most of you know, Admiral Naftur was seriously injured immediately before the mission to Location Dagger began. Fortunately, he was still able to briefly participate in a parley with four Resistance cruisers tasked with guarding their original rally point. A fifth, much larger warship, the *Baldev*, arrived shortly thereafter. Long story short, negotiations quickly broke down and hostilities ensued. At that time, Admiral Patterson dispatched two additional squadrons of *Reapers* for a total of seventy-two.

"Admiral Naftur had warned of the possibility that the *Baldev* was equipped with a gravitic beam weapon of unknown capabilities. During the course of the battle, *Theseus* discovered that the purpose of the weapon is to prevent an enemy ship from transitioning to hyperspace. Everything we have learned about this 'grav beam' weapon is contained in your briefing materials and I highly encourage you to review it in detail if you have not already done so. Fortunately, all of the information we have in hand at the moment indicates that the *Baldev* was the only ship in the Sajeth Collective inventory equipped with this type of weapon. In the event, however, that we run into more of these weapons in the coming battle, our only option will be to destroy those particular ships as quickly as possible. As you've all heard a thousand times, flexibility is the key to naval power. So, as always, be prepared for the Flag to quickly adjust our strategy to counter emerging threats in real-time.

"Wrapping up the engagement at Location Dagger, the *Theseus* and her escorting fighters destroyed one of the enemy cruisers and disabled two others. Ultimately, the remaining Resistance defense cruiser, the *Hadeon*, under Wek Commander Yuli Takkar, elected to join Admiral Naftur and subsequently assisted the *Theseus* in disabling the battleship *Baldev*."

Although virtually all of the officers attending the briefing had full access to the information being presented by Captain Davis, most of them had not had the opportunity to learn the details of what had been taking place at Location Dagger. After many weeks under the stress of hastily preparing their ships for battle, then waiting in a high state of readiness for the attack they all knew to be inevitable, the news of any sort of victory was welcome indeed. The spontaneous round of applause and words of congratulations for Captain Prescott and all those who had taken part in the battle were immediately recognized by the *Navajo's* AI. In response, the vidcon's audio feed was automatically adjusted to compensate, resulting in a gratifying uproar that sounded almost as if all the participants were gathered in a single, large auditorium.

Captain Davis had briefly joined in the applause to recognize Terran Fleet Command's second official combat victory, but now continued with a more somber expression on his face. "While it is absolutely appropriate to celebrate every victory in the defense of our homeworld, we must also acknowledge that such things are rarely achieved without sacrifice. Unfortunately, this battle was no exception, and the losses on our side were significant as well. A total of twenty-eight of our F-373 fighters were destroyed … and I'm sorry to report that all twenty-eight of their brave pilots were killed in action. Another seven fighter spacecraft were damaged. The *Theseus* herself has also sustained significant damage, but remains mission effective and on station at Location Dagger along with the remaining fighters and the defense cruiser *Hadeon*.

"The acting captain of the *Hadeon* indicated that the Resistance warships at Location Dagger were still expecting two more battleships — sister ships to the *Baldev* — to arrive at any time. Upon their arrival, both will be ordered, via automated communications device, to depart immediately for Earth without engaging our forces in the immediate area. Whether or not they will comply with that order remains to be seen.

"The battle at the secondary rally point, Location Crossbow, was much larger in scope and, unfortunately, resulted in significantly greater losses on both sides. Admiral Patterson dispatched seventeen *Theseus*-class destroyers under the command of Captain Bruce Abrams to engage the main body of the Resistance task force. Once again, Captain Abrams attempted to negotiate an alternative to open hostilities, but his attempts were rejected by the Resistance commander, Commodore Naveen Sarafi. A preliminary reconnaissance conducted during the negotiation process indicated that the enemy task force consisted of fifteen standard cruisers, two defense cruisers of similar configuration to the *Hadeon*, three destroyers, and six battleships. Based on the cruisers' known vulnerability to C-Drive-equipped missile attack by the stern, they were targeted during the first round of attacks. As a result, Captain Abrams' ships destroyed thirteen standard enemy cruisers and disabled two others. One of the two defense cruisers was also disabled. TFC forces suffered no losses up to this point in the battle.

"Captain Abrams had received information from the *Theseus* indicating that the battleship they had encountered, the *Baldev*, had corrected its aft shield vulnerability through the use of supplemental shield emitters installed around the perimeter of its drive section. In spite of these modifications, all Sajeth Collective vessels encountered thus far have shown some vulnerability to kinetic energy penetration rounds. Accordingly, Captain Abrams divided his ships into six groups and closed with the Resistance battleships with the intention of destroying enough emitters to bring down their supplemental aft shields. As they approached, the battleships opened fire with heavy kinetic energy weapons of their own. You will note that this is the first time we have seen weapons of this type aboard Sajeth Collective warships. Commander Takkar of the *Hadeon* has now confirmed for us that these vessels — *Rusalov*-class battleships — are of an older design. The projectiles they fired were relatively slow at just under 1.7 percent c, but that's fast enough at close range. Four of our *Theseus*-class ships were destroyed outright and three others were heavily damaged. Our undamaged vessels then C-Jumped away to regroup for another attack, at which time two of the three damaged vessels

— adrift and without power at the time — were intentionally targeted and destroyed by Resistance forces."

There were audible gasps and expressions of anger mixed with disbelief in the background, and several participants immediately signaled their desire to ask questions. After a few seconds, Davis raised his hand to quell additional discussion, then continued. "I assure you that we will provide an opportunity to ask questions at the end, but Admiral Patterson has asked us to keep things moving during —"

At that moment, Captain Davis was distracted by movement in the *Navajo's* Combat Information Center that was not visible to the vidcon's remote attendees. "Ladies and gentlemen, the Chief of Naval Operations," he announced as Admiral Kevin Patterson took his place beside the holo table.

"Good morning everyone. I apologize for my being delayed, but after several weeks of waiting for something to happen, the situation is now developing very rapidly. It sounded like Captain Davis was describing our losses at Location Crossbow. I know you have a number of questions, and I will do my best to give you an opportunity to ask them. For the moment, however, I would appreciate your continuing to hold them until the end of the briefing. With any luck, I will be able to anticipate most of what you would like to ask, and avoid having to repeat things as we go."

Patterson paused, zooming the holographic table to a view of one of the *Theseus*-class destroyers immediately before it had been destroyed by the huge shells fired by the enemy battleships.

"My first question was probably the same as most of yours, and that is: 'How the hell did this happen?' Some of you might also wonder why Captain Abrams didn't simply order an emergency C-Jump immediately after the *Rusalov* battleships opened fire, so let's start with that.

"Before Abrams engaged the battleships, we had already seen Captain Prescott and the *Theseus* make an initial attack run at the stern of the *Baldev* back at Location Dagger. The AI projected, and battle experience later confirmed, that it would take concentrated and sustained heavy fire at a single point location to effect a localized field disruption, ultimately leading to a cascading failure of the target's aft shields. In the course of her battle, *Theseus* ended up making three such attack runs before finally — with the help of the *Hadeon* — destroying most of the *Baldev*'s drive section. There is simply no way for a *Theseus*-class destroyer, or three of them, for that matter, to put enough energy into those aft shields to cause this type of failure without exposing themselves to an extended period of enemy fire. So, just as many of you are likely to encounter in the coming days, Abrams was in one of those 'pay me now or pay me later' situations. He knew that there was a possibility of taking damage or even losing some of his ships, but no other viable strategy had presented itself.

"We were, of course, hopeful that our new shield systems would prove effective against whatever those battleships could throw our way, but it turns out that there was something about these projectiles that proved more than they could handle. So far, we have no idea whether the problem was related to the shells' size, shape, composition … we just don't know yet. The Science and Engineering Directorate is working on discovering the source of the vulnerability, as well as hardening our shield emitters in response to the area denial pods encountered by the *Theseus* and her fighters at Location Dagger. More on that in a moment.

"I have one more important item to note about the battle at Location Crossbow. After the attack on the battleships was unsuccessful, Captain Abrams saw that his remaining damaged destroyer was unable to C-Jump, but was attempting to clear the combat area at its best possible speed using its sublight engines. Three Resistance *Gresav*-class destroyers gave chase, and were so intent on intercepting our ship that they presented him with another opportunity to exploit their aft shield vulnerability. Captain Abrams had the foresight to put two of his ships in flanking positions on either side of the damaged ship — 'sweetening the deal,' you might say — and making it less likely that the enemy destroyers would break off their run before they themselves could be attacked from astern.

"His tactics were sound, his decision-making was swift, and his execution was flawless, resulting in the destruction of two of the enemy task force's newest and most powerful warships, as well as the rescue of TFS *Aeneas*. There is much that I don't know about how the Resistance plans to conduct its attack once they arrive in system. What I do know, however, is that decisive, smart action like this is exactly what it takes to win battles, regardless of the size of your enemy's fleet or the sophistication of their weapons. Hooyah?"

"Hooyah!" came the enthusiastic, congratulatory response from the admiral's remote audience.

"There is no doubt that Captain Abrams faced a couple of tough calls, but the important thing for us to recognize is that he *took action* — executing the best plan he could put together quickly using the information he had available at the time. Although his attack on the *Rusalov* battleships ultimately proved ineffective and costly, I can't fault him for anything he did. If I had been in his place, I only hope I would have had the fortitude to do the same thing.

"Any further questions on either portion of the battle at Location Crossbow?" Patterson asked, knowing full well that his previous statement had rendered any additional comments extremely unlikely.

Marine Rescue Flight 901, Location Dagger
(3.3 light years from Earth)

"Marine Rescue Flight niner zero one, *Theseus* Flight Ops. Clamps released. Expected flight time to the *Keturah* is zero six minutes," the controller announced over the secure tactical comm channel used by First Lieutenant Jacks and his squad of fourteen spec-ops Marines.

"Niner zero one acknowledged," Jacks replied absently, still heavily engaged in the process of preparing for a mission that had commenced with virtually no warning and at least a couple of hours earlier than he had anticipated.

Anytime *Theseus* was engaged in combat operations — and even when she wasn't, for that matter — at least one of her three Marine squads was on alert and prepared to go into action at a moment's notice. At this particular moment, however, some of the platoon's most important equipment was not. With the ship hurrying to conclude its recovery of the fourth damaged F-373, her aft flight deck and hangar bay were in a state of organized chaos. Although she was capable in her own right as a platform for conducting various forms of naval aviation, *Theseus* was no carrier. Her standard complement of twenty-four *Hunter* RPSVs (which were surprisingly compact in their stowed configuration), four *Gurkha,* and two *Sherpa* ASVs took up very nearly all of her available space.

This morning's battle with Resistance forces had reduced the destroyer's complement of *Hunter* RPSVs by six, freeing up a significant amount of room in the hangar bay. Shortly thereafter, however, all of that space and more had been taken up by three of the much larger F-373 fighters — with a fourth about to be brought onboard within the next half-hour. As a result, when the order had come down to prepare for an immediate launch and begin providing assistance to the Resistance cruiser *Keturah,* the status of all four of the Marines' *Gurkha* assault shuttles had been listed as "occluded."

Upon further investigation, Jacks had found that all four of his ships were so severely boxed in by equipment and other spacecraft that they were not even in a position to take on the required cargo of relief supplies, let alone be relocated to the flight apron for launch. Even after an impassioned plea to the on-duty spacecraft director, it seemed that there was simply nothing that could be done to quickly extricate the heavily armed and armored

Gurkhas within the required launch window specified by the XO. So, rather than waste any additional time, not to mention his own credibility, by taking up the matter with Commander Reynolds, Jacks had acquiesced and instead had the two *Sherpas* loaded and prepped for immediate launch.

"Listen up, Marines," he said, having just finished compiling enough information to provide at least some semblance of an adequate mission brief. "I'll take the hit for getting our rides stuck in the hangar bay. I assure you that it won't happen again. In any event, we don't have a lot of time, so let's brief this up with a standard estimate of the situation."

With only two *Sherpas* at their disposal and much of the shuttles' cargo capacity being taken up by relief supplies, Jacks had room for only a single squad of Marines on the mission. As a result, his fourteen troops were divided into two sections of seven aboard each spacecraft. Fortunately, their "universal" combat EVA suits were designed with small unit tactics in mind, and their ability to communicate and seamlessly share information with each other as well as with friendly forces in the area amounted to a significant force multiplier. Now, as Lieutenant Jacks ran through his standard, METT-TC briefing, supporting visual aids and textual information were displayed within the fields of view of each member of his squad.

"*Mission*: the primary mission is to stabilize the situation aboard the *Keturah* to the maximum extent possible within the next six zero minutes. Even though we're classified as a 'rescue' mission, that is not our objective at the moment. Using the information

Commander Takkar provided, we will approach the cruiser's four primary external access points at these locations."

As Jacks spoke, a model of the Resistance BD cruiser appeared to hover in space before each of his troops, rotating and zooming in on each area of interest.

"The security system protecting each of these access points will issue a series of 'challenge' codes when you arrive in front of the door. Your suit's AI has all of the data it needs to provide the correct response. Once that happens, you should have access not only to the door itself, but also a fair amount of general information regarding the status of that section of the ship. Unfortunately, the system is smart enough to recognize whether someone is actually prepared to enter once it opens the door, so it requires that you not only have the key, but also that you are in the immediate vicinity of the airlock before it will grant access. The access routine will kick off when you are within about three meters of the door. After that, the first thing your AI will do is attempt to determine if the section of the ship beyond the airlock is still pressurized. If so, proceed and attempt to deliver a portion of our relief supplies. If not, move on to the next access point. Again, we are not equipped to conduct rescue operations at this time, so regardless of what you find inside that ship, right now we are just here to help stabilize the situation and prevent further loss of life. Understood?"

Although questions of this type have traditionally been intended more to ensure that at least part of a commander's audience was paying attention and were generally rhetorical in nature, this was no longer the case. Jacks paused momentarily as he waited for every member of his squad to mentally respond to the question — their understanding positively confirmed by their individual suit's AI via its neural interface.

"Somebody slap Montaño," Jacks said after noting that the Marine's response, while indicating an adequate understanding of the mission, was thirty-seven percent slower than his personal average. Fifty meters away aboard shuttle niner zero two, Corporal Montaño's closest neighbor happily complied, delivering a sharp blow to the side of his helmet with an open hand. "Very good," Jacks said after allowing a few seconds for the cursing and accompanying laughter to subside.

"*Enemy*: the status of enemy troops aboard the *Keturah* is largely unknown. There has been no contact and very little power output from the ship since she took one of the *Baldev's* anti-ship missiles by the stern and shortly thereafter jettisoned her reactor's containment unit. Her normal complement is around four hundred. She's what they refer to as a battlespace defense or BD cruiser, so most of her personnel are *not* combat troops. Most Sajeth Collective warships do, however, carry a small Marine security force with approximately three zero troops. Keep in mind that most of their personnel are Wek. From what we know about their species so far, you can count on them to be quick and resourceful in a scrap. Do *not* underestimate them, even if they're not wearing any sort of combat armor.

"It is important for us to do everything we can to clearly communicate to any survivors we find that we are here to offer assistance. Even though we are in an active combat zone, we are *not* authorized to use lethal force unless they attempt to do so first. If that happens, listen closely for orders, but my expectation is that we will simply withdraw and return to the *Theseus*. As always, do *not* let your guard down.

"*Troops*: Initially, we will operate as a single squad to provide each other with fire support, if necessary. This is especially important on this mission since we do not have our *Gurkhas'* AIs backing us up with their heavy weapons. Once again, we are conducting a relief mission, but the *Keturah's* crew may not see things that way. Watch each other's backs — particularly during ingress. The external access points and airlocks are large enough to accommodate our pallets of supplies, but still small enough to create a choke point if we find ourselves in a hostile situation. You will not — repeat will *not* — close the external airlock and proceed into the ship's interior spaces without coordinating through me. And I don't expect we'll be in a position to do that unless we can make contact with members of the *Keturah's* crew and receive credible assurance that they won't attack us. If things are going well, I may decide to split us up into two sections to speed up delivery of our supplies, so listen up for instructions.

"*Terrain*: Commander Takkar provided schematics of the ship, so your AIs will be able to provide navigation in the unlikely event that we do end up proceeding farther than expected inside the ship. Remember your training, people. Always be alert for the 'absence of the normal' or the 'presence of the abnormal.' If you see something, sing out. Keeping something to yourself because you think it's probably no big deal can very easily get us all killed.

"*Time*: As usual, time is short. Captain Prescott wants us to do everything we can to stabilize the situation within an hour of our arrival and then hightail it back to the *Theseus*. We are expecting two enemy battleships to arrive in the area shortly. They are being given orders via comm beacon from their commodore to avoid contact with our forces and depart the area immediately. After they're gone, I'm sure we'll be headed back to the *Keturah* to evacuate any survivors, so be thinking about what kinds of additional supplies and equipment we will need to bring with us when we return. If the enemy battleships happen to arrive *while* we are here ... I suppose we'll plan to shelter in place and request further instructions from Captain Prescott. Hey, it's a Resistance warship, right? I figure we should be safer out here on the *Keturah* than we would be if we were back aboard the *Theseus*.

"*Comm*: Pretty standard ops for comms. Use your neural interface for most basic communications and keep radio chatter to a minimum. Our call sign is simply 'Rescue 11.' If I split us up into two sections, we'll be 'Rescue 11' and 'Rescue 12.'

"That's it for now," Jacks concluded. "Questions?"

The only response over the tactical comm was the sound of Lance Corporal Dario Montaño stifling a yawn.

"Jeez, Montaño," Jacks chuckled, "you do realize that Master Sergeant Rios sees and hears everything you say and do, right?"

"Aw, come on, LT, this is a milk run. Surely he has something better to do than —"

"Top, how do you read?" Jacks interrupted.

"Five by five, Lieutenant," his platoon sergeant responded without hesitation.

"Any *other* questions?" Jacks asked.

This time, there was absolute silence over the comm channel, and Lieutenant Jacks was gratified to see that a query of his squad's physiological state showed that all fourteen of his troops were now fully alert and focused on the mission at hand.

Chapter 13

TFS Navajo, Earth-Sun Lagrange Point 2
(0845 UTC - Combat Information Center - 1.5×10^6 km from Earth)

Satisfied that his comments regarding Captain Abrams' actions at Location Crossbow had prevented a round of unnecessary second-guessing from his audience, Admiral Patterson pressed on with his briefing.

"Captain Davis may have mentioned this earlier, but the shells fired by the *Rusalovs'* main guns appear to have some guidance capabilities built in. They are extremely accurate at close range — certainly anything inside of one hundred thousand kilometers — and they're also nuclear-tipped with an explosive yield several times that of their standard anti-ship missiles. Obviously, none of our ships are going to be able to stand up to that kind of firepower for long, so our goal is to find a way to take them out before they have the opportunity to make use of those weapons again. Fortunately, they're not the only ones with big guns at their disposal," he smiled.

Patterson waited a moment for the chorus of satisfied grunts and comments of approval from his audience to subside before continuing. "The *Navajo's* AI is still working to formulate the most effective strategy for conducting an attack based on our order of battle, and you'll have it as soon as it's available. I suspect, however, that we will continue to focus on taking down their aft shields so that they become vulnerable to C-

Drive-equipped missile strikes. That task will most likely fall primarily to our cruisers, but I would prefer to hold off on providing any additional details until our plans are finalized.

"I'd like to reiterate that the primary lesson learned from the battle at Location Crossbow is that we cannot allow shells from the *Rusalovs'* main batteries to impact our hulls ... to the extent that it's possible to avoid it. For the purposes of the coming engagement, that applies equally to ships equipped with gravitic shielding since the shields have proven largely ineffective against these very large projectiles. Accordingly, your AIs will be configured to warn you of any incoming rounds, then force an emergency C-Jump, if necessary, to get you out of their way. Any questions on that, specifically?"

"Admiral," Captain Davis spoke up from off-camera, "just to clarify, this AI tweak applies only to incoming shells fired by *Rusalov*-class battleships, correct?"

"That's right. The two *Baldev*-class battleships we believe will also be headed our way do not appear to have kinetic energy weapons at all, and *Theseus'* shields fared much better against their big energy cannons ... at least until she got hit by the area denial weapon. Thank you, Captain Davis, that was a good segue. Does anyone else has any questions regarding the *Rusalovs?*"

Hearing none, Patterson continued. "This," he said, gesturing to a rotating cylindrical device suspended above the holographic table, "is the Carrada Area Denial Weapon System. Although we don't have much in the way of detailed information regarding its full capabilities, Commander Takkar did at least provide us with some basic specs. Each of these pods carries twelve

kinetic energy interceptors. The interceptors themselves
are fired via an electromagnetic launcher not unlike what
our railguns use. Thankfully — and whether this is due
to inferior launcher design or limited onboard power, we
don't know — the interceptors do not achieve anything
like the velocities our railgun projectiles reach. Based on
what we have seen so far, we believe they travel at
approximately 2.4 percent light. Just before impact, each
one sets off a series of charges designed to distribute
fragmentary submunitions along the flight path of its
target. The pattern actually looks a bit like that of a
traditional shotgun. And, just like a shotgun, it's simple
but damned effective.

"Two of these pods were responsible for thirty of the
thirty-five fighters that were either damaged or destroyed
at Location Dagger. Two other pods were able to hit
Theseus so hard and so fast that her shields were
completely overwhelmed. The good news is that the
armor we use on our capital ships proved sufficient to
absorb all of those impacts without any critical damage.
Theseus took over thirty thousand hits, which is probably
something close to a worst-case scenario since both pods
hit her with all twelve of their interceptors. As you can
imagine, she's a mess, but she's still in the fight. So I
suppose we should all thank Captain Prescott and crew
for graciously volunteering to test Science and
Engineering's latest armor tech … again."

Patterson managed a pleasant but reserved grin as he
waited a moment for the smattering of chuckles and
commentary to subside. "Don't get me wrong," he said,
his expression and tone quickly returning to its previous,
rather solemn state, "I don't mean to make light of these

weapons, or anything else in the Sajeth Collective's inventory, for that matter. While we are very thankful that there were no casualties aboard *Theseus*, let's keep in mind that twenty-three of our pilots lost their lives to this same system. And, as far as our capital ships go, once all those fragments start hitting your hull, there's almost no chance that enough shield emitters will survive to allow the shields to be brought back online. There's also a good chance you could lose weapons mounts, gravitic field emitters, your comm array, or pretty much any other system with key components mounted on the hull."

The admiral paused once again, this time scanning a portion of his audience displayed in a grid-like pattern on a nearby view screen. Although he generally liked to look people in the eye as he spoke in order to gauge the impact of his words, the faces on the screen were too small to provide much in the way of useful feedback.

"Everything we know about this weapon system is included in your briefing materials, so that's all I was planning to say about it for now. All of our AIs will be keeping an eye out for these pods from here on in. It goes without saying that if you detect one, you should destroy it immediately. I don't think I can make it any more succinct than that. Any questions on the Carrada Area Denial System?"

"Admiral Patterson, do we have any idea how many of these systems they have available, or how they are deployed?" asked the captain of the frigate TFS *Industrious*.

"Yes, good question, thank you, Captain." Patterson was irritated that he couldn't remember the man's name, recalling only that he had proven a bit of a sore loser after taking a shellacking from *Ingenuity* — under the command of her XO at the time — out at the Live Fire Training Range. "According to Commander Takkar, we can expect that each of their newest warships will have four of these pods available. That means their remaining *Gresav*-class destroyer, their remaining *Keturah*-class defense cruiser, and both of their *Baldev*-class battleships each have the potential to deploy four more of these things as they prepare to conduct their attack. The pods themselves can operate autonomously, but they generally aren't fast enough to keep up with their ships. That means they will most likely be either deployed by fighters, or launched from their host ships after they reach their destinations.

Standing just a few feet away but intentionally remaining off-camera, Captain Davis motioned for Patterson's attention, then tapped his wrist in the still universal, but now anachronistic signal for running short on time.

"Alright, folks, Captain Davis is telling me we need to move things along, so I'd like to cover a couple of additional things we have learned over the past several hours and provide a high level summary of how I see our defensive strategy shaping up. As I'm sure most of you know, the remaining Resistance warships that departed Location Crossbow appeared to be on their way to Earth, so, obviously, we must assume they intend to commence their attack as quickly as they can make the trip. If we proceed under that assumption, I think we can also assume that Commodore Sarafi is not expecting any additional reinforcements beyond the arrival of the two

Baldev-class battleships we discussed earlier — or at least none that he plans to wait for. This agrees with what our new ally, Commander Takkar, has told us as well. After a bit of cajoling from Captain Prescott, Takkar provided two additional pieces of valuable intelligence, both of which are critical to our defensive preparations. First, the Sajeth Collective's newest vessels are capable of traveling at approximately eleven hundred light. At that speed, they would arrive here from Locations Crossbow or Dagger in just over twenty-six hours. Their older warships, however, including the *Rusalov* battleships, are capable of only about half that speed. Since Sarafi took a pretty big risk by waiting for the three *Baldev*-class battleships in the first place, my best guess is that his main body will travel directly to Earth at approximately five hundred and fifty light, rendezvousing with the two *Baldev*-class vessels here at approximately 1125Z — that's just over forty-eight hours from now. Even though I believe that's the most likely scenario, we'll also call it our best-case, since it provides us the most time to prepare our defenses. Our worst-case would be that Sarafi proceeds directly to Earth at the best speed of his fastest two ships, perhaps hoping that the two additional *Baldevs* will still arrive shortly thereafter. That scenario would put him here by approximately 0900 tomorrow.

"The other important thing we learned from Commander Takkar is that Sarafi's flagship, the destroyer *Gunov*, may be carrying some sort of biological weapon. He had no specific information regarding its effects, but he indicated that the Lesheerans, another member of the Sajeth Collective that we have only rarely heard mentioned by the Wek, are adept at creating such weapons. The biological agent would most likely be targeted at something specific to our genome, using a highly modified virus to act as its vector. So we have to assume that, once released, it would spread rapidly via person to person contact, and even a single Human infection could have catastrophic consequences for the entire planet.

"Since we obviously don't want to find ourselves struggling to cope with a global pandemic while at the same time fighting an interstellar war, our only real hope of defending against this type of weapon is to prevent it from ever being used in the first place. On this point, Takkar's ship provided us with a data dump containing some information regarding how the bio weapon might be employed.

"The delivery system the Lesheerans created is called Sazoch — a wicked-sounding name that apparently refers to some sort of winged demon from their mythology. Charming, right? If it works as advertised, however, I'll be the first to admit that it's quite an impressive system. It's relatively compact, very stealthy … you might even say elegant in its design. In fact, it's so small that I'm sure the only reason they haven't equipped every ship in their fleet with the system is due to the long-standing ban the Wek have imposed on weapons of this type.

"Before I go any farther, keep in mind that our people have only taken a cursory look at Takkar's data so far, so all I'm really able to provide here today is a quick summary. Hopefully, I'll be able to offer significantly more information before 0900Z tomorrow, particularly how we might go about stopping it — even after it's launched.

"Remember that the *Gunov*, the ship carrying the bio-weapon, is also one of the two Resistance vessels previously located at Location Crossbow capable of traveling at eleven hundred light. As I stated earlier, my gut tells me that Commodore Sarafi intends to arrive here with *all* of the vessels he has at his disposal, which will take him a couple of days. We must also consider the possibility, however, that he has decided to press on with only two vessels in the hopes of executing a 'Hail Marry' biological attack. Unfortunately for us, those are two very different scenarios, each requiring its own unique defensive strategy."

The thought of an enemy willing to kill not just those Humans tasked with defending their world, but *all* Humans — now well over twelve billion of them — caused an involuntary chill to travel down the length of his spine. How does one even respond to such a threat? Patterson glanced once again at the view screen displaying members of his audience, and although their facial expressions were difficult to gauge, their posture and body language were clear enough. These were men and women nearing the limits of their mental and physical endurance. Most of them had worked around the clock for months preparing their ships and crews for combat. The demands placed upon them had been totally unreasonable, and the inevitable effects of such prolonged stress were beginning to tell.

Ever a student of history, Patterson's mind immediately recalled a military situation in Earth's past that appeared hopeless to some degree, yet Human beings not unlike them had persevered in spite of the odds.

"Do any of you ever remember reading the story of American Brigadier General Anthony McAuliffe during the Second World War's Battle of the Bulge?"

Patterson saw a few nods here and there, but mostly just blank stares. "It doesn't matter, I was going to tell you the story anyway," he grinned. "Towards the end of the war, McAuliffe — who was acting commander of the 101st Airborne Division at the time — was deployed with a relatively small group of glider infantry troops when they became encircled by a much larger German force at Bastogne, Belgium. I'm summarizing a bit, but when the German commander sent him an ultimatum threatening the annihilation of his troops as well as innocent civilians in the area if he refused to surrender, McAuliffe famously sent the following reply:

To: The German Commander

NUTS!

From: The American Commander

"Now, many of you who have worked with me probably know that I'm not a big fan of foul language, and neither was General McAuliffe. In fact, his personal aide said that General Mac was the only general he ever knew who didn't speak using a steady stream of profanity. Sadly, I guess it's safe to say that a general officer with a clean mouth was as rare in 1944 as it is today. So when the typed message was delivered to the

German lines, the receiving officers were confused by the rather enigmatic, one-word response. When asked for an explanation, the American colonel who delivered the message replied simply, 'In plain English? It means go to hell.'

"What we face here today is similar in many respects. You and I might be tempted to think that the consequences of our failing in the coming battle makes any comparison to the Battle of the Bulge seem a bit trivial. But to the soldiers on the ground in Bastogne, I can guarantee you that it was absolutely no different. Their lives, and the safety of their families back home, were on the line every bit as much as ours are today. So if nothing else, my friends, take comfort from the fact that we are by no means the first commanders to face this kind of situation, and I'm every bit as confident as General McAuliffe was that we will prevail in the end."

"Sir," one of the vidcon participants spoke up, "what happened to General Mac and his troops?"

"Ah, well, the German general in command of the artillery they had threatened to use on Bastogne had been so confident that the Americans would surrender that he had already moved his forces out of range. German infantry made a number of attempts to take the area, but without their supporting artillery, they were unable to dislodge the American defenders. General McAuliffe's troops managed to hold on for four days until being reinforced by the 4th Armored Division on the day after Christmas. So the point of my story is that it's very often courage, perseverance, and even a little defiance thrown in that tends to be decisive in battle, not ships and weapons … unless, of course, you truly are *hopelessly* outgunned," he chuckled. "And, ladies and gentlemen, we are most certainly *not* hopelessly outgunned."

Taking in a deep breath and consciously drawing himself up to his full height, Patterson was pleased by the apparent changes in his audience he noted on the view screen. "Anyway," he said after a momentary pause, "we all have lots of work to do, so let's wrap this up, shall we? Back to the Sazoch bio weapon … the delivery system works a lot like the interceptors I described earlier that are fired by the Carrada Area Denial pods. The most obvious differences are their slower speed and significantly increased size. This is probably due to the fact that they carry a much larger payload as well as the same engines used by their standard anti-ship missiles.

"To begin an attack, the 'vehicle,' as they refer to it, is fired from its host ship towards the target planet. At first, it's essentially just a large, unpowered projectile. As it approaches atmospheric entry interface, however, fairings covering the engine nozzle detach, allowing its engine to engage for a long-duration deceleration burn. This results in a relatively low speed — and, thus, low temperature — reentry profile. At first glance, it looks as if the entire design of what we might call 'stage one' of this thing is focused on maintaining a relatively low temperature throughout the reentry process. We might be able to infer from this that the biological agents onboard are at least somewhat vulnerable to extreme temperature changes.

"Once the vehicle reaches relatively low altitude, say six thousand meters or so, it deploys small wings and its primary focus becomes that of a drone delivery vehicle.

Again, it looks as if the designers intentionally kept the speed relatively low at just over four kilometers per second — roughly the same speed as some of our older hypersonic cruise missiles designed for purely atmospheric flight. The vehicle 'sprints' at this speed between release points, decelerates, deploys a number of small, autonomous drones, then accelerates again for the trip to the next release point. The drones themselves are capable of high subsonic speeds, and they are what actually deliver the biological agent — most likely targeting heavily populated areas first.

"Now I understand that for our latest generation of fighters, particularly the F-373, this sounds like a relatively straightforward exercise in air defense, but, as you might expect, it's not quite as simple as it sounds. First off, the delivery vehicle itself is designed to be all but invisible, and I mean from just about any sensor you can name — visible light, infrared, radar, whatever. We've already done some analysis and believe the best opportunity for detection will be during its deceleration burn … if it has one, that is. If the host ship slows sufficiently to allow for a relatively low-speed deployment, however, we may literally never see this thing before it starts deploying drones. Note that the delivery vehicle itself can be targeted to reenter — or simply be released — at any location above the planet's surface. Once inside the atmosphere, four kilometers per second is still fast enough to fly from one side of Australia to the other in just over sixteen minutes. And if the bio-agents are as lethal as Commander Takkar indicated, how big of an area it covers is probably a moot point anyway. A single successful deployment of one of these Sazoch drones might well be sufficient to kill off virtually every Human being on the planet inside of a few months.

"When I first started looking at this thing, my first thought was that we should focus our initial attacks on destroying the *Gunov* as quickly as possible after she arrives. Once she has escorted her task force to the immediate vicinity of Earth, however, she will no longer be burdened with providing navigational assistance for her consorts. That means she will have the capability to execute rapid transitions, if necessary, just like our ships.

"Frankly, I don't think Commodore Sarafi will risk allowing his flagship to be brought into the battle early on. Instead, I think he will transition repeatedly, if necessary, to avoid combat. That being the case, if we immediately go after the *Gunov*, we run the risk that he might elect to proceed with his Sazoch attack while the rest of his forces are still engaged with ours. His older battleships, on the other hand, do not have the capability to make rapid transitions, and even if they did, I expect their strategy will be to stand and fight.

"Taking all of that into account, in order of priority, we must attack and eliminate the six *Rusalov* battleships, followed by the two *Baldev* battleships, the single remaining defense cruiser, then, finally the destroyer *Gunov*. I will begin issuing deployment orders within twelve hours, and I need each of your ships prepared to execute your orders immediately.

"That's really all I have for the moment. I know we've only scratched the surface of many of these topics, and ignored many others that also require our attention. That means I'm relying on each and every one of you to perform at your absolute best, and I know that you will do exactly that. Now, all of us need to get moving, but is there anything remaining that any of you feel urgently needs to be addressed at this time?"

Since it was clear that Admiral Patterson was hoping to avoid further questions, it took several seconds before anyone among the audience of mostly senior officers had the courage to speak up. Just as he was about to sign off, the admiral heard the distinctive chime indicating that one of the participants had a question.

"Yes, someone had a question?" he asked. Throughout most of the briefing, Patterson had been looking over the top of his glasses to allow him to read his notes. Now, raising his chin so that he could glance at the distant view screen in an effort to identify the source of the question, he had the look of a particularly irritated college professor. "Oh … Commander Reynolds from the *Theseus*," he said, his tone immediately softening as if to recognize a favored student. "Go ahead, Commander."

"Admiral, what about the Guardian spacecraft. Has it given us any indication of how it will react once we come under attack? It has said many times that it has defended the Earth for hundreds of years, so can we not expect that it will continue to do so?"

"Thank you, Commander, I'm glad you brought that up because I had intended to mention it. The short answer is that we have no idea what, if anything, the Guardian will do. If it really *has* been defending us for hundreds of years, it doesn't seem to make much sense that it would choose now as the moment to stop doing so. Even if it allows us to do most of the fighting, it seems reasonable to expect that at some point it would provide some level of assistance, particularly if things were going badly for our side. Having said that, however, it has also referenced the fact that its defensive mission was to last 'only until we had the means to defend ourselves.' It has also at least implied that its continuing in that role required that we make a decision as to whether we intended to join the Pelaran Alliance. That decision process, as you know, will most likely take many months to complete, so I suppose it's possible that we're in some kind of probationary, pre-membership limbo period at the moment. In any event, Admiral Sexton and I are planning to attempt contact later today to see if we can get some idea of its intentions. Frankly, if it doesn't plan to help, my preference is that it leaves the immediate area before the shooting starts. We have enough to worry about without having that thing in our way while we're going toe to toe with the Resistance."

"Thank you, Admiral," Reynolds replied.

"Of course. Now, if there is nothing further …" Patterson paused very briefly, but had no real intention of waiting for further questions. "Very good. Expect deployment orders by 2000Z. Once you receive them, move smartly to get your ships into position and be prepared for additional instructions. Godspeed to you all. Patterson out."

Marine Rescue Flight 901, Location Dagger
(Near SCS *Keturah* External Access Point One - 3.3 light years from Earth)

The *Sherpa* ASV shuttle had no windows in its passenger/cargo area. Instead, two large view screens were installed on the forward bulkhead that separated the aft spaces from what was still referred to as the "cockpit." Rather than rely on such a limited view of the situation outside the ship, however, Lieutenant Jacks and his Marines had configured their helmet displays to simply ignore the presence of the shuttle in which they were traveling. Much like the view commonly preferred by *Reaper* fighter pilots, the effect was so immersive that — after taking a few seconds to adjust — it was difficult for the Human mind to grasp that they weren't already operating their EVA suits outside the confines of the shuttle.

"I've got the first access point," Jacks announced, commanding his helmet display to zoom in on the area while also highlighting it with a pulsating green oval within the other squad members' fields of view. While Jacks wasn't actually in control of the *Sherpa* shuttlecraft itself, the ship's AI responded to his very thoughts — much like a Human pilot might react to requests and updates from a mission commander riding in the back of his ship. In fact, ASVs were rarely controlled by an onboard crew (although it was still possible to exercise "local" flight control during an emergency). In most situations envisioned for either the *Sherpa* or her militarized cousin, the *Gurkha*, it was considered unlikely that even an experienced pilot could handle the small ship any more effectively than its onboard AI. Now, as Lieutenant Jacks surveyed the area surrounding their first point of entry, he was able to get a better feel for how his troops would access the external hatch, offload their supplies, and defend themselves in case of attack. In response, the two shuttlecraft banked smoothly to starboard, then slowly closed the remaining distance to put themselves in precisely the positions he had in mind.

"Squad displays local," Jacks commanded using his neural interface, instantly switching his team's integrated helmet displays back to a view inside their shuttles as they prepared to dismount. "*Theseus* Flight Ops, Marine Rescue Flight niner zero one preparing for EVA. Any changes in the target?"

"Negative, niner zero one," the Flight Ops controller responded. "No changes in emissions or power levels detected and no response to hails."

"Niner zero one copies. Proceeding with EVA. Call sign change to 'Rescue 11.'"

"Rescue 11, *Theseus* Flight Ops acknowledged."

Just under two minutes later, the Marines in both shuttles had completed a final set of equipment checks and received their go order from Lieutenant Jacks. Unlike the *Gurkha*, which was tailored specifically for missions of this type, the *Sherpa* was not equipped with side-mounted cargo doors, forcing all of the Marines to dismount via the shuttle's aft cargo ramp. The fact that there were only fifteen troops present, however, expedited the process, and moments later, all but two members of the squad had taken up positions initially placing the two shuttles between themselves and the nearby access point on the *Keturah's* starboard hull. The remaining two Marines stationed themselves atop one of the *Sherpas* and quickly improvised a mount for their R229 Squad Light Railgun (SLR) utilizing a hardpoint typically employed for securing external cargo containers.

Continuing to scan the side of the massive cruiser, Jacks noted several heavy beam emitter apertures close by, most likely of the same type the *Hadeon* had used to take down forty-eight anti-ship missiles in just a few seconds during their battle with the *Baldev*. At such short range, the huge energy weapons looked as though they were aimed directly at his small, absurdly exposed force. Jacks wondered briefly whether his mind would even have the chance to register what was happening if one of them discharged. *Probably not, so probably not worth worrying about* he thought darkly, then pushed the notion out of his mind and pressed on with the business at hand.

"SLR online," the railgun team lead announced. Unlike many of the other basic status updates that passed between members of the squad, this particular one was always done verbally, largely because the readiness of the unit's heavy weapon tended to immediately precede the order to execute the next phase of the mission. A powerful weapon with a long, distinguished lineage, the R229 could trace its origin all the way back to famous designs from the likes of Richard Gatling, Sir Hiram Maxim, and John Browning. Unlike those weapons, however, the SLR used a miniaturized version of the electromagnetic launchers used aboard Fleet's warships, providing a level of firepower that would have been inconceivable during the long reign of gunpowder-based propellants. Too small to include a gravitic generator capable of counteracting the inertia of its kinetic energy rounds during launch, the weapon still produced a recoil significant enough to require it to be secured in place. In this case, mounting it atop the *Sherpa* meant that the shuttle itself would be required to use its Cannae thrusters to precisely maintain its position in space once the SLR opened fire. The relatively compact weapon was served by a crew of two: the team lead — generally a corporal who managed the accompanying power and ammunition supplies, and a gunner — normally a private first class who was responsible for the weapon itself. During combat ops, the team lead took on a number of additional roles including acting as a spotter, equipment manager, and communications specialist, all while working to ensure the weapon's perimeter and rear security.

With a final quick check of his squad's position, Lieutenant Jacks designated two Marines to accompany him on the short trip to the first access point before arcing up and over the top of his shuttle in the direction of the *Keturah*.

Chapter 14

TFS Theseus, Location Dagger
(3.3 light years from Earth)

"Report," Captain Prescott said as he and Commander Reynolds emerged from his ready room.

"Sir, the hangar deck reports that they will have the last F-373 secured within the next one four minutes," Lieutenant Commander Schmidt reported, vacating his captain's command chair and relieving the standby crew lieutenant who had been sitting in for him at the Tactical 1 console. "We also have a crew of five from Engineering performing an EVA at the moment, including Commander Logan himself. He said to tell you that he would have everyone back onboard by the time the Flight Deck completes their recovery operation."

"Commander Logan is outside ... right *now*?" Prescott asked, suppressing the urge to sound irritated. Although his chief engineer could sometimes act in a manner that bordered on impulsiveness, Prescott had never known him to exercise poor judgment or take a risk without a good reason for doing so.

"Yes, sir. He said to tell you that they needed to take care of an urgent problem with one of the heat exchangers that was damaged during the battle with the *Baldev* and that the repair should only take a few minutes. He also said that he was taking a couple of extra people with him in hopes of replacing some shield emitters while they were out there."

"And he didn't want to interrupt the XO and me during our secure vidcon, right," Prescott smiled.

"Yes, he said that too, sir."

"Alright, fine. Lieutenant Dubashi, will you please keep tabs on Commander Logan's team and hurry them along as best you can?"

"Aye, sir, will do."

"Thank you. Okay, Schmidt, please continue. What's the status of our Marine rescue mission?"

"They were forced to take the two *Sherpas* because of the situation in the hangar bay, but everything seems to be going fine so far. They appear to be getting pretty close to trying the first access point. Otherwise, no changes in the past couple of hours. All systems in the green. The ship remains at General Quarters, but we have set Condition 2 due to the various EVA ops currently underway. The individual departments are in the process of rotating in fresh crewmembers to relieve those who have been on duty the longest. Both the C-Drive as well as our sublight engines are temporarily offline while Commander Logan's team completes their repairs."

"Very good, thank you. We should probably work on getting ourselves fed and rested as well," Prescott said, raising his voice to address the entire bridge crew, "but I would prefer to wait until all of these pending operations are wrapped up first. For now, I'd like us to — one at a time — call in a replacement from the standby crew, stretch our legs, grab something to eat for a few minutes, and then head back up here. I'll do my best to get us all some rack time as soon as possible. Can everyone hang in there a little longer?"

In spite of enduring several days of heavy stress, including extended combat operations with very little time for rest from one crisis to the next, *Theseus'* first watch bridge crew replied with the usual chorus of "yes, sirs" in response to their captain's largely rhetorical question.

Commander Reynolds had yet to take her seat at the rear of the bridge, and had been looking over Lieutenant Lau's shoulder at the Tactical console during the status update. Now, she placed a hand on Lau's shoulder and silently gestured for him to be the first to take a break. Within seconds, his replacement emerged from the portside standby lounge and took his place at Tactical 2.

"Lieutenant Lee, without the Marines' assault shuttles I know we have a somewhat diminished view of the rescue mission, but please see if you can call up some additional video feeds for the view screen," Prescott said. "Give us their tactical comm audio as well if you would."

"Aye, sir. We're mostly limited to the feeds from their individual EVA suits, but we do have a pretty good view of the first external access point from the nearest *Sherpa,*" Lee replied, opening two windows in the center of the bridge view screen. "The window on the right is the feed from Jackson's ... sorry, First Lieutenant Jacks' suit. The audio is live as well, but these guys tend to say very little during an op. There actually is a display I can show you that will give us a representation of what they're communicating to each other with their neural interfaces, but unless you're familiar with the symbology they use —"

"Yeah, I've seen it and you're right. It's like watching a group of twelve-year-olds playing a video game. They know exactly what they're doing, but it's largely incomprehensible to anyone else."

As they watched, Lieutenant Jacks and two other Marines approached what looked like a fairly standard external hatch measuring approximately three and a half meters on each side. Although there was a keypad of some sort visible to their right, Jacks halted their approach just short of the door, raising his right hand in a fist out of sheer force of habit.

On Fleet vessels, cargo doors of this type were spaced fairly evenly around the hull to facilitate the loading of cargo and provide points of access for equipment and personnel when the ship was moored. The doors always included an airlock of some sort and could be opened from the outside during an emergency.

Reading quickly through a transcript of the briefing Lieutenant Jacks had delivered to his squad before their EVA, Prescott made a mental note to discuss external access procedures with Commander Reynolds and eventually Admiral Patterson. Clearly, Wek warship designers considered access from the outside by hostile forces a serious enough threat to build in some fairly sophisticated security measures. In a situation where TFC ships were either unable to move due to battle damage or because they were conducting some sort of operation that prevented them from moving — very much like *Theseus* was at the moment — an enemy boarding action might become a very real possibility.

As Prescott continued to watch the Marines conducting their relief operation, he couldn't help but picture a similar group of heavily armed Wek troops easily gaining access to critical, yet largely undefended areas of his ship. Such troublesome thoughts, coupled with fatigue, left him feeling uncharacteristically impatient to conclude all three of the missions taking place outside and get *Theseus* back into a state where she could fight or flee, if necessary. After what seemed like a long delay, Prescott was more than happy when a call from Lieutenant Jacks refocused his mind on the Marines' rescue mission.

"Bridge, Rescue 11," Lieutenant Jacks called over the tactical comm channel.

"I got it," Prescott responded immediately, preempting Lieutenant Dubashi's response. "Rescue 11, *Theseus*-Actual. Go ahead, Lieutenant."

"Sir, we're using the codes provided by Commander Takkar, so as far as the *Keturah's* AI is concerned, we're friendlies and have the same access from out here as their troops would."

"Understood. Are you having a problem getting their system to respond?"

"Negative, it's not that, sir. It's just that … according to their AI, there are only seven survivors aboard."

Prescott paused for a moment, the terrifying image of a nuclear weapon detonating near the center of her hull quickly forming in his mind.

"I'm sorry to hear that, Rescue 11. Do you have a route that will allow you to reach them quickly?"

"Affirmative, Captain. They're in two separate groups, not far from the second and third external access points. With your permission, we'll plan to go ahead and recover them all, if possible. With such a small group, we can split into two sections and access both areas simultaneously."

"Be quick about it, Lieutenant. We have two other EVA ops concluding here within one zero minutes. As soon as that happens, we'll try to get a little closer. Either way, I want you headed back to the ship within half an hour max. Understood?"

"We'll make it happen, sir. Rescue 11 out."

Marine Section "Rescue 11," Location Dagger
(Near SCS *Keturah* External Access Point Two)

When he had told Captain Prescott that the Wek survivors were located "not far" from the external access points, he might have been just a little optimistic, Lieutenant Jacks admitted to himself. That was particularly true for the members of the *Keturah's* crew currently represented in his field of view by four red pulsating ovals accompanied by a single text block indicating that they were still over forty-five meters from his current position. In the lower right corner of his helmet display, a timer relentlessly counted down from the original thirty minutes Captain Prescott had given him to recover the enemy warship's survivors and have his squad on its way back to the *Theseus*.

"You do see how much time we have remaining, right?" his EVA suit's AI asked aloud. It was both an odd and irritating question, given that the AI knew precisely where he was looking at all times.

I see it. Surely you have something more useful to contribute to this effort, Jacks thought, communicating his response via the suit's neural interface without the need to even fully form the words in his mind. *If that's the best you've got, do us both a favor and bugger off.*

"Oh, nice talk, mate. Kiss our mum with that mouth, do you?" the suit asked indignantly using a perfect facsimile of his own voice.

Jacks rarely verbalized his conversations with his suit's AI, and chose not to allow it to synthesize the voice of some famous actor, athlete, or military leader. Since first beginning the complex training required to interact with TFC's military-grade version of the standard neural interface, his preference had always been to use the suit's default internal communications setting — typically referred to by the manufacturer as "conscience mode."

"I'm just trying to keep us out of trouble, that's all," the AI continued. "We've already been in here for nearly twenty minutes. That leaves us only ten to reach our group of survivors, provide whatever first aid is required, then get them back to the access point and prepped for the trip over to the shuttle. At the moment, it seems unlikely that we'll be able to meet such an aggressive timetable."

When first introduced to their EVA suit's many capabilities, Marines were shown an orientation video provided by the multinational defense contractor that handled most of the AI's Pelaran tech integration. In what seemed like a ridiculous insult to their intelligence, "conscience mode" was depicted by an eight-centimeter, miniaturized version of the Marine wearing the suit. During various combat operations, the mini-Marine doppelgänger stood steadfastly on the EVA suit's shoulder and provided the user with sage advice (its traditional angel's wings were omitted to avoid any appearance of religious affiliation, of course). Jacks had always found the comparison to a "shoulder angel" particularly fitting, since Marines tended to ignore their suit's advice nearly as much as Humans in general ignored the urgings of their own conscience. In reality, however, the data overwhelmingly showed that an ever-present AI not only improved the user's ability to cope with stressful situations, but also increased the likelihood that they would make better choices when faced with morally ambiguous situations.

It's important that we save these people if we can ... and you know very well that Mum swears much more often than I do. Besides, swearing in my head doesn't count anyway, does it? Jacks thought distractedly as he continued his slow progress down the rubble-strewn corridor leading to his objective.

"It *is* important, Jackson, but so is following orders," the AI replied earnestly. "Captain Prescott is concerned about what might happen when the *Zhelov* and the *Serapion* arrive. That could happen at any moment. If we're still out here, we've compromised our own safety and quite possibly that of the *Theseus* as well. If we don't have time right now, we can come back and complete our rescue mission after those two battleships leave the area."

I understand all of that, but it might be too late for the survivors if we wait. Now do your job and help me complete this mission successfully. The corridor up ahead is a mess. We can probably get through it just fine, but I'm not sure about coming back through here with wounded. Is there an alternate route?

"Yes, there is," the AI sighed. "Stand by while I check the environmental systems in the adjoining spaces."

You do that, Jacks thought, gratified that he had once again managed to temporarily distract the AI. "Rescue 12, Jacks," he called over the tactical comm.

"Rescue 12 here. Go ahead, Lieutenant."

"It looks like your section is back at access point three already, Sergeant. What's your status?"

"We got 'em, sir. Most of the area surrounding this access point is unpressurized, but we managed to close off a section of corridor adjacent to where our three Wek personnel were located and then repressurize it before entering their room. The room itself looked like it was used for food storage. It was right next to their galley."

"What's the status of the survivors?"

"There were no life-threatening injuries, but all three do need medical attention. They also weren't very happy to see us at first. Fortunately, they were all mess staff of some sort — not the kind of folks who were likely to put up much in the way of resistance. We just kept talking to them and trying to convince them that we were here to help. We also told them what we knew about Admiral Naftur. I'm not sure they entirely believed us, but they did finally allow us to zip them up in their triple EPs for evac."

Expandable Emergency Evacuation Pods, or "triple EPs," as they were commonly called, were two-and-a-half-meter-long cylindrical capsules that were just over one meter in diameter. When originally developed in the late twenty-first century, the inflatable pods were primarily intended to provide a simple (and, therefore, inexpensive) lightweight means of escaping a damaged spacecraft. Each was equipped with its own power supply as well as enough water and emergency rations to keep a single occupant alive for up to a week, if necessary. Even though early versions were derided as little more than a "one-person space tent," crewmembers who found themselves in a situation where they were forced to choose between using one of the pods or subjecting their bodies to a hard vacuum universally selected the EEEP as the better of the two options.

TFC's latest version of the triple EP, while similar to the original in some respects, had a number of enhancements intended to facilitate the evacuation of injured military personnel. The pod's onboard computer now included a specialized AI capable of performing a surprising number of medical procedures, from administering antibiotics and pain medication to laser suturing wounds. Each pod also included a small gravitic field generator, allowing the entire device to "hover" in the same manner as the ubiquitous "grav chair" now used in hospitals worldwide. This feature alone had revolutionized the concept of medical evacuation — allowing a single, uninjured person to both treat and transport a much larger colleague, if necessary. In addition, although they could still be used by an individual to escape a damaged ship, the pods were much more commonly used by military personnel during rescue operations — often to stabilize their injured occupants and transport them from one spacecraft to another. The addition of a small, three-axis Cannae thruster allowed the pods to accomplish short journeys of this type entirely on their own once outside the damaged vessel.

"Good work, Sergeant," Jacks replied. "Now here's what I need you to do next. Rescue 11 has run into some difficulty reaching our survivors. We can get there, but it's going to take us a little longer than expected. The captain wants us back aboard *Theseus* ASAP, and there's no reason for you to delay out here waiting on us."

"Sir," the Marine sergeant replied, "how about I send three or four guys in there to help clear the way? That should speed things up quite a bit."

"Negative, Sergeant. Now listen up. We don't need that SLR team outside. Dismount the railgun, load up your section and your three survivors, and head back to the ship immediately. I've got six of my section's seven guys with me. That will be more than enough to handle getting these four survivors out. Any questions for me?"

"No, sir, but I don't like it … and Top's not gonna like it either."

"I'd say you're right about that, but you'll notice that he isn't commenting over the radio. That's because he knows it's the right call. He also knows that you two work for me," Jacks replied in a joking tone that still left little room for additional debate. "Now get moving, Marine."

"Yes, sir. See you back onboard."

"No worries, Sergeant. We'll be along shortly."

Jacks paused momentarily, knowing full well that the bridge might also be listening in on their tactical comm channel. Given how much time they had already burned, he half-expected to receive orders to abort the remainder of the mission at any moment. In his short time working for Captain Prescott, however, Jacks had seen no evidence that he was the kind of commander who was inclined to "micromanage" his people. So far at least, he seemed to trust their judgment and expect them to make the right call without his constantly needing to look over their shoulders or second-guess their decisions. Jacks appreciated this kind of leadership style, but understood that it implied a greater burden of responsibility on his part. In his mind, that really left him with only two choices at the moment. He could either abort the mission and return to the ship, or, within the next few minutes, contact the bridge and make the case for taking a bit more time. Disregarding the captain's instructions and pressing on without reporting in was just not an option under the circumstances. *Living up to professional obligations really is a pain in the arse sometimes,* he reflected.

"Okay, I've got an alternate route for us," his AI reported. "Unfortunately, with the *Keturah* running on spotty emergency power, there's no way I can confirm whether it's any better than our current route. We'll just have to check it out and see. One thing I can say for sure, however, is that we'll have to put our survivors inside their triple EPs for the trip back to the access point. No matter which way we go, we'll have to cross though at least one unpressurized section."

Humph, Jacks grumbled inwardly, *I don't see us getting past the end of this corridor humping four of those pods unless we take the time to cut our way through some of the debris, so let's take a look at your alternate. Is it something we can check quickly?*

"Actually, yes. Take the next right. There should be a short, ten-meter corridor that ends in an entrance to another that runs parallel to the one we're in now for another fifty meters."

Great, that should be long enough to reach our survivors, he thought, fully aware that this was mostly likely their last shot at completing the rescue successfully.

It took Lieutenant Jacks only a moment to update his section on the change in plans, after which they quickly cleared the intersecting corridor and moved up to the bulkhead door leading to their alternate route. Jacks then paused to once again allow his AI to access the *Keturah's* security system. With so much of the ship open to the vacuum of space, it was necessary to override safety protocols, gaining access one section at a time. Not surprisingly, the overall result was painfully slow progress.

"Significantly reduced pressure in this area — most likely due to a small leak somewhere between here and one of the major hull breaches just aft," Jacks' AI reported. As the door slid open, water vapor in the surrounding air instantly condensed into a cloud of fog with a disconcerting WHOOSH as air rushed past the Marines and into the adjacent hallway to equalize the pressure. "The environmental system is attempting to compensate, but it's fighting a losing battle at this point. Gravity is still steady at their standard .8 G."

Glancing furtively around the corner, Jacks was gratified to see that the corridor was largely free of debris. At the same time, it struck him how similar the view was to a scene from any one of a hundred sci-fi movies he had watched over the years. Although his suit obviated the need for ambient lighting, several light panels dangled from the ceiling, flashing randomly. To complete the effect, a myriad of cables hung loosely from several locations — all of which he was sure would be arcing wildly if the ship's reactors were still online. The only things strangely missing were bodies. Upon their arrival, *Keturah's* AI had indicated that over three-fourths of her crew had been killed within moments of the nuclear detonation. Most of the rest had suffocated shortly thereafter due to the innumerable breaches that had occurred along the entire length of her hull. Ironically, as some of the last members of her crew had attempted to make their way to areas they believed might offer them the best chance of survival, they had found their way blocked by doors sealed in an effort to preserve the few remaining pressurized areas of the ship.

With less than five minutes remaining before Captain Prescott's deadline, Jacks made his call back the *Theseus*.

"Bridge, Rescue 11."

"Rescue 11, *Theseus*-Actual. How much more time do you need, Lieutenant Jacks?" Prescott asked, preempting his question.

"The corridor ahead looks pretty clear, sir. If all goes well, I'd say an extra ten to fifteen minutes will probably do it. The biggest problem we're likely to have from this side is pressurization. If we can't seal off a section of the corridor outside the room they're in, we'll cause a rapid decompression when we open the door. They're accustomed to slightly higher air pressures than we are, and the pressure out here is currently around thirty kPa and dropping. That's well below the atmospheric pressure at the summit of Mount Everest. Our survivors will go hypoxic almost immediately and will most likely be unconscious in less than thirty seconds."

"Won't that be enough to cause decompression sickness?"

"Maybe so, sir. There are lots of variables, including the amount of time they are exposed to the lower pressure. At thirty kPa, we're well above the Armstrong limit, though, so there won't be a problem with exposed bodily fluids boiling away. As long as we get them into their triple EPs pretty quickly, they should be fine. The pods will get them back to standard atmospheric pressure and provide one hundred percent oxygen until we get them back aboard the *Theseus*. After that, the doc will need to evaluate them to see if they require hyperbaric treatment. Bottom line, it's still better than staying here, sir."

"Agreed. Fifteen more minutes, Lieutenant … and don't bother asking for more. We're on borrowed time as it is and I'm just not willing to risk having you and your people out there any longer than that. Understood?"

"Understood. Thank you, sir. Jacks out."

Knowing that he would still need every moment of the additional time Captain Prescott had given him, Jacks issued a rapid series of orders for four members of his section to secure the surrounding area — which, he admitted to himself, seemed somewhat pointless under the circumstances. If training and experience had taught him nothing else, however, it was how following well-established procedures could keep you alive when something unexpected happened. And in situations like this one, it often did. At the same time, Jacks' two remaining Marines set about preparing to deploy the inflatable evac pods while he worked with his AI to determine if there was anything that could be done to avoid the need to depressurize the room containing the remaining four Wek survivors.

"The problem is that the first pressure door we can close is just beyond the room where they're located," Jacks' AI reported after a few minutes spent in a fruitless search of the surrounding area. "Unfortunately, closing that one doesn't help us since all that would do is cordon off an area that's already losing pressure. We could, of course, use an inflatable barrier, but I estimate that doing so will require at least ten minutes more time than Captain Prescott has given us to complete our mission."

Yeah, I assumed that was the case. Here's the thing, we're not likely to hurt anyone in there when we open the door, right? Jacks asked.

"Most likely not," his own voice replied. At times like this when the situation demanded extensive interaction with his suit's AI, it really did start to feel like he was carrying on a two-way conversation with himself, and the fact that his own words were rarely spoken aloud lent a somewhat surreal air to the entire conversation. "Now that I've had a little more time to interface with their environmental systems," the AI continued, "it appears that their pressure doors have the capability to micro-advance, much like ours do. When we breach, we can command the door to open just enough to break the seal. The pressure will still equalize pretty quickly, but it won't be nearly as traumatic as it would have been had we just opened the door all at once.

As far as hurting anyone inside goes, that really depends on their condition. Unless they're already gravely injured, however, it's unlikely we'll do them any additional harm. Since we have little choice in the matter at this point, I recommend we attempt to communicate our intentions beforehand."

Good idea. Can you patch me through to some sort of intercom system?

"Surprisingly, yes, it's still working. Stand by." Seconds later, a chime indicated that an active intercom connection had been opened. "Go ahead, Lieutenant," his AI prompted.

"Hello in there. Can anyone hear me?" Jacks began tentatively. He knew that his words were being translated on the fly by his AI, and thought it best to avoid mentioning specifically who he was for the moment.

"Yes, we can hear you," a male Wek replied after a slight pause. "Who is this?" he asked in what Jacks took to be a suspicious, if not openly hostile tone.

So much for establishing trust up front, he thought darkly.

"If I may, Lieutenant," his AI interrupted, "they almost certainly know of Admiral Naftur. Although they are unlikely to believe you if you mention him alone, perhaps also including the fact that we are working with Commander Takkar from the *Hadeon* might engender some trust."

Yeah, I'm also not going to stand around out here begging them to let us continue to risk our lives to save theirs, he thought, then continued aloud, "This is Lieutenant Jacks from the starship *Theseus*. We are here on a rescue mission at the request of Commander Takkar of the *Hadeon*. Admiral Rugali Naftur is also a guest aboard our vessel. We have already rescued three other members of your crew. Unfortunately, we have very limited time to get you evacuated back to the *Theseus*.

"The fact that you know the name of Commander Takkar carries little weight, Lieutenant," the Wek growled in response, "and we all know that Prince Rugali was killed by your forces months ago. Why should we willingly agree to come aboard your vessel and become prisoners of the Pelaran Alliance?"

Jacks sighed inwardly and rolled his eyes in response, then took a moment to compose his thoughts before continuing. "Sir, I'm assuming that, since we are near your ship's medical bay, some of your group may be civilians. You, however, sound like a military man to me, so please allow me to do you the honor of shooting it to you straight," he said, wincing as he realized that his last statement might result in an awkward translation. "I only have a few minutes to get each of you inside emergency evacuation pods for transport back to our shuttle followed by a short ride over to *Theseus*. If I leave without accomplishing this task, I don't know whether I will get the opportunity to come back for you. As I'm sure you know, the *Keturah* is dying, and you will surely die with her if you remain aboard. As far as your status as prisoners goes, it's true that I am required to treat you as enemy combatants for now — that's for your protection as well as that of my unit — but you have my word that you will not be mistreated in any way. We have a Wek surgeon aboard the *Theseus* who can see to your medical needs and, although you will be escorted by Marine guards while onboard, as long as you conduct yourselves as guests, that is precisely how you will be treated. It will, of course, be up to Captain Prescott to decide what to do with you after that, but my guess is that you will be given the opportunity to transfer to the *Hadeon* as soon as it is safe for you to do so."

There was silence on the intercom, indicating that the feed from inside the room had been muted. Jacks took advantage of the lull in conversation to note the progress of the two Marines working feverishly behind him in the corridor. He was gratified to see that they had three pods deployed and were already preparing to inflate the fourth.

"Lieutenant Jacks?" the Wek male called from inside the room.

"Yes, sir," he replied immediately.

"We agree to your terms. I warn you, however, that I am armed and will not hesitate to open fire if I see any evidence that your intentions are other than what you have described. All four of us are injured to some degree, but one of the medics here has sustained serious burns and needs immediate attention. We did what we could to stabilize him, but we were unable to reach the supplies and equipment we needed inside the medical bay itself."

"Understood. In just a moment, I'm going to need you to stand clear of the door while we equalize the pressure between the hallway and your room. There is a leak in the adjoining compartment, so I'm afraid you are going to experience a brief period of low pressure and oxygen content once we open the door. It will be uncomfortable, and you should expect to start feeling lightheaded shortly after we enter the room. Again, we will need to place each of you in your own evacuation pod in order to transfer you back to the *Theseus*. The pods have their own medical AI that is familiar with Wek physiology, so please relax, lie still, and allow the system to begin administering whatever treatment it deems necessary. Regarding your weapon, I will allow you to keep it as we enter the room, but, for your own safety, I ask that you place it on the floor once we begin loading your most seriously injured colleague into his evacuation pod."

"And will you also be armed, Lieutenant?" the Wek asked.

"Yes, I will, but don't let that alarm you. We are Terran Fleet Command Marines, sir. We never go anywhere without being heavily armed." Jacks chuckled to himself in spite of the gravity of the situation. "You will also see that we are wearing a type of combat armor that allows us to operate in all environments. It can be a little intimidating when you see it for the first time, but you have my word that the only reason we are here is to help get you safely off this ship. So do I have *your* word that you will not attack us when we enter the room?"

There was another brief period of silence during which, Jacks assumed, the survivors were giving final consideration as to whether they had any choice at this point other than cooperation. "You have my word, Lieutenant. Let's get this over with," the Wek said, sighing resignedly.

Chapter 15

Exclusion Zone, Location Dagger
(3.3 light years from Earth)

Had an observer been in the unenviable position of witnessing the arrival of SCS *Zhelov* and *Serapion* at close range, the sight would almost certainly have inspired a sense of awe replaced shortly thereafter by fear. The starfield near their points of hyperspace interface seemed to blur and twist convulsively, then turn completely black in the instant before two spectacular flashes of gray light heralded the battleships' arrival.

Hyperspace transitions in the immediate vicinity of other ships are inherently dangerous, but centuries of naval operations experience had allowed the Sajeth Collective to develop procedures designed to minimize risk and render such activities largely routine. One example of just such a procedure required the two *Baldev*-class battleships to arrive in what was considered a tight formation for warships of their size. Doing so allowed for a predictable interface footprint, followed by an equally predicable pathway for their deceleration burn.

"Tight" formation flying was something of a relative term, the definition of which tended to vary with the size and configuration of the ships involved. In this case, the two-ship formation had maintained a separation of just over ten kilometers during the final leg of their journey to the Resistance rally point. This was done primarily to avoid any potential for the fields generated by their massive hyperdrives to interfere with one another, but also to provide a little room for the ships to maneuver as necessary after transitioning back into normal space.

Although the speed and range of modern naval weaponry made the idea of "formation flying" seem like something of an anachronism, there was still value in the mutual support two or more ships of war could provide for each other. As powerful as each individual ship was, there was still safety in numbers, particularly when there was the potential to encounter hostile forces immediately upon arrival at their destination.

Now, as the two, thirteen-hundred-meter-long warships streaked downrange at nearly ten percent the speed of light, four forward-facing panels slid into recesses in their hulls, each one revealing the presence of two massive sublight engine nozzles. Much like the retrograde engines employed by the BD cruiser *Keturah* during her battle against the *Theseus* — but significantly larger due to the battleships' size — all eight flared to life as they engaged at maximum power. When viewed from the side, a ghostly blue aura issued forth from the two battleships in their direction of flight, allowing the formation to decelerate at a surprising rate for ships of their size.

As the pair neared the end of the exclusion zone, the captains of both ships noted that the situation at their rally point was not as they had expected it to be. In response, both began an intense scan of the area utilizing their entire suite of both active and passive sensors. Even with the limitations imposed by the speed of light, the distances involved were relatively short, and it took only a few moments for the two captains to assess the situation and settle on an initial course of action.

On the side of each battleship facing the center of their formation, the forward-facing engines vectored their thrust to begin increasing the distance to the other ship while the engines on the opposite side ceased operation entirely. At the same moment, the stern of each ship was lit by a bluish-white glow as a total of twenty-four enormous sublight engines added their colossal thrust to the task of positioning the two ships for imminent combat operations.

From the opposite end of the exclusion zone near their original transition point, the two *Baldev*-class ships had the appearance of an eerie duplicate of the star Sirius, which just happened to be located just above their current plane of flight at the moment. Shortly thereafter, the false star created by the combination of the two ships' huge drive sections separated into two distinct points of light, then rapidly diminished in brightness as the battleships completed their turns and settled on their new courses — both aligned perfectly to intercept the starship *Theseus*.

TFS Theseus, Location Dagger
(3.3 light years from Earth)

With Lieutenant Lau still away from the bridge, his replacement jumped involuntarily as a series of urgent-sounding warning tones issued from the Tactical 2 console, none of which she had ever encountered outside of the simulator.

"Contact!" she reported, excitedly but without hesitation.

"What do you have, Lieutenant?" Commander Reynolds asked immediately. Although the XO tried to sound as casual and relaxed as possible, the first thought that had entered her mind was the hope that they were detecting the arrival of several replacement fighters rather than the long-anticipated appearance of *Zhelov* and *Serapion*. Just as the eager young lieutenant from the standby crew was fully qualified to sit in for Lieutenant Lau at Tactical, Commander Reynolds was more than capable of commanding the destroyer in combat. But with Captain Prescott off the bridge and three separate EVA missions underway, she couldn't help but feel a chill of dread run down the length of her spine at the thought of being faced with a completely unmanageable set of circumstances.

"I don't think it's one of ours, Commander," the lieutenant replied gravely. "The AI is still working to classify it, but the point of hyperspace interface corresponds with the exclusion area outlined by Commander Takkar."

Reynolds glanced to her right at the tactical plot, noting with some relief that there appeared to be only one new ship — currently displayed with the yellow icon reserved for unknown contacts. Realizing that, at this range, *Theseus'* AI could be expected to provide additional details rather quickly, she paused momentarily to observe the new arrival. In the back of her mind, she still harbored a faint hope that the contact would turn out to be a friendly — perhaps even one of the *Theseus*-class destroyers that had taken part in the battle at Location Crossbow.

"Can we get a decent visual from here?" she asked, not directing the question to anyone in particular.

"We can try, ma'am," Lieutenant Commander Schmidt replied from Tactical 1. "It's heading away from us at the moment, so assuming it's a ship, we should be able to see the light given off by its drive section."

Reynolds' gaze now shifted to the center of the bridge view screen, which shortly thereafter displayed a pulsating green oval surrounding an otherwise unremarkable section of the starfield to port. After a brief pause, the oval pulsed red three times before the entire view screen zoomed in on that section of the sky. It took several seconds for *Theseus'* AI to focus its optical sensors on the distant, rapidly moving contact. With a growing sense of anxiety, Reynolds divided her attention between the tactical plot and the slowly sharpening image on the view screen.

"Captain Prescott to the Bridge ... Flight Deck, bridge," she announced in rapid succession. Although they had detected the new contact just ten seconds earlier, Reynolds was unwilling to wait any longer to begin taking definitive action.

"Bridge, go for Flight Deck," came the immediate reply from the on-duty flight operations officer — currently standing just forward of the destroyer's main aft airlock that led out to the stern flight apron.

"We're working a contact up here that may be another hostile. What's the status of our ... stand by one."

It was at that moment that *Theseus'* AI had finally processed sufficient information to both classify and positively identify the contact. Reynolds heard several expressions of recognition from members of the bridge crew as the image on the view screen resolved into near perfect clarity. Although the two massive warships displayed were currently headed away from the *Theseus*, the configuration of their drive sections were now all too familiar. On the tactical plot, the single yellow icon divided into two distinct contacts now represented by diamond shapes outlined in the angry red color indicating that both were hostile warships. Inside each icon, the traditional, two-letter code of "BB" indicated the enemy vessels' platform type, while the accompanying text blocks provided an even more specific identification — SCS *Zhelov* and SCS *Serapion*.

"AI, resume General Quarters for combat operations, Condition 1," Reynolds ordered. "Set status of all EVA activities to 'Terminate Until Further Notice.'"

"General Quarters for combat operations, Condition 1 set," the AI's synthetic female voice responded in a businesslike tone. "EVA status change acknowledged. Please note that EVA activity is currently in progress."

"Uh huh, tell me something I don't know," Reynolds muttered under her breath as the AI began announcing the status change over the ship's intercom. "Flight Deck, are you still there?"

"Yes, ma'am," the duty officer replied. "I believe you were about to ask about our EVA status."

"Yes, I was. Who do we still have outside?"

"The last of the damaged fighters is aboard and being secured as we speak. We have all four of them pushed as far forward as we can get them now, so they are no longer interfering with flight ops. Commander Logan and his team came in with the last fighter, so they're all back aboard as well. I just spoke with him briefly and he said to tell you that he would report in as quickly as he can get back to Engineering."

"That's all good news. And what about the Marines?"

"One of the *Sherpas*, that's Marine Rescue Flight niner zero two, is on final approach and will be aboard in zero two minutes. They have eight of the fifteen Marines aboard plus three Wek survivors from the *Keturah*. The other *Sherpa* — with six other Marines plus Lieutenant Jacks — was not yet en route back to the *Theseus* at last check."

"Yes, that's still the case. I need you to get that first *Sherpa* onboard and secured as quickly as possible. We have two battleships just like the one we fought earlier headed our way and unless we get underway before they have a chance to open fire —"

"Understood, Commander. And what about Lieutenant Jacks and the other shuttle?"

"I'm afraid they're on their own for the moment. His team is aboard a Resistance ship, so I suspect they're a lot safer than we are right now. Reynolds out."

Marine Section "Rescue 11," Location Dagger
(Near SCS *Keturah* External Access Point Two)

"Rescue 11, bridge," Commander Reynolds called over the tactical comlink.

"Bridge, go for Rescue 11," Lieutenant Jacks replied, sounding uncharacteristically winded.

"You're out of time, Lieutenant. What's your status?"

"We're nearly there, Commander. We have all four Wek survivors secured in triple EPs. Three of them should be fine, but one is in pretty bad shape with third degree burns. The medical AI on his pod says he's stable for now, though. We ran into some trouble on egress. I think our pressurizing and depressurizing several large compartments caused some additional structural instability and we ended up needing to clear quite a bit of debris on the way out. We'll have everyone aboard the shuttle in zero three minutes."

"I'm sure you received an alert that the *Zhelov* and *Serapion* have arrived."

"Yes, ma'am. Are you still planning to move *Theseus* in closer to pick us up?"

"I don't think we have time," Reynolds sighed, the stress and frustration of the current situation clearly evident in her voice. "We're in the process of recovering your first shuttle as we speak. In the meantime, those two battleships are headed right at us and will be well within weapons range before you can get back aboard *Theseus*. I'm afraid our moving in closer might actually put you in more danger than just having you stay put. Stand by one, Lieutenant. Captain Prescott just stepped back onto the bridge."

"Careful, there," Jacks' AI interjected after ensuring that they were no longer broadcasting over the comlink, "she sounds calm enough, but I'll wager she's as mad as a cut snake."

Nah, she's just in a tight spot, that's all. She's a pro, that one ... I wouldn't want to cross her, though, and that's a fact.

For the next few minutes, Jacks continued to supervise final preparations for his team's departure from the *Keturah*, assuming (correctly) that his captain and XO were in the middle of a discussion regarding precisely what, if anything, they could do to help him. The prospect of being left aboard the dying ship, while a bit unsettling, didn't pose much of a problem for his section of Marines — at least not in the short term. The power supplies in their EVA suits would last pretty much indefinitely, and would continue to generate plenty of oxygen for far longer than they would need it. The limiting factor, as usual, was food and water. Having exerted themselves over the course of the past hour, he assumed that most of his troops would have already run through the two liters of water in their suits' onboard drink bags, and a quick status check of his own supply showed it to be less than half full. It would be at least a day before lack of water posed what he would consider an "emergency" situation, however. If they reached that point, there were several metric tons of survival rations, water, and medical supplies aboard their *Sherpa*. Even in the unlikely event that they somehow lost access to the shuttle, he felt sure they would be able to locate additional supplies aboard the *Keturah*, if required. Finding a safe place to eventually remove their helmets in order to eat might prove a problem, but it was one he could afford to ignore for now.

Jacks also knew that, in a worst-case scenario, their EVA suits were capable of traversing significant distances in space — perhaps allowing them to set out for one of the other damaged ships, if necessary. The suits' integral Cannae thrusters were certainly capable of providing a steady acceleration over an indefinite period of time, hopefully achieving the speeds required to cover the vast distances involved before their occupants died of dehydration. Very few things frightened First Lieutenant Jackson "Jacks" Lee, but the idea of such a desperate journey across open, interstellar space sent a forbidding chill coursing down the length of his spine.

The Wek survivors represented an even bigger problem. Having risked his own life as well as those of the six other Marines in his section in an attempt to rescue them, losing even one at this point would represent the worst imaginable type of mission failure — perhaps in some ways even worse than losing a member of his own unit.

Pushing these rather morbid, unproductive thoughts from his mind, Jacks straightened his back, drew in a deep breath, and surveyed the situation just inside the large airlock that serviced access point two. The four triple EPs as well as what little equipment they had brought onboard were arranged neatly on one side of the small cargo bay, and the members of his section were prepared to depart. All that was required at this point was an order from the bridge to either hunker down and shelter in place, or embark for the trip back to *Theseus*. Either way, seeing all of his people as well as the Wek survivors safely back to the ship was both his singular focus as well as a point of professional and personal pride. No other outcome was acceptable.

"Rescue 11, *Theseus*-Actual," Captain Prescott's voice sounded inside his helmet, interrupting his stream of consciousness.

"*Theseus*-Actual, Rescue 11. Go ahead, Captain," Lieutenant Jacks replied, hoping to hear that the massive destroyer would soon be waiting right outside to evacuate his team.

"Jackson, I'm sorry to have to do this to you, but I'm going to have to ask you to sit tight for the time being. Those two battleships are coming on fast, and unless they change course, we don't have time to bring you aboard before they're likely to start shooting at us. Under the circumstances, I think I'd be putting you at more risk by pulling you out now than just having you wait it out there."

"Understood sir. I'm sure we'll be fine," Jacks replied with more enthusiasm than he felt at the moment.

"With any luck, the two ships will receive their orders from Captain Yagani's comm buoy shortly and be on their way before they have the opportunity to open fire. If possible, we don't want them to know that we have people aboard the *Keturah*, so I've asked Flight Ops to tuck the *Sherpa* in tight against the *Keturah's* hull on the opposite side from the approaching enemy ships. I don't know if that will prevent them from detecting it, but it can't hurt. In any event, the shuttle is still only about two hundred meters from your point of entry, so it won't take long to get it back when you're ready for it."

"Will *Theseus* be departing the area, sir?" Jacks asked.

There was a brief pause on the comlink as Prescott considered the meaning behind the young lieutenant's question and how best to answer.

"They seem to be headed our way at the moment, so my hope is to draw them away from the *Keturah*. Having said that, we're in no condition to engage one of those ships at this point, let alone two. The good news is that we don't believe either of them is equipped with the gravitic beam weapon the *Baldev* used against us, so, yes, once they get within weapons range, we will C-Jump clear. I know it's a little uncomfortable being left out there, but rest assured we'll be back for you shortly."

"I'm not worried, sir. My guys never pass up a chance for a nap, so take your time."

"Very good, Lieutenant," he chuckled, appreciating the young officer's effort to stay positive while facing a difficult situation. "Prescott out."

TFS Theseus, Location Dagger
(3.3 light years from Earth)

"Bridge, Engineering," Commander Logan's voice sounded from the overhead speakers.

"Prescott here. Go ahead, Commander."

"Things are looking a little better down here, Captain. While we were outside, we repaired a coolant leak on one of our main ventral heat exchangers. It's back online now and working fine. We also took a bunch of spare gravitic emitters with us in hopes of bringing more of the shields back online. It turns out that quite a few of the emitters we assumed were destroyed were just dismounted. When they take an impact, they're designed to break free and fold down into a shallow recessed area built into their base. When they're in this 'conformal' state, they're supposed to be much less susceptible to additional damage. Frankly, I never believed it would work, especially against a fragmentary weapon like the Carrada —"

"So are you telling me we have our shields back?"

"It's by no means a hundred percent, but yes, they're mostly back online. Unfortunately, we did lose quite a few emitters completely, and the hull damage in those areas was generally too severe to mount any of our replacements. As you know, most of the worst damage is forward, so our shields are likely to be weakest near the bow. I strongly suggesting doing whatever you can to avoid taking fire head-on."

"That's still good news, Commander, and I'll do everything I can to avoid taking fire from any direction at this point," Prescott said. "I don't suppose you were able to do anything about the plasma torpedo tubes and railguns we lost?"

"No, sir. Two of each are out of commission until we get back to Yucca. The torp tubes are fused shut and the two railgun mounts look like pieces of modern art at this point."

"Alright, nice job. Thank you, Cheng. Prescott out."

For the past few minutes, *Theseus* had been proceeding along a course that — assuming the enemy battleships continued their pursuit — would put as much distance as possible between them and the various other vessels in the area.

"So how do we go about drawing them away from the *Keturah* while still avoiding a confrontation?" Reynolds asked, still feeling unusually relieved to have Prescott back on the bridge.

"Well, fortunately, since we were still recovering the damaged fighters when we sent out Lieutenant Jacks' team, we weren't very close to the *Keturah* when *Zhelov* and *Serapion* arrived. Hopefully, they will assume that we would have been much closer if our intention had been to board her. If that's the case, they may well ignore her completely. So far, they only seem to be interested in us, and I'm perfectly happy to drag them along until they realize they're supposed to be somewhere else."

"Sounds reasonable, I suppose, but don't we have to assume they realize what we're trying to do?"

"Absolutely, they do," Prescott chuckled. "Don't misunderstand me, Commander, I don't mean to give you the impression that we are in any way controlling how this unfolds. We're simply playing for time. They just happen to be playing along — for now. Perhaps Lieutenant Lau can give us some idea of whether they will continue to do so. What do you have for us, Lieutenant?"

"I just finished it, sir," he replied, opening a window on the bridge view screen to display a rather complex-looking diagram indicating the relative distances between all of the ships in the vicinity. Irritated at having been off the bridge when the two enemy ships arrived, Lau had immediately thrown himself into the task of attempting to predict their movements upon his return to the Tactical 2 console. The result was a modified version of a three-dimensional situational awareness diagram commonly used for training purposes. Lines intersected at each vessel to form a series of triangles, all of which were slowly moving to both track and predict each ship's relative position in space. In a further effort to provide perspective, the entire diagram slowly rotated about both its horizontal and vertical axes. Understandably, both Prescott and Reynolds' first reaction was to tilt their heads slowly to the left in an attempt to make sense of what they were seeing.

"Okay, I know," Lau said, noting the expressions on their faces and then turning to look at the diagram for the first time on the huge bridge view screen. "It's a little confusing to look at, so let me break it down and point out a couple of things. We're right here, of course," he said, causing a red oval to temporarily flash around one of the vertices on the diagram. "*Zhelov* and *Serapion* are here. As you can see, they are continuing to increase the distance between them, but they're still generally heading in our direction. They modified their courses slightly when we started moving, and they're still accelerating, but not as quickly as our model indicates that they could be. They're also executing some random course changes as they go, so I wouldn't bet on a C-Drive missile strike being very effective."

"We're not planning to engage them," Reynolds said, "but that doesn't sound good at all. So you're saying that they are trying to give the appearance of pursuing us, but they aren't really trying to overtake us and bring us to action, right?"

"Yes, ma'am, that's the way it looks to me right now. If they really wanted to catch us, one of them could have easily transitioned to the opposite side of the battlespace to box us in."

"Their behavior may also be consistent with their taking the time required to digest their orders from Commodore Sarafi before they commit themselves to any course of action," Prescott added.

"That's true as well, sir, but let me show you one more thing that worries me." Lau turned to enter a series of commands at his console, causing a shaded polygon to be superimposed across the region of space formed by all of the vessels with the exception of the two battleships. "If we project the positions of the *Theseus*, *Keturah*, *Hadeon*, *Baldev*, and *Babayev* onto a single plane ... this," he said, highlighting a single point in space, "is its geometric center. And then if we project the courses of *Zhelov* and *Serapion* —"

"Well," Reynolds replied, "there's no way *that's* a coincidence. See how they're continuing to spread out as they get closer to that point?"

"It's probably not a coincidence," Prescott sighed, rubbing the bridge of his nose between his thumb and index finger, "but what, if anything, does their behavior tell us about their intentions?"

"Two possibilities stand out for me," Reynolds said. "They're either hedging their bets while they figure out what they want to do — in which case, holding the center of the battlespace gives them the most options, kind of like sailing ships working themselves to windward of their opponents in order to take the weather gauge. Or ... they already know what they plan to do — and holding the center of the battlespace still gives them the most options."

"Lau, did you say that point was the geometric center of *all* of the vessels in the area?" Prescott asked.

"Yes, sir, with the exception of the two battleships."

"Including the disabled Resistance ships?"

"Yes, sir."

"Show me the *Zhelov* and *Serapion's* beam weapons range based on the data from our battle with the *Baldev*."

"What are you thinking?" Reynolds asked, noting a rising tone of urgency in his voice.

"Why would they take into account the range to their own ships — especially the disabled ones that are adrift and relatively isolated — even if they are positioning themselves to mount an attack?"

Lieutenant Lau immediately simplified his diagram to place the centroid of the battlespace in the center of the display window. The two enemy battleships were now surrounded by large red bubbles to indicate the maximum demonstrated range of their energy weapons. With the exception of the *Theseus* herself, it was clear that all five vessels would be in range once the two-ship formation reached the point at the center of the diagram.

Although Prescott could still conceive of several possibilities that might fit the current scenario, the one that now seemed by far the most likely was one he had not even considered prior to the two battleships' arrival. With chilling objectivity, the rational side of his mind judged that it was probably already too late to change the outcome of what was about to take place, but the emotional side screamed with righteous, indignant fury for immediate action — demanding vengeance for an act that had not yet taken place.

"Lee, position the *Sherpa* to pick up our Marines and tell your brother to get his people off the *Keturah* immediately," Prescott ordered urgently. "As soon as they're aboard the shuttle, head them in the opposite direction at best possible speed. Dubashi, warn the *Hadeon* that we believe the two battleships are about to open fire and order them to depart the area immediately. Ensign Fisher, on my mark, C-Jump us right in the middle of those two battleships. Tactical, all we're trying to do is hold their attention long enough to get Rescue 11 out of harm's way."

A chorus of "aye, sirs" filled the bridge, followed a few seconds later by an update from Ensign Fisher at the Helm console. "Completing our turn back, Captain. Ready to C-Jump in zero niner seconds."

"Did we get a response from Commander Takkar on the *Hadeon*?" Prescott asked impatiently.

"Yes, sir," Dubashi replied. "They were just about to break contact with the *Baldev* when the two enemy ships arrived. They're already on the move and should be clear shortly. He indicated that they will be awaiting further instructions at Location Willow."

"Good. Go ahead and signal our fighters to rendezvous with us at Willow as well. I don't think there is much they can do for us here at this point."

"Aye, sir."

"Sir," Lieutenant Lee said from the Science and Engineering console. "I'll have the *Sherpa* ready to evacuate Rescue 11 in two two seconds. Lieutenant Jacks is ready to go, but reports that it will take him a couple of minutes to get everyone aboard."

"I trust you impressed upon him that he may not *have* a couple of minutes?"

"I did, sir. He said the only way to speed things up is to abandon the survivors. And I can promise you that's not something he will be willing to do."

"Captain," Lieutenant Lau announced from Tactical 2, "the *Zhelov* and *Serapion* are now in beam weapons range of the Resistance ships."

"They've also engaged their supplemental aft shields," Schmidt added. "They've stopped accelerating, but are continuing along the same course as before."

"Ready to C-Jump," Fisher announced.

"Tactical, hit them both as hard as you can with the railguns and directed energy weapons. Pretty much everything we have should bear on one target or the other. Helm, execute your jump," Prescott ordered.

"Aye, sir," Fisher replied. "C-Jumping in 3 … 2 … 1 …"

On the bridge view screen, *Theseus'* AI automatically minimized a number of previously open windows in order to provide an unobscured view of their arrival between the two Resistance battleships. With just over five hundred kilometers now separating the *Theseus* from each of the two enemy vessels, neither was as close as the *Baldev* had been during her earlier attack runs. Given the speed and power of the weapons involved, however, the three warships were still within what might be referred to as "point-blank range" from one another. Just as Captain Prescott had predicted, every operational weapons mount aboard *Theseus* had a clear line of sight at one or the other of her two targets and, within seconds of her arrival, she was showering both with a steady hail of railgun penetrator rounds and energy weapons bolts.

"No response from either ship, Captain," Schmidt reported as *Theseus* passed aft of her targets. "They have not returned fire and are continuing on course."

"Any apparent damage?"

"Superficial only, sir. Their shields are more effective from the sides — even against the railguns."

"Keep it up. Helm, extend this run downrange so that we have a little more time to concentrate fire on their sterns, then give us another pass right down the middle."

"Aye, sir," Fisher said.

"Captain, the *Hadeon* has transitioned to hyperspace." Lau reported.

"Thank you, Lieutenant."

"I have to say that I'm a little surprised that they aren't bothering to return fire," Reynolds observed, looking up from her touchscreen for the first time since their C-Jump.

"At this point, I'm guessing that's a combination of their following orders while at the same time making the point that there's nothing we can do to stop them from doing whatever they like," Prescott replied. "Captain Yagani said that the battleships were being told to 'avoid contact with enemy forces here and depart immediately for Terra.' Their not bothering to fire on us is consistent with having received such an order. The problem is, they could have stayed in the exclusion zone and immediately transitioned back to hyperspace — but they didn't."

"Instead, they calculated a flight profile out of the area that would take them within weapons range of their own disabled ships," Reynolds continued. "I suppose it makes sense that the commodore didn't share that particular piece of information with Captain Yagani …"

"Sir, both enemy ships are firing," Lieutenant Lau reported gravely. With most of the bridge view screen occupied by an aft-facing view of the two warships, his report was largely unnecessary as the bridge was once again lit by the hellish, orange-tinted flash of energy weapons fire. There were several seconds of silence on the bridge as every member of the crew watched, transfixed by the horror playing out in front of them.

"Schmidt, give us visuals on the *Keturah*, *Baldev*, and *Babayev*, please," Prescott ordered.

Though it had been only seconds since the *Zhelov* and *Serapion* had opened fire, their two most distant targets were already taking tremendous damage. Their immediate prey — the *Baldev* and the *Babayev* — were completely defenseless against the onslaught, adrift and with no shields to protect their most vulnerable internal components. Accordingly, the two battleships focused their fire on the areas most likely to result in secondary explosions in an effort to bring about the ships' complete destruction as quickly as possible. Unlike their Terran counterparts, Sajeth Collective warships were still required to carry large quantities of propellant for use in their sublight engines. The volatile chemicals used for this purpose were typically stored deep within the most heavily armored and shielded sections of the hull. In this case, however, the two battleships had the additional advantage of knowing precisely where to concentrate their fire for maximum effect.

Aboard *Theseus*, Captain Prescott continued his attempt to draw the enemy battleships' fire, but it was now painfully obvious that the entire effort had been in vain. A stunned silence seemed to permeate the bridge as the *Zhelov* and *Serapion* methodically disassembled their targets with a cold, calculating precision that might have engendered a sense of admiration were it not for the realization that they were witnessing the senseless, brutal murder of thousands. On the view screen, both enemy warships maintained a continuous, heavy bombardment — energy weapons fire issuing relentlessly from beam emitters mounted all along the sides facing their respective targets. In the windows displaying the *Baldev* and *Babayev,* it was clear that their hulls had already been torn into several large sections, each one tinged with a wicked, red glow of twisted, molten metal — and still the energy weapons fire continued. What possible justification, military or otherwise, could ever be put forward for such an act, they wondered … what leader, bound by any reasonable system of morality, could live with the repercussions of issuing such an order?

"Lieutenant Lee, what's the status of Rescue 11?" Prescott asked with a weary tone of resignation in his voice.

"I've been monitoring their tactical comm, sir. They made more rapid progress than expected in getting everyone back aboard their *Sherpa.* I've got them headed in the opposite direction now, but the shuttle's painfully slow, sir. Shall I patch them through?"

"Yes, please. Ensign Fisher, do you have them?"

"Yes, sir."

"C-Jump us as close as you can to put us in a position to bring them aboard. Put us between the *Sherpa* and the two battleships. Make sure our bow faces the enemy ships so that we can shield the aft flight apron from incoming fire."

"Understood, Captain. Projecting two six seconds to C-Jump. I'll get us as close as I can, but after we're over there it will take some time to get us in a good position to make the recovery."

"Just do it as quickly as you can. The most important thing is to protect the shuttle from enemy fire. Execute when ready."

"Aye, sir."

"If both of those battleships open up on our bow, our weakened forward shields may not last long," Reynolds said.

"You're probably right, but our armor hung in there pretty well against the *Baldev's* energy weapons — and at much shorter range. With any luck, we won't have to sit there for long. In any event, I'm not sure we have much choice in the matter. The *Sherpa* would never survive even a single hit."

"Sir, we're up on Rescue 11's tactical comm channel again," Lieutenant Lee reported, accompanied by the obligatory chime over the ceiling speakers.

"Lieutenant Jacks, this is Prescott. Are you clear on what we're about to do?"

"Yes, Captain, and I can tell you that we're all quite anxious to get back onboard at this point."

"I'm sure you are. Hang in there just a bit longer and we'll make that happen."

As if on cue, Ensign Fisher completed *Theseus'* turn and announced their imminent transition to hyperspace for the short trip back to the *Keturah*. "C-Jumping in 3 … 2 … 1 …"

Chapter 16

TFS Navajo, Earth-Sun Lagrange Point 2
(Combat Information Center - 1.5×10^6 km from Earth)

"It's good to see you, sir," Admiral Patterson said as he addressed the vidcon image of his immediate superior, Admiral Duke Sexton, Commander in Chief, Terran Fleet Command. "Before we get started, I wanted to let you know that the two Resistance battleships we have been expecting for some time have just arrived at Location Dagger."

"It's good to see you as well, but perhaps it might be better if we postpone this conversation until the situation at Dagger is resolved."

"No, no, it's fine. Captain Prescott remains in command of our forces in the area, supported by Captain Zhukov and Commander Waffer from the *Jutland*. They are more than capable of handling the situation without my looking over their collective shoulders. Having said that, we never stop looking over their shoulders, of course," Patterson said with just a hint of a smile. "At the moment, Captain Davis is managing our oversight of active operational areas while I continue to prepare our defenses in system. The truth of the matter is that there is very little we can do to help them at this point anyway. All of our C-Drive-equipped capital ships have already been deployed. Our strategy at Location Dagger at the moment is to simply allow the new Resistance arrivals to transition through the area and deal with them once they arrive near Earth — hopefully, on a more equal footing."

"As always, your judgment in such matters is beyond reproach. I know you're bound to be feeling an unbelievable level of stress right now, but just know that you have my — and the Leadership Council's for that matter — absolute confidence. Now don't get me wrong," Sexton continued, with a raised eyebrow, "we both know that I'm actually the best man for the job —"

"You'll get no argument from me there, sir, but, even under these circumstances, I don't think I would switch places with you if I were given the opportunity to do so."

"No, I would say not. There's a big part of me that can't help but envy all of you still fortunate enough to be doing operational work. The battles I'm fighting down here are of an entirely different sort."

"I can imagine. In fact, when we didn't hear from you for a while after *Theseus* departed, I was beginning to think I was going to have to put together another evac mission and pull you out of there like we did with Naftur."

"In all seriousness," Sexton replied earnestly, "I know you're kidding, but I also know that you'd be willing to do just about anything that didn't violate your own ethical standards to help me, if needed. I certainly appreciate the sentiment, but no matter what happens down here, please don't even consider doing something like that. We were walking a very fine line when we took Naftur and Turlaka off-world without specific permission from the Leadership Council to do so. At this point, I'd say about half of the Council's representatives have made public statements accusing me of masterminding some sort of military coup that resulted in the Wek 'escape.' They're also blaming me for

Chairwoman Crull's removal from office. The rest of them are up to their eyeballs trying to hold things together long enough to deal with the current situation. Right now, I have the sense that we're a heartbeat away from disbanding as an organization, and we absolutely cannot afford to provide Crull's people with any additional 'evidence' that our military forces are operating outside of the Council's control."

"Understood, but how is it that she still has so many followers on the Council after everything that's happened? I would have thought that after she brought in her own private army to take over the Headquarters campus … to say nothing of the attempted murder of the Commander in Chief in front of fifty plus witnesses —"

"That they might start to question her motivations?"

"Hell, question her sanity for that matter. Surely they have to realize that she's not fit to hold public office, particularly one with such far-reaching responsibilities. She's under arrest at this point, and one would have to assume that she'll at least be indicted for the shooting."

"Oh, Crull is not one you would ever want to underestimate. As you know, her late husband had a long and distinguished career — first as a businessman, then as a politician — and he was phenomenally successful at both. He was generally well liked, and those who didn't like him, feared him. There was a persistent rumor, however, that Karoline was the brains behind his success. I think that's probably nonsense, since they were obviously *both* brilliant people. Based on my interactions with the two of them, however, I'd say it's fair to say that he was the one who was liked, and she was the one who was feared. As to her quote, unquote 'arrest,' I'm surprised they've managed to hold her as long as they have."

"I don't understand. Surely you don't think she will get away with what she's done."

"She might very well be permanently removed as Chairwoman — although she's technically just on 'administrative leave' at the moment — but her status as a Leadership Council representative provides her with diplomatic immunity. This has never been challenged in court, to my knowledge, but all TFC member nations, including the United States where the incident happened, agreed to grant this status when they originally signed the charter."

"So she's free to do pretty much whatever she pleases and the host country can't even so much as issue her a parking ticket," Patterson observed wryly.

"Hah," Sexton laughed, "interestingly enough, I think that's actually something the host country *can* legally do, but if they did, there would be precious little they could do about it when the tickets went unpaid. In all seriousness, the Council is keeping her status very much under wraps at the moment, as you can well imagine. It's possible she could be indicted by the authorities back in the Central and South American Union, but —"

"Uh, right, let's see," Patterson interjected, reading from a biographical summary on the adjacent wall-mounted view screen, "third wealthiest woman in the world, owner of a controlling interest in the second largest corporation in South America, globetrotting philanthropist with world-spanning political ties — not to mention celebrity status in all of the countries that make up the CSAU."

"Exactly, so don't expect to see her standing trial for attempting to knock off some 'rogue military officer' anytime soon," Sexton said. "In fact, a couple of international news outlets have already referenced 'unnamed sources' who claim she is being illegally detained after attempting to thwart a military takeover of Terran Fleet Command Headquarters."

"Jeez, now *that's* rich, under the circumstances," Patterson replied, rolling his eyes.

"Well, there's how things should be … and then there's how things are," Sexton smiled. "Alright, regarding the business at hand, your last update indicated you intended for the two of us to attempt to make contact with the Guardian. I think I understand what you have in mind. Your primary goal is to ascertain its intentions once we come under attack, correct?"

"That's right. We need to have some idea regarding what, if anything, we can expect it to do when the Resistance ships arrive. The last thing we need is for one of our ships to inadvertently do something that it interprets as a hostile action, so if it's going to participate in our defense, there needs to be some sort of coordination to prevent any misunderstanding of intentions."

"And if it has no wish to participate, you need some assurance that it will remain clear of your operations," Sexton added.

"That's correct. Frankly, I'm not sure which of these two options I prefer, but since we have no control whatsoever over what it does or doesn't do, I would at least like to see if we can get it to agree to cooperate with us on some level."

"It has made a number of rather ambiguous statements along those lines, as I recall," Sexton observed. "One day it makes reference to how it can no longer defend us without our participation, the next it says something about us now having everything we need to defend ourselves without its help. I have to say, however, that it seems strange to consider that it might simply stand by and allow us to be attacked without intervening in any way. Why would it allow something like that to happen after sitting on us like a mother hen for five hundred years? In my mind, that seems like the ultimate in wasted efforts."

"I suppose," Patterson said pensively. "Unless the mother hen knows that at some point, we have to be able to fend for ourselves. And if we're unable to do so —"

"It's time to cut its losses and move on. I guess that does make sense if you consider that the Pelarans seem to be all about playing the long game. You have to figure that if they've completed their 'cultivation' program enough times, there must have been instances where late stage failures have occurred. Anyway, we're just speculating at this point, but I agree that it's worth a try to see if we can get … what are they calling it again?"

"'Griffin,' but you won't catch me calling it that," Patterson scowled.

"Oh, right … get 'Griffin' to play along," Sexton continued, smiling in response to his long-time colleague's occasionally cantankerous attitude. "Do you think it will answer our hail?"

"I do, although there's still so much radio traffic aimed in its direction that I think we'll try a laser comlink like we used during the so-called induction meeting. At last check, the *Navajo* was just coming into range. Shall I give it a try?"

"No harm in trying it," Sexton replied.

Patterson nodded in the direction of Ensign Fletcher, waiting dutifully at her Communications console nearby. With no appreciable delay, the view screen displaying the vidcon image of Admiral Sexton opened an additional window containing the smiling Human avatar of the Pelaran Guardian spacecraft. As if he had guessed the topic of conversation, he was once again wearing what appeared to be a close facsimile of the black flight suits worn by TFC pilots.

"Well hello, Admiral Sexton … Admiral Patterson. This is indeed a rare pleasure," 'Griffin' greeted them in a particularly amiable tone. "I expected that I would hear from a TFC representative at some point, but I will freely admit that I did not anticipate that it would be the two of you. How can I be of service?"

"Thank you for taking our call," Admiral Sexton began with the odd sense of uncertainty that always seemed to accompany a conversation with the sentient machine. "As you know, Admiral Patterson is our Chief of Naval Operations. For the duration of the current crisis, I have placed him in operational command of all of our military forces. We have some questions for you of an operational nature, so I would like to turn the conversation over to him momentarily. Before I do so, however, I want to assure you once again that we have absolutely no hostile intent towards you — now, or during any combat operations that may occur between TFC forces and those of the Pelaran Resistance."

"Not to make light of such a serious subject," the Guardian replied, smiling pleasantly, "but don't you find their choice of names a little odd? 'Pelaran Resistance' makes me think of a group of Pelarans *resisting* something or someone — not some odd cross-section of the Sajeth Collective *resisting* the Pelarans. Clearly, they could have used some marketing help at the outset of their ill-conceived little movement. I'm sorry, I don't mean to get us off-topic right away. Yes, I understand that you harbor no hostile intent towards me. I appreciate your taking the time to reiterate this fact, although it would be strange if we considered one another anything less than the closest of allies, given our long and very successful history together."

You're certainly an authority on marketing, Sexton thought. *Everything that comes out of your virtual mouth sounds like a propaganda-laden campaign ad for the Pelaran Alliance.* "We just want to avoid any potential for misunderstanding one other's intentions," he said with a polite smile.

"A sensible precaution. So, Admiral Patterson, is there something specific you would like me to do?" the Guardian asked.

"I hate to answer a question with a question," Patterson replied, "but can I first ask that you clarify your intentions? You have told us that you defended the Earth against attack for centuries. Are you still acting in that capacity?"

"Ah, yes, that is the question, is it not? You face an imminent attack from an enemy that until very recently you didn't even know existed. Worse still, it's an ambiguous enemy, elements of which appear to share much in common with your species and profess to offer you friendship — perhaps even membership in their alliance at some point. At the same time, you struggle to come to grips with my choosing this point in time to openly reveal myself — and the Pelaran Alliance I represent — to your world. Unfortunately, and I know you're not going to like this answer, there are long-established rules governing what I can and cannot reveal to a species that has been offered membership in our Alliance, but has not yet made its decision to join. Specific details regarding my continuing role as a defender of your world certainly fall within this category."

Patterson stared at the Guardian's synthetic, albeit completely lifelike, image for several seconds, thinking through his options before continuing. "As you say, we have a well-established history of successful cooperation with you during our species' vetting process — a process that you personally supervised over a period of hundreds of years. And even though we have not yet elected to join, you have graciously extended the offer of membership — and full membership at that, based on our genetic ties to the Pelarans."

"To my knowledge, there is simply no higher honor that could be conferred upon a civilization," the Guardian said proudly.

"Of that, I have little doubt. So, then, is it logical that, having invested so much time and effort in preparing Humanity to take its rightful place in the Alliance, you would now abandon us in the face of possible destruction at the hands of the Resistance?"

"From your perspective, probably not, but I am simply not at liberty to provide specifics regarding what actions, if any, I might take in the event you are attacked. What I will tell you, however, is that you have been provided everything you need to defend yourselves from this particular threat with no further assistance from me."

"If you will forgive the observation," Patterson said, "it almost sounds as if you are implying that you see this as some sort of test."

"Oh, come now, my dear Admiral, surely there are few challenges in life to which that term does not apply. 'Tests' come in many forms, and on scales that range from the individual to the civilization and beyond. As the old saying goes, it's a 'much of a muchness.'"

"Could we, then, impose on you to remain clear of the combat zone once our ships engage enemy forces?" Patterson pressed, undeterred by the Guardian's typically evasive comments. "We would also appreciate having a commitment that you will refrain from attacking any vessels we designate as friendly or neutral. We will, of course, be happy to share a tactical data link with you so that you will have this information in real-time."

"I'm glad you mentioned sharing data, Admiral Patterson," the Guardian replied, ignoring his question. "I am transmitting a data stream as we speak that your AI will be able to display for you. Consider it an advance on the technological bounty your world will receive once you make the decision to join the Alliance."

"Alright," Patterson replied suspiciously. "And what sort of data are you sharing?"

"It's nothing particularly exciting, I'm afraid. In fact, I believe your scientists are already working on something similar based on the technology used in your long-range NRD network comm beacons. I think you will find, however, that it will be of great utility in the coming days."

Patterson looked in the direction of Ensign Fletcher, who had become accustomed to his habits when working in the *Navajo's* Combat Information Center, particularly those where data communications were concerned. After initially setting up the vidcon with the Guardian, she had been closely monitoring the call, anticipating the next glance from the CNO indicating that he expected something to be handled immediately — preferably with no further explanation on his part.

Initially, his constant presence in the CIC and his rather exacting demeanor had been nerve-racking for the young officer to say the least, but now that she had a better idea of what to expect, she took tremendous pride in staying one step ahead of the "old man." Perhaps even more importantly, the more time she spent in the company of Admiral Patterson, the more she respected and admired him — he was truly the kind of officer whose personal example inspired those around him to offer nothing less than their best.

"I have the Guardian's transmission, Admiral," Fletcher replied immediately. "It's formatted just like our standard Fleet data exchange streams."

"I recommend displaying it on your holographic table," the Guardian commented offhandedly. "You'll need to set the scale for three light years or so."

Patterson nodded his agreement to Ensign Fletcher, then turned back in the direction of the holo table just in time to see the display reformat itself per the Guardian's recommendation. Sol itself was now depicted as a yellowish-white pinpoint of light on one side of the table. On such a large scale, the entire solar system out to the far edge of the Oort cloud now reached only halfway across the display, with no other astronomical features of any significance beyond. After a momentary delay (almost certainly for dramatic effect, Patterson assumed), eight red diamond icons appeared within the dark area beyond the system's outer boundary, each one bearing the two-letter code indicating the type of enemy vessel it represented: one destroyer (DG), one cruiser (CG), and six battleships (BB). As usual, the *Navajo's* AI provided some additional information in small text blocks adjacent to each contact, including their current speed as well an estimated time to reach a point within weapons range of the Earth.

"Are you able to see this as well, Admiral Sexton?" Patterson asked.

"I'm sure it doesn't have quite the impact as it does on the holo table," Sexton replied, "but yes, I see it. I assume that these are the remaining Resistance ships from Location Crossbow. Is this some sort of an estimate, or an actual, real-time display of their positions?"

"Really, Admiral Sexton, do you think I would bother offering you an *estimate*?" Griffin asked, seemingly offended by the implication. "Of course it's a real-time display. And, as a continued example of our good faith, I will continue providing you with access to this information until the Resistance ships are no longer a threat. Note that this data feed will only display ships currently in hyperspace. Ironically, it was the Sajeth

Collective's repeated forays in and around the Sol System that allowed me to develop this tracking technique."

"Wait, you're telling us that you somehow *invented* this yourself?" Patterson asked, incredulous.

"My, you two are full of implied barbs today, aren't you? Is it such a surprise that I would be capable of such a thing?"

"Oh, please. If we're going to work together effectively, you've got to develop a little thicker skin than that. Hell yes, it's a surprise," he laughed. "That's a monumental scientific achievement, and it's a surprise that anyone would be capable of such a thing, particularly on your own."

"Ah, well, the truth is that I did have some help … in a manner of speaking. There has been a significant amount of research done on this topic within the Alliance. Their basic technique was sound, but they had difficulty overcoming some problems with signal processing and ultimately abandoned the effort."

"And, what … you just happened to have plenty of time on your hands to work through the problem yourself?"

"As I said, your scientists were already working on something similar by applying existing hyperspace communications technology."

"You stole their work, didn't you?" Patterson asked with triumphant smile.

"I did nothing of the sort. I merely monitored some of their ongoing tests. But I will admit to gaining valuable insight based on some of the emissions I detected. Besides, it can hardly be called 'stealing' since their work is based on technology I provided in the first place," he scoffed, dismissing the accusation with a wave of his hand. "As I mentioned, Sajeth Collective ships have been making incursions in and around the Sol system for months. Some of the data I gathered while attempting to monitor their vessels proved invaluable in perfecting the technique I'm sharing with you today. Bear in mind that it is a relatively short-range system — accurate out to only ten light years or so. Tracking ships in hyperspace over larger distances requires a much more sophisticated approach. Unfortunately, information regarding that particular topic is restricted to members of the Pelaran Alliance with appropriate security clearances. I'm sure you two, of all people, can appreciate that."

"We certainly do, and we thank you for access to this information," Patterson said. "I'm sure it will be of tremendous help in placing our ships to defend the planet. Returning now to my original question … will you provide us with some assurance that you will remain clear of active combat and refrain from attacking friendly vessels?"

The Guardian paused for a moment, rubbing his chin thoughtfully. "Those do sound like reasonable requests, Admiral, and I understand your concerns, so how about this … I will endeavor to remain clear of active combat inasmuch as doing so will not prevent me from accomplishing elements of my own mission. I take full responsibility for my own safety if I do enter a live fire zone, and will hold your forces blameless for any damage I might suffer as a result of doing so. This includes fire from all TFC sources as well as any vessels you choose to designate as friendly. And, yes, I will make every effort to avoid destroying any of these quote, unquote 'friendly' ships you mention, although before all of this is over, I doubt you will ever again make the mistake of placing any Sajeth Collective vessels into that category. Is that an acceptable compromise position, sir?"

"Short of a commitment to actively participate in our defense of the planet, yes, I suppose it is. Thank you," Patterson replied.

"Very good," the Guardian chuckled, shaking his head in mock admonishment. "I mean this is a compliment, of course, but it's stunning to me how similar you Humans are to the Makers — the Pelarans, that is. You both seem to have an abiding love of all things legalistic."

"I'm not sure I can agree with you there," Sexton replied. "Perhaps we both just have a certain level of, shall we say, *discomfort*, with ambiguous situations. Spelling things out in such precise terms provides us with at least the illusion that events will unfold in a predictable manner."

"What you're describing is an attempt to impose order on a naturally chaotic universe that has no regard whatsoever for your comfort. So, yes, 'illusion' is precisely the word I would use," the Guardian smiled. "On a related subject, I truly hope that the situation you find yourselves in today provides the two of you with some additional perspective regarding the existential dangers faced by your world. As I have said many times, Earth need not stand alone against these threats."

"Our opinions matter very little in the grand scheme of things," Sexton replied. "And if we do have as much in common with the Pelarans as you say, it surprises me that you would expect our species to be comfortable with forfeiting so much of our sovereignty, particularly just as we begin taking our first steps away from home."

"Ah, there's that word 'comfort' again. Gentlemen, please ask yourselves how many worthwhile endeavors from Earth's history — be they scientific discoveries, great voyages of exploration, or the formation of grand alliances to conquer the forces of tyranny and oppression — were accomplished from a position of *comfort*?" the Guardian asked, smiling triumphantly as if he had just provided incontrovertible proof in support of his argument. "As to your good opinions, I believe that if the two of you voiced your public support of Earth's entrance into the Alliance, it would have a profound impact on a great many of your people."

"I'm sure you can appreciate that most of Earth's nations have a long tradition of civilian control over military forces. That implies that, as officers, we are not at liberty to voice our personal opinions on political matters. Don't get me wrong, there are a great many who have done exactly that, but it was and still is highly inappropriate for us to do so. Our role is to act as servants ... instruments, if you will, of public policy, rather than its creators."

"Besides," Patterson added, "all of this is academic anyway if we don't manage to survive what happens over the next few days."

"Take heart, Admiral," the Guardian said facetiously. "All of the simulations I have put together thus far indicate that you have a reasonable chance of prevailing in the coming battle. But make no mistake … this is only the beginning."

Chapter 17

TFS Theseus, Location Dagger
(3.3 light years from Earth)

"Transition complete, Captain. Range to our *Sherpa*, one zero kilometers. Adjusting course and speed for recovery," Ensign Fisher reported from the Helm console. "We'll have them aboard in approximately five eight seconds."

"The faster the better, Ensign," Prescott replied. "At your first opportunity, plot a C-Jump to Location Willow."

"Aye, sir, already entered."

At the Science and Engineering console, Lieutenant Lee had been closely monitoring every aspect of Marine 11's departure from the *Keturah*. Having worked feverishly to ensure that the shuttle was in the optimal position to evacuate the Marines and their cargo of Wek survivors, he now found himself with nothing remaining to do but simply watch and wait as *Theseus* maneuvered to place herself between his brother's team and the distant enemy battleships.

My brother's team, he scolded himself. *There are ten other lives at risk aboard that shuttle, but when it comes down to it, my brother's life is really the only one I'm worried about.*

In a desperate attempt to pass the remaining seconds as quickly as possible, Lee allowed his mind to reflect momentarily on the nature of Human compassion — on the assertion that all Human life is endowed with fundamental value … equality … importance. He wasn't entirely sure that he had ever taken the time to consider the topic in quite this manner before. Now, however, with his brother facing imminent danger, it struck him as strange how most of us seem to agree to such lofty notions from an intellectual standpoint, even though they in no way reflect what is truly in our hearts. Once our emotions are taken into account, it simply isn't possible to assign the same level of importance to *all* Human lives as we do to those with which we have a personal connection. Was this a hypocrisy, or evidence that such complex concepts are not so easily distilled down to the bite-sized statements often seen in governmental documents and corporate vision statements?

In his peripheral vision, Lee noticed a flashing icon indicating that an urgent, text-only message had been routed to his console. It was uncommon for "private" messages of any sort to be delivered to Fleet personnel during their duty hours. But for those rare instances requiring that urgent information reach specific crewmembers, the comm system onboard retained the capability to route messages directly to their intended recipients in real-time. Desperate to pass the remaining seconds until *Theseus* could depart the area with Rescue 11's shuttle safely secured within the confines of her hangar bay, Lee tapped the message icon. In an open section of his console's screen, a window opened to display the following message:

To: Lee, Jayston (Lieutenant, Junior Grade, TFC)
From: Lee, Jackson (First Lieutenant (Marines), TFC)
Subject: Just in Case

Theseus just transitioned in to pick us up, but even though I know you're just a few seconds away from bringing our shuttle aboard, I just got the strangest feeling that this might be my last chance to talk to you. I think I understand now what Nanna meant when she talked about someone "pointing the bones" at her. Anyway, I obviously don't have much time and don't know what to say anyway, but if something happens, please tell Mum and Dad that I never had to hurt anyone in my job, and I was doing my best to save lives on my last mission rather than take them. That should please them. Make sure they understand that we both love what we do and wouldn't change a thing if we had it all to do over again.

Love all three of you heaps and I'll see you in the Dreamtime,
Jackson

The message was so unlike anything he had ever heard Jackson say that it caused an involuntary chill to run down the length of his spine. Squirming uncomfortably in his seat as he fought to overcome the empty, sick feeling that had materialized in the pit of his stomach, Jayston realized with inexplicable certainty that he would never see his twin brother again.

***

It had taken the *Zhelov* and *Serapion* a few moments to alter their relative positions slightly in order to ensure that as many of their starboard beam emitters as possible would bear on their third and final target. Their captains had been given explicit orders from Commodore Sarafi that they were to ensure the complete destruction of all three of the disabled Resistance ships — and to such an extent that there would be little chance of any useful materiel or technology being recovered by the Terrans. Accordingly, several minutes' worth of uninterrupted energy weapons fire from the two enormous battleships had reduced both the *Baldev* and the *Babayev* to a pair of rapidly expanding debris fields. Now it was the *Keturah's* turn.

With the methodical attacks being handled almost exclusively by the two warships' AIs, their bridge crews simply monitored the rate of progress while making the necessary preparations for their imminent departure for Terra. As the commodore had instructed, neither vessel had engaged the Human warship that had boldly (albeit foolishly) chosen to attack their formation shortly after they had opened fire on the *Baldev* and the *Babayev*. Both captains did notice, however, that once the Human warship had broken off its attack, it had transitioned to a location just beyond the *Keturah*. Unsure of the reasons behind this suspicious behavior, both battleships had commenced a high-resolution scan of the area around the damaged BD cruiser. Within seconds, their scans revealed the presence of a small, previously undetected spacecraft that appeared to be preparing for a rendezvous with the Human warship. Additional analysis by *Serapion's* AI also revealed an open external access hatch, amidships on the *Keturah's* port side.

Both the letter and the spirit of Commodore Sarafi's orders were intended to prevent the Humans from acquiring valuable intelligence and technology that could be used against the Sajeth Collective. Based on the evidence now in hand, both AIs calculated a high probability that the crew of the small Terran spacecraft had indeed been aboard the *Keturah* — most likely engaged in precisely the type of operation they had been ordered to prevent. With cold objectivity, the AIs immediately recommended to their respective crews that the small spacecraft be destroyed before it had the opportunity to reach the larger Human warship.

Since Sajeth Collective vessels had never before encountered a *Sherpa* ASV, the small ship's capabilities — hyperdrive, weapons, shielding, etc. — were entirely unknown to them. Accordingly, to ensure the small spacecraft's complete and immediate destruction, and with limited time remaining before it reached the Human destroyer, a total of forty-seven beam emitters targeted the small ship and fired simultaneously. At the same instant, the larger attack on the *Keturah* itself got underway, as both battleships opened up with all of their remaining energy weapons that had a direct line of sight to the stricken cruiser.

With no shielding whatsoever and only the minimal hull thickness required for all commercial spacecraft, the *Sherpa* had little hope of escape as the first wave of energy bolts slammed into its aft port quarter. Occurring far too quickly to be seen with the naked eye, the shuttle had first been enveloped in what appeared to be a single stream of coursing, orange-colored energy. Microseconds later, the ship's hull at the center of each beam's point of impact reached four thousand kelvins — seventy percent of the average temperature at Sol's surface — before flash boiling then briefly vaporizing into a cloud of metallic gas.

Once stripped of the scant protection offered by the ship's thin hull, the internal components and living occupants inside succumbed instantaneously to the massive quantities of energy still streaming in from the two distant battleships. Even the tough armor of the Marines' EVA suits delayed their demise by only a few additional milliseconds. In the end, none of the shuttle's passengers even had time to realize that they were under attack as, only a fraction of second after the *Zhelov* and *Serapion* had opened fire, the *Sherpa* simply ceased to exist.

In concert with one another, the AIs aboard each Resistance battleship assessed a better than fifty percent chance that significant intelligence information had already been transmitted from the Human shuttle back to its accompanying warship. After a brief discussion on the merits of pressing their attack, however, both captains determined that their orders would best be accomplished by completing the destruction of the *Keturah*, then departing the area immediately to join the remainder of their fleet for the attack on Terra.

This decision made, both ships resumed their grim work in earnest, completely ignoring the Human warship nearby. The dark, silent vacuum of space was once again pierced by thousands of energy weapons flashes punctuated by secondary explosions as the two massive battleships continued the process of grinding the once-proud BD cruiser to pieces.

***

Silence also permeated *Theseus'* bridge as the crew struggled to come to grips with what had just transpired. They had been tantalizingly close to recovering Rescue 11 — so close in fact that some of the enemy battleships' final energy weapons bolts intended for the shuttle had been deflected by the destroyer's shields. As officers in positions requiring them to place others in harm's way are wont to do, Prescott had begun the process of reexamining the series of decisions and events that had led them to this point well before the *Sherpa* had been destroyed. There had been less than twenty seconds remaining before the shuttle and its Marines would have reached the relative safety of *Theseus'* hangar bay, and it was all too easy to assume that some decision more quickly communicated, some action more efficiently executed, might have made the difference. In spite of this, Prescott felt strangely at peace. As far as he could tell, every decision had been the right one — given the information they had at the time. Every action had been crisply and professionally executed. It simply had not been enough in this case. Now, with only *Theseus* and the two enemy battleships remaining near Location Dagger, there was nothing left for them to do but depart for their rendezvous with the *Hadeon*.

"Helm, execute your C-Jump to Location Willow," Prescott ordered quietly.

"Aye, sir," Fisher responded in the same hushed, mechanical tone.

Prescott made eye contact with his XO, nodding first in the direction of Lieutenant Lee then towards the aft entrance to the bridge. Reynolds nodded her understanding, then stood and walked the short distance to the Science and Engineering console, placing her hand softly on the young Lieutenant's shoulder. Lee jumped involuntarily at her touch, clearly not even sensing her approach.

"C-Jumping in 3 ... 2 ... 1 ..." Ensign Fisher announced in the background.

"Come on, Jayston," Reynolds said, squeezing his shoulder reassuringly as his replacement from the standby crew emerged from the lounge nearby.

Lee drew in a deep breath to steady himself, then stood and turned in the direction of the exit, Commander Reynolds' left hand resting on his lower back to offer comfort and support as she slowly escorted him off the bridge. As he approached the captain's command chair, Prescott stood, nodding respectfully at the young lieutenant as he passed. In his peripheral vision, Lee noticed that all of the other officers on the bridge were standing as well. Unsure what, if anything, he should say, he stopped momentarily and turned back to offer the room a weak smile.

"Thank you," he said, mouthing the words more than actually saying them aloud. As he turned back in the direction of the door, he stopped again and looked back at Captain Prescott. "What they were doing was important, wasn't it, sir? I mean ... it *mattered*," he said with tears in his eyes.

"You're damn right it did," Prescott replied without hesitation. "And every member of their team did as well: Mario Rojas, Private; Sheila Barks, Private First Class; Vincente Vega, Private First Class; Priya Bakshi, Corporal; Elon Dyer, Corporal; Eduard Kazan, Staff

Sergeant; Jackson Lee, First Lieutenant. They *all* mattered, as did the four Wek survivors they gave their lives trying to save. Your brother knew it better than any of us. He could have easily called it quits and headed back to the ship without making the effort to get them out, but he knew that would have left them almost no chance of rescue. Instead, he made the tough call that put himself and his team at risk because that's what Marines do ... that's what *heroes* do."

"Thank you, sir," Lee said, nodding gratefully.

"Go and get some rest, Lieutenant. We'll talk more later."

As Commander Reynolds followed Lee off the bridge, she looked back at Prescott and nodded respectfully.

"Alright, Ensign Fisher," Prescott said after the two of them had left the room, "status, please."

"Transition complete, Captain. All systems in the green. The ship remains at General Quarters for combat ops and ready to C-Jump. C-Jump range 100.6 light years and stable. Sublight engines are online, we are free to maneuver."

"Very good. We've been at General Quarters for quite some time," he said. "It's time we started working on getting everyone fed and rested. Tactical?"

"No enemy contacts, sir," Lieutenant Lau replied. "Range back to *Zhelov* and *Serapion,* approximately five light hours. Range to the *Hadeon,* just over one hundred thousand kilometers. Also, I'm only seeing two niner of the three one remaining fighters that departed Location Dagger just before we did."

"Understood. I'm sure we'll hear from them shortly. They're most likely just rotating more of their ships back to the carriers," Prescott replied. "AI, set Condition 3. All departments are to maintain general wartime manning and readiness."

"Securing from General Quarters for combat operations. Condition 3 set," the AI's synthetic female voice acknowledged.

"Captain, Commander Waffer is hailing us," Dubashi announced.

"Put him through, please," Prescott replied, then paused momentarily to allow the comm channel to be established before continuing. "Go ahead, Commander."

"Just checking in, sir," Waffer said. "I also wanted to let you know that Captain Davis aboard the *Navajo* had us send a two-ship formation back to Location Dagger to observe the departure of the two battleships."

"I assume they will be remaining in hyperspace then?"

"That's affirmative, sir. Captain Davis says the AI has pretty much worked out how to determine a ship's direction of flight when it transitions out of the area."

"Right, that's how they found the secondary rally point so quickly," Prescott responded, swearing silently for not thinking to issue the same order himself.

"Other than that, can you tell me what the plan is from here?" Waffer asked.

"Your guess is as good as mine at the moment. If possible, I'd like you to maintain a full squadron here at Willow until we get a read on what the Flag wants us to do with the *Hadeon*. Otherwise, continue to rotate your ships back to base as needed."

"Will do, Captain. Badger 2 out."

Graca, Dru Tinari - Ancestral Home of the Dynastic House of Naftur
(Twenty-eight years earlier — 494.7 light years from Earth)

"I never said or even implied that I was disappointed in you, my son. And if I were, that would clearly be due to a fundamental lack of vision and sound judgment on my part, not any fault of yours. What I said is that I believe you are making a mistake," Javir Naftur said. The statement had been delivered with a pleasant smile, but it was clear that his words were heartfelt and of the greatest personal importance. "In my long lifetime, I have never seen a better opportunity for Graca to free itself of this loathsome Collective and declare that we are a free and independent world once more — as is our birthright. This simply will not happen without your leadership."

Rugali Naftur stood with his back to his father, staring out of the enormous, floor-to-ceiling windows making up the entire outside wall of their home's "observation room." Situated atop a series of low hills that were the closest thing this region had to a mountain range, Dru Tinari had been constructed just over one hundred meters above the sweeping plains that stretched to the horizon in every direction. Compared to a similar vista on Earth, Graca's twenty percent larger planetary diameter provided an even more dramatic view. On a clear day like this one, the horizon was nearly fifty kilometers away, sometimes more when atmospheric conditions were ideal. Rugali had spent countless hours in this room as a child simply watching the wildlife on the plains below — now a part of the expansive Kalek Expanse Conservation Zone. At just over one million square kilometers, the reserve was nearly three times as large as the Kavango-Zambezi Conservation Area in Africa, its closest analog on Earth.

Although his eyes were no longer as keen as they had been during his youth, Rugali still took note of a large herd of Banea, doubtless over a thousand strong, moving slowly off to the south. Taking in a deep breath and pausing to appreciate the view once more, he considered how best to respond in a decisive yet respectful manner. He had, after all, heard all of these arguments many times before, and not just from his father.

Graca was arguably the most prosperous and easily the most powerful member of the Sajeth Collective, and always had been, but it was also the most isolated. Just as it had originally been with Earth, Graca's relative isolation had provided a degree of protection during the Wek species' technological development, allowing them to mature and advance with little to no external interference. Unfortunately, well before any star system in the Orion Spur had ever even heard of the Pelaran Alliance, there had still been regional threats that had required their attention. As was often the case, Graca's prosperity had attracted the greedy attention of two of their slightly more advanced neighbors, shortly after they had acquired the capability to travel between the stars for the first time. And although the Wek people had never been ones to shrink from a fight, when necessary, it had quickly become clear that they simply did not have the resources required to continue their development as an interstellar species while at the same time fighting a perpetual war to maintain their sovereignty.

When first courted for membership in the Sajeth Collective, opponents had argued that Graca's isolation made such alliances both unnecessary and impractical. After all, their nearest allies might take years to offer any meaningful assistance, when needed. Ironically, it had been the persistent threat of attack from their two aggressive neighbors that had finally pushed Graca into alignment with the Collective — neighbors that would ultimately join the alliance themselves. The names of these two worlds: Damara and Lesheera.

"You honor me with your confidence," Rugali said, turning to look his father in the eyes, "but my sense is that the time has not yet arrived when our people are truly ready to stand on their own once more. Indeed, we seem to learn day by day that our galaxy is far more dangerous than we once naively believed. You once believed strongly in the wisdom of sharing the burden of defending our world with others. Why is this no longer the case?"

"Humph," Javir growled, "I have simply come to understand that what I believed in was an ideal — an unattainable goal wherein worlds of roughly equivalent strength of will, arms, and above all integrity work together to ensure one another's collective security. While we might have been closer to that ideal early on in our association with the Sajeth Collective, it grows less so with every passing year. Now, it is our fleet that ensures their safety, while Graca's resources are systematically squandered by faceless Damaran bureaucrats — funneled, without our consent, to our so-called allies with little or no benefit accruing to our own people. I ask you, Rugali, how is the current state of affairs any different than being occupied by a foreign power?"

Rugali stared at his father for a moment, weighing his words carefully before continuing. "There is undeniable truth in what you say, but have you fully considered the likely chain of events we would be putting into motion were we to withdraw from the Collective? As you say, the very structure of the organization depends heavily upon our fleet. Without it, they would be relegated to something more akin to a trade association than a true collective security alliance. I have seen an intelligence analysis that attempted to model just such a scenario. It predicted that the six remaining worlds would be engaged in open warfare with one another within eighteen months of our departure. Do you believe we are prepared to deal with the regional instability that would inevitably result? We are also just beginning to understand the threat posed by the Pelaran Alliance, the scope of which appears to dwarf anything we have ever faced in the past. Surely, now is not the time for a return to the inward-looking, isolationist views that dominated our early years as a space-faring world."

"*No,*" Javir replied emphatically, "it certainly is not. What I am telling you is that, for an alliance to have lasting value for *all* of its members, each must have similar goals, values, and common societal threads binding one to another. The benefits of the alliance must accrue to each in a mutual and roughly equivalent manner. This also implies that each member must *contribute* equally in order to receive said benefits. Nothing could be further from the truth in the Sajeth Collective where, unfortunately, it is Graca that contributes the most and receives the least benefit in return. You know all of this to be true, Rugali, so why do you feel compelled to resist taking your rightful place in the leadership of our world?"

"Please, Father. You need never doubt my esteem and love for you, but you now tread perilously close to foolish talk of 'destiny.'"

"As well I should, Rugali. Do not be so quick to dismiss such notions, for doing so in no way grants you the mantle of enlightenment that you seem to believe it does," he scolded. "We can disagree on the semantics of the word if you like, but one need only study the history of our world — or any other, for that matter — to find examples where combinations of timing and circumstance conspire to place an individual in a truly unique position."

"'Conspire' is an interesting word choice in this case, is it not?" Rugali replied with a raised eyebrow.

"Sarcasm is a form of humor well below your station, my son," his father replied, then continued, undeterred. "We have offers of coalition in hand from five of the seven houses of Graca, and it is clear that the other two will close ranks soon enough if you would but agree to put yourself forward as prince regent."

"Prince regent? So now we discuss not only our withdrawal from the long-standing alliance that has helped ensure the safety of our world for generations, but also a return to a primitive, regressive system of governing our people."

"Please do not act as if you can mask your true feelings on this subject from me, Rugali. I know, for example, that neither you, nor the vast majority of our people believe that our membership in the Sajeth Collective serves to enhance Graca's safety and security in any way. If anything, *we* ensure the security of the other six member worlds while their incessant saber-rattling often puts ours at unnecessary risk. Furthermore, as you know, the concept of dynastic, monarchial rule has always been fundamental to the fabric of our society. Many argue that it is literally encoded in our genetic makeup. As you say, however, a true monarchy has its drawbacks, and the other houses favor the establishment of a system more akin to a 'crowned republic,' wherein the monarch's role is more ceremonial in nature. Do not misunderstand me, a Gracan king would still wield enormous political influence, serving as the commander-in-chief of all of our armed forces as well as casting tie-breaking votes in Parliament. Personally, I believe that the simple act of reestablishing Wek 'home rule' is far more important than the practical aspects of governing. The representatives we have sent to the Governing Council on Damara for all these years have done little more than allow us to offer our *opinion* on how our world should be governed. The Wek people need a Wek leader, Rugali, and you are their clear choice."

"As to that, I would think that there are any number of others who would be better suited to the role," his son said absently, turning once again to stare out across the plains below. "Besides, the title of 'prince regent' implies that it should be *you* who takes up reins of power, not I."

"Well," Javir chuckled, "there is some truth in that statement … and it is also true that I cannot help but envy the respect and admiration you have earned for yourself. At the same time, however, I could not be more proud of the leader you have become. Your military and civil service accomplishments are widely known, your integrity is beyond reproach, and you are easily the most recognizable public figure on Graca. It is largely because of this that House Naftur alone has the support required to reestablish the crown."

"You did not answer my implied question, Father. Why not you?"

"Simply put, I am far too old and not seen as the compelling choice that you are. The other houses also believe that having you ascend to power as prince regent is politically more desirable than immediately naming a new king. You would rule in my stead and by my choice, but I would not officially abdicate the crown until the timing was considered more appropriate."

"I see," Rugali sighed, turning back to his father with a somber expression.

"Do you indeed?" Javir asked after a long silence. "And is that all you have to say on the subject?"

"For the moment, yes," his son replied, a thin smile forming at the corners of his mouth, "but you have my word that I will give serious consideration to all that you have told me. If you truly believe in the concept of 'destiny' as you say you do, however, then you must understand if I ultimately decide that the time has not yet arrived for this to come to pass."

"I will respect your decision, of course, but I must say that I cannot imagine the timing ever being better than it is now."

"That may be true from a political standpoint, Father, but my heart tells me that the reasons for such a momentous change should be obvious to such an extent that our people will naturally understand and accept that it is the right choice — *their choice*, not one that was in any way imposed upon them."

"Your faith in our people is commendable — perhaps misplaced in some ways — but commendable nonetheless. You know my feelings on this matter, so I will say no more. When you do feel that the time is come, however, I pray that you will act swiftly and decisively, and that you will hear the whispers of your ancestors so that you may know exactly what you must do."

***

Admiral Naftur awoke with a start, forcing himself to breathe deeply while the sedative-induced haze cleared from his mind like fog lifting from the plains surrounding Dru Tinari at the beginning of a new day. Under the circumstances, it took him a few moments to remember that he was in the medical bay aboard the Human destroyer *Theseus* — then a few more for the events of the past few days to fall back into place. Even as his thoughts began to coalesce and organize themselves, he had the distinct impression that, somehow, his entire perspective had changed. Pressing the button to call the nurse, he first sipped, then drank greedily from the stainless steel cup of water on the table beside his bed.

"Ah, good morning, Admiral," the duty nurse said warmly as she entered the room. Without further comment, she immediately set about preparing to help the Wek officer out of bed for the first time since shortly after his surgery.

"How long was I asleep?" he asked, speaking slowly so that the AI had at least some hope of properly translating his dry, raspy voice.

"I wasn't on duty at the time," she replied, glancing at her tablet, "but it looks like it has been just over thirty-six hours since they brought you back from your brief visit to the bridge."

"Expletive," the AI growled emphatically from the room's ceiling speakers using an apparently censored facsimile of Naftur's own voice. Although it could not locate a database entry to provide a precise, literal translation of the Wek word the admiral had used, the AI had little difficulty guessing its intent from context alone. "I am needed back on the bridge immediately," Naftur urged, "and I would prefer to be in uniform if you would be so kind as to help me —"

"Really?" Nenir Turlaka interrupted from the doorway, "I never would have guessed." Her words were delivered in a tone that left little doubt that she was still acting in her capacity as a physician rather than as a diplomat. "And what makes you think you are ready to just leap out of bed and resume your duties?"

Irritating though it was, Naftur was well aware of the necessity of convincing his doctors that he was both mentally and physically capable of leaving the medical bay and returning to duty. He was also aware that failing to do so might well result in further confinement — under sedation, if necessary. With the renewed sense of purpose that seemed to be growing of its own accord in the back of his mind, he knew with absolute certainty that he could not afford to waste any additional time convalescing in a hospital bed.

"I am actually feeling surprisingly well, Doctor Turlaka," he said, swinging his feet off the side of the bed.

"I am sure you do. Doctor Chen and I do good work," she said, taking the offered tablet from the duty nurse. "We have been keeping a very close eye on the repairs we made to your aorta, and I am happy to report that we have been very pleased by your progress. Our hospitals on Graca have access to some equipment that is perhaps a bit more advanced than what the Humans have, but their gene-based therapies are far better than ours … certainly beyond anything I would have expected them to have at this stage. I am sure that you are uninterested in hearing the specifics, but we were able to genetically encode a group of your own cells to essentially regenerate much of the damaged tissue in your chest — and at an astoundingly accelerated rate. That process is still ongoing, of course, but I believe it is accurate to say that the crisis has now passed."

"I am pleased to hear it. So I am cleared for duty, then?" Naftur asked, smiling optimistically.

"We will *see*," she said, narrowing her eyes. "If everything checks out this morning, I will allow you to resume some light duties, but only for short periods of time. Understood?"

"Of course, Doctor," he replied soothingly.

"Mm-hmm. Let the nurse get you disconnected from everything and help you freshen up a bit, then I will look you over. Keep in mind that *you have been shot*, Rugali Naftur, and if you do not wish to find yourself back in surgery — or worse," she said, pausing meaningfully, "you will follow your doctors' instructions to the letter."

"I will endeavor to be a model patient," Naftur replied, testing his weight on his legs for the first time since his surgery. Gratified to be back on his feet, he inhaled deeply, expanding his massive chest and stretching to his full height of just over two meters.

Doctor Turlaka had been preoccupied entering information on her patient's chart, but now looked up into Naftur's eyes for the first time. What she saw there touched her emotionally, and in an almost primal way that she was certain she had never experienced before. Her practiced, authoritarian bedside manner evaporated in an instant. Without another word, she closed her eyes and bowed her head in a manner that, although she had never done so before, felt completely natural — spontaneous — *instinctive*.

Chapter 18

TFS Navajo, Earth-Sun Lagrange Point 2
(0007 UTC - Combat Information Center - 1.5×10^6 km from Earth)

"At this point, the fact that your shields may not be fully operational is of little consequence, Captain," Admiral Patterson stated flatly, struggling to avoid losing his temper with the two officers on his view screen. "Both of you are fully aware of what happened to Captain Abrams' destroyer force at Location Crossbow. Every one of his ships were shield-equipped, but the shields were largely ineffective against the Resistance battleships' heavy guns. I'm confident we will soon learn why that was the case, but it won't be today ... and certainly not within the —" Patterson paused to glance at a different screen, "less than eleven hours we have remaining before we come under attack. This is not a matter of meeting some arbitrary production schedule, gentlemen. We still have only four cruisers in space, along with three carriers, perhaps eight available destroyers, and a handful of frigates. Look, I have worked with both of you before and know you both to be competent, professional naval officers. So you tell me, does the force I just described sound in any way sufficient to deal with as many as eight Resistance battleships as well as this vague threat of some sort of biological attack?"

"No, Admiral," both men replied in unison.

"I was fine with the original decision to launch the first four cruisers out of the Yucca Mountain Shipyard

— again, based on the original configuration with no C-Drive and no shields — while delaying the ships at Pine Gap and Yamantau Mountain for upgrades. But we made that decision based on an aggressive schedule that the two of you assured the Admiralty staff you could meet. You said that if we allowed you to delay three of the four cruisers at each location, you could instead deliver one cruiser each with all of the latest upgrades installed. Now by my count, if you had met that schedule, I would have a total of six *Navajo*-class cruisers in space — two of them presumably with working shield systems — and we wouldn't be having this conversation right now. Correct?"

"Yes, Admiral," both men replied again, feeling very much like first year midshipmen at this point, but also keenly aware that now was not the time to offer anything that sounded even vaguely like an excuse for the delay.

"Alright, then, so let's hear it. When can I expect to see those additional cruisers making their initial climbs to orbit?"

Both men naturally paused for a moment to see if the other would speak first, but it was Captain Marko Budarin, Facility Commander of the Yamantau Mountain Shipyard facility in southern Russia, who rose to the challenge.

"Admiral Patterson," he began carefully, "holding the remaining *Navajo*-class cruisers in port for upgrades was, as you know, a calculated risk. But —" he paused, raising both hands placatingly to head off Patterson's anticipated objection, "as is often the case with such complex projects, there were several unforeseen difficulties that conspired to delay their launch.

Fortunately, we now have the *Cossack* at Yamantau as well as the *Koori* at Pine Gap preparing to launch within the hour."

"I am pleased to hear it. That should have happened a week ago, of course, but under the circumstances, late is most definitely better than never."

"If I may return to the subject of their shields for a moment, sir, I didn't mean to give you the impression that the shields are not operational. They will certainly work as well as those installed on the *Theseus*-class destroyers, but they still suffer from the same vulnerabilities as well."

"As I alluded to earlier, that's largely irrelevant at this point," Patterson interrupted. "We need them up here immediately, regardless of the state of their shield systems."

"Yes, sir, I understand," Budarin persisted. "If you will allow me, however, to address your point about finding out why the shields were ineffective against the *Rusalovs'* heavy guns, I believe I have an answer for you."

"Make it quick, Captain, but yes, please proceed."

"Thank you, sir. As you know, most of the Science and Engineering Directorate's shield development work was accomplished on site here at Yamantau. Within an hour of their receiving performance data from the shield failures at Location Crossbow, I had their team lead knocking on my door insisting that he be allowed direct access to the *Cossack's* AIs. He said they had a theory about why the shields had failed to deflect the large projectiles and thought they might be able to implement a fix."

"Captain Budarin," Patterson said, shaking his head, "you, of all people, fully understand how overly optimistic our engineers can be when it comes to implementing a so-called 'quick fix.'"

"Very much so, sir, but they showed me their data, and it did look like something that could be fixed pretty quickly with a software change. The problem with the large projectiles is that the AI was underestimating their kinetic energy due to their relatively low speed compared to other ordinance — our small penetrator rounds, for example. The rounds from our railguns travel at roughly six times the velocity that the *Rusalovs'* shells achieve. For the same size projectile, that means ours are carrying thirty-six times the energy that theirs are. The problem is that the *Rusalovs'* shells have a mass of around eight hundred kilograms. That's nearly double that of our cruisers' main guns or sixteen times that of our standard railgun mounts. Long story short, our designers simply did not anticipate our shields encountering any high-velocity projectiles with that much mass, so they were consistently underestimating the energy required to deflect them."

Patterson drew in a deep breath and considered how best to respond. TFC was in the business of combining military operations and space flight — two Human endeavors where the loss of Human life had always been expected to some degree. He also knew that the men and women who were designing and building Fleet's warships were the best and the brightest engineers and scientists that Earth had to offer. On a daily basis, they performed technological miracles that would have been considered impossible just ten years earlier — and on a schedule that often bordered on the absurd. Still, the idea of such losses due to what amounted to a simple oversight was difficult for the old admiral to accept.

"This seemingly small mistake has cost us six ships thus far. That's over nineteen hundred lives lost — not to mention the fact that our destroyers might well have been able to prevent the attack on Earth altogether had their shields functioned properly," Patterson said, pausing again to allow the gravity of his words to fully register with both captains. "While we cannot allow ourselves to slip into the mode of assigning blame, we absolutely must find a way to learn from this mistake and hopefully make it less likely that something like this will ever happen again … assuming any of us survive long enough to do so, that is."

Both men nodded solemnly, realizing that there was nothing further to be said on the subject.

"So, Captain Budarin," Patterson continued, "I assume you are telling me all of this because you believe the shield development team may be able to implement their fix before the Resistance ships arrive?"

"Yes, Admiral. It would, of course, apply only to the *Cossack* for now. The *Koori* will still have essentially the same configuration as the *Theseus*-class destroyers."

"And is there a risk of the *Cossack* not making it into space at all if we allow them to proceed?"

"Unfortunately, yes. The team has completed their simulations and believe the fix will work, but integrating it into the ship's gravitic system will require the AI to be taken offline temporarily."

"Oh, come on, Marko, that's easily a twelve-hour procedure, and once the AI is offline, it's an all-or-nothing proposition. They will either finish on time, or they won't — in which case she'll still be sitting in her berth during the battle, just like the other three *Navajo*-class cruisers at your shipyard. So why are we wasting time talking about this?"

"I know, I know, sir," Budarin replied apologetically. "Under normal circumstances I wouldn't have even mentioned it, but they insist they can get it done in time to launch and have her in position to meet the Resistance battleships."

Patterson glanced at the holographic table, noting the positions of the two groups of enemy ships converging inexorably on the Earth. "If they're wrong, the absence of that one ship, with or without shields, could tip the balance against us," he said, half to himself.

"Yes, sir. But if they're right, her presence alone could well prove decisive."

"It sounds to me as if you are recommending that we take the risk, Captain. And are you literally willing to bet *all* Human life on the outcome?"

Budarin swallowed hard, feeling the truly staggering implications of the decision resting temporarily on his shoulders alone. "I do not presume to comprehend the full scope of the situation as you do, Admiral Patterson, but yes, under the circumstances, I believe the potential benefits outweigh the risks."

Patterson stared intently at both officers as his mind ran through a long series of possible scenarios — each one tending to sway him in one direction or the other. In the end, however, his mental "pro and con" list remained frustratingly well-balanced.

"Very well," he sighed. "Please make it abundantly clear to everyone involved exactly what's at stake. Also make sure they know that the words 'there's not a moment to be lost' have never been more applicable. I'll expect to see the *Koori* in orbit within the hour and the *Cossack* no later than 1000Z."

"Aye, sir," both men replied.

TFS Theseus, Location Willow
(3.3 light years from Earth)

"Ah, good timing, sir," Reynolds said as Prescott arrived back on the bridge after seven hours of blessed sleep. "Admiral Naftur is on his way up."

Since the departure of *Zhelov* and *Serapion,* for Earth, *Theseus* had received no new orders from the Flag other than keeping an eye on the original Resistance rally point for additional arrivals while ensuring that their newfound ally, the *Hadeon,* continued to hold her position at Location Willow. On the plus side, the full day of downtime had allowed her exhausted crew to temporarily stand down from General Quarters and rotate off duty for some critically needed rest.

"I'm amazed that Chen and Turlaka are allowing him back up here so soon. Then again, it surprises me they've managed to keep him down for this long," Prescott said.

"I stopped by once to check on him. He's done exceptionally well, but they didn't give him the option of getting out of bed until this morning."

"Knocked him out, did they?"

"Cold," she chuckled.

"Listen up, folks, we will render honors to Admiral Naftur when he arrives to welcome him back," Prescott announced, receiving a chorus of "aye, sirs" from around the bridge in reply.

"By the way," Reynolds asked, "I assumed it was okay for him to be back on the bridge, but we've got this new hyperspace tracking feed posted up on the view screen all the time now. Do we have any restrictions on what we should and should not allow him to see?"

"That's certainly a valid question, but Admiral Sexton fired off an order right after the shooting that both Admiral Naftur and Ambassador Turlaka are to be extended all the courtesies and access privileges of senior allied officials. So, clearly our commander in chief trusts them both at this point. Granted, we're not going to be sending them home with engineering schematics or anything, but there shouldn't be any problem with having them observe operations on the bridge."

"Understood. I'm assuming they still require escorts, though?"

"Yes, but a single Marine is adequate while aboard ship. At this point, that's primarily just for their own security and as a simple courtesy. Overall, I think it's safe to say that they have earned our trust at this point."

"Agreed. Being willing to lay down your life for someone you only recently met will do that," Reynolds said.

During their conversation, Prescott noticed that Lieutenant Lee had returned to his post at the Science and Engineering console. Surprised to see him back on duty so soon after his brother's death, he nodded in

Lee's direction while giving Commander Reynolds a questioning look.

"He's okay," she mouthed, nodding silently in reply to the captain's implied question.

At that moment, the aft bridge entrance door opened to admit Admiral Rugali Naftur, dressed once again in his freshly ironed and mended gray and black utility uniform.

"Admiral on deck!" Prescott announced, prompting every officer present to rise and stand at attention while Naftur made his way to the row of command chairs lining the rear of the bridge. Arriving in front of Prescott and Reynolds, he executed a crisp left face, then returned the two officers' salutes before offering his hand.

"Good morning, Captain … Commander. It is a pleasure to see you both," he said, shaking each of their hands vigorously. "It is good to see you all," he repeated, raising his deep, powerful voice to address the entire bridge. "Please, as you were."

"I must say you're looking remarkably well, sir," Prescott said, looking him over while wearing an expression of amazement that clearly pleased the Wek admiral. It immediately occurred to Prescott that the last time he had seen Naftur looking so energized had been during the heat of combat at the Battle of Gliese 667.

"Hah!" Naftur laughed aloud with a deep, satisfied rumble from inside his massive chest. "You are too kind, young Captain. I do feel quite well, all things considered. I can assure you, however, that in spite of the exemplary care I have received, my body does not hesitate to remind me of my injuries if I venture to move too quickly. The doctors say that most of this will pass within a week, and I should then be allowed to return to more strenuous physical activities."

"That's fantastic, sir," Reynolds said, equally astonished by Naftur's imposing presence so soon after the shooting. "We're all very pleased to see you up and around, but I'm sure the doctors have told you to take it easy and not overdo it," she said, ushering him to a vacant command chair.

"Oh, of course," he sighed, taking his seat, "as they are wont to do. As I am sure you are aware, Doctors Chen and Turlaka are formidable indeed. Failing to follow their instructions is not a course of action I would recommend. Now," he continued, his brow furrowing as his piercing eyes took on a grim, purposeful expression, "may I impose on the two of you for a brief update? I have read through the AI's log entries and believe I have a reasonable sense of what has transpired, but it grieves me to know that I have been unable to offer much in the way of assistance thus far."

"On the contrary, sir ... there," Prescott replied, nodding to a magnified image of the *Hadeon* on the view screen, "lies proof of your invaluable contributions thus far. Your conversation with Commander Takkar persuaded his crew to withdraw from the Resistance task force and assist us during our battle with the *Baldev*. It is unlikely we would have been able to prevail without their — and your — help."

"Be that as it may, I keenly feel the losses suffered thus far on both sides. I also cannot help but wonder whether I might have been able to convince Captain Yagani to stand down as well. The destruction of the *Baldev* and the *Keturah* alone represent the loss of nearly twelve and a half thousand souls … all of them surrendered needlessly to the unchecked power of an insidious lie." Naftur breathed in deeply, attempting to remain calm in spite of the smoldering rage that at times threatened to overcome his normally disciplined mind.

"Together, my friends," Naftur continued, "we shall protect your world from Commodore Sarafi's forces. Once that danger has passed, both he and all of those in positions of power who were responsible for bringing about this so-called 'movement' will answer for their crimes. You must know, however, that I bear some responsibility in allowing all of this to transpire. I allowed myself the indulgence of believing that my military career represented the highest and best form of service that I could offer the Wek people. I arrogantly ignored traditional leadership obligations, somehow convincing myself that they were outdated, primitive relics with no relevance in a 'modern' space-faring society. Worst of all, I recognized the fundamental lack of morality that had become rampant within the Sajeth Collective, but did nothing to stop it. There is little doubt in my mind that my lack of action played a significant role in bringing us to where we are today."

"Sir," Reynolds began after a long pause, "we are largely unaware of the details of your military service, let alone the other leadership obligations you mention, but from what we do know, you have dedicated your entire life to honorably serving your people. How much responsibility or blame can be reasonably attributed to a single person for corruption and misdeeds on such a grand scale? You didn't personally participate in the

Resistance movement, so how can you consider any of what they have done to be your fault?"

"Ah, I can answer that question with the words of a gifted Human statesman from another age: '... *when bad men combine, the good must associate; else they will fall, one by one, an unpitied sacrifice in a contemptible struggle.*'"

"That's Burke, correct?" Prescott asked.

"Edmund Burke, yes indeed," Naftur said. "And his words are as true on Graca today as they were on eighteenth century Earth. Unfortunately, the 'good men' to whom he was referring have all too often allowed ourselves to become convinced either that evil does not truly exist, or — even worse — in the moral equivalence of those who justify evil deeds in pursuit of a 'just' outcome. I give the two of you my most solemn word that I will never again fail to meet my obligations along those lines. If they will still hear it, I will offer the same promise to the Wek people at my first opportunity."

"Well said, sir," Prescott replied, "and for what it's worth, I feel confident that they will support you in whatever role you envision for yourself going forward — just as we do."

"Thank you, Captain Prescott. Both of you do me great honor with your kind words, but enough with all of this lofty rhetoric for now," Naftur said with the hint of a smile returning to his face. "Back to more pressing matters, I could not help but notice the information on your display screen. I still have much to learn regarding your language and symbology, but I believe I understand the fundamentals well enough. Is this data current?"

"If the Guardian spacecraft is to be believed, yes, it is," Prescott said. *That sure didn't take him long,* he thought, both pleased and a little surprised at the return of the admiral's keen powers of observation so soon after his near-fatal injuries.

"Once again, I am astounded by your world's technological progress. I have never seen any means of tracking vessels traveling in hyperspace that approaches this level of fidelity."

"Well, as much as we would like to take credit for developing this technology, it doesn't really belong to us … not yet anyway," Reynolds replied. "The Guardian is simply providing us with access to the data while the Earth is under threat of attack. As you can see, the eight remaining ships from the secondary rally point as well as the two *Baldev*-class battleships we encountered here at Location Dagger will arrive simultaneously in just under eight hours. We assume that the point where their projected course lines meet is their approximate destination. If that is the case, they will transition at 1125Z at a distance of just over seven million kilometers from Earth."

Naftur stared at the display in silence for some time before speaking again. "Regardless of how you gained access, I believe this information may prove decisive in the coming confrontation."

"That is certainly our hope," Prescott replied. "One item of concern we wanted to bring to your attention, however, is the absence of the *Gresav*. She should have arrived here at Location Willow by now, but she has never appeared on this display, nor have we heard from Captain Jelani."

"*That*, my friends, is very good news," Naftur replied with a satisfied smile.

"You're not surprised by this at all, are you?" Reynolds asked, eying him suspiciously.

"Surprised? No, I do not believe that is the word I would use. Unfortunately, where the Pelaran Guardian is concerned, we can never be certain of its capabilities without putting our people at great risk. When my small squadron arrived in the Sol system, for example, we knew there was a very real possibility that we would come under attack at some point. Although we went to great lengths to ensure Ambassador Turlaka's survival in a worst-case scenario, under no circumstances did we expect that our squadron would be decimated within seconds of our arrival — with no warning and no possibility of escape."

"And yet, the *Gresav* did manage to escape," she pressed.

"Yes," Naftur replied gravely, "and I was forced to watch helplessly as thousands died. The details of that story I will save for another time, Commander. We have become friends, and I sincerely hope that our two worlds will soon become allies. Even if that does happen, however, there will still most likely be *some* secrets that we choose not to share openly with one another. As I have mentioned before, one of the *Gresav's* primary missions was to gather data on the effectiveness of several new technologies. She was equipped to test the effectiveness of various deceptive techniques using hyperdrive transition signatures, for example. She was also fitted with a number of low-observable technologies. Suffice it to say that, if successful, similarly equipped ships might ultimately be capable of executing a surprise attack against a Pelaran ship, hopefully destroying it before it has the opportunity to return fire."

"So it sounds like the technologies worked pretty well," Reynolds said with a raised eyebrow.

"The analysis will take some time, as you can imagine, but, as you said yourself, Commander Reynolds, the *Gresav* survived the Pelaran Guardian's attack," he said with something approaching a look of playful amusement on his face. "I would not, however, have expected to see her arrive here at Location Willow."

"And why is that, sir? Those were the instructions we gave Captain Jelani when our two ships encountered the Guardian near Earth."

"Yes," Naftur replied, the corners of his mouth now turning upwards in a rather cunning grin, "but those were not, however, the instructions that *I* gave him."

Chapter 19

TFS Navajo, Earth-Sun Lagrange Point 2
(0403 UTC - Combat Information Center - 1.5×10^6 km from Earth)

"Let me make sure I understand what Naftur is asking," Admiral Patterson said wearily, struggling to process yet another demand on his already overtaxed attention. "He's saying that the *Gresav* never left for Location Willow. Instead, it's waiting nearby for his signal — most likely somewhere within an hour or so of Earth."

"Yes, sir," Captain Davis responded, "that's my understanding as well."

"So he wants Prescott to give him a ride back into the system, where he will rendezvous with his ship. After that, he wants us to stay clear of the arriving Resistance warships and allow him one last chance to talk them out of attacking?"

"That's about the size of it, Admiral," Davis replied with a half-hearted smile.

"I guess a number of responses come to mind, but none that I would utter in polite company. Help me out here, Captain, does any part of that sound like a good idea to you at this point? Haven't we already tried this approach and failed?"

"That was my first thought as well, sir, and it seems exceedingly more risky here than it was out at Location Dagger. But, if you will recall, Naftur really only got the opportunity to address the captain of one Resistance ship, the *Hadeon*, and she did ultimately stand down and assist *Theseus* in the battle against the *Baldev*. So from that perspective, he's one for one so far."

"So you're saying we should actually consider giving him another opportunity?" Patterson asked, unconvinced.

"Here's the thing. If we believe what Naftur has told us about their naval doctrine — and assuming, of course, that they follow it — their battleships are unlikely to begin a bombardment of the planet's surface until all of our forces are out of their way. Sterilizing a planet is apparently a time-consuming process, and they seem to require the establishment of space superiority in the vicinity of their target before they will even attempt it."

"Right, but that doesn't seem particularly relevant in this case once you throw the Guardian spacecraft into the mix. Surely they don't expect to be able to waltz in here and destroy *all* of our forces ... the Guardian included."

"That's really my point. I don't think they know what to expect any more than we do. The Guardian was largely noncommittal when you and Admiral Sexton contacted him, but it's still difficult for me to imagine its doing nothing at all to help. The planetary bombardment scenario assumes that it will allow the Resistance ships to eliminate our forces in detail, and then sit idly by while they methodically destroy the Earth. Why would the Guardian do that after investing so much time grooming Humanity for membership in the Pelaran Alliance?"

"Unlikely perhaps, but then again why not? Hell, at this point, anything is possible, right?" Patterson said, shaking his head.

"Absolutely, and that's why I think Commodore Sarafi will try to keep all his options open for as long as possible until he sees how things are going to play out. If the Guardian stays out of his way, I expect a traditional attack using the battleships' heavy guns will be his first choice. As strange as it sounds, I think they might see an orbital bombardment as somehow being more 'civilized' than a biological attack."

"So you believe the biological attack is something of a last resort then?"

"I don't think they will lead with that option, no. But I obviously don't have much data on which to base that opinion. If I'm right on this, however, giving Naftur a little time up front probably doesn't introduce much in the way of additional risk. The truth is that Sarafi has far more options than we do. Once his forces arrive, our *only* choice is to destroy all of his ships, or at least remove them from the fight somehow. So if there is any chance that Naftur might be able to take a few of them off the table without the need for us to destroy them outright —"

"Alright, give Prescott the go ahead, but make sure Naftur understands that we are not changing our attack plans. He will have very little time to do whatever he can before we open fire. If any Resistance ships elect to withdraw, they need to make their intentions abundantly clear to our forces. At a minimum, they should turn away from the planet and all TFC vessels immediately — preferably transitioning to hyperspace and clearing the area altogether. The *Gresav* is the only Sajeth Collective vessel I intend to designate as a friendly unit. The rest will be subject to immediate attack for as long as they remain in system."

"Aye, sir."

"Oh, and tell Prescott that he is to take command of our reserve forces once he sends Admiral Naftur on his way. *Theseus* has taken a beating, so I would rather not put her back into the fight unless it's absolutely necessary. He is to stand by at the reserve staging area designated by the Flag and await further orders. If all goes well, I should be able to give him at least one additional destroyer and a couple of frigates."

"Aye, sir, I'll tell him."

"Admiral," Ensign Fletcher called from her Communications console, "TFS *Koori* just checked in. They have completed their post-climb system checks and are reporting a 'mission effective' status."

"Best news I've heard all morning. Thank you, Ensign. Tell them to move out to their designated position in the line and stand by for action."

SCS Gunov
(1125 UTC - 7.3x10⁶ km from Earth)

"Disengaging hyperdrive in 3 … 2 … 1 … mark," the Wek officer at the Helm workstation reported as the display screen returned to a view of the local starfield. "Commodore, we have returned to normal space. Location confirmed, 7.3 million kilometers from Terra, all systems nominal."

"We are receiving data from all nine of our ships, sir, including the *Zhelov* and *Serapion*," the tactical officer reported.

"Excellent," Sarafi replied with a satisfied smile. "Let us take a look at the Humans' homeworld, please."

"It is right … there," Commander Freyda replied, highlighting the small, vaguely bluish white dot inside a flashing red square. From the *Gunov's* arrival point, all of Earth features, even her vast oceans, blended smoothly into a single blur of light set against the inky blackness of space. The planet's moon, barely visible at all just off to the left, appeared as little more than a white pinprick of light. "I am afraid it is not much to look at from here."

"Magnify," Sarafi ordered.

With a quick command at Freyda's workstation, both the planet and her moon seemed to leap from the screen in vivid shades of light reflected from blue oceans, white clouds, and the greenish-brown land masses of the western hemisphere. From the *Gunov's* position, both bodies appeared in a gibbous phase, with just over three-fourths of their disks illuminated by their distant star. To the right of the terminator inside the planet's shadow, the yellowish-white lights of Human civilization were clearly visible.

"The pictures I have seen did not do it justice," Freyda commented. "It is breathtakingly beautiful."

"Multiple contacts," the tactical officer reported. "As expected, there are quite a few of them, sir."

"No need to call them all out, Lieutenant, just post the situation display on the starboard side of the screen please."

"Aye, sir," he replied as an overhead schematic of the battlespace appeared on the screen. "A couple of items to note, however … the closest warships are a group of four that the AI is classifying as heavy cruisers. They are spread along a line directly between our current position and the planet."

"What? At what range?" Sarafi asked, incredulous.

"Just over five hundred thousand kilometers. We are most likely within range of their weapons already."

"That is simply not possible," he scoffed.

"It is if they had some means of tracking us in hyperspace," Freyda stated flatly.

"I also have two small groups of destroyers just like the ones we encountered at the secondary rally point. They are standing off to either side of the cruisers."

"Most likely the exact same ships, Lieutenant. Anything else?"

"Ten smaller vessels classified as frigates. Nothing else in range at the moment, sir."

"Any sign of the Pelaran spacecraft?"

"No, sir, not yet."

"Well," Sarafi began, standing and raising his voice to address the entire bridge crew. "It looks as if they were expecting us ... but as impressive as that may seem at first glance, it is of little consequence. We will make short work of the Human forces, accomplish our mission, and return home victorious. I am confident that each of you —"

"Attention all Wek vessels. Stand by for an Emergency Defense Message duly authorized by the Royal Dynastic Houses of Graca," the *Gunov's* AI interrupted in an urgent, commanding tone. In the center of the bridge display screen, a large window opened and immediately displayed a circle formed by a series of six different coats of arms. In the center of these, a larger family crest was adorned by a banner bearing text in an ancient Wek tongue with which no member of the bridge crew was familiar. At the bottom, however, was a smaller banner with a single word that every crewmember recognized immediately: "Naftur."

"Comm!" Sarafi roared. "What is the meaning of this inane drivel?"

"Please forgive the intrusion, Commodore," the comm officer replied apologetically. "It is from an external data stream that appears to have overridden all of our standard security protocols. Shall I attempt to terminate the feed?"

"Yes, of course! And if the other ships are receiving this as well, jam the signal immediately."

"Sir, I do not think we will be able to terminate the stream," Freyda said in a low voice.

"What? Nonsense, Commander, of course we will. Why would you think that?" Sarafi asked, clearly agitated at the unexpected turn of events.

"The introduction said that it was an EDM. I have heard rumors of such things since I first began my studies at university — hidden, so-called 'back door' code included in all Wek-designed AIs — but I honestly thought that it was all nothing more than idle talk … tech folklore, if you will."

"Commander Freyda, I should not have to tell you that now is not the time to try my patience. Your point, please?"

"Yes, sir. As you know, during the period when Graca was considering membership in the Sajeth Collective, a great many Wek opposed it, fearing that we were giving up our independence and cultural identity in order to ally with other worlds — a few of which were even former enemies. In an effort to assert some degree of sovereignty, the dynastic houses originally insisted upon the ability to remotely control all Wek-constructed vessels in the event of an emergency."

"Surely you are not implying that the Humans are going to somehow take control of our ships."

"No, sir. In fact, the original proposal was overwhelmingly voted down for a number of obvious reasons. The legend persisted, however, that the royal houses still managed to force some concessions that allowed for certain 'privileged' access to all Wek-manufactured ships in case a time ever came when they were being used in a manner they deemed … unacceptable. One of these was supposedly the capability for a representative from one of the original seven dynastic houses to publicly address the crews of the ships. If that is indeed what this is, it is hard-coded into our systems, so we are unlikely to be able to shut it down."

"Eton Ulto!" Sarafi swore under his breath as the potential implications of such an intrusion rushed through his mind. "So you are saying that whatever this is could be appearing at other locations aboard the *Gunov* as well as the other ships in our task force?"

"I am speculating, sir, but yes — potentially aboard every Wek ship within range of the signal — most likely on every screen where it can be displayed without posing an immediate danger to the safe operation of the ship."

Before there was sufficient time to further investigate the source of the transmission, the EDM introductory screen was replaced by the face of a commanding Wek male. It was a face that practically every crewmember aboard all of the Resistance task force's vessels recognized immediately, but very few had ever expected to see again.

"Brothers and sisters," he began with a steely resolve evident in his voice, "I am Rugali Naftur, former First Admiral of the Sajeth Collective Fleet and Crown Prince of the Dynastic House of Naftur. Time is short, so I will come straight to the point. I just introduced myself as a *former* admiral because I have very recently come to realize that I can no longer in good conscience serve both Graca *and* the Sajeth Collective. The very existence of this so-called 'Resistance' movement — based entirely on lies and the disgraceful exploitation of the Wek people — has been a major factor in helping me arrive at this decision.

"You have been told that the Humans have allied themselves with the Pelaran Alliance. While it is true that they have been solicited for membership, they have not yet made the decision to join. And now that I have had the opportunity to meet the Human people, learn some of their history, and even fight alongside them, I sincerely doubt that they will become an enemy of the Wek people, even if they do ultimately make such a decision. And yet, you have been brought here with the intent of bringing about their utter destruction. You have been told that the Terrans represent such a grave, existential threat to the Sajeth Collective that *all* actions are justifiable … including the genocide of a species that has done absolutely nothing to warrant such an unspeakable fate. To stoke the fires of your fear and hatred, you were told that the Humans killed me and all of the brave men and women who accompanied me to the Sol system several months ago. My friends, I stand here before you now as proof of this deception … a deception that the cowards driving the Resistance movement were so anxious to maintain that they sent two of our own warships to intercept and destroy the *Gresav* once they learned that I had survived the Pelaran Guardian's attack.

"Many thousands have already perished on both sides in this wholly unnecessary conflict with the Humans. But I tell you now that it is still not too late to end the bloodshed … end it now before our world is forever darkened by a shame so heinous that we shall never again regain our honor. Just as I have done, I call on each and every one of you to renew your commitment to our homeworld. Take back your vessels in the name of the Dynastic Houses of Naftur and follow me home. If you will do so, I commit to you now that it is my intention to restore home rule to Graca. I am sure you understand that this course of action poses its own perils and risks, but I am now wholly convinced that this is the right choice for our people.

"I implore you to act without delay, for there is little time remaining to put a stop to this madness. The Resistance task force has backed the Humans into a corner, forcing them to fight for the very survival of their homeworld. They *will* fight, my friends, … with every bit as much tenacity and perhaps even a bit more cunning and guile than we would if faced with the same situation. Their technology is also far more advanced than you have been led to believe. And while I do not mean to imply that we should fear them, we would be foolish indeed to underestimate either their resolve or their military capabilities.

"I have included coordinates for a rendezvous point with this transmission. As quickly as possible, each of you must turn your ship away from Terra and her military forces. To avoid drawing fire, simply rotate about your vertical axis and transition out of the area immediately. I will be in contact as quickly as possible to provide further instructions once the situation here is resolved."

Naftur paused, his face taking on the confident, bold expression of a military commander well-accustomed to having his orders followed without hesitation. "Now, my friends, the time has come for you to act. Do what I have asked of you here today ... and then, tomorrow — together — we shall return Graca to the Wek people."

There was utter silence on the *Gunov's* bridge as Naftur's face was replaced once again with an image displaying the emblems of the seven houses of Graca. Sarafi's eyes remained focused on the display screen for several seconds, sensing the stares he was receiving from both his XO as well as every other officer on the bridge. Although he had handpicked his flagship's crew for the most part, the same was certainly not true of the other vessels that made up what remained of his task force. In each case, their commanding officers had given him the impression that they were reliable converts to the Resistance cause, but what of their crews? Many of them, he knew, had simply acquiesced to their officially unsanctioned mission ... perhaps believing themselves insulated from any resulting consequences because they were following their superiors' orders. What, then, if anything, should he say regarding Naftur's comments?

After what seemed like a long pause, Sarafi looked Commander Freyda directly in the eyes, then slowly, methodically shifted his gaze to each crewmember present before looking back up at the situation display. The internal conflict and questions of duty to the Collective he had struggled with over the past several months no longer troubled his mind. In its place, there was only rage. Rage for Naftur's interference — at the prospect of a return to an archaic, backward form of government on his homeworld — and at the very real possibility of his own colossal failure.

"We will commence our attack," he growled defiantly.

TFS Navajo, Earth-Sun Lagrange Point 2
(1130 UTC - Combat Information Center - 1.5×10^6 km from Earth)

"Still nothing from the *Cossack?*" Admiral Patterson asked in a loud, irritated voice without turning to address anyone in particular.

"Not a word for over an hour now, sir," Ensign Fletcher replied from her Communications console. "Based on what they were saying when they last checked in, we should be seeing them anytime."

"We should have been seeing them *before* their last call," he replied angrily. "Signal Captain Budarin at Yamantau Mountain that we urgently need that ship — with or without shields at this point."

"Aye, sir."

"We've got movement, Admiral," the young tactical officer announced loudly from the holographic display in the center of the CIC.

"I see them, Commander, thank you," Patterson replied, still staring intently at a bank of view screens nearby. "I need to know exactly what each of them is doing before we start issuing attack orders." A distant part of his mind made the observation that, under the circumstances, his own voice sounded composed to an almost absurd degree — not at all in keeping with the surge of adrenaline-induced emotions he was dealing with at the moment. *At least the waiting is over and we can finally get this behind us,* he thought, trying and failing to provide himself with a quick, inspirational thought.

"I'm showing three of the *Rusalovs* and the *Keturah*-class cruiser in a slow rotation to port — I think they may be withdrawing, sir!"

"Maybe so, but let's not start counting our proverbial chickens just yet. Even if that *is* what they're doing, that still leaves us with five battleships and a destroyer to contend with. Just in case, however, change our status to 'weapons tight' until further notice. Designate the four ships that seem to be responding to Naftur's instruction as neutrals, for now, but if they're not obviously heading out of the area within the next few minutes, I want them designated as hostiles once again. Clear?"

"Yes, sir. Done. I'll keep an eye on them for any changes."

"Very well. Any response from the Guardian spacecraft?"

"None whatsoever, sir."

"Alright, let me know if that thing so much as flinches. Initially, this is shaping up to look a lot like a classic naval artillery battle, and we don't need any ships in the general vicinity of the engagement zone that we don't intend to destroy."

"Sir, all of the remaining Resistance ships appear to have engaged their sublight engines and are accelerating. Since the *Cossack* isn't here, should the *Navajo* join the line?"

"We may have to, depending on how this first attack goes, but right now we're the only backstop between our line of battle and our carriers … not to mention Earth itself. Do we have a clear field of fire for our four cruisers' main batteries?"

"Yes, sir. Our destroyers and fighters are well clear of the engagement zone and all four cruisers have signaled that they are ready to execute their attack plan."

"Make your target Bravo 1 and execute. Jump fire jump, Commander."

"Aye, sir."

***

As one, the battle line of four cruisers: *Shoshone*, *Chickasaw*, *Shawnee*, and *Koori* — each named to honor indigenous warrior cultures from the areas near their respective construction sites — disappeared in spectacular flashes of grayish-white light. At virtually the same instant, the line of ships reappeared in the same dramatic fashion, but now less than one hundred thousand kilometers from their first target. Before their transition to hyperspace, each ship had altered its course slightly so that their formation was perfectly aligned to concentrate its firepower on the first *Rusalov*-class battleship in the enemy line.

The *Navajo*-class cruisers had been designed from the ground up as a platform for their primary weapons — a total of eight massive railguns dual-mounted atop the largest fully articulated turrets ever constructed. Both the dorsal and ventral mounts were capable of turning a full three hundred and sixty degrees, and in spite of their nearly seventy-five-meter length from hull mount to the tips of their barrels, could rotate at just over fifteen degrees per second. With their first target lying directly ahead, however, all four mounts were currently trained forward along each cruiser's longitudinal axis.

The railguns themselves were not unlike their much smaller cousins mounted on virtually every Fleet vessel, and a munitions engineer from as far back as the early twenty-first century would easily be able to recognize most of the weapon's primary components. What differentiated this gun from countless generations that had come before was its scale, as well as its ability to accelerate a projectile rivaling the size of those fired by World War I battleships to relativistic speeds. Now, just before the rails lining the inner walls of each gun were energized, a series of emitters produced an intense gravitic field along the entire length of the barrel. Within each gun's breech, it took less than three milliseconds for the four-hundred-and-twenty-five-kilogram kinetic energy penetrator to be forcefully centered between the launch rails with an audible *PING* as its mass was temporarily reduced to zero. The ship's fire control AI then took over, completing and verifying the calculations required to optimize the conditions within the railgun itself as well as ensuring that the projectile would hit its target nearly one hundred thousand kilometers away within centimeters of its intended point of impact. With all required tasks now completed, the AI issued its final clearance to fire. The end result was a tremendous burst of energy being shunted directly from the cruiser's reactors to each railgun turret — instantly propelling the round out of each weapon's muzzle at just over ten percent the speed of light.

Unlike the main batteries mounted on the enemy *Rusalov*-class battleships, the Terran *Navajos* made much more efficient use of gravitic fields. This allowed their guns to fire more rounds simultaneously (eight versus six) at a higher rate of fire (five salvos per minute versus two), all while transmitting negligible 'recoil' forces back to the warship itself. While the *Rusalovs'* guns did fire larger (eight hundred and twenty-five kilogram) rounds, the *Navajos'* projectiles crossed the intervening space to their intended targets at six times the velocity of the *Rusalovs'* shells. This fact alone meant that the Terran cruisers enjoyed a significant advantage in both accuracy and firepower compared to the older Sajeth Collective battleships.

The first salvo took less than three and a half seconds to reach the first Resistance battleship, with each shell initially carrying over two hundred petajoules of energy — roughly that of the largest nuclear weapon ever tested on the Earth's surface.

***

"Multiple impacts, sir!" Patterson's tactical officer reported.

"Very well. We need to assess as quickly as possible whether or not the first target is neutralized. Based on what we've seen before, Wek shields have some difficulty stopping railgun rounds, but they still do manage to reduce their effectiveness quite a bit."

"That may have been the case here as well, Admiral, but I can confirm solid hits from all thirty-two rounds on the first battleship. I'm seeing significantly reduced power output, secondary explosions, and her engines appear to be offline."

Thank God, Patterson thought, daring for the first time to consider that his forces might actually have the upper hand in this fight.

"The remaining two *Rusalovs* just fired their main batteries," the commander continued. "One two rounds in flight. Time to impact, one eight seconds. Our cruisers have adjusted course and are transitioning to hyperspace."

"Excellent. Designate Bravo 2 as the new primary target and have them set up as quickly as possible for another shot," Patterson ordered, turning to check the status of his small reserve force, now consisting of two destroyers and two frigates. For the moment, he still believed that allowing his cruisers to continue firing on the enemy battleships was a reasonable course of action — for as long as their current tactics remained effective, that is. After all, just a few more salvos like the last would reduce the Resistance task force to such a degree that they might well withdraw. The real problem was the *Gunov.* In his mind, she still represented the most significant threat against the planet itself, and he was impatient to bring her to action as quickly as possible — hopefully either disabling or destroying her before she could launch her Sazoch bio weapon. Unlike the *Rusalovs*, however, she was capable of rapid hyperspace transitions, and would almost certainly do so immediately if she were targeted by his cruisers. Further complicating the situation was the fact that Captain Abrams' destroyer force was largely useless at the moment. It was simply too dangerous to allow them to engage the *Gunov* as long as the cruisers were blazing away with their main guns.

Patience, he counseled himself. *No rash decisions ... no mistakes.*

"Sir, we've got a problem," the commander said, calling his attention back to the holo table. "*Shoshone* and *Chickasaw* transitioned to their next initial point, but *Shawnee* and *Koori* did not. They are maneuvering in an attempt to avoid the incoming rounds, but —"

"Time to impact?" Patterson interrupted.

"Six seconds ... missile launch, sir!" the tactical officer reported tensely as the holographic table automatically zoomed in on a series of strobing red ovals moving rapidly away from the two largest enemy battleships. "I've got multiple missiles in flight — launched from both of the *Baldevs*."

"Damn," Patterson said under his breath, fearing that he already knew the reason his two cruisers had failed to transition.

Chapter 20

TFS Theseus
(2.5×10^6 km from Earth)

"Something's wrong," Commander Reynolds said in a low voice that only her captain could hear. "Two of our cruisers didn't transition."

Since returning from their rendezvous with the *Gresav*, Prescott had been working with the other captains in his small reserve force to strategically position their ships. Although they represented only a small fraction of TFC's available firepower in the immediate area, he knew that their presence could become critically important, depending on how the battle progressed.

"Are *Shawnee* and *Koori* still firing their main guns?" Prescott asked, glancing up at the tactical plot. "It could be that their captains saw an opportunity to get in another salvo or two before moving to the next IP ... particularly since the two *Baldevs* haven't opened fire yet."

"No, sir, they are not. And if they don't get out of the way within about ten seconds, they're going to get clobbered by incoming rounds from the two remaining *Rusalovs*."

"Sir, the signature is pretty faint from here, but I think the *Zhelov* and *Serapion* are using the same gravitic beam weapon that the *Baldev* did at Location Dagger," Lieutenant Commander Schmidt reported gravely from Tactical 1.

"Missile launch!" Lieutenant Lau announced from Tactical 2. "*Zhelov* and *Serapion* are launching missiles, sir. Our cruisers are taking evasive action to avoid the incoming rounds, but —"

"But it won't be enough," Prescott replied. "The *Rusalovs'* shells are self-guided … there's not enough time."

"Multiple impacts," Schmidt reported. "Our AI indicates five nuclear-enhanced naval artillery impacts on each cruiser, Captain."

"Dear God," Reynolds gasped.

From *Theseus'* current position, the port sides of each cruiser were visible, allowing her crew to witness all five of the flashes produced by the shells' warheads. On each ship's ventral surface — currently shaded from the light of the sun — the plumes of fire erupting from the location of each impact were as spectacular as they were terrifying.

"Time to impact on the missiles?" Prescott asked.

"They were fired too close to their targets for a direct flight path, sir," Lau said, "but the first will still arrive in three zero seconds. Both of our cruisers have opened fire with their weapons in point defense mode, but their overall power output has dropped by about six zero percent."

"Dubashi, send an Emergency Action Message to all Fleet vessels as follows: One. Believe two largest Resistance battleships of the *Baldev*-class equipped with gravitic beam weapon. Two. Beam prevents a single target from transitioning to hyperspace. Three. Demonstrated range of at least five hundred and fifty thousand kilometers. Got it?"

"Yes, sir, transmitting now."

"Look sharp, everyone," Prescott said in a tone intended to refocus his crew's attention. "We obviously were not expecting to see the gravitic beam weapon employed by these two *Baldevs*, but the admiral has a couple of contingency plans in place for this situation. I suspect we may be called into action shortly."

Reynolds shot him a dubious look, knowing full well that the "contingency plans" he was referring to were risky, "worst-case" options at best.

TFS Navajo, Earth-Sun Lagrange Point 2
(Combat Information Center - 1.5×10^6 km from Earth)

"Belay my previous targeting order," Patterson said. "Designate Bravo 4 as the new primary target. Signal *Shoshone* and *Chickasaw* to fire as soon as they are in position — danger close. Remind them to also check their field of fire beyond their targets. They'll be firing back in our general direction this time ... and the Earth itself is a *very* big target. They are to hold this new position and fire continuously until ordered to do otherwise. With any luck, we'll either take the two *Baldevs* down or at least force them to discontinue their attack. Oh, and have Captain Abrams move his two destroyer groups around to cover the flanks of the second firing location and tell him I want C-Drive-equipped missiles in flight, just in case. Either way, we may need to commit his ships to battle shortly."

"Aye, sir," the tactical officer replied. "There are seven six hostile missiles in flight at this time. Time to impact for the first of these is one four seconds. The inbound missiles should begin reaching the cruisers' point defense barriers anytime. Still no energy weapons fire from the two *Baldevs*, sir."

"They probably figure it's unnecessary at this point. Our cruisers have already taken several major artillery hits and right now each one has thirty-eight anti-ship missiles inbound."

"Admiral," Ensign Fletcher called, "Captain Prescott aboard the *Theseus* confirms that the two *Baldevs* are using a gravitic beam weapon to prevent our two cruisers from transitioning."

"Acknowledge and tell Prescott that he is to monitor the *Gunov* closely. If she makes any indication of commencing her attack on the planet, the reserve force is to pursue and destroy. Make sure Prescott understands that his ships are not to approach the primary engagement zone."

"Aye, sir."

"The *Rusalovs* have fired again," the tactical officer reported, his steady stream of dire reports now taking on the cadence of a judge delivering a lengthy, monotone death sentence to Patterson's ear. "Time to impact, one eight seconds. All four Resistance battleships have engaged their supplemental aft shields."

"I'm not surprised," Patterson said resignedly. "They're worried about us launching C-Drive-equipped missile strikes, but they also think they have us on the ropes. So they've throttled back, raised their aft shields, and now they're planning to sit tight and slug it out until all of our major combatants are out of the fight."

Patterson paused, forcing his disciplined mind to ignore the frightful destruction being visited on his forces while taking in the vast quantities of information being presented on the various displays around the Combat Information Center. As he struggled to distill multiple data sources into some sort of strategy that might still offer a means of salvaging the situation, his glance paused momentarily on the holographic table. The two groups of anti-ship missiles were highlighted in an angry red as they completed their final, relentless approach to the two already heavily damaged cruisers. On the far left side of the table, he also noted the approach of the next salvo of nuclear-tipped shells fired from the *Rusalovs'* main guns. Whispers of despair were playing at the edge of his consciousness when his peripheral vision detected a flashing blue icon displayed on a nearby bulkhead-mounted view screen.

"I'm afraid we may well lose the *Shawnee* and *Koori*, Commander," he said solemnly, "but I think Sarafi may have just made his first big mistake. Weapons hold on *Shoshone* and *Chickasaw!*"

***

To the extent that current Pelaran and Grey-enhanced technology allowed, TFC's engineers had designed all of their combat vessels to keep their crews alive while remaining in the fight for as long as possible — even after sustaining heavy damage. At nine hundred and fifty meters in length, the *Navajo*-class cruisers' tremendous size had provided her designers with an unprecedented opportunity to construct the ultimate expression of this design philosophy.

The ships were equipped with a large hangar bay, as well as the cavernous internal spaces required to embark a Marine Expeditionary Unit of approximately twenty-three hundred troops along with all of their accompanying equipment. Still, the ships' size had been dictated primarily by their massive main guns, resulting in the unusual situation of the engineers having met all of the various mission requirements while still having internal space to spare. Rather than "waste" that unused space on such luxuries as more spacious accommodations for the relatively small crew, the designers had instead opted to roughly double the thickness of the ships' outer armor. Design decisions such as these, while seemingly minor at the time they were made, could sometimes produce unexpected, far-reaching results — occasionally even changing the course of history. Now, as the already heavily damaged cruisers shook violently from the impacts of multiple anti-ship missiles, the fate of the entire world hinged on their ability to remain in the fight for just a short while longer.

SCS Gunov
(7.1x10^6 km from Earth)

"Why have *Zhelov* and *Serapion* not opened fire with their energy weapons?" Sarafi asked impatiently. "Better yet, why are they not ignoring the first two targets altogether and shifting their fire to the undamaged enemy ships? Surely the first targets no longer represent a significant threat. If we continue this leisurely pace, however, the other two will soon be in position to resume their attack."

"Based on the catastrophic damage cause by the Humans' first round of artillery attacks, the two *Baldevs'* AIs automatically rerouted power from their energy weapons to their shields," Commander Freyda replied without looking up from her Command workstation. "It assumed, incorrectly, that the targets were likely to be destroyed by the missile strike and *Rusalov* artillery impacts. With your permission, I will override this precaution. The data indicates that the Terran cruisers' main guns have more than enough energy to penetrate our shields, even if we drive them well beyond their design limits."

"Of course, do it!" Sarafi bellowed, sensing the outcome of the battle still teetering precariously between overwhelming victory and ruinous defeat.

Freyda took a moment to enter the necessary commands, then returned her attention to a high resolution image of one of the damaged Terran warships. With a quick gesture, she opened the same view on one side of the bridge display screen, then slowly panned the hull of the ship in an effort to better gauge the damage that had been inflicted thus far.

"Tactical, has our AI completed an interim battle damage assessment on the first two targets?" she asked.

"Yes, Commander," the young lieutenant replied. "Both of the Human cruisers have sustained a total of nine main battery hits from the *Rusalovs* and approximately twenty hits each from the anti-ship missile strikes conducted by the *Zhelov* and *Serapion*. Power levels on both ships have dropped significantly, but, as you can see, both are still managing to sporadically return fire with their energy weapons. Our AI indicates that both ships still represent a diminished but significant threat and recommends that we continue our attacks to fully neutralize them before shifting fire to the other Terran ships."

"I want both of those ships destroyed *immediately*," Sarafi said in a low, menacing tone. "The *Zhelov* and *Serapion's* field interdiction capabilities obviously caught the Humans totally unaware, but they will quickly regroup if we fail to exploit the situation. Unlike the ships we faced two days ago, these Terran cruisers clearly have no shielding whatsoever. The fact that these first two are still offering resistance is beyond ridiculous at this point. Concentrate all four battleships' main battery and energy weapons fire and finish them *now,* then immediately move on to the other two."

"Yes, Commodore," several Wek officers replied at once.

Believing she might have seen movement against the otherwise static view of the Terran cruiser's hull, Commander Freyda paused momentarily, then panned the optical sensor back in the previous direction. Pausing once again on the warship's massive forward dorsal gun mount, she could clearly see that it was traversing ominously in the direction of the *Zhelov.*

***

During the thirty seconds following Commodore Sarafi's order ensued some of the most violent ship-to-ship combat that had occurred on or near the Earth since the days when seventy-four-gun ships of the line would fire broadside after broadside within pistol shot range of one another. Although severely damaged, both Terran ships had maintained a steady, albeit ineffectual, fire with what remained of their starboard bank of energy weapons. The *Shawnee* had even managed to restore power to one of her four main railgun mounts and was preparing to fire on the lead Resistance battleship when the space surrounding her hull flared brilliantly with the discharge of over one hundred and fifty heavy beam emitters.

With full power now available for their energy weapons and their AIs now having completed an extensive damage assessment, *Zhelov* and *Serapion* concentrated their fire with the intention of causing the complete structural failure of both Terran cruisers as quickly as possible. Bolts of intense, orange-tinted energy peeled back layer after layer of their targets' hulls, focusing on locations that had already sustained heavy damage from the *Rusalovs'* artillery rounds as well as their own missile strikes.

Ironically, *Koori* was the first to succumb, becoming (in spite of her modifications) the shortest-lived major combatant warship in Human history. Just before being hit by a final salvo of six nuclear-tipped artillery rounds, her hull buckled and failed just forward of her aft dorsal gun mount. The breech vented a number of the ship's most critical internal compartments to space while also allowing *Serapion's* energy weapons to penetrate deeper and deeper within until, finally — her reactors destroyed and all of her major systems offline — she simply ceased operation, drifting helplessly. By the time the final wave of artillery rounds arrived, their additional destructive power was largely redundant. As each round penetrated the *Koori's* hull, the bodies of her remaining crew were instantly vaporized as much of her recently completed interior was reduced to brightly glowing masses of molten metal.

Less than six seconds later, TFS *Shawnee* suffered a similar fate. Just before the last salvo of artillery rounds reached her battered hull, however, she did manage to let fly with two final rounds of her own. Each huge kinetic energy penetrator reached the *Zhelov* just over three seconds later. The first round passed easily through the battleship's shields before slicing through her armored starboard side and entering her cavernous hangar bay. The entire compartment was instantly consumed in an enormous fireball as the shell's energy was transferred to thousands of tons of what had been hull material, spacecraft, and maintenance equipment just moments before. The second round, although beginning its flight only twenty meters from the first, was deflected slightly upward as it penetrated its target's outer armor. Fortunately for the crew of the *Zhelov*, this new trajectory dramatically reduced the amount of damage inflicted on her internal spaces. Passing briefly through an unpressurized maintenance corridor, the round exited through a relatively flat section of the battleship's hull — completely destroying her dorsal gravitic beam weapon array in the process.

Although one of their number had been effectively destroyed and another seriously damaged, the Resistance ships now seemed to rally — spurred on by the elimination of the first two Terran warships. With no appreciable delay, all four battleships altered course in an effort to better position themselves for a final assault against the remaining two undamaged enemy cruisers. Simultaneously, the two Human cruisers completed their turns back towards the engagement zone in preparation for resuming their own attack. Inexplicably, however, neither ship opened fire.

The two *Rusalov* battleships, having the benefit of rotating "gunhouse" mounts for their main guns, were the first to shift their fire to the remaining two Terran cruisers. A total of twelve rounds immediately streaked away at over five thousand kilometers per second, this time aimed to converge on the cruiser *Shoshone* just under nineteen seconds later. Eight seconds into their flight, however, the starfield ahead of the projectiles seemed to blur and distort convulsively, followed by a flash of grayish-white light as yet another, seemingly identical Terran cruiser appeared directly in the shells' path. What at first appeared to the captains of the Resistance ships to be a stroke of good luck quickly proved otherwise as all twelve rounds reached the location of the new Human warship and — amid brilliant flashes of white light — were deflected harmlessly away into space.

TFS *Cossack* had joined the battle.

TFS Navajo, Earth-Sun Lagrange Point 2
(Combat Information Center - 1.5×10^6 km from Earth)

"Alright, alright, pipe down, people!" Admiral Patterson bellowed, trying to restore order to the normally tranquil Combat Information Center. Having witnessed the destruction of both the *Koori* and the *Shawnee* just seconds earlier, the arrival of TFS *Cossack* — followed immediately thereafter by a successful demonstration of her gravitic shields — had incited the room to something just short of a riot. "We will celebrate when *all* enemy forces have been destroyed. Until then, I need this room quiet, focused, and each of you on point." Patterson paused and glanced around the room for a moment at all of the smiling, triumphant faces turned his way. "Hooyah?" he prompted, with just a hint of a smile.

"HOOYAH!" came the thunderous, enthusiastic reply.

"Very good. Now get back to work!" he concluded, turning back to his tactical officer at the holographic table.

"Sir, the battleship that took two rounds from the *Shawnee's* main guns ceased fire on her gravitic beam weapon immediately afterwards. Based on the timing of the damage, I'd say she's lost the capability to stop our ships from entering hyperspace."

"That's good news, but I don't know if we can be certain that's the case. *Theseus'* data seemed to indicate that the beam came from one of two separate arrays, depending on their position relative to the *Baldev*. I think it's safe to say, however, that as long as our ships remain above her dorsal surface, she won't be able to use the weapon."

"Shall we send that information, sir?" he asked.

"Absolutely," Patterson replied, nodding to Ensign Fletcher.

"Sending now, sir," she responded immediately.

"Our goal is to take no more *Rusalov* main battery hits on our unshielded ships, Commander," Patterson continued. "*Cossack* is to continue to close with the two remaining *Rusalovs* and take them out as quickly as possible. If her upgraded reactors are working as advertised, her rate of fire should be increased as well. As long as the incoming artillery rounds can't get through her shields, she should be more than a match for both of them."

"And the two *Baldevs*?"

"Are in serious trouble," Patterson replied with a savage grin. "They are primarily energy weapon platforms and, although quite powerful in their own right, are much more effective against our ships when paired with kinetic energy weapons. I think it's safe to say they will be losing access to those shortly."

"So *Shoshone* and *Chickasaw* should resume their attack against the *Baldevs*, then? Sorry, sir, but won't they simply transition to hyperspace to avoid our heavy railgun fire?"

"They might, but I'll be surprised if they are able to do so. That's the mistake I mentioned earlier. Based on the analyses from Dagger and Crossbow, we believe that once their aft supplemental shields are engaged, they're essentially stuck where they are. We know for sure that the additional shields encumber their sublight engine nozzles, but we have also seen indications that they prevent the ships from transitioning to hyperspace. And if they drop their supplemental shields —"

"Yes, sir," he replied, nodding his understanding.

"One more thing, Commander. I want *all* enemy ships destroyed in detail. Understood?"

"Understood," the tactical officer replied gravely.

"I'm not saying we won't give quarter … we're not about to start behaving like them. What I *am* telling you is that we will continue our attacks until all enemy ships have either surrendered unconditionally or are completely destroyed."

"Yes, Admiral. Does that include the *Gunov* as well?"

Patterson considered the question for a moment, replaying the merciless destruction of severely damaged Human and Resistance vessels in his mind. "Let's cross that bridge when we come to it, Commander. I can't imagine any circumstances where Sarafi would surrender. And even if he did, we would have no way of ensuring that he wasn't preparing to launch his bio weapon under a flag of truce."

Chapter 21

SCS Gunov
(7.1x10^6 km from Earth)

Commodore Naveen Sarafi stared impassively at the spectacle playing out in real-time on his bridge display screen. He had watched with pride as the first two Terran cruisers had met their demise — portents, he had assumed, of victory's inevitable approach. That had been just minutes ago, had it not? Yet, what he now saw on the *Gunov's* various situation displays foretold not of his enemies' destruction, but rather his own. By his AI's count, the shielded Human warship had now absorbed at least twenty-six direct hits from his two *Rusalov* battleships' main guns. He surmised that there was likely only one such vessel available to attack his forces, but it had immediately become obvious that one would be more than enough. In a last ditch effort to overwhelm its shields and retake the initiative, Sarafi had ordered the *Zhelov* and *Serapion* to ignore the remaining two Terran cruisers and concentrate their fire on the newcomer. Even with a combined barrage from the two *Rusalovs'* main batteries supported by enfilade energy weapons fire from the two *Baldev*-class battleships, however, the new Human warship had proven to be all but indestructible. Predictably, the two remaining Terran cruisers had taken full advantage of the opportunity, sending their own deadly streams of railgun and energy weapons fire streaking downrange to slam into his two most powerful remaining warships.

"Forgive me, Commodore, but should we not consider a strategic withdrawal at this point?" Freyda asked, bracing herself for a wide range of possible responses. "You have spoken to me before regarding the importance of demonstrating the danger posed by the rapid Terran military buildup thanks to their Pelaran allies. As distasteful as it is to settle for anything less than a total victory, we can now return home with undeniable proof that the Sajeth Collective must unify and commit itself to eliminating this threat once and for all."

"No, Ragini," he replied with a weary sigh, "I am afraid it is far too late for that at this point. You heard Naftur as well as I did. Even after generations of relative peace and prosperity under the banner of the Sajeth Collective, Graca's participation in the alliance has never been particularly popular among our people. A great majority of them favor a return to home rule, and we would have certainly seen that come to pass many times in the past were it not for the tacit support of the dynastic houses. Regardless of what you may think of Rugali Naftur, he is precisely the kind of leader who could unite the houses in coalition."

"And you believe he would end Gracan participation in the Collective?"

"I believe he will do much more than that, Commander. The Sajeth Collective was little more than a loosely organized economic development and trading partnership prior to Graca's accession. Even now, there is little chance that it would survive Graca's withdrawal. In fact, our world's exit from the Collective will be so catastrophic that it would not surprise me to see several of the remaining members declare war in a last ditch effort to protect their interests."

"If they do, they will surely be destroyed," Freyda declared flatly.

"In the case of open military conflict, that is almost certainly true," Sarafi replied, as exclamations of dismay and anger erupted from various locations around the *Gunov's* bridge.

Both officers glanced up at the display screen just in time to see SCS *Zhelov* — fire belching from the open wounds caused by over one hundred impacts from the Terran cruisers' main guns — flare brilliantly as her drive section exploded. Both officers observed silently that the primary source of the blast's destructive power must have been the ship's propellant storage tanks. Perhaps due to their arrangement deep within the hull, the resulting blast wave traveled in a rapidly expanding "V" shape as it struggled ferociously to break free of its confinement. Watching from the *Gunov's* position, it was as if the hands of a colossal giant had grasped each end of the battleship, then snapped it into two pieces like nothing more than a dry, brittle twig. The entire bridge crew stared at the screen for a long moment, transfixed as the two halves of the enormous ship tumbled away in opposite directions. Judging by the state of the three remaining battleships, every officer in the room knew that they too would be destroyed in short order.

"As I was saying," Sarafi continued in a strangely detached tone, "conventional military operations are of little utility against a superior enemy force. This will obviously be the case if the less powerful members of the Sajeth Collective seek to force Graca to remain in the alliance. I believe that it is now also the case for our struggle against the Terran puppets of the Pelaran Alliance. History has repeatedly taught us that when situations like this occur, the less powerful belligerent is often forced to resort to some form of asymmetric warfare."

Freyda felt a chill travel the length of her spine as she realized the commodore's intentions. She had, of course, known from the beginning that deploying the Sazoch delivery system was a potential option, but she never truly believed that it would come to that. Like most Wek officers who had volunteered for the Resistance task force, she had always assumed that any military conflict with the Terrans would be short-lived. The powerful Sajeth Collective would simply deal with the Terrans, then just as quickly find a means of dispatching the Pelaran Guardian. The entire conflict would be over in short order, with the Sol system coopted as a new, albeit involuntary, associate of the Sajeth Collective.

As one of the two remaining *Rusalov* battleships was declared combat ineffective by the *Gunov's* battle management AI, Freyda was forced to acknowledge how utterly naive she had been from the outset. "We do not have to do this, sir," she began again.

"You are correct, Commander. *We* do not." Sarafi smiled. "Just as the destruction of the disabled Terran vessels at the secondary rally point was my responsibility alone, I also bear the burden of the decision on how best to complete our mission. You are a good and moral officer, Ragini, so it is only natural that you would be uncomfortable with being forced to make such a difficult decision. Consider, however, how far the

Humans have come in a relatively short period of time. Granted, if a larger portion of our fleet had been here fighting alongside us today, we would almost certainly have made short work of their relatively small force. But the question you must ask yourself is whether that will still be the case a year from now — even if we assume that an opportunity like this presents itself again. No, Commander, this is our one and only chance. We must deliver the Sazoch weapon and then depart immediately for Damara."

TFS Theseus
(2.5×10^6 km from Earth)

"Sir, the last of the *Rusalov*-class battleships has been destroyed," Lieutenant Commander Schmidt reported from Tactical 1.

The sense of elation experienced by the bridge crew while watching TFS *Cossack, Shoshone,* and *Chickasaw* go about the methodical, almost businesslike elimination of the Resistance warships had been short-lived. Each now took a moment to glance up with conflicting emotions at the destruction their forces had wrought on their enemies while at the same time looking forward to finally putting this battle behind them. On the view screen, several huge pieces of the once-mighty Resistance battleship rotated at varying rates as they moved steadily away from one other — each one riddled with dimly glowing holes where artillery rounds had either penetrated or exited her armored hull. At her peak rate of fire, the fully-upgraded cruiser *Cossack* had achieved nearly eight salvos per minute — a total of sixty-four shells — each of which had slammed into her targets with a shocking level of accuracy and destructive power. Out of curiosity, Commander Reynolds had placed the newest cruiser's hull impacts counter on the tactical plot, just below that of the *Theseus*. In spite of the massive volume of main battery artillery and energy weapons fire she had received, the ship's AI had registered only four hits — none of which had caused any significant damage.

"Thank you, Schmidt," Prescott replied after a long pause.

"The Sajeth Collective — the Wek in particular — have been building starships for hundreds of years," Reynolds observed quietly, in awe of what they had all just witnessed on the bridge view screen. "I would never presume to tempt fate by making comments about a battle that has not yet been won, but does it not seem strange that the Pelarans would have provided weapons technology that is far in excess of what they believed we truly needed?"

"I don't suppose I've ever thought about it that way before. So you think they expect that we will ultimately be facing more dangerous enemies than the Sajeth Collective?"

"Maybe … then again, they didn't provide *all* of the technology that has gone into our warships. But I can't imagine they would ever want us to have access to more military capability than they thought absolutely necessary. Why set us up as a potential rival before we've even joined their alliance?"

"Lieutenant Commander Schmidt," Prescott continued without further comment on the subject, "I expect Admiral Patterson will clear the cruisers to open fire on the *Gunov* shortly. When that happens, he believes she will transition to hyperspace immediately. The question is whether she will retreat or press on with her attack on the Earth itself. Watch her closely and report any changes immediately."

"Aye, sir."

"Helm, if she decides to attack, we expect she will jump directly into low orbit — perhaps even just inside the upper atmosphere. Can you plot an atmospheric C-Jump from our current position?"

"Yes, sir. In fact, I've already got several rough-plotted, just in case. With your permission, however, I'd like to put us in a little better alignment. That way, once she jumps, we'll be just a few seconds behind her."

"Excellent, do it. Once you are satisfied, pass the data along to the other three ships in our reserve squadron. I'd like them to follow us in, if possible, but we don't need them transitioning inside our hull when they do."

"Will do, Captain."

"Tactical, our primary objective is not to attack the *Gunov* herself, but to intercept and completely destroy the Sazoch. The intel we have on the biological agent involved leads us to believe that it may be susceptible to heat, so once we find it, we will engage with energy weapons only."

"Aye, sir," Lieutenant Lau replied, "… if we can find it."

"True enough," Prescott sighed. "I wish I had more to offer you on that subject, but there just hasn't been enough time for our Science and Engineering Directorate to develop anything like a 'sure thing' detection strategy.

All I can tell you is to hammer the hell out of the area with every active sensor we have and hope that we find it in time. The flagship will be attempting to coordinate with some ground-based detection systems as well, but …"

"But there's not a lot of time for that kind of thing, sir," Schmidt offered.

"No, I'm afraid not, but if Fisher puts us right on top of the *Gunov* immediately after she jumps, I have to believe we'll see *something*."

"There she goes, sir!" Lieutenant Lau reported excitedly as the Tactical console emitted a series of urgent-sounding warning tones.

Four and a half million kilometers away — with *Serapion* now in her death throes and TFS *Cossack* maneuvering to begin her attack on the Resistance flagship — the *Gunov* transitioned to hyperspace once again.

"Fisher?" Prescott said expectantly.

"Almost there, sir. One zero seconds."

SCS Gunov, Low Earth Orbit
(Approaching the Philippine Islands)

"Hyperdrive disengaged," the Wek helm officer reported, although he need not have done so with Terra's largest ocean now completely filling the bridge display screen. "Deceleration burn commencing," he continued, as the destroyer's forward-facing retrograde engines quickly deployed and engaged at their maximum rated thrust.

"Confirming launch commit of the first Sazoch delivery vehicle. Firing in ten seconds," Commodore Sarafi said, mostly to himself out of force of habit as he entered the required launch authorization codes at his Command workstation.

Sitting less than two meters away, Commander Freyda felt paralyzed by indecision. Since unexpectedly hearing Prince Naftur's voice addressing the Resistance task force upon their arrival, she had been silently replaying his words over and over again in her mind: *"... it is still not too late to end the bloodshed ... end it now before our world is forever darkened by a shame so heinous that we shall never again regain our honor."* But it truly *was* too late now, wasn't it? The first Sazoch weapon would be launched regardless of any actions she chose to take at this point. The sense of inevitability that accompanied this thought caused a wave of relief to wash through her mind — relief that, for better or worse, she was now freed from any personal responsibility for what was about to happen.

But you know that to be a lie, do you not? she asked herself. *A convenient lie of self-deception told in silence by every witness to such atrocities throughout history. All of them cowards who had the opportunity to take action, but were too weak and afraid to do so.* As her own thoughts echoed in her mind, the bitter sense of relief she had felt ignited a white hot rage deep within her chest. With no time for further contemplation, she was spurred into action by the fundamental conviction that she could not allow herself to indulge in the denial of her own role in what was happening around her. *I am Ragini Freyda,* she thought, as her fingers flew over her workstation's touchscreen, *child of Graca ... born of the house Jelani ... and I am no coward.*

As she finished entering commands, she looked up at Commodore Sarafi wearing an expression of anger mixed with a vague sense of pity. Although she felt somewhat vindicated in the knowledge that she might well have saved the entire Human species from extinction, she knew with almost absolute certainty that she would pay for her actions with her own life, as well as the lives of many honorable Wek officers aboard her ship.

"The first Sazoch is away, Commodore," the tactical officer announced.

"Sir, the ship is no longer responding to control inputs," the helm officer reported in an urgent, but controlled tone.

Sarafi looked up from his own screen and immediately noticed his XO's stare. "Manual override," he ordered, sensing that things were by no means as they should be.

"Our shields are down!" the tactical officer bellowed.

"Alright, everyone," Sarafi said, raising his voice in a calm but firm tone, "let's work the problems one at a time. The AI will manage the helm momentarily while we sort out the control problem. Regarding the shields, a couple of overlapping emitters get taken offline during a weapons launch. Perhaps this is what you are seeing."

"No, Commodore," the Wek officer replied, still rapidly entering commands in an attempt to isolate the problem. "Immediately after the Sazoch launch, rather than bringing those emitters back online, the entire system disengaged. Our shields are completely down."

Sarafi turned to look his XO directly in the eyes. "Oh, Ragini," he whispered, "what have you done?"

TFS *Theseus*, Low Earth Orbit
(North of Papua New Guinea)

"Transition complete, Captain. Range to the *Gunov*, one zero kilometers dead ahead," Ensign Fisher reported from the Helm console as their quarry appeared in the center of the bridge view screen.

"Nice job, Fisher, just hold this position," Prescott replied. "Tactical, give us an active spherical scan at maximum power. With the exception of the *Gunov* herself, take out anything you don't recognize as a friendly target."

"On it, sir," Schmidt replied. "Nothing so far."

"Captain," Lieutenant Lau said excitedly, "they just dropped their shields!"

"By all means, fire!" Prescott said with a spontaneous involuntary laugh in spite of the urgency of the situation.

"Firing all weapons," Lau replied, entering commands as fast as possible in a near frantic effort to keep up with the rapidly changing situation.

"Contact!" Schmidt bellowed from Tactical 1. "Not a Sazoch, Captain, it's the *Gresav* … thirty kilometers to starboard. She's firing as well."

On the view screen, *Theseus'* three remaining forward plasma torpedo tubes as well as all available railgun and energy weapon emplacements opened up on the *Gunov's* fully exposed drive section. At almost precisely the same moment, the *Gresav's* heavy keel-mounted energy weapon fired — its enormous stream of focused energy stabbing through the darkness to pierce the Resistance flagship directly in the center of her sublight engine cluster. With her shields offline, the *Gunov* never even had the opportunity to return fire. In a scene eerily reminiscent of the Battle of Gliese 667, the *Gresav's* energy weapon appeared to maintain a single discharge until its beam had literally burned its way through the entire length of its target to exit near the ship's bow.

Knowing all too well the danger posed to the Terran population below from the dreadful weapons the *Gunov* had been carrying, Admiral Naftur had intentionally placed his shot in an effort to initiate an antimatter release. As the hellish, orange-tinted beam penetrated the destroyer's reactor containment unit, nearly six kilograms of antihydrogen — stored in the form of ice crystals — flash vaporized before coming into contact with the surrounding normal matter. The resulting annihilation event had an explosive yield exceeding ninety megatons of TNT, completely obliterating the *Gunov* and sending a massive cloud of superheated debris tumbling into the Earth's upper atmosphere from the Solomon Islands to the Antarctic Peninsula. At the same time, gamma rays produced from the explosion interacted with the Earth's magnetic field, generating a significant electromagnetic pulse. Although both warships were hardened against its effects, a roughly three-thousand-kilometer-long stretch of the South Pacific Ocean suffered power outages and widespread damage to electronic equipment as a result. Fortunately, the relatively low altitude of the blast confined the worst of the damage to one of the least populated sections of the planet's surface.

"The *Gunov* has been destroyed, Captain," Schmidt reported evenly. "We never detected any sort of weapons launch. If they did get one off, there's so much debris in the atmosphere right now that I doubt we'd ever see it."

"Understood, but keep trying. Comm, signal the rest of our ships to fan out and continue the search. We will also need to update the Flag on our situation shortly."

"Aye, sir," Lieutenant Dubashi replied from the Comm/Nav console. "Also, Admiral Naftur is hailing us."

"Thank you. On-screen, please."

"Aye, sir, opening channel."

A window opened on the left side of the view screen to display an exuberant Rugali Naftur.

"Once again, I have the pleasure of being the first to wish the two of you joy of our great victory, Captain Prescott and Commander Reynolds," he greeted warmly.

"To you as well, Admiral. We arrived in low orbit less than thirty seconds after the *Gunov*, but detected no Sazoch weapons being launched."

"Humph," Naftur growled. "They are exceedingly difficult to detect, but Sarafi would most likely have been entering the required authorization commands himself, so it seems unlikely to me that he would have had time to complete a launch sequence. In any event, we will, of course, assist you in your search. The *Gunov* herself, however, experienced temperatures exceeding twenty million kelvins, so I do not believe your people have anything to fear from any devices that remained onboard."

"Agreed," Prescott nodded. "Sir, I don't know how we will ever repay you for all of the assistance you have provided our people. There is no doubt in my mind that none of us — and by 'us' I mean our entire species — would have survived without your help."

"Any man of honor, yourself included, would have done the same in my place, but I appreciate the sentiment in any case. Regarding how you may, as you say, 'repay' me," he paused, smiling fiercely, "fear not, young Captain, you will be provided with that opportunity soon enough."

Guardian Spacecraft, Earth
(0059 Local - South Pacific Ocean - 123 km Above the Island of Tonga)

With a blue flash of light easily visible from the ground over a huge, but still relatively remote section of the Earth's surface, the Guardian spacecraft transitioned from hyperspace less than two kilometers from its target. A quick scan of the rather utilitarian Sazoch delivery system indicated that, in spite of its having been launched, the onboard AI had been ordered to place its containment system in a "fail-safe" mode and had not been granted authorization to deploy its deadly payload. After a brief interaction with the weapon, it all but abandoned any attempts at preventing the unauthorized access to its most sensitive systems. As a result, the Guardian was able to assess that there was little danger that biological materials would be released — even in the event of an unpowered descent to the surface. The weapon was aware that it could not return to its host vessel and further indicated that it intended to seek a remote location near the planet's southern pole to set down and await its recovery by friendly forces. As had so often been the case throughout Terran history, dumb luck — or perhaps divine providence — had served their species far better than any knowledge or technology they had managed to acquire.

Thousands of possible scenarios flashed through the Guardian's consciousness, even as it powered up its weapon systems and prepared to fire on its target. The Makers generally discouraged outright dishonesty. Deception, on the other hand — particularly the omission or purposeful delay of certain key pieces of information — was permissible under certain circumstances. The Humans were very fond of the notion that morality was a flexible concept, tinged with shades of grey rather than absolutes. Surely, then, they could hardly fault others for similar thinking … particularly their allies or those seeking to become their allies. Membership in the Alliance was, after all, wholly in their best interest.

Structural analysis of the Sazoch delivery system — *a fine name for such a weapon,* it thought — indicated that the safest method of forcing a landing at a given location was removal of its drive section at a precise instant during its descent. Once this occurred, the engines would continue to provide thrust for a few additional seconds, followed by an uncontrolled plunge into the South Pacific Ocean, just off the southernmost tip of South America. The payload section would then follow a fairly predictable descent profile utilizing a series of emergency gravitic generators and small thrusters to prevent a hard landing.

Approximate landing area selected … four seconds remaining. *A "test," then, as Admiral Patterson said — or, more accurately, the application of a specific set of circumstances to better illustrate the benefits of Alliance membership*, the Guardian thought, as it opened fire on the Sazoch delivery system.

***

Just over one hour later, the following "Flash" Emergency Action Message was received via the reserved command and control channels of the NRD network:

Z1303
TOP SECRET MAGI PRIME
FM: GUARDIAN SPACECRAFT - SOL SYSTEM
TO: EAM — TFC FLEET OPS
INFO: SUCCESSFUL ATMOSPHERIC INTERCEPT OF SAJETH COLLECTIVE SPACECRAFT

1. SMALL SPACECRAFT BELIEVED TO BE CARRYING WEAPONIZED BIOLOGICAL AGENTS INTERCEPTED OVER SOUTHERN PACIFIC OCEAN.
2. NO SUBMUNITIONS OR DRONES WERE DETECTED DURING INTERCEPT, BUT RECOMMEND EXTREME CAUTION.

3. AREA IN THE VICINITY OF ANY WRECKAGE
SHOULD BE QUARANTINED PENDING
DECONTAMINATION.
4. RECOMMEND TWO HUNDRED KILOMETER
SEARCH AREA CENTERED AROUND -56.17333, -
67.83410.
5. GUARDIAN SPACECRAFT AVAILABLE FOR
IMMEDIATE CONSULTATIONS REGARDING
REMEDIATION EFFORTS.

Epilogue

Earth, Patagonian Desert
(128 km Northwest of Tres Cerros, Argentina)

Although the cold, dry air is still breathable and the local gravity hovers very near the planetary standard of 9.81 m/s², there is little else about the Earth's fourth largest desert that most Humans would recognize as "home." Once a vast, temperate forest, the formation of the Andes Mountains to the west a mere forty-five million years prior covered much of the region with volcanic ash. As the mountain chain rose ever higher, its jagged peaks impeded the flow of moisture from the Pacific Ocean — a "rain shadow" that ultimately created one of the most barren, inhospitable locations that planet Earth has to offer.

With a near constant stream of cool mountain air descending down the leeward side of the Andes, the Patagonian Steppe experienced strong winds throughout the year. And over the past hour, its ever-present, mournful howl had served to mask the low, rumbling sounds of four *Sherpa* Autonomous Space Vehicles operating in the area. The first of these had arrived from the north, immediately beginning a series of overflights in a precise, grid-like search pattern. Although there was no way to know precisely what kind of pathogen they were looking for, the shuttles were equipped with a broad range of sensors capable of detecting even the most minute traces of chemical or biological agents. Based on the intelligence currently in hand, a modified virus of terrestrial origin was deemed the most likely delivery vector. In this at least, the Sazoch's crash site had been something of a lucky break for the personnel tasked with securing the area. With the region's extremely sparse Human population and relatively sterile biome, it was hoped that even the smallest release of weaponized biological materials would be easily detectable.

Once multiple sweeps of the area had been completed with no signs of contamination detected, three additional *Sherpas* had arrived, along with a high altitude combat air patrol of eight Argentinian fighter aircraft. Although the fighters had clearly been dispatched by the Argentinian government, the four *Sherpas* each bore an emblem that was neither that of Terran Fleet Command nor the Argentinian component of the Central and South American Union.

After the *Sherpas* had finished deploying troops at several strategic locations to establish a defensive perimeter, a much larger group disembarked and set to work on the crash site itself. All of the obviously military personnel wore full body armor that appeared to be of similar design to earlier versions of TFC's combat EVA suits. Combat operations seemed unlikely at such a remote location on the Earth's surface, but the suits also offered protection from all known chemical and biological agents, which seemed by far the most likely threat to their occupants at the moment. All of the other personnel in the area had donned the latest in "Level A" hazmat suits, although there had been some debate as to whether such precautions would ultimately prove futile if a release had indeed occurred.

The Sazoch spacecraft itself was in surprisingly good condition, considering how it had arrived at this location. Its main propulsion unit had been sheared off with almost surgical precision during the Guardian's attack, landing nearly a thousand kilometers to the south near Cape Horn. Here, however, the weapon system's heavily armored payload module was still largely intact, and appeared to have landed under power to some degree — perhaps even utilizing a form of gravitic braking in order to arrest its rapid descent to the desert floor. Intact or not, the team processing the crash site was taking no chances. Two of the four shuttles had situated themselves just upwind, allowing technicians to uncoil several long hoses from their cargo bays. Each hose fed a bank of nozzles that immediately began dousing the entire site with a fine spray of chemicals in an effort to eradicate anything that might be released during the next phase of their recovery operation.

Now, less than thirty minutes after the last of the four *Sherpas* had landed and secured the area, a gigantic military transport arrived, touching down in a cloud of dust just south of the crash site. Within minutes, an additional team of technicians attached a series of gravitic maneuvering units to locations on the Sazoch's payload module deemed structurally sound enough to allow it to be lifted off the ground. Once satisfied that there were sufficient GMUs to minimize the risk of additional damage, the entire assembly was maneuvered — with such infinite care that its movement was barely perceptible to the Human eye — until it rested once again in the center of what appeared to be a huge, tent-like structure. After being secured in place, lightweight, structural "ribs" were quickly installed above the payload module before the entire assembly was enclosed in an enormous, inflatable cargo container not unlike the expandable evacuation pods used by TFC.

Colonel Mateus Rapoza, the officer in overall command of the operation, had made it a point to stay well clear of the Sazoch itself, choosing instead to monitor progress through binoculars and via comlink from a low hill just west of the crash site. With the most dangerous portion of the recovery now complete, he breathed a long sigh of relief while establishing a secure comlink via his tablet.

***

Over ten thousand kilometers to the northwest — just outside the Terran Fleet Command Headquarters campus — a contingent of twenty-five heavily armed private military contractors exited their small fleet of nondescript, black vehicles. Moving with practiced efficiency, they quickly established a security perimeter between their "principal" and the high-speed executive transport idling on the adjacent landing pad. Each member of the team understood all too well that a delay of any sort would not be tolerated. Accordingly, those unfortunate enough to be stationed in the immediate vicinity of their charge's vehicle glanced around nervously behind their dark sunglasses — anxiously awaiting clearance to complete the final leg of their brief escort mission.

After a tense twelve-minute administrative hold due in part to a last ditch legal challenge from TFC's Judge

Advocate General's office, permission to depart was finally granted. Everyone present expected nothing less than a spectacular tongue-lashing upon opening the vehicle's door, so they were pleased to see that their charge had just accepted a call via her tablet, and paid them no attention whatsoever as she brushed past on the way to her aircraft.

"Is the device secured?" she asked without preamble.

"Yes, ma'am. The coordinates you provided were spot-on. I'm pleased to report that we have detected no contamination, and the device itself is largely intact. The entire assembly has been isolated in a sealed cargo inflatable that meets all of the requirements for Biological Safety Level 4 containment. We are preparing for departure now, and should be clear of the area in fifteen minutes."

"Well done, Colonel Rapoza. Please proceed with transport as quickly as possible. I will be en route shortly and should be able to meet you at our facility as planned. TFC is still somewhat in disarray at the moment, but it won't take them long to realize that there is nothing of value at the southernmost crash site. Before you leave, make absolutely certain that no evidence remains to indicate that you were ever there."

"Understood. Thank you Madame Chair —"

"Mrs. Crull will do for now, Colonel," she interrupted.

"Yes, ma'am. Thank you, Mrs. Crull."

"Keep the operation moving, Colonel. We absolutely cannot allow this abomination to fall into the wrong hands."

———————————————

End of Part 1

THANK YOU!

I'd like to express my sincerest thanks for reading *TFS Navajo*. I hope you have enjoyed the story so far and will be interested in the next installment of The Terran Fleet Command Saga (expected release: spring of 2017).

If you did enjoy the book, I would greatly appreciate a quick review at Amazon.com, or wherever you made your purchase. It need not be long or detailed, just a quick note that you enjoyed the story and would recommend it to other readers. Thanks again!

Have questions about the series? For example: How long will the "saga" be? Why is the story divided into multiple books? How do I find out about the next release? Please visit my FAQ at:

AuthorToriHarris.com/FAQ/

While you're there, be sure to sign up for the newsletter for updates and special offers at:

AuthorToriHarris.com/Newsletter

Have story ideas, suggestions, corrections, or just want to connect? Feel free to e-mail me at Tori@AuthorToriHarris.com. You can also find me on Twitter and Facebook at:

https://twitter.com/TheToriHarris

https://www.facebook.com/AuthorToriHarris

Finally, you can find links to all of my books on my Amazon author page:

http://amazon.com/author/thetoriharris

OTHER BOOKS BY TORI L. HARRIS

The Terran Fleet Command Saga

TFS *Ingenuity*
TFS *Theseus*
TFS *Navajo*

ABOUT THE AUTHOR

Born in 1969, four months before the first Apollo moon landing, Tori Harris grew up during the era of the original Star Wars movies and is a lifelong science fiction fan. During his early professional career, he was fortunate enough to briefly have the opportunity to fly jets in the U.S. Air Force, and is still a private pilot who loves to fly. Tori has always loved to read and now combines his love of classic naval fiction with military Sci-Fi when writing his own books. His favorite authors include Patrick O'Brian and Tom Clancy as well as more recent self-published authors like Michael Hicks, Ryk Brown, and Joshua Dalzelle. Tori lives in Tennessee with his beautiful wife, two beautiful daughters, and Bizkit, the best dog ever.

35560652R00229

Made in the USA
Middletown, DE
07 October 2016